"LOOK HOW FAR I'VE COME. I'M A THIRTY-TWO-YEAR-OLD MULTIMILLIONAIRE— AND YOUR BOSS."

Rebecca aggressively leaned over and slipped her hand up firmly between David's legs. She suddenly felt like doing something crazy, and forbidden. "So if I were you, I'd shut up and take my clothes off. The mourning period is officially over." Her voice seductively dripped with urgency. "We've got at least twenty minutes to kill, and I know how I want to do it."

David swallowed with a frown. "Rebecca, come on. Here, in a funeral limousine? For God's sake we just left the graveyard of your dead husband. Show a little respect. That's morbid."

Rebecca leaned down into David's lap. "Sure I can't change your mind? I see at least part of you is interested."

David looked toward the front of the car. "Can he see us?"

"No," Rebecca lied. The glass was transparent and only stopped sound. She didn't care what the chauffeur saw in his rearview mirror as long as he didn't hit any inopportune bumps. . . .

ANTICIPATION

Paris Hall

POCKET BOOKS

New York   London   Toronto   Sydney   Tokyo   Singapore

An *Original* Publication of POCKET BOOKS

POCKET BOOKS, a division of Simon & Schuster Inc.
1230 Avenue of the Americas, New York, NY 10020

ISBN: 0-671-74759-2

First Pocket Books printing June 1993

10 9 8 7 6 5 4 3 2 1

POCKET and colophon are registered trademarks of Simon & Schuster Inc.

Cover art by Kam Mak

Printed in the U.S.A.

ANTICIPATION

Prologue

April 1990

Dallas, Texas

THE WHEELS OF THE TWIN ENGINE LEAR EAGLE GLANCED ONCE against the runway with a brief, whining protest of rubber, then settled down firmly as the nose of the private jet leaned forward into a picture-perfect landing, The pilot reversed the pitch on the twin turbines and throttled the engines hard to slow their speed down to a comfortable roll. As the flaps retracted and the copilot received ground instructions from the Dallas/Fort Worth International Airport air traffic control center, Nicole unbuckled her seat belt. She opened her pocket book, took out a small cosmetic mirror and touched up her makeup, then ran her long smooth fingers through her auburn hair, smiling quietly to herself. Her excitement was already building; she could feel her heart rate accelerating even before her jet stopped on the tarmac and her captain opened the door. In less than an hour it would begin again; and this time for just over a full week. Her imagination was already running wild with anticipation.

Captain Brian Weaver turned around in his seat as the aircraft came to a halt and smiled. "Right on time, Ms. Prescott. Just like we promised."

The shrill tone of the private jet's engines rapidly sank in

1

pitch as its twin engines slowed to a halt. Nicole looked out her window at the approaching ground crew. Her white 500 Series Mercedes limousine stood ten yards away, ready to receive her; the rear door and trunk were open and waiting. Phillip, her Dallas chauffeur, walked up to take her bags. Turning to Captain Weaver, she nodded with approval, "Excellent, Brian. Thank you."

Captain Weaver had refused to let the rain at Boston's Logan International Airport impede them, despite a departure delay of forty-five minutes. Copilot Joel Parnell had adjusted their flight plan en route to arrive at DFW precisely at 3:00 P.M., according to Ms. Prescott's wishes. Parnell unclasped his shoulder strap and swung his legs away from the control panel, glancing down at Nicole's long, graceful legs, sheathed in sheer, black silk hose. He discretely watched her slip her Gucci heels back on.

"When shall we expect you, Ms. Prescott?" Parnell asked, deliberately looking her in the eye.

Nicole suppressed a grin. She caught him looking. "Not until next Sunday." She picked her suit jacket up off of the seat next to her, along with her black and gray ostrich-skin portfolio, throwing the gray tweed jacket which matched her skirt over her arm. The jacket was appropriate in Boston, but the weather was too warm for it here in Dallas. She had hoped to change before heading for the airport, but it had taken much longer to complete the Trident Corporation antitrust brief than she had anticipated. She had no alternative but to come straight to Logan from her office near South Station, hastily leaving her candy-apple-red Lamborghini Diablo with her Boston-based ground crew to park. Besides, she thought with a chill of delight rippling through her, in a couple of hours clothes would not be an issue.

"Day after tomorrow?" asked Captain Weaver as he concluded all of his postflight instrument checks, pulled his gold-rimmed aviator sunglasses out of his shirt pocket and slid them on.

"No," she corrected, making her way toward the open doorway. "Next Sunday, nine days away." Phillip took her hand as she made her way down the two small steps onto the concrete tarmac.

"Nine days?" Parnell looked at Weaver as the copilot made his way to the open door.

Nicole stopped and turned around, reached into her purse and removed a legal-sized envelope. Looking back at Weaver, who was just making his way down the small steps after Parnell, she smiled and said, "Here's some cab fare. I had Katy make reservations for you and Joel at the Westin-Galleria. It's over off of the North Dallas Parkway just north of Loop 635. I'm confident you two will be able to keep yourselves entertained for a week. But do check the hotel for messages in case I need you." She turned back toward her car without waiting for a reply.

"Yes, ma'am," Weaver said, nodding after her. Parnell took the envelope and peered inside it, his fingers quickly thumbing through a stack of cash. Inside was four thousand dollars, all in one-hundred-dollar bills.

Phillip had no sooner closed the door and pulled away when Nicole picked up the platinum-cased telephone and pressed speed-dial button number one. A soft voice answered on the second ring. "North Dallas Women's Center, Stephanie speaking. How may I help you today?"

"Stephanie, this is Nicole Prescott. Advise Dr. Brighton I have landed in Dallas and will be arriving at the center within the hour." Nicole noticed a slight trembling in her hand as she held the receiver next to her ear. She reached up and removed her earring to more comfortably hear the other party.

"Yes, Ms. Prescott. You're expected at four o'clock. All the arrangements you've requested have been made. Your suite has been prepared as usual." The voice was matter-of-fact but courteous.

"And my itinerary for the week?" Nicole watched Phillip pay the parking fee at the north exit of the airport. The attendant tried to peer into the dark privacy glass to see who was inside.

The soft voice paused for a second. "Yes, Ms. Prescott,

everything seems to be in order. However, Gerald is still in the process of reconditioning your saddle for your riding lesson on Tuesday. He left a note saying that it might have to be rescheduled for Thursday. Is that a problem, ma'am?"

The image of Gerald flashed across Nicole's mind: tall, sandy-haired, muscles toned with a working man's daily labors, always wearing skintight knee boots and riding breeches. Yes, the wait would be worth it. "That's fine, Stephanie. Move my golf game to Tuesday if you have to."

"Certainly, Ms. Prescott. We appreciate your understanding." The phone crackled as they left one cellular zone and entered the next. "I'll inform Dr. Brighton that you are on your way. Will there be anything else?"

"Sounds like I'm all set. If I think of anything, I'll call you back. Thank you for your help." Nicole returned the receiver to its cradle and sat back in the rich burgundy water-buffalo hide seat. The sumptuous leather filled the car with its aroma like a finely stitched garment. The ornate silver champagne bucket mounted in the recessed niche between the two rear-facing seats was properly iced down. The bottle of Dom Pérignon nested inside it was open as usual. She leaned forward, pulling one of the long-stemmed flutes from the oak rack below the bar, smartly filling it halfway. The rich, sparkling foam cascaded over the rim and dripped lightly onto the thick white carpet beneath her. The warm Texas afternoon prompted her to reach over and adjust the climate control a notch. With a long, luxurious sip of her glass, she raised the volume of the precision sound system, filling her spacious compartment with the expressive melodies of Schubert. As the delicate enchantment of the music swelled around her, Nicole marveled at the silver, gold, and bronze panorama of the monolithic glass towers of North Dallas passing by on either side of the eight-lane expressway.

The ride to the North Dallas Women's Center would take just under an hour. Phillip would proceed down Loop 635 to the recently completed expansion of Central Expressway north, through Richardson and Plano, east on Parker Road out past the historic Southfork Ranch, winding through two-lane back roads to the north shore of Lake Lavon. There, on the one-hundred-acre grounds of the lakefront retreat, she would find the delightful relaxation and exhilarating fulfillment she had come to crave week after week. Normally, Nicole would summon her jet to make the three-hour journey from Boston to Dallas on Friday evening, enjoy a satisfying weekend, then return Sunday evening ready to start the week. But this week she conceded to let Dr. Brighton apply a specialized treatment to the tiny wrinkles that had appeared around her eyes.

Even at age forty-two, Nicole was a stunning beauty, with her long, chiseled features; and she knew how to use her appearance and demeanor to her advantage. She didn't really care about the faint crow's-feet around her eyes; what had appealed to her most was the thought of spending a full week convalescing at the Women's Center—if convalescing is what it could be called. With a shiver of delight, she wondered if she had the stamina to endure a full week of their *special* care.

After another hearty sip of champagne, her tongue wiping the sweet juice from her lips, she nodded with satisfaction. She deserved this vacation. It was a victory celebration. On Wednesday the judge in the Dalmar Corporation trial had awarded her client, Ball Petroleum, a $6.5 million settlement. That meant $2.15 million in attorney's fees for her two months worth of trouble. And with an extra two million dollars in your pocket, you can afford a few pleasantries— like nine days at the North Dallas Women's Center.

Nicole loved to practice law. Her law firm was not only revered, but feared by any potential adversary. Her sharp mind, flawless analytical logic, and fluid public speaking skills never failed to dazzle both judge and jury alike. Over the years, she had developed a reputation of success second to none. And with the conquests of war come the spoils. This week she was ready to be spoiled.

Phillip stopped the long white Mercedes under the wide stone porte cochere in front of the Women's Center. The drive had taken just under an hour, conveniently timed just ahead of the North Dallas rush hour. Nicole's anticipation had feverishly swelled as they came through the artistically sculpted wrought-iron gates, snaking down the immaculately landscaped drive past flawlessly manicured grounds to the magnificent complex.

The uniformed doorman opened the rear door of the limousine as Phillip proceeded to the rear of the car to unload Nicole's luggage. Nicole took the white-gloved hand of the young, smiling, dark-haired attendant as she swung her long legs out of the car, rising gracefully into the warmth of the Texas air, an atmosphere graced by the inviting fragrance of a wide spray of blooming honeysuckle billowing over the waist-high stone wall between the massive columns of the porte cochere.

"Ms. Prescott, welcome once again to the center," offered the young man with the bright red uniform jacket and tight black trousers, holding her hand at shoulder height as he promptly closed her car door behind her.

"Thank you." Nicole nodded politely and quickly strode into the foyer of the main complex building, leaving the doorman to help Phillip with all of her bags. The dark glass doors silently slipped closed behind her as she passed. Inside the richly appointed foyer, decorated with classic antiques and warm, hearty woods, she stopped at the circular reception desk. A young woman in her early twenties wearing a small earpiece and clear boom microphone, looked up at her from a computer console and smiled.

"Ms. Prescott. Right on time," came the familiar voice.

"Hello, Stephanie." Nicole could not restrain the eagerness in her voice, nor her wide-eyed grin.

Stephanie mirrored her joy with a warm smile of her own. "Dr. Brighton said to proceed directly to the clinic. She'll see you in examination room five."

Nicole walked past the reception area into the main gallery of the central complex. The great room was two and a half stories in height, one hundred feet from front to back, and two hundred feet wide. The rear wall was all glass to the peak of the roof overlooking the two outside terraces and the waters of Lake Lavon below. The other three walls were tastefully appointed with original art treasures from around the world, mostly Renaissance impressionists' work. The gallery's breathtaking inlaid wood floor was lavishly adorned with Oriental carpets, attractively arrayed with numerous plush, comfortable sitting groups. Several women were gathered in clusters of two or three, engaged in conversation, sipping their favorite blends of teas, exotic coffees, or deliciously prepared cocktails. Periodically a ripple of laughter would erupt in one of the groups, eclipsing the light strains of Mozart which filled the air. Young, attractive, uniformed waiters quietly moved around the guests of the Women's Center, attentive to their every need.

In the center of the room was a circular fireplace covered by a great bronze hood extending up and through the vaulted ceiling. Surrounding the bronze flue at the top were massive beams running down in four directions to the separate corners of the room. The afternoon sun filled the entire room with its relaxing hues. Nicole stood for a moment, drinking in the majestic ambience, then made her way to her left, out of the great room to the long corridor extending to the medical facilities.

Examination room five looked more like an artist's studio than a medical clinic, sparsely furnished with a wide skylight overhead. Yet its lack of intimidating antiseptic austerity was comforting. An antique oak armoire held all of the medical supplies. Nicole laid her jacket on the back of a bentwood armchair and took a seat at a small, round, country-styled kitchen table which matched the china cupboard against a side wall. She heard footsteps.

Dr. Alicia Brighton came into the room with a smile and an apology. "Nicole, my dear. I'm so sorry to keep you waiting. Delores Fennery does like to talk so, and I feel so guilty telling her to shut up and bother someone else." Alicia didn't look like a doctor either. She wore a bright print blouse and a comfortable looking knee-length dark skirt. She came over and gave Nicole a familiar hug of welcome.

Nicole laughed. Alicia always seemed to be able to make her laugh. In fact, Alicia seemed to bring a smile to everyone's face at one time or another. "It's all right. I've just arrived."

"Nonsense," protested the older doctor, light streaks of gray coursing through her short black hair. She pushed her wire-rimmed glasses up on her nose, looking intently at Nicole's face. "This is supposed to be your special week, and I'm keeping you from enjoying it. You must hate me with a passion."

"Alicia!" Nicole frowned. "Don't be ridiculous." Actually, she did hope her consultation would be quick.

"Now, let's see." Dr. Brighton set her metal flipchart down on the table and pulled a chair directly in front of Nicole. She sat down and took Nicole's cheeks in her hands, turning her head to the left and slowly to the right, peering out of the lower lenses of her bifocals. Nicole straightened her back and leaned forward.

"Umm." Alicia furrowed her brow.

"Is that a good umm or a bad umm?" Nicole squirmed on her chair.

"Let's try to hold still and relax our face shall we?" admonished Dr. Brighton. Nicole complied. "Yes, Nicole, I think we can have you tuned up and ready to go with only two applications. I'll schedule you for the first one tomorrow morning and the second on Wednesday." Alicia picked up Nicole's chart, extracted a pen from behind her right ear and began to make some notes.

Nicole leaned back in her chair and smiled. "Is it going to hurt?"

Alicia smiled and patted Nicole's hand in a motherly way. "Of course it will, dear. We use very long, sharp needles."

Nicole's smile faded, her eyes growing wide.

Alicia laughed out loud. "Gotcha."

Nicole smacked the older woman's hands playfully. "You're wicked!"

"So I'm told," retorted the doctor. "Don't worry about a thing, my dear. All we have to do is give you a small injection right about here." Alicia touched the forward part of Nicole's temple. "The medication will then do the work. Within a few days you'll see the results. The small lines will disappear and you'll look like you did when you were twenty-five."

Nicole's memory jumped back to when she was twenty-five, back at Harvard Law School, living in Cambridge. That's when she first met Rae, back in the early seventies. That's when it all started. Had it really been seventeen years?

"What is it, dear?" asked Alicia, looking at her friend's pensive expression.

"Nothing. Is that all for today?" Nicole reached for her coat.

Alicia was smiling again. "I can see you're eager to get settled in. Don't let this old woman keep you any longer. I expect you have a therapy session scheduled for this evening?"

"Indeed," announced the powerful Boston attorney as she rose. "Actually, I had planned to be in therapy for the entire week."

"Oh, my." Alicia's eyebrows arched. "You always were an ambitious thing. Well, I'll see you here in the morning."

Nicole swung her jacket over her shoulder. "Not too early in the morning."

"Of course not." Alicia walked with Nicole to the door. "Say around ten?"

"I'll try." With a mischievous wink, Nicole sauntered off down the corridor, back through the great room, her heels clicking rapidly against the polished inlaid woods, to the elevators on the opposite side. Her private suite was on the third floor.

Nicole forced herself not to run when the elevator opened on the third floor. She was a trained professional. She could control her emotions and actions. The problem was, she had no desire to do so. When she turned the key in the lock of room 314 and swung the door open, the scene was just as she had imagined it. Her luggage was neatly arranged on the

ceramic tile landing. A long white terry-cloth robe was laid
out for her on the king-sized brass bed in the raised niche to
her right. To her left, the drapes were drawn, allowing the
sunlight to come in off the terrace, illuminating the overstuffed leather couch and sitting group by the fireplace with
warm, sultry hues. An open bottle of 1967 Chateaux Lafite-
Rothschild was breathing on the bar of the kitchenette.
Quietly in the background, a solo pianist rendition of
Chopin was playing on the entertainment system. And
across the room, in front of the sunken hot tub, behind the
waist-high massage table, folding a towel, stood Brett.
Everything was perfect.

"Hello, Brett," she said softly, the words coming forth
hesitantly, expectantly.

A disarming smile preceded the tall man's reply. "I've
been waiting for you. Everything is ready for your treatment."

Brett leaned against the long table upholstered in rich,
black leather, the well-defined muscles of his tanned upper
body and arms standing out nicely from his royal-blue tank
top. The matching sweatpants covered legs Nicole knew
were like pillars of polished marble. His piercing blue eyes
held hers as she closed the door and walked into the room,
stopping at the foot of the wide brass bed. Her heart began
to race again. The athletic therapist walked around the table
and approached her. She stood silently still as he came
within twelve inches and stopped.

"I trust your flight was pleasant?" he asked, never taking
his eyes off of hers. She felt his hands reach up and unbutton
the top button of her blouse, then slowly moving on to the
second and third.

"Yes," she whispered, wanting him to hurry, but relishing
each moment of his patient manner.

"Good." He nodded once, genuinely pleased. "But I can
tell you need to relax. I would like to help you relax."

He finished the last button and methodically pulled the
two tails of her shirt out of her skirt. She watched his eyes
glance down at the delicate black lace brassiere she wore. He

reached down and took her hands in his, gently unbuttoning her cuffs. His hands felt warm and strong. Then, with an alluring smile, he stepped behind her and slid the blouse off her shoulders and carefully laid it over the brass footboard of the bed to his right. She could feel his breath on her shoulder and the back of her neck while his hands unbuttoned and unzipped her skirt. His haunting fragrance filled the air, and she breathed it in deeply.

While Chopin's pianist ran his fingers lightly along the keyboard, a slight push of Brett's palms against Nicole's hips sent the conservative tweed skirt into a gray pool at her feet. He ran his hands back up her hips, over the lace edges of her French-cut panties and black lace garter, along the gentle curve of her waist, teasingly slow across her breasts and around to her back. A wave of electricity tingled up her spine; but she held still, letting her head tilt back slightly, resting against his cheek, knowing her patience would soon be richly rewarded.

She felt him unclasp her bra, his fingers carefully cupping the fine lace straps and moving them forward until the delicate garment fell to the floor, landing on top of the tweed skirt. She kicked off her shoes when she felt his left forearm gather up her legs and his right arm pull her shoulders to him, lifting her up off the soft, white carpet. She rocked her head back, her respiration rate climbing with the pace of her heart. He carried her over to the warm, leather-covered table and gently sat her down facing him. With meticulous care he unclasped her garter and slipped her black stockings off each leg. She cherished the feel of his powerful fingers sliding along her legs. She caught his gaze looking up at her, smiling, as his hands pulled at the edge of her panties.

She playfully grabbed his wrists; her eyes flashed. "Do it with your teeth."

He laughed softly. "I'm afraid if I did, you wouldn't get to enjoy your massage. The oil is ready. But it's up to you."

With a shudder of delightful anticipation she released his wrists, put her palms against the soft, electrically warmed leather beneath her, and lifted her bottom off the table. He slid her undergarment off and tossed it in the pile with her bra and skirt. She allowed him to turn her onto her stomach, knowing that getting the full treatment was vastly superior to rushing things to a premature conclusion.

Nicole folded her arms under her left cheek and watched him walk around the massage table to the accessory stand. She could hear the electric motor of the tall black hot-oil dispenser filling his cupped hands with the hot, sebaceous liquid. She gasped slightly as the succulent heat dripped onto the small of her back. Warm, strong hands spread the glistening oil up her spine, over her shoulders, back across her shoulder blades, down her sides, around the firm curves of her hips and buttocks, up over the small of her back, and returning up her spine in a subdued, deliberate, hypnotic pattern. Nicole felt each muscle melting away in the path of Brett's experienced touch, as meticulous as the pianist's delicate technique pleasing her ears.

After spending ten minutes on her back, with a fresh handful of the hot, coconut-scented oil, Brett worked on each leg, kneading the muscles of her feet, calves, knees, thighs, and hips. After each leg was done, she felt him part her knees slightly and tenderly begin to rub her inner thighs, his thumbs just barely making contact with her velvety pubic hairs. It was almost more than she could stand. A fine layer of her own perspiration beaded up on the oil across her back. Her breathing was now long and relaxed.

With a gentle pat on her rear she heard him say, "Time to turn over."

This was the part she loved the most. Nicole had never received a hot oil massage before coming to the North Dallas Women's Center. And after her first, she had not found a better way to relax or become more sexually aroused. And the front side was always the better of the two. With an almost sleepy moan she rolled over onto her back, just as the hot oil landed on her stomach, filling her navel and running down her sides. She closed her eyes and let her arms drop to her sides.

Standing to her left, he began with her arms, gently

rubbing the oil between each finger, into her palm, around her wrist, down her forearm, upper arm, shoulders and neck. After spending a few minutes on each arm, he rubbed the intoxicating lubricant over her cheeks and forehead, her skin drinking it in. His hands flowed down her neck and chest, cupping each breast in both hands individually, working the firm tissues around and around. A rapturous moan eased past Nicole's lips; she knew her nipples were growing erect beneath his touch. He was so tender, so gentle. Brett was always like that. It was almost mystical how he knew exactly where to touch, to rub, to please.

Chopin's étude swelled again with the musician's passion as Brett's hands pressed the liquid heat into her abdomen and down her long legs, always defining a rotating pattern of intense pleasure, up to her shoulders, around and over her breasts, down her stomach, over each thigh, again and again. The tempo of his rhythm increased along with the pressure of his hands. Her tongue delectably encircled her lips, her mouth agape; she knew she was not going to be able to contain the kindling heat inside her much longer.

Once again she felt his hands serenely push her knees slightly apart. Only this time as his left hand pressed and massaged along the inside of her thighs, she felt his right hand move under her lower back, sliding easily in the oil between her back and the now well-lubricated leather. She sensed his hand stop in the center of her back, lifting her into a gentle arch. Her breath stilled as, in the same moment, she felt his mouth close over her left nipple as his left hand rose up between her legs. She raised her right hand and ran her fingers through his dark brown curls, pressing his face firmly against her. His fingers softly teased her moist loins, carefully brushing the hairs aside to allow him to explore further.

He lifted his head slightly, running his lips and tongue down the incline of her left breast, up the right one, then playfully encircling her erect right nipple with the tip of his tongue. Now both of her hands held the back of his neck, running her nails up into his scalp and caressing his ears.

She held her lower lip between her even white teeth, her eyes clamped shut, as her hips began to move in rhythm with his probing left hand. With soft featherlike kisses, his lips moved down her right breast across her stomach, his tongue lingering for a teasing plunge in her navel, foreshadowing his intentions, bringing her nearly to a climax at the thought.

Without lifting his face from her gently writhing body, she sensed him move his body around the end of the table, and felt his hands reaching under her hips and carefully lifting her knees apart. As Chopin's étude crescendoed in a shower of intertwined melodies, Nicole pulled her knees up toward her chest, feeling his warm, darting tongue disappear inside her. Her eyes snapped open as the early waves of a thunderous orgasm began to crest. She gasped in air through clenched teeth, her legs stretching up toward the ceiling, toes pointed, muscles tightening—and then he stopped, a moment before she went over the precipice of ecstasy.

All was still.

The pianist began another movement of the concerto.

"What's wrong?" she asked incredulously.

Brett stood up and pulled the royal-blue tank top over his head and used it to playfully wipe his face of the oil, sweat, and savory juices from her body. Nicole's eyes drank in the beauty of his washboard stomach and glistening chest.

"Not yet," he whispered.

He walked around the right side of the table and scooped her up into his arms, his moist lips covering hers. Nicole floated in his arms over to the bed, where he laid her down on the quilted spread and stood once again. She leaned on one elbow watching him kick off his huarache sandals and slide the sweatpants down, kicking them away from the bed. Nicole bit her bottom lip again in anticipation. Brett was gorgeous. And it was obvious that he wanted her. She laid back and held out her arms. As he leaned over her, she reached down and guided him inside her, filling her completely. Their hips slowly rocked together in unison for several minutes as his mouth alternated gifts of euphoric sensation between her mouth, neck, earlobes, and breasts, sending her to the brink of the precipice yet again. And yet each time he sensed her about to explode, he would slow down, force her to relax, and teasingly whisper, "Not yet."

Brett masterfully varied the pace of his lovemaking, picking up speed to tease her, then gracefully backing off. Each plateau short of orgasm he brought her to, heightened her feelings of near delirium. Finally she knew she couldn't be denied any longer.

Nicole grabbed his solid buttocks in both hands, wrapped her legs tightly around him, and forced him inside her faster and faster, deeper and deeper, hotter and hotter, accelerating into a blinding fury. The music around her increased its volume and tempo. She was barely aware of Brett's hands reaching around her perspiring body, taking hold of the small of her back and beginning to work the rhythm of her hips at an even greater pace, faster than the pianist's hands upon the keys, fantastically increasing the direct pressure on the exact spot that pleased her most. Again his mouth closed over her left breast, drawing on it more and more as the tempo of both the lovers and the musician grew white hot.

With the resounding base octave crash of the classical pianist's thundering fortissimo of Chopin's finale, the lightning struck. Like a devastating collision of locomotives, Nicole took four desperate breaths, held the last one, every muscle in her body instantly immobilizing her lover, her mouth locked agape, eyes locked shut, a throaty moan penetrating the entire room, her loins throbbing and contracting in transported rapture for a full half minute. And just as the crashing waves upon waves of euphoric gratification began to ebb, Brett suddenly accelerated the tempo of his thrusting back to fever pitch, sending Nicole soaring back up the next hill of the roller coaster of unbridled sensuality.

"Yes!" she cried out, her bodily appetite ravenously gorging on the feast of raw passion. Without mercy he kept her in a state of almost constant orgasm for several minutes, till at last her body fell back limp on the bed in utter

exhaustion. Drenched and glowing with oily beads of perspiration, she looked into his eyes and panted, "I can't go
on. I can barely breathe. You're going to kill me."

He smiled down into her glassy expression, kissing her
tenderly. "But my beautiful Ms. Prescott, we've only begun."

The peaceful strains of the next movement of the concerto played on the sound system while Brett tenderly and
silently held Nicole in his arms for over twenty minutes,
letting her heartbeat settle down. She loved being just held,
feeling him still joined to her. Over the next hour he slowly
made love to her, letting her just relax and enjoy the gentle
closeness. He brought her to orgasm three more times,
patiently, easily—not so furiously as when they began, but
tenderly. And when he knew that she had been fully
satisfied, he allowed himself to climax. When Nicole felt the
warm rush inside her, his body pulsating within her, it sent
her into one last delicious contortion. She savored every
moment.

Brett kissed her softly once more, rose from the bed, and
grabbed a towel from under the massage table. He wiped off
his body and quietly put his sweats and tank top back on.
"I'll be back after dinner if you desire."

Nicole rolled over on the soiled quilt. "Yes. I desire."

Brett nodded with a gratified smile and left.

Two hours later, long after Nicole had showered and
dressed in a sheer white gauze caftan, she sat on her terrace,
sipping a glass of the deep red Rothschild wine, watching the
sun set to the west. It was incredible that a place as fabulous
as the North Dallas Women's Center, a place where a
woman's most intimate needs and fantasies were fulfilled,
could exist. She began to have doubts if she really could live
through a week of pure pleasure. It was certainly worth a try.
But what was most incredible was that she was here as a
favor to the center's founder, Dr. Rae Taylor.

Nicole resigned herself to the fact that Rae, Marsha, and
Alicia apparently seemed to know what they were doing.
The fruits of their work were certainly proven. They had

helped so many women, many cases nothing short of miraculous. Alicia's surgery and Rae's genetic therapy could make any woman beautiful. Certainly the treatment was expensive, but it was worth it. But they went beyond the outer woman. They also knew how to care for the inner woman, how to make her *feel* beautiful, alive, vital, and fulfilled. It was hard to imagine how anyone could put a price on that. And who could have ever known that it was all here because of that bitch Rebecca Danforth.

Part I

BYGONES

Friendship is constant in all other things
Save in the office and affairs of love:
Therefore all hearts in love use their own tongues;
Let every eye negotiate for itself
And trust no agent; for beauty is a witch
Against whose charms faith melteth into blood.

—William Shakespeare
Much Ado About Nothing

1

February 1972

Cambridge, Massachusetts

THE FRESH SNOW MADE IT EVEN MORE DIFFICULT FOR RAE TO maneuver her little green 1968 Volkswagen Beetle into the parking space at her apartment. The tiny rear engine groaned, making the tires spin as she eased the clutch back, doing her best to thread the little round vehicle into the slot between her neighbor Judy's Camaro and her roommate Rebecca's Corvette. The front bumper thumped against the ice-covered brick wall of the four-story brownstone tenement, letting her know she could go no farther. The condensation on the small flat windshield in front of her had completely frozen. She could only see to drive by smearing a six-inch-wide hole with her glove. After a firm tug on the emergency brake, she killed the lights and the engine, glad to hear an end to the Carpenter's "Rainy Days and Mondays" on the radio. It depressed her. It was only six o'clock, but already completely dark outside. The parking lot was poorly lit, so she turned on the little round dome light to find her apartment key before she got out of the car.

Readjusting her scarf around her neck and pulling her toboggan firmly around her ears, Rae grabbed the sack of groceries from the seat next to her and opened the thin metal door. A blast of cold air cut through her navy-blue wool overcoat, prompting a violent shudder. The metal cans and jar of mayonnaise clattered together as her door banged sharply against the side of Rebecca's car. It was too cold to worry about a nick in Rebecca's precious gold paint job. But Rae didn't care. Actually, she hoped she cut all the way through the primer. Besides, Rebecca probably had ten *other* things to rant and rave about when she arrived. Steeling herself against the wind, Rae closed her car door and carefully plodded through the ice and snow to the entrance of her building.

Grateful to be inside, out of the bitter cold, Rae threw her keys down on the dining table and carried her bag into the small kitchenette, placing it on the counter by the porcelain-covered iron sink. She glanced down at the tall stack of dirty dishes. Rebecca didn't do dishes. In fact, Rebecca didn't do much of anything she didn't want to. It became apparent after only the first week sharing the apartment at Harvard Yard that the only reason Rebecca tolerated a roommate at all was because her family refused to buy her a maid. But the arrangement had been tolerable over the past two years. In exchange for a little housework, and listening to Rebecca bitch and whine about any and every conceivable topic, Rae could afford to live at Harvard Yard and complete her education. It was one of life's little sacrifices.

The television was on and Rebecca was flopped down on the couch watching the news while she painted her toenails. The apartment was filled with the pungent chemical smell of the bright red polish and the overly loud drone of the television.

"Hi. Have you eaten anything?" Rae asked, taking the knitted cap off her straight brown hair and unbuttoning her coat.

Rebecca ignored the question, waving her hand at Rae in a gesture of irritation and a demand for silence as she strained to catch every word of the newscast. Rae shrugged her shoulders, opened up the food cabinet, and began to empty her grocery bag. After she got all of the items put away, she took her coat off, walked back into the living area, and hung it up on the wooden coat peg on the back of the front door—right next to Rebecca's full-length leather trench coat with fox-fur collar. Her hands were still cold, so she briskly rubbed them together. Even after four years of undergraduate work on a biochemistry scholarship at Radcliffe, a Ph.D. at Harvard, and now just over halfway through her first year of postgraduate work at MIT, she had not acclimated to the New England winters. Rae had grown up just south of Houston, Texas, in Pasadena, where the greatest climatic threat was the humidity.

"Can you believe that?" Rebecca shook her shiny black ponytail in amazement, gesturing at the nineteen-inch color screen with the palm of her hand. The television was a birthday present from Rebecca's mother.

"Believe what?" Rae came around the end of the orange Herculon couch and sat down in the green overstuffed chair by the window. Both the chair and the couch matched the burnt-orange and green shag carpet that ran throughout the entire two-bedroom, one-bath apartment, with the exception of the kitchen, which had the one-foot-square checkerboard black and white linoleum tiles.

"President Nixon," Rebecca pointed. "He's in Peking opening up diplomatic relations with the Chinese."

Rae frowned. "So what. They're communists. I thought you hated communists."

"Yes," Rebecca snapped. "But this is the first time an American President has recognized the Chinese since Chairman Mao's takeover."

"So what happens now?" asked Rae. "Is he going to get them to make the North Vietnamese get out of South Vietnam?"

Rebecca shot Rae a cold glare. They had undertaken numerous unproductive discussions on the "police action" in southeast Asia. Rae always complained of the ridiculousness of the conflict, and Rebecca always defended the current administration's actions, citing the communist threat and our strategic Pacific interests. "Look, Rae. I know you don't understand world politics. But just be happy that we have a good man in the White House who has the tenacity to take on the communists directly and make them listen. I expect China to have a complete democratic government and a free market economy before 1980."

"I don't know." Rae looked at the smiling face of the balding, sagging-jowled statesman on the screen as she pulled her legs underneath her, straightening out the wrinkle in her bell-bottomed jeans. "He looks too shifty to me. I don't trust him."

"You're just paranoid," Rebecca countered. "He's bringing back the men from Vietnam, isn't he?"

Rae looked at her nails; she knew she should stop chewing them. "Yeah, but why were they there in the first place?"

Rebecca screwed the cap back on her bottle of nail polish. "I'm not going to explain it to you again. If you haven't grasped it by now, it's because you are incapable of doing so. You spend all of your time at that stupid laboratory, or at the library, or God knows where, and you're out of touch with world affairs."

"The news is boring," Rae offered, taking her brown-framed glasses off and cleaning them with the loose material at the bottom of her red cowl-necked shirt.

"You think that way because you're out of touch." Rebecca smugly sat back on the couch and folded her legs underneath her. She was wearing her long blue satin house robe over her blue pajamas. "I study and analyze the news because when I'm running my own company, I'll need to be in touch with changing trends and markets. You see, I *need* to be aware of who the shakers and movers are. I've only got three more months before I've got my MBA finished, and I plan to blaze out of this place into glory. I'm ready to write my own ticket—and mark my words, no one's going to stop me. Learn a good lesson, Rae. You get ahead in this world by knowing what to do, when to do it, and who to do it to."

Rae raised her hands in mock surrender. "You can have

the rat race. I just want to finish my research and go to work in a good hospital or clinic where I can do some good."

Rebecca made a patronizing face and affected the tone of her voice, "Well, isn't that sweet, little miss Florence Nightingale. Have you found your Nobel-prize-winning cure for cancer yet?"

An angry surge of energy flashed through Rae's body; her eyes narrowed. Her mother had suffered from ovarian cancer six years ago, undergoing a hysterectomy and numerous painful chemotherapy treatments in the years since. Rae indeed had a vested interest in using her gifts and talents in fighting terminal diseases. "Almost. I think in another year I'll at least have cervical cancer, ovarian cancer, and breast cancer licked."

Rebecca rolled her eyes and looked back at the television. "You're so full of shit, Rae. Sometimes I don't know why I let you hang around here."

Rae did not appreciate her roommate's vulgar insult, prompting her words to tumble out with quick, terse venom, "Well, Miss Danforth, for your information, curing major diseases is not as complicated a task as you might think. You, who pride yourself on being so *in touch* with everything that's going on in the world. Well, *obviously* you haven't bothered to pick up on the work that's being done in DNA regeneration and cell mapping."

Rae flipped one hand up emphatically. "Every cell in the human body has a preprogrammed image of the entire makeup of the human physiology. If that programming becomes disturbed, chemically or genetically, then things like cancer can occur. But with the right chemical stimulus to unmutated cells, an idealistic pattern can be used to restore cancerous tissue to its original state."

Rebecca sniffed, obviously unimpressed. "Are you finished with your little dissertation, Dr. Louise Pasteur?"

Rae just shook her head in disgust. She was in no mood to spar with Rebecca tonight. Both of the nucleic acid regression tests had failed today, and an entire new culture series would have to be started all over again tomorrow. The laborious preparation and documentation was beginning to wear down her nerves. She had been researching the inner working of the cell for almost five years; and just when she thought she was near a breakthrough, setback after setback had cropped up. First the temperature variances in the incubators had invalidated the first six months' results. Then there was the specimen contamination caused by some careless lab technicians. Then the grant money hold-ups. She wondered if it would ever end.

Rebecca smiled at her plain-looking roommate. "Rae, what you need to do is get your nose out of your books and find you a good man. You're becoming a drag. Let your hair down. Have a little fun."

Rae didn't respond. She was twenty-two years old, and still a virgin. Her work was too important to be distracted by boys. At least that's what she constantly told herself. But the sharp edge of Rebecca's remark did its damage. Rae wouldn't admit the real reason her social life was nearly nonexistent was due to the fact that rarely did anyone of the opposite sex ever bother to notice her. But then there was Matthew.

"I do go out on occasion," Rae offered defensively.

Rebecca laughed. "Really? With who?"

Rae cleared her throat. She didn't like talking about this subject, but she hated Rebecca's arrogant attitude even more. "I've gone out a few times with Matthew Tobias."

"Really?" Rebecca turned on the couch to face Rae, her voice eager, as though she was genuinely interested. "What's he like?"

"He's nice." Rae held back a slight smile. "He's a second-year divinity student at Harvard. I met him in a philosophy class last year I had to take to complete my Ph.D. We've had dinner together a few times. In fact, he called me this week and asked me to dinner on Saturday."

Rebecca shook her head. "No, dear. I mean what's he like *in bed*? How big is he? Does he make you scream?"

Rae's eyes flashed in outrage. As far as she was concerned, Rebecca was a slut. She paraded her paramours in and out of the apartment with no shame whatsoever. "I'm sorry, Rebecca, but we don't have *that kind* of a relationship."

"Too bad," Rebecca mocked, then mused, "Perhaps Matthew wants to have *that kind* of relationship and you just don't know it."

Rae huffed, "Wrong. Matthew is not that kind of a guy. For Pete's sake, he's a seminary student!"

Rebecca tossed her shoulders, suggestively writhing her curvaceous body. "Sometimes the quiet ones are the best. They know how to take their time and make it last."

Rae scowled. "You're disgusting."

Rebecca ran her fingers back through her hair. "No, my dear, sweet, innocent, virginal, Dr. Rae Taylor. I'm a realist. I learned years ago that we women have something that men want. And I know how to use it to get what *I* want. There's no free lunch out there in the real world, dear academic sister. So you'd better open your eyes and realize that if you want a piece of the action, you've got to march out there and take it. No one's going to give it to you. And you'd *better* learn what it takes to get ahead."

"I don't want to get ahead if it means I have to be a whore . . ." Rae's eyes were cold and unflinching. ". . . like you."

Rebecca held her gaze for several seconds, then burst into laughter, mocking Rae's slight southern accent. "Why, Miss Taylor, I do declare, you just might have some spunk buried down deep inside that cold asexual exterior after all. That's good." Then her smile faded and her voice lowered. "But don't get too self-righteous. You'd sell your soul as quickly as I would if it would bring you what you really wanted."

"You're wrong," Rae rasped, her anger growing.

"Am I?" Rebecca stood, pulled her robe about her and walked toward the kitchenette. "Like I said, I'm a realist. I know how to get what I want."

Rae crossed her arms and looked back at the television.

The weather was coming on. "Well, I'm happy with what I have right now."

"Are you?" Rebecca taunted. "You never know, Rae. You could lose everything in an instant if you're not careful."

"I'll take my chances," Rae said through pursed lips, pushing her glasses back in place once again.

"Suit yourself." Rebecca shrugged apathetically. "But you might try being nicer to your friend Matthew. You never know, he just might decide to go after a *real* woman."

Rae glared at Rebecca again, not dignifying the comment with a reply.

"Who knows?" Rebecca mused, pulling open the refrigerator door and propping her elbow on it. "I might give him a ring just to let him know what he's been missing."

Rae forced a laugh, trying to sound genuine. "Be my guest. He has enough common sense than to eat out of the gutter."

Rebecca set a jug of apple juice on the counter and pulled a glass out of the cupboard. "My, aren't we bitter this evening. Settle down, Rae. I won't take your precious little preacher-boy away. I've enough men in my life to keep me satisfied. But take my advice and learn to enjoy him. It'll keep you from coming home every night so . . . so . . . frustrated."

Rae was at a loss. She didn't dare let Rebecca have the last word, especially with her condescending attitude of superiority. Sure she was rich, sure she was beautiful (and worst of all knew it), sure she had men calling the apartment at all hours of the day and night; but Rebecca was still a spoiled bitch. Rae consoled herself in the knowledge that if you opened any unabridged dictionary and looked up "Spoiled-self-centered-slutty-bitch," you would find a picture of Rebecca. It was a simple scientific fact.

After a moment of thought, Rae formed her expression into a look of sincere concern. "Rebecca, on the way in I noticed someone put another scratch on your car."

2

August 1979

Daytona Beach, Florida

THE WINDOWS OF THE 1970 DODGE CHARGER WERE COMPLETELY
fogged, but the full moon outside cast a dim luminescence
inside the car parked just off the two-lane Route A1A on a
desolate strip of sandy beach just north of Tomoka State
Park. The ignition key had been turned half on, allowing the
radio to continue playing the golden oldie "Help Me
Rhonda" by the Beach Boys; but the soft rush of the Atlantic
waves could still be heard washing against the moonlit
sands. At eleven-thirty at night the heat of the summer day
had passed, dropping comfortably into the mid-seventies
with a gentle breeze; but inside the car, Sabrina was
sweating. She wanted Tommy to hurry up; she was ready,
she was more than ready—she was becoming impatient.
Her red bandanna-styled halter was untied, draping around
her exposed breasts; her cutoff jeans and panties lay crumpled on the floorboard below her. The blond, well-tanned
young man leaning between her uplifted legs awkwardly
fumbled in his efforts to unroll a condom on his throbbing
erection.

"Come on," the nineteen-year-old blonde urged, rubbing her breasts back and forth against his chest and reaching her left hand down playfully to his testicles. "I want
it."

"I'm trying," panted the eighteen-year-old boy with three
cans of Budweiser on his breath, fresh beads of perspiration
breaking out across his forehead. After a few more futile

moments, he finally determined it was upside down and corrected the problem.

With a blunt stab, he plunged inside her and began pumping as fast as he could go, with his belt buckle flapping against the edge of the backseat. Sabrina winced slightly as he entered, but pulled him close, desperately wanting to feel the heat inside her. She could feel the bony edge of his stubbled chin pushing down on her bare right shoulder as he strained in his frantic motion. He had been eager to climb in the backseat and kiss and fondle her, but she wanted more. She wanted to feel it all, the rush, the ecstasy, the thrill of young passion. When they stopped the car, she couldn't wait to pull her clothes off and feel a warm body against hers. Even in the darkness of the car she could tell her young lover's eyes grew wide with desire when she opened the crisscrossed bandanna covering her generous breasts and thrust his face between them, just minutes ago.

She dug her short, grease-stained fingernails into his back, running them down to his surging buttocks. In her right ear she could hear his breathing growing more labored and short. The movement inside her felt good; she was just beginning to feel a swell of pleasurable sensation. Suddenly the young man froze, his body went rigid, the tendons in his neck stood out, and a strained breath seethed through his grinding teeth. She could feel the dull pulsing inside her and the subsequent slow fade of his erection.

"That's it?" Her voice was filled with unmasked irritation.

His eyes blinked with confusion. "What's the matter?"

"That's all you've got? Two minutes and puny squirt?" She pushed him back away from her, his latex-covered penis flopping out onto the vinyl seat already looking like a withered two-day-old balloon from the carnival.

"Hey look," he protested with an obviously bruised ego. "Y-Y-You were great. I thought you were really getting hot, you know, really getting into it." His expression grew smug. "Look, I'm sorry if you don't know how to really enjoy it. *Other* girls do."

Sabrina was livid. "Get your bony little ass out of my car."

"What?" Tommy looked at her in disbelief, his faded blue jeans still wound around his thighs as he knelt on the floorboard straddling the drive train.

"You heard me," she snapped, grabbing her panties and shorts off the floor and pulling them up over her legs. The acrid smell inside the car, a mixture of beer, sweat, and spermicide-covered latex, was starting to make her feel ill.

"Look, *babe,* I'm sorry." The blond surfer held up his hands in sarcastic defense. "What do you want me to do? Give me ten or fifteen minutes and I'll give you some more?" He reached out to fondle her breast again.

"More? More of *what?* No thanks. You had your shot." She pushed his hand away in disgust and climbed past him, between the bucket seats and back into the driver's seat, buttoning her fly. He awkwardly rolled over, sitting on the backseat, and started to pull up his pants, suddenly realizing he still needed to attend to the soiled prophylactic.

"Hang on a minute," he groaned as he leaned forward and opened the passenger side door, pushing the front seat forward as he climbed out. "I'll be right back. I gotta dump this thing and take a leak."

Sabrina watched him walk a few steps away from the car, carefully squeeze the rubber off his shriveled organ and toss it in the sand. His head turned around sharply when he heard the sound of the modified 454-cubic-inch engine roar to life. He didn't have time to pull up his pants before Sabrina popped the clutch, slamming her custom transmission into gear, sending a skyward shower of sand spinning from beneath her high performance tires. The passenger side door slammed shut of its own accord from the sudden forward movement.

Sabrina laughed at the sight in her rearview mirror, watching the helpless boy fall forward in an attempt to chase her with his pants around his knees. She could just make out his enraged expression, his mouth bellowing unheard ire, and his upraised right hand with extended middle finger.

The fourteen-inch Goodyear radials squealed across the blacktop as she cornered hard to her left and headed south, back toward Daytona.

When the high-distortion, high-energy rock-and-roll strains of Tom Shulz's guitar ripped into "Don't Look Back" by Boston, Sabrina's hand automatically moved to the volume knob of the radio and cranked it up loud enough to compete with the deep roar of the engine. She lowered her window a few inches to let the cool night air rush through the car. She didn't even know Tommy's last name. He was just a good-looking thing that had approached her at the time trials that day at the track. His bright smile and good sense of humor had led her to believe that he might be a lot of fun; but he was as disappointing as most of the others.

She shook her head in silent disbelief as her Charger flew down the coastal highway at just over a hundred miles an hour. Why couldn't these assholes see what she needed? Why did they always just jump on, have their thrill, and climb off—some without so much as a thank-you? She knew there was more. Deep down inside she knew there was a height of pleasure she had never been to, a place as exhilarating as her racing. She knew exactly what it felt like to move at life and death speeds, roaring between tons of screaming metal machines. But that titillating thrill wasn't enough. She wanted that feeling of raw power in all aspects of her life—especially when it came to her own body.

Her voice melodically scratched along, accompanying Boston's lead singer as her powerful V8 engine hummed on an even tone, blazing through the night. She had personally rebuilt and enhanced that engine herself. Even before Sabrina had her own driver's license, she had been working on cars—an only child helping her perfectionist father, John Doucette, a professional auto mechanic, in his garage in Jacksonville.

John Doucette never let Sabrina get away with second-class work. He relentlessly pushed her to do things right, even if it meant going back and repeating steps until the job was done. He was never a very affectionate man, was always hard on her, criticized her mercilessly, always with a Marlboro hanging out of one corner of his mouth. But he didn't treat her any different than any of the other professional mechanics in his shop. And in a strange way, she liked that. By the time Sabrina was fifteen, she could tear down a block, optimize a transmission, tune a carburetor, and custom turbocharge an engine to perfection. She was versed in everything from struts to fuel injectors. She was an excellent mechanic, but she was an even better driver.

As soon as she climbed behind a wheel at age fifteen, she became addicted to speed. The entire Jacksonville police department knew her 1965 Ford Mustang convertible on sight; and she was on a first-name basis with three-quarters of the traffic officers. When her mother and father soundly refused to pay her weekly traffic tickets, she accepted a well-meaning auto-shop teacher's advice and took her passion for speed to the racetrack. All throughout her last two years of high school, she spent every afternoon and weekend either in a garage or out at the raceway. At seventeen she entered her first race and came in third. The little bronze loving cup she was awarded became one of her most treasured possessions, and represented a key turning point in her life.

Sabrina never had any desire to hang out with the "feminine crowd" of cheerleaders and panty-hosed socialites at her high school. They used to unmercifully tease her, singing the jingle of that damned cartoon, calling her the "Teenage Witch." Her real friends were auto mechanics, part-store clerks, pit-crew technicians, and young racers with big egos and fast cars. However, if there's any justice in the universe, mother nature and her parents' genes had been kind enough to give the young blonde a stunning figure, deep smoldering green eyes, and a classic face. Many people had told her if she didn't spend "so much time messing around with those silly cars" she could easily have a successful career in modeling. The Florida sun had made its contribution to her bright blond hair; and it wasn't long before her male acquaintances caught the scent of fresh blood. And she didn't mind. It was nice to feel wanted for a change.

The "track talk" she heard so often made her so curious about sex, she lost her virginity at sixteen to a dark-haired, swarthy racer with a devilish smile—just to see what it was like. The painful experience in the cab of his Ford pickup left her mystified as to what all the attraction was. But over the last three years she had had a few sexual episodes that made her feel good enough to want to explore the subject further. Yet each time, she kept expecting something more that never seemed to happen. A few times she actually felt like she was going to lose control, but just before it happened, everything would usually stop and the guy would be zipping up his pants and bumming a cigarette. No one understood her, of that she was certain. She was a woman of passion—dark, untamable passion. But so far it lay totally undiscovered, or selfishly abused by insensitive brutes who used her more as an act of masturbation than any act of mutually pleasurable lovemaking. And yet her own personal frustrations fueled her desire to win, serving as an outlet of raw power on the battlefield of high-speed competition.

Two days after her eighteenth birthday, she had her first win. With the completed modifications on her restored Dodge Charger, she had taken the checkered flag at Daytona in a minor league race. It wasn't the big time, but it was a start. The prize money had been fifteen hundred dollars, and to her it was a fortune. In that victory, she received her first taste of blood, and wanted more. At that point in her life she could truly say that the thrill of victory was "better than sex."

Her father sternly lectured her to put her winnings aside for a college education, but she routinely used them to buy parts, fuel, and protective clothing. One of her happiest memories was opening the UPS box containing her special-ly ordered, custom-fitted fire suit. The skintight crimson unitard fit her like a glove, accentuating her dangerous curves and hard lines. She wore it around the house the entire first day and slept in it that night.

She remembered standing in front of the full-length mirror hanging on the back of her mother's bedroom door, holding her helmet under her arm, imagining standing next to her Formula-One racer in the checkerboard winner's circle at Indianapolis on Memorial Day. No other woman in history ever held that honor. She knew, even as a teenager, one day that glory would belong to her. That image often came to mind, almost daily. There she would be, her oil-stained face being washed with flowing champagne and tears of joy as Paul Newman kissed her and conceded defeat, handing her the wreath of roses and the tall silver-plated trophy. It would happen someday, or she would die trying.

But reality told her it would be many years before she climbed into the cockpit of a multimillion-dollar wing car. You had to have huge corporate sponsors and be part of a world-class racing team. Those things were far away on the horizon. She had managed to get a few articles written about her in the local papers; and a racing magazine once had her picture in it after she won a stock-car race in Louisiana the previous spring; but no national attention had ever come her way. But that could all change the following Saturday. Saturday she would be racing again at Daytona in the Sea World charity race to benefit the American Cystic Fibrosis Foundation. The world-famous NASCAR champion Richard Petty would be in poll-position number one. And based upon the results of the time trial today, she would be right on his tail in poll-position three.

Sabrina downshifted the Charger's V8 into third as she saw an approaching red traffic light a mile down the road. As she pulled further into civilization, she saw where Route A1A widened into four lanes. Her car came to a rolling stop at the light on the right side of a dark blue pickup with three young men inside and a radio turned up as loud as hers to some hard-rock station. With her eyes impatiently locked on the traffic light, she absently reached over in the bucket seat next to her, grabbed the last unopened can of Bud, and popped the top. It was getting warm, but still tasted good.

The throaty growl of her revving engine brought the attention of the bearded young man in a black T-shirt sitting on the passenger's side of the pickup, hanging his arm out the window, holding an open gold can of Michelob. Sabrina turned her head when she heard the pickup's horn honk and the three young men break into juvenile whistles and catcalls. Noticing they weren't admiring her car nor her pretty face, it suddenly dawned on her she had neglected to tie her red bandanna halter back in place. Her firm breasts stood out at prompt attention in the light of the nearby amber streetlamp. But rather than entertain any sensation of embarrassment, Sabrina felt a rush of wicked teasing wash over her.

She rolled her window the rest of the way down and turned her shoulders toward the door to give the three ogling spectators a better look. She ran her tongue over her full red lips, her words dripping with sensuality, "Catch me and you win a taste."

The stunned young men sat there in shocked silence until the light turned green, then were simultaneously startled by the sudden, ferocious roar of the V8. Sabrina's tires smoked and screamed between the friction of the asphalt and the torque of a nearly four-hundred horsepower engine. She broke into peals of laughter watching the frantic little truck going as fast as it could, fading away in her rearview mirror. But miles down the road, as she turned off of A1A onto McKensie Blvd., she wondered if perhaps three might have been better than one.

3

March 1972

Cambridge, Massachusetts

DR. CALVIN "CALL ME CAL" DOMINSKI COURTEOUSLY OPENED
the door of the Chemistry Building for Rae as she exited,
quickly following along beside her as he continued his
critique of the findings report she had turned in earlier that
week. It was still cold outside, the spring thaw a month or
two away; but recent temperatures in the forties had gener-
ated several inches of dirty slush throughout the streets and
sidewalks. Both Rae and Cal bundled their coats tightly
about their shoulders, hands buried in their pockets, as they
walked together through the crisp night air toward the
apartment buildings of Harvard Yard.

Dr. Dominski's breath frosted with every word coming
out of his mouth. He was obviously excited. "I'm telling
you, Rae, you must submit your report not only to JAMA
and NEJM, but to the U.S. patent office as well, before
someone runs off with your idea."

"You really think that's necessary?" Rae didn't know
whether her long-time thesis advisor was just being flattering or whether she really did need some legal protection in
her work.

"Absolutely," he insisted. "With the gene displacement
results we saw this week, I don't think it's premature to say
we may well have 'broken the code' to finally eliminating
many of the replicative infirmities." The magnitude of that
statement made them both shudder with excitement. It was
like finding the vaccine for polio, or maybe even better.

Rae was beaming behind her freezing, rosy cheeks. When it looked like they were getting nowhere, a breakthrough finally came. Almost by accident she found the right catalyst compound that stimulated DNA replacement in cancer cells. They had tested the serum-based formula on a volunteer who had been diagnosed with a small malignant tumor in the right breast. Attending physicians at Boston General Hospital had prescribed a radical mastectomy for the tumor, but the woman had graciously volunteered to let Rae try her treatment on her over a four-week period, prior to the scheduled surgery. X-rays that week had revealed the tumor completely gone, each cancerous cell replaced by the normal surrounding tissue that the DNA pattern said should be there. Seeing the woman's tears of joy was all Rae needed to confirm her conviction that what she was doing was the most important work in the world. Not even Rebecca could take away that joy.

"And it's all so simple," Cal went on. "We let the cell's own internal intelligence directly attack the physical anomalies and return it to the ideal state. Why, it's miraculous!"

Rae giggled. "No, it's science, Cal. And it's a treatment that we need to see developed into a clinical procedure that can bring the same hope of success to all women that we saw in Mrs. Donnely."

"Indeed, Rae. Indeed." Dr. Dominski nodded vigorously, his tweed Gatsby cap flapping up and down. "But please, take my advice and see a lawyer. You could be a rich lady some day if you do, or a very poor one if you don't."

Rae shook her head as they turned the corner and headed toward her four-story apartment building. "I'm not interested in money, Cal. I just want to see people helped."

Cal Dominski coughed and stumbled slightly over a chunk of ice, chuckling to himself. "Well, it may sound callous, but you had better think about money. If you don't, your work may end up sitting on someone's shelf who doesn't want to see it developed. You know, like all those oil companies buying up car engines that don't break or that don't need very much fuel. All because their existence would threaten their financial empires. Rae, I've been in biochemical research for many, many years, and I've seen many discoveries, some big, some small. And each one represented a threat to someone's empire. Don't forget that."

Rae smiled to herself. "I won't." She appreciated the slightly overweight Cal Dominski. His personality was akin to the jolly old uncle in everyone's family, whom you see once or twice a year at Thanksgiving and Christmas, who has the magical ability to make everyone laugh, recounting the embarrassing escapades of your cousins, parents, and other relatives. But he was more than that; he was a good friend. Even though, at first, he thought her theories on cellular mutation and DNA pattern identification were completely insane.

But over the last three years Cal had grown to respect the conscientious young woman from Houston. And Rae dearly liked being treated like a colleague instead of a student. On several occasions Cal had come to her asking for advice on some of his research projects and theories. She had been delighted to steer him in the right direction more than once. And he wasn't too proud to accept the criticism or the help. She appreciated that most of all.

They continued to revel in the implications of the discovery all the way down the narrow street to Rae's apartment building. As she turned to go up the icy steps, she stopped and looked at her friend. "Thanks for walking with me, Cal."

The older man looked around almost absentmindedly. "Oh, are we here already?" He chuckled softly to himself again.

She smiled at him, then leaned over and gave him a hug. "Thanks for all your help."

"Oh!" He leaned back jovially, his hands still stuffed down in the pockets of his overcoat. "Don't let the neighbors see you doing that. I have enough trouble keeping tenure as it is."

This time she laughed. "Good night, Cal. I'll drop by your

office tomorrow and we can start going over the testing procedures. We still don't have those finalized."

He nodded. "That's right. Well, don't let this old man keep you out in the cold. Until tomorrow, Doctor?"

"Until tomorrow, Doctor." Rae gave him one more warm smile, pushed her glasses up on her nose again, turned and carefully ascended the concrete stairs. Quickly pulling off her mitten, she fished her key ring out of her coat pocket just as she made it to the second-floor landing. As she walked down the freezing hallway, she separated her jingling keys, pulling the apartment door key out between shivering fingers. But at her door she stopped with an annoyed frown.

There on the doorknob was the red T-shirt. That was the agreed-upon signal that one of them had company and the other needed to stay away. Rae had come to see that T-shirt quite often over the past two years. Rebecca entertained to the point of excess. Rae looked at her watch. It was only 10:45. Their own self-appointed curfew was midnight. The thought of having to go back out in the cold and find something to do for an hour and fifteen minutes bordered on cruelty. But that was just like Rebecca. And it wasn't like she couldn't afford a nice motel room for her little escapades. Why did she have to do this tonight?

With a huff and a shrug, Rae turned around, plodded back down the stairs, and walked across the street to the all-night coffee shop. Unfortunately, Cal was nowhere in sight. He would have been nice to have around. She took a seat near the window so she could see when Rebecca's guest left, in the highly unlikely event she abided by the curfew. On a couple of occasions in the past Rae had asserted her rights at midnight and boldly entered the apartment at her own risk. But each time she had merely found Rebecca's bedroom door closed and had to lie there in bed listening to all sorts of obscene sounds emanating from the next room. She was not in the mood for it tonight. The thought of a chastising phone call came to her, but she knew Rebecca would just bitch her out and hang up. And that would only make things worse.

The waitress brought her a cup of coffee and the daily newspaper. She read the comics, did the crossword puzzle, looked at what was for sale in the classifieds, and even forced herself to peruse the sports page. Four cups of coffee later she looked at her watch. It was five minutes till twelve. No one had left the building since she sat down. She thought about the phone call again but decided against it. Once more the image of Mrs. Donnely's face came to mind. The thought quickly melted away the frustrated feelings she had for Rebecca. In light of what had happened this week, Rebecca didn't matter. What the hell? Let her have her fun. Great things were happening in her own life, and none of them concerned the precious Miss Rebecca Danforth.

At precisely midnight Rae paid her tab and plodded back across the street to her building. When she arrived at the door, the T-shirt was still in place. She hesitated for a moment. People lose track of time, she thought, still in a generous mood. It happens all the time. A confrontation tonight, especially with four cups of caffeine coursing through her veins, would not be pleasant. So with a martyr's sigh she plodded back across the street to the coffee shop. The waitress looked at her with concern. Rae just gave her a futile shrug and reclaimed her seat by the window.

Wide-awake, she passed the next thirty minutes thinking about Cal's advice. Who could she see about a patent? She didn't know any lawyers. Her best friend, Nikki Thompson, was about to graduate from Harvard Law this semester, but Rae wasn't sure she knew anything about patents or legal liability for medical procedures. She resolved to call Nikki anyway. Even if her friend didn't know, she at least might know who to call.

Rae looked at her watch again. It was 12:35. Time was up. Confrontation or no confrontation, it was her apartment too. Even if she had to listen to Rebecca's orgasmic moans all night, she was going to her own warm bed and call it a night. Once again she plodded back across the icy cold street to her building and retraced her steps up the stairs to the apartment door. The sentinel T-shirt still kept its silent vigil.

Rae grabbed the shirt and pulled it off the doorknob, stabbing her key in the lock with intentional disdain, hoping the sound of it would alert whoever was inside of her arrival. She threw open the door, and the rich melodies of a string symphony playing on the stereo flooded out into the hallway. What she saw made her abruptly stop in the doorway.

There in the middle of the living room floor on the ugly shag carpet, Rebecca lay naked on top of a man. Rae had never actually seen someone having sex. She had seen love scenes in movies and imagined it from books and conversation, but never just walked in and beheld two people engaged in the act. At least that's what registered in her mind in the first instant; but something was not right according to the mental image of what she thought sex was supposed to look like. A moment later her startled, tired, caffeine-wired brain registered what she was actually seeing.

Rebecca was laying on top of the man with her thighs wrapped around his head, while her head was buried between the man's legs, slowly bobbing up and down. From either end of the couple she could hear the wet, juicy noises of their mutual body feast. Rae just stood there for several seconds not saying anything, still holding the red T-shirt in one hand, her keys in the other. The writhing couple in front of her obviously were too engaged to notice her presence. After a few more awkward seconds, Rae watched Rebecca toss her long black hair over her shoulder with her hand and lift her head up with irritation. The man's swollen penis slowly slid out of her mouth.

"Close the door, Rae, you're letting the cold in." Rebecca twirled her tongue around the man's organ and began to resume her activity.

Utterly appalled, Rae couldn't believe Rebecca could be so unconcerned about her presence. However, the man lying on his back beneath her was obviously more concerned that he and his lover were no longer alone. Rae watched him frantically squirm underneath Rebecca, obviously trying to get up.

Rebecca began to laugh, offering little cooperation to her partner's sense of panic. "Hold on, loverboy. Calm down. It's only my roommate."

With an awkward shove the man moved Rebecca's body off of his face and rolled away toward the far wall, hastily grabbing at a pile of discarded clothes near the television. Rae's mouth dropped open even wider when she suddenly recognized the young man as Matthew Tobias.

Rae slammed the door behind her, throwing the T-shirt to the floor in disgust. Matthew awkwardly refused to look her in the eye, putting his clothes on as quickly as he could. Rebecca just sat cross-legged on the floor with a devil-may-care look on her face.

"Don't worry about it," Rebecca commented to the embarrassed young man. "She doesn't care."

Matthew looked down at Rebecca with a mixture of embarrassed anger and frustration in his voice, trying to whisper through clenched teeth, "I thought you said she wasn't coming home tonight."

Rebecca just shrugged. "I thought she wasn't. But like I said, it doesn't matter. Right, Rae dear?"

Rae looked into Rebecca's cold dark eyes. "You did this on purpose, didn't you?"

"I do everything on purpose, little Rae." Rebecca stood up, grabbed her blue robe from the back of the couch and threaded her arms through the sleeves.

With his bright polyester shirt and bell-bottomed corduroy pants back in place, Matthew grabbed his coat and shoes and ran out of the apartment, not bothering to say good-bye to either woman. Just as the door closed, Rebecca mockingly fired at Rae, "Now look at what you've done. You've frightened the poor boy away. And he was just about to finish too."

Rae took her coat off and hung it up behind the door. "Well, Rebecca, I was certainly wrong about one thing. Matthew *was* low enough to eat out of the gutter."

Rebecca spun around and flopped down on the couch. "Witty. Very witty, dear."

Rae put her hands on her hips defiantly. "What did you hope to accomplish by staging this little show, Rebecca? Do you really think I care who you contract your venereal diseases with?"

Rebecca's expression grew cold, her tone more terse. "What you saw here tonight, Dr. Taylor, was proof that I know what I'm talking about, and I know how to get what I want."

"And you wanted Matthew?" Rae demanded, feeling a sense of outrage and betrayal; not because of any existing relationship she had with Matthew Tobias, but for the simple audacity of Rebecca taking the time to seek him out, just to spite her.

"I was curious. After we last spoke of him I wondered if he really *did* know what he was missing. And oh, by the way, your friend Matthew *was* a lot of fun," Rebecca began to tease. "And I was certainly right about him—one of the slow, patient ones. He definitely had more on his mind than his studies. Rae, you really don't know what you've been missing."

"You seduced him," Rae snapped. "And you did it just to embarrass me. Well, I'm sorry, Miss Danforth, it didn't work. All you've done is show me what a filthy slut you really are."

"Didn't it work, Rae dear?" Rebecca's tone became patronizing. "I saw your eyes when you looked down at me. What was the matter? Haven't you ever tasted a man yourself? Never had anything warm and wet in your mouth? No? Of course not. Who would want a skinny little Texas girl that's never even seen a man without his clothes on except perhaps on a dissection table! Oooh, but maybe that's how you like your men, cold and hard."

"What *is* your problem, Rebecca?" Rae demanded, shaking her head in disbelief. "Has your gonorrhea finally deteriorated your brain to this level?"

Rebecca's eyes flashed with fury. "Get it straight, little

miss peaches and cream. I can, and will, do as I please, when I please, and with whomever I please. You're right! Tonight's lesson was for your benefit! But apparently you've missed the moral of the story, so I'll explain it more clearly for the simpleminded in the room. I not only took what I wanted from dear little Matthew, but I wanted you to know that I can have anything I want, including what belongs to you. Anything or anyone. Anything you possess, I can have if I desire it. And one of these days you are going to drop this academic superiority bullshit and realize who's really in charge here."

Rae laughed in amazement. "That's it, isn't it? You're so damned insecure it's incredible. Someone with a brain instead of just a body intimidates you." She laughed again. "I guess the truth finally comes out. We both know you're a stupid cheese-brain with an IQ somewhere between a rock and plant life, and the only way you've made the grades this far is by screwing every teacher you've ever had. And the only way you're ever going to succeed in life is literally by the seat of your pants. Or should I say what's *inside* them?"

Rebecca forced a laugh, then jumped up from the couch and stormed over directly in front of Rae, shouting at the top of her lungs, "Is that what you think, little Rae. Little flat-chested, immaculate Rae. Is it? Guess again, you stupid bitch! I'm going to succeed beyond anything you could ever imagine! And in the process I'm going to watch you shrivel up and die in your lonely little world of books and test tubes! In fact, I'm going to enjoy watching you fail, Rae. Almost as much as I enjoyed sucking your little boyfriend dry tonight."

Rae slapped Rebecca's face as hard as she could. Rebecca staggered from the force of the blow. In the next instant Rae expected Rebecca to lunge at her with her claws fully bared. But instead Rebecca lifted her head with a quick snap, tossing her dark black hair over her shoulder, massaging her left cheek, which was rapidly turning bright red. She let out a slow, macabre, malevolent laugh of pure evil.

"You made a choice to do that, Rae Taylor. We all make

choices." Rebecca controlled her vehement breathing with an eerie resolve. "If I were you, I'd watch your back."

"Don't threaten me," Rae retorted, lowering her voice to the same blood-chilling tone. "I'm not afraid of you."

Rebecca's eyes narrowed. "You ought to be. Remember. No matter what you do, or what you have, I can always be there to take it away and watch you cry."

"You'll never see me cry." Rae lifted her chin defiantly. Her emotions were spinning at such a feverish pitch, it was hard to resist the urge to burst into tears, warm tears of release, tears that would wash away all of the anxiety, hatred, and fear she was feeling at the moment.

"We'll see about that," Rebecca sparred. "When you see me running some of the most powerful corporations in America and you're still trying to find a job at some back-alley mercy mission, we'll see if you won't cry."

The phrase "mercy mission" triggered Rae's memory. She remembered the face of Mrs. Donnely. Her last words were those of thanks for Rae's mercy upon her. It brought back a small portion of the good feelings she had all day. The memory jarred her mind back to reality. For a moment she couldn't believe Rebecca actually managed to spoil her near-perfect day. However, the thought of her doing so fueled her ire and bolstered her courage.

"I've had it with you, Rebecca." Rae shook her head, turned around and walked toward her room. "You're a spoiled, rotten little slut, and I have no desire to spend another moment under the same roof with you. Have a nice life. I'm sure it'll be a *ball* for you, if you'll forgive the pun."

Rebecca followed her. "Fine! I wanted you out of my apartment anyway. Couldn't you get the hint? Good luck finding a room anywhere in the Yard on your miserable little stipend from Mommy."

Rae wasn't listening anymore; she was gathering up her belongings. Rebecca continued to harp and taunt her as she hauled down all of her earthly belongings to her Volkswagen. It took half a dozen trips. When she was sure she had everything, she came back up and tossed her apartment key on the kitchen table. Rebecca had apparently run out of insults for the time being; she just stood in the kitchenette glaring.

"Well, I believe that's everything," Rae said almost pleasantly. And then, with an insincere smile, just before she closed the door, she shot, "And if you find anything else that belongs to me, do be so kind as to shove it up your butt so far you choke on it."

Rae slammed the door and raced down the apartment stairs, desperately wanting the satisfaction of having the final word. She was unaware of Rebecca going to the window and watching her drive away, had no idea of the smoldering blaze that was burning beneath deep inside the Connecticut debutante's heart.

"Build your fortune, dearest Rae. Build it well," Rebecca muttered with a half laugh toward the vanishing Volkswagen. "And before you taste a moment of its pleasure, I'll be there to make it mine."

4

April 1990

Dallas, Texas

THE UNIFORMED ATTENDANT OPENED THE DOOR OF THE SPACIOUS office and admitted a handsome woman in her early fifties, elegantly dressed in a basic black day-wear dress with tapered bodice and a knee-length flared skirt. A tasteful array of custom-crafted Cartier gold jewelry graced her ears, neck, and wrists. The woman stopped inside the office door, visibly impressed with the interior office. It was thirty feet by thirty feet, with a high ten-foot classic ceiling accented with ornate crown moldings. The opposite wall was all glass, facing the gardens by the lake. In the center of the glass wall was a chrome-edged sliding glass door which opened to a private terrace above the gardens. Out on the inlaid tile terrace the woman could see a six-foot-diameter sunken hot tub flanked by amber flagstones. A small stone waterfall splashed down into the steaming waters.

The side walls of the room were lined with bookshelves, graced with various art treasures of brass and bronze. Positioned diagonally, between the rear glass wall and the ornately carved credenza on the left wall, was a massive oval writing desk made of a single sheet of two-inch-thick beveled glass, perched atop two polished marble pedestals on either end nestled softly in the high-pile rose carpet that covered the entire floor. The room contained the rich, oiled scents of mahogany and teakwood, plus the delicate fragrances of the plants and flowers that accented the perimeters. Seated in the high-backed cordovan leather chair behind the desk was Marsha Collins. She smiled and stood as the woman entered.

"Ms. Halliran, do come in. I've been expecting you." Marsha rose and walked around her desk with her hand extended, dressed conservatively in a dark business suit with pleated skirt. She wore a stunning diamond brooch on her lapel, which Louise Halliran was certain she had seen at Tiffany's in their "African Treasures Collection" on her last visit to Manhattan. Marsha's dark red hair was neatly folded back in a French braid.

The older woman came in and took Marsha's hand. "Good afternoon, Ms. Collins. I'm so delighted to finally meet you. I've read several of your books."

"Oh please, call me Marsha." Marsha's smile was infectious, and Louise Halliran quickly caught it. "Won't you please have a seat."

Marsha showed Ms. Halliran to the white leather couch on the front wall of her office, and took a seat herself in one of the two Queen Anne chairs that were part of the matched sitting group. A silver tea service had been set on the dark cherrywood coffee table between them.

"Thank you," the older woman said, nodding as she sat down. "But please call me Louise."

"Very well, Louise." Marsha picked up a burgundy portfolio from the coffee table and opened it. "Before we get started, I trust you have found your accommodations to your liking?"

"Oh, my, I must say." The woman put her hand out on her knee. "It's the finest suite I think I've ever seen. I've seen nothing like it anywhere in the world."

"Nor will you." Marsha lifted the teapot. "Tea?"

Louise nodded with a polished, genteel smile. "Please."

As Marsha poured the steaming blend into one of the antique bone-china cups, she asked, "And I hope you found the service to your liking?"

The older woman blushed slightly. "I must say so. But you must tell me," she said, her voice lower, as if she didn't want to be overheard, "how do you find so many beautiful young men to work here?" She dropped a lump of sugar into her cup and stirred it with one of the small silver spoons. "They're all so thoughtful and considerate."

Marsha filled her cup. "They're all highly trained professionals, Louise. And they're highly paid to see that each moment here is enjoyable for you. But we'll discuss that more in detail in a moment. First, I need to go over a few items on your membership application."

"Yes?" Louise nodded as she sipped her tea, holding both cup and saucer together, her little finger pointing as it was properly bred to do.

Marsha sipped her steaming, aromatic cup and carefully set it down. "As you may know, I am the senior administrator here at the North Dallas Women's Center, and my responsibility is twofold. First, I see to it that you receive the exact care and treatment you require to your utter and complete satisfaction. And secondly, I make sure that the center remains profitable."

Louise smiled. "Do you do this full time now, or are you still lecturing?"

Marsha rolled her eyes. "I still travel and give motivational lectures from time to time, but my work here at the center occupies most of my time."

"Do you still dabble in real estate?" Louise inquired with an eager tone of gossip.

"I still maintain a few investments. But we're here today to discuss your needs today, Louise, not mine." Marsha did her best not to sound scolding.

The older woman sounded apologetic, "I'm sorry. I've read about you for so many years, I was just thrilled to have this chance to finally get to meet you in person."

"I'll tell you what," Marsha offered politely. "After our interview, I'd be delighted to treat you to lunch in the Montressor Salon. The decor is Italian Renaissance, bright regalia motif, that sort of thing; and the chef there prepares a sole almondine that will melt your palate. We can chat about anything you'd like then."

"Oh, that sounds marvelous," cooed the older woman.

"Now, let's see here . . ." Marsha began looking over the forms inside the portfolio. "Louise, you've stated here that your husband has been deceased for three, almost four years. I trust you're stable financially?"

"Oh, yes." Louise nodded, her tone suddenly turning very professional and businesslike. "Frank was CEO of Amtex Oil over in Forth Worth. My estate holds more than sixty percent of the outstanding shares of public stock, and I have ten percent of the preferred shares. After Frank's death I assumed the chairmanship of the corporation, and I have been seeing to its affairs ever since."

"Profitably?" Marsh asked, her pen poised to take a few notes on the application.

Louise laughed. "Yes! And even more so than before Frank died. He was very old-fashioned in his thinking. As a matter of fact, it was after reading one of your books that I began restaffing many of my key corporate executive and managerial positions with fresh thinkers and innovators.

Just like you said in *Harnessed Ambition,* 'New ideas and new methods should flow in just like every fresh breath rejuvenates the blood.' I have to tell you, Marsha, some of your recommendations have been the very spark of life my company needed to really succeed."

Marsha graciously accepted the flattery with a courteous smile. "That's wonderful, Louise. Because to be quite frank, the reason I ask is that our highly specialized treatments here at the North Dallas Women's Center are very costly. We openly recognize that fact, and we want to be very up front with you from the outset. None of the unique medical or therapeutic services is covered by any insurance plans, so all payments must be in the form of cash or cashier's check."

Louise's face grew puzzled. "Well, exactly what kind of money are we talking about here?"

Marsha's eyes scanned the membership application again. "I don't see anything unusual here on the application, so short of Dr. Taylor's input, I can quote you the customary fees. We require an annual membership fee of $250,000 plus ten thousand dollars per day service fee. Medical treatments are additional."

Louise Halliran's eyes grew wide, her cup and saucer sinking to her lap. "That's incredible. And what, pray tell, might I expect for such an amount of money as that?"

Marsha closed the portfolio. "Louise, here at the center we do some very amazing things. In addition to the resort atmosphere you've seen, you will have an opportunity to receive special counseling and treatment by Dr. Rae Taylor and Dr. Alicia Brighton. Dr. Brighton is a cosmetic surgeon. She can do anything from breast augmentation and nose jobs, to lyposuction, bone and skin grafts. In a nutshell, she can fix the machine and make it shine like you never thought possible. Then there is Dr. Taylor's special gift. She has a chemical therapy treatment that can make all of those age spots on your hands and face disappear. The wrinkles around your eyes and on your cheeks and forehead will be gone. In fact, your whole appearance will go through an amazing metamorphosis, causing your entire body to look like it did when you were in perhaps your early to mid-thirties, and most likely even better."

Louise gasped. "I don't believe it!"

"We guarantee your satisfaction in writing. Here." Marsha handed Louise a brochure. "Look at this information at your leisure. It's the testimonials of some of the most prominent and reputable women in the country who have benefited from the services here at the center. We actually call this particular treatment Aging Regression, for in reality that's what it is. In a very real way, we can actually turn the clock back for you."

Louise opened the booklet and began to glance through it. "Why, here's a picture of Gladys Jacobs! I know her. I thought she just had a face-lift and colored her hair."

"You haven't seen her undressed. Aging Regression affects the whole body, not just the face." Marsha knew the woman was intrigued. "But there's much more you need to know."

Louise looked up, her expression growing more eager.

Marsha continued, "Our service here at the Women's Center goes far beyond the mere superficial. We endeavor to treat all of the needs of a woman. In addition to the medical treatments, should you decide to pursue membership here, you will be assigned a personal therapist. We firmly believe our medical treatments can do miraculous things for the outer woman, but the inner woman must progress in pace with the changes going on outside. Does that make sense, Louise?" Marsha leaned forward, looking for Louise's concurrence before going on, the lecturer in her coming out again.

Louise nodded. "Absolutely." She was savoring every word that came out of Marsha's mouth.

Marsha nodded and continued. "Right! Therefore, we must ask you to fully take advantage of the therapeutic sessions. Your personal therapist's sole job is to find the real woman in you and bring her to the surface. He's there to help you feel alive, full of vitality, and eager to live life to the fullest, or . . . have that 'spark of life,' as you put it."

Louise was beaming. "That sounds wonderful. But how does he possibly accomplish that?"

Marsha's eyes flashed knowingly. "Any way you want him to."

The two women just stared into each other's eyes for a moment. In a few seconds the weight of Marsha Collins's statement registered with Louise.

"You don't mean they . . ." she began, trailing off shyly.

"As often as you desire," Marsha said, finishing her thought for her. "In ways you've never dared to dream. Louise, there is nothing you can't have or do here at the Women's Center. This is the place where your most intimate fantasies can be realized and indulged in, as much as your mind and body can stand. And your Aging Regression treatments will help you stand quite a bit."

Louise's face was starting to flush slightly. "Well, I don't know about that. I mean, I've lived a long time, and . . . I come from a generation that, well . . . doesn't . . ." She set her cup and saucer down on the coffee table, folding her hands in her lap, unconsciously covering her virtue.

Marsha laughed. "And that's why you're here today. Isn't it? To discover something new, a part of yourself that you've only dreamed about. Louise, face it, you're successful, powerful, and you deserve the richness of life that your success affords you. You said yourself that my principles have helped you in the past. Here is an opportunity for you to see what life's really like for the complete woman."

Louise's eyes were hesitant. "But isn't what you're suggesting illegal?"

"Not at all," Marsha corrected with a trace of indignance. "We're a licensed health clinic. Our therapy, whether it be physical, mental, or . . . otherwise . . . is state approved and regulated—just like the Mayo Clinic or Masters and Johnson. But the decision is yours, Louise. It's very simple. The North Dallas Women's Center is here to help women be beautiful, inside and out. Isn't that what you want?"

Louise nodded slightly. She knew what years of loneliness

felt like, watching herself grow older. Even before Frank's death, she experienced the pain of being left at home while he went out into the world to slay the dragons and conquer new empires. But now she was in charge; she ran the machine and had made it shine where he couldn't. Marsha was right, she did deserve the best. She had worked for it, and earned it. Her eyes strayed over Marsha's shoulder, out to the hot tub on the terrace. She watched the sparkling water of the waterfall rush over the rough stones into the steaming waters below. She wondered what it would be like lounging inside it with the handsome dark-haired attendant who had taken her arm so politely and walked her down the hall to Marsha's office.

"Do I have my choice of . . . *therapists?*" Louise asked timidly.

"Of course." Marsha nodded with a playful grin. She stood up and walked over to her desk, retrieving a leatherbound picture album. "Here is our current available staff. The selection is yours—anyone you like."

Louise took the book and opened it. It looked like a men's fashion catalog, but without the wording and prices. A girlish thrill ran through her as she paged through leaf after leaf of athletic-looking young gentlemen, some with light hair, some dark, some with curls, some straight, all of them athletically built, tanned, and well-groomed. Louise muttered to herself, almost giddy, "This is amazing."

"If you'd like," Marsha said softly, closing the sale, "we could schedule your first therapy session for later this afternoon."

Louise looked up suddenly. "Could you?"

"It's up to you, Louise." Marsha was already pulling out the contracts from her portfolio. "Everything here is up to you. Whether you let us take a little of gravity's cruelty out of your bustline; or whether you just want to come by for a hot-oil massage by your therapist; or if you just want a relaxing round of golf, a game of tennis, or a cup of tea—we're here to serve you. And whatever your innermost needs are, you'll find them deliciously met here at the North Dallas Women's Center."

Louise reached down on the coffee table and picked up the ebony Mont Blanc pen lying next to the contract Marsha had placed there. "I think I can get to the bank and be back by three o'clock. Would that be convenient?"

Marsha smiled. "Everything will be prepared to your liking. But you need to select a therapist before we can schedule your appointment for this afternoon. I can have Stephanie set you up for an initial consultation appointment with Dr. Brighton and Dr. Taylor later in the week."

Louise dotted the i's in "Louise" and "Halliran" with two quick stabs, put the elegant pen back down and picked up the photo album again for several seconds. Finally she giggled. "Oooh, I like this one here with the blond hair. It says his name is Benjamin?"

Marsha absently wet her lips, a delightful warm rush of recollection washing over her. She had hired Benjamin personally last month. He was a Southern Methodist University graduate student, a business major working his way to an MBA. His talent with his hands alone had merited him a special incentive bonus to come to work at the Women's Center. So far he hadn't been assigned any clients. Rae still had him in training. "Excellent choice, Louise. I'll call him and make sure he's available at three. Shall I put you down for a massage, and then dinner in your room with Benjamin?"

Louise's heart was racing. "That will be fine. Would you be so kind as to have the young lady out front summon my car?"

Marsha looked at her new customer awkwardly. "You've changed your mind about lunch?"

"Lunch?" Louise looked dazed. "Oh, yes. Sorry, perhaps another time, Marsha dear. My bank is in Fort Worth, and I'm sure you know traffic is terrible at the noon hour. I'll be lucky to be back by three." She stood with marked urgency. Marsha politely rose with her.

Louise put her hand on Marsha's arm. "But please accept my apologies. I really would love to stay and chat, but I completely understand your financial policy."

Marsha couldn't resist, "Then I take it you find our fees acceptable?"

"Oh, quite, quite," said Ms. Halliran as she did her best to give Marsha a quick handshake and a courteous smile. Then she hurried out of the office, and practically ran down the corridor.

Marsha walked back to her desk chuckling softly to herself. She called Stephanie at the front desk, had her summon Ms. Halliran's limousine, then plopped down in her desk chair, pensively looking out over the lake. A speedboat pulling a water skier cruised by. She glanced at her watch; it was almost time for *her* therapist to arrive. One of Rick's massages and a dip in the hot tub before lunch was definitely on the agenda today. She mused with another half laugh, "This sure beats the hell out of selling real estate."

5

September 1981

Ontario, California

SHE FELT NUMB AGAINST THE ENDLESS, DEAFENING THUNDER; THE constant body-bruising vibration; her shoulders burning against the webbed harness; her back throbbing against the molded seat, knuckles bone-white, leather-sheathed palms and fingers aching, wrists locked, forearms screaming with pain—all steeled against the torque of the wheel. Each short breath was strained through her clenched teeth and an oil-stained fire mask; the pungent fumes of the nitro-alcohol fuel mixture still stung her nasal membranes, even after two hours of punishment. Rivulets of perspiration burned down into her eyes behind the tight face mask and oil-smeared glass, melding together the river of vibrant colors washing by on either side of the never-ending, left-banking and straightening black asphalt stripe. Her reflexes sidestepped blurred machines by pure instinct; the agony of endurance held in constant check by the electric sensation of raw power—and the insatiable drive to win.

The crackle of the radio headset in Sabrina's helmet jarred her concentration. "Pit Five! Pit Five!"

"Roger-One!" she screamed above the storm.

Five laps later her Pontiac Grand Prix wound into the pit area, screeching to a halt in front of her crew. Five bodies in crimson coveralls leaped over the safety wall and flew into their assigned tasks like worker bees swarming their queen, changing tires, refueling, and clearing the windshield. The voice of her crew chief came into her earpiece again. "How's it holding?"

"We can do it," she garbled into the microphone installed in her helmet, taking a moment to flex her fingers and rotate her wrists.

"Sabrina, you've got half a lap up on Conner. He's already had his last pit," came the mechanized-sounding voice amid the sounds of air wrenches and the high- to low-pitched furies randomly screaming by on the track to her right. "He won't be stopping before the finish line."

"Neither will I," she yelled. "Call clear!"

"Clear!" came the voice at the same instant her right foot stepped into the accelerator for the last time. It wouldn't come off until the checkered flag.

The torrential river of color with a bed of black washed around her once again; the ringing in her ears resumed its constant tone. With ten laps to go at the Ontario Motor Speedway, fifteen competitors were left in the three-hundred-mile race. The winner would be crowned NASCAR champion for 1981. Sabrina Doucette's Pontiac now held a quarter of a lap lead on the rest of the field.

This year had certainly been Sabrina's year for pro-stock competition. After her wins in Florida at Daytona, she was able to get some local businesses to sponsor her in bigger and bigger races. As her prize money grew along with her reputation, so the quality and performance of her cars improved in direct proportion. This year alone she had taken the checkered flag in five major pro-stock races. Her picture had appeared on the cover of *Car and Driver* magazine. People in the deep South were beginning to hail her as a folk hero. But her biggest break came in the fall of 1980, when Margaret Banks, owner of Consolidated Foods Corporation in Minneapolis, took notice of her success.

Margaret's vice-president of advertising signed Sabrina to a promotional campaign which put her adorable, smiling face on billboards across the country. In return, Consolidated Foods fit the bill for the customized Pontiac Grand Prix plus the salaries of the mechanics and crew. Her winnings in 1981 had already exceeded $400,000. If she could maintain her lead at Ontario, the purse would more than double that. But even with a potential NASCAR championship under her belt, Sabrina still had her sights set higher—much higher.

The image of her standing in the winner's circle next to the Formula-One wing car at Indianapolis was never very far from her mind; but the door to that universe was still closed. Not even the coffers of Consolidated Foods could play in that league. No, one day she would try out for one of the Formula-One racing teams, like the legendary Penski, Foyt, Andretti, Marks, or Unser. Their teams all had the resources to compete—huge oil companies, tobacco empires, major breweries, and auto manufacturer's budgets sponsoring them, ready to spend millions of dollars just to prepare for a single race. One day she would find a way to join them.

Sabrina's heart pounded even harder when she saw the white flag waving from the marshal's stand. One lap to go. Eugene Conner was somewhere behind her, but that didn't matter; all that mattered was pure concentration. Four turns to the checkered flag and the race was history.

"He's right on your ass! Drafting," came the muted voice in her earpiece, from her spotter in the grandstand. "Steady in turn one. Congestion ycllow."

Just ahead, two racers flanked either side of the track, both a lap down. Sabrina came out of turn number one threading easily between them, but quickly discovered the traffic she had been warned about. She swung wide to her right to avoid one car, slowing slightly against the outside wall, riding high all the way down to turn number two. Another racer positioned on the center of the track prohibited her from diving in low on the second turn—but not Eugene Conner.

His dark blue Chevrolet ducked down, hugging the white infield line, using gravity from the bank of the turn to slingshot himself into the lead. Sabrina was livid.

"Bogey left, bogey left," came the voice.

"I see him, dammit! Shut up and let me do my job!" she screamed into the microphone, her eyes sharply scanning the straightaway just ahead like a bloodthirsty animal looking to pounce upon some unsuspecting prey. Her foot held the accelerator flat to the floor. With three more lane changes, she had successfully negotiated her way through the scattered field, and was now drafting behind the dark blue Chevy. Two turns to the flag. The risky strategy, whirling through her mind would have to be timed perfectly.

At speeds in excess of 185 mph, her bumper stayed within inches of the dark blue Chevy's down the backstretch, through turn number three, along the far side of the track, and barreling headlong into turn number four. It was now or never; the move could not be conscious, but instinctive, timed with raw nerves and a conqueror's passion.

As the two cars approached the turn, the Chevy began to drop down low. But just as he made his move, Sabrina downshifted, red-lining her tortured engine, swinging her left fender out to the right, moving her vehicle high in the turn. Conner was instantly alerted to the move by his spotter and defensively swung his car to the right to block the pass attempt. In the same instant, Sabrina upshifted, her forearms flexing against the wheel with all the strength she had remaining, swerving her car to the left, diving in low, her right front fender barely easing by Conner's left rear.

Her crimson Pontiac pulled alongside the Chevy as they exited the last turn, heading for the finish line in a dead heat. Now it was purely a matter of which General Motors engine wanted it the most. Sabrina could feel her knuckles about to burst through the flesh of her steel-gripped hands on the wheel. Her eyes could see the finish line less than a quarter of a mile away. It would be over in seconds. The crowd in the grandstand was on its feet shouting in near delirium, the impassioned announcer's voice bellowing to the end.

Sabrina felt a slight jolt to her right, accompanied by the high-pitched scream of metal. The two cars had made incidental contact, but not serious. She knew better than to look, but in that instant an idea came to mind. There was no time to think about it, just a split second for the body's voluntary muscles to instinctively react. Her hands began moving to her right, and the screeching sound of metal was heard again. She kept her grip steady, increasing her angle toward the grandstand wall. Less than fifty yards from the marshal's already-waving checkered flag, the dark blue Chevy's engine decelerated to keep from being driven into the concrete wall.

The crimson Pontiac flashed across the finish line a full car length ahead of the Chevy, sending over 67,000 screaming fans at the raceway into a near riot. Sabrina's pit crew leapt into the air with hands raised high in victory, jumping, screaming, laughing, hugging one another, hugging bystanders and fans, hugging each other again, and then collecting themselves enough to run over to the victory stand to meet their triumphant racer.

Sabrina proudly held her left arm out the window in victory as she took one more lap around the Ontario raceway, amid the raucous adulation of thousands. When her car pulled into the victory lane, two of her red-uniformed pit crew helped her unbuckle the full-body harness and climb out of the driver's side window. Fountains of champagne were showering into the air even before she pulled her crash helmet and fire hood off her head, letting her long blond, sweat-drenched hair cascade over her tired shoulders in the California sun. The crew lifted her up on their shoulders, chanting and singing. It was the greatest moment of her racing career. Sabrina Doucette—NASCAR champion of 1981.

But now, hours later, as she lay on the soft sheets of the king-sized bed in her suite at the Hyatt Regency Hotel in Hollywood, staring up at the ceiling, the agony and ecstasy of the race were just memories—wonderful memories. She knew there would be many more.

A hand reached under the sheet, touching her right leg just above the knee, and slowly made its way up between her legs—gentle fingers, but eager. She closed her eyes and let the fondling massage arouse her fully. It had been at least fifteen minutes of lying quietly, side by side, relaxing, reflecting, cooling off, letting the thin layer of perspiration from the first time evaporate. But her hunger had not been satisfied the first time. He had been too eager, too anxious. This time she would be in command.

Sabrina rolled over on her right side, reaching down with her left hand, finding his muscular stomach. The muscles were tight and strong. She ran her fingers over the soft hairs leading from his navel down between his legs. As she took him in her hands, tenderly rubbing, she felt him swelling larger and larger until he was fully aroused.

With a playful moan she rolled over on top of him, still holding him in her hand, gently stroking. She could see his eyes close tight with pleasure. He licked his lips with a savory arc. With patient care she slid him inside her, straddling his lap, pushing herself up into a sitting position. Her back arched slightly as her hips began to rock forward and back, her hands moving back from his stomach to his knees. She felt his fingers delightfully rise up her legs, across her stomach and up to her prominent breasts, massaging and kneading. Her hips rocked faster.

A few moments later she leaned forward again, rotating her pelvis down to increase the contact between his body and the sensitized spot that gave her the greatest sensation of pleasure. After several years of backseat romances, she had discovered that she could finally experience something distinctly pleasurable if she were allowed to control the action. She loved controlling the action, her emotions swelling with an aura of power, not in a sense of manipulation, but rather a gratifying sense of uninhibited, unrestricted indulgence. Her rocking motion began to pick up tempo as her breathing became more labored. She tilted her chin back with eyes closed—the warm, softly ticklish sensation slowly working its way from her loins to her spine with a tide of sensual tingles. She felt him sit up and eagerly bring his mouth to her right nipple, at first tasting it lightly with his tongue, then closing his lips over it, drawing it fully into his mouth. A fresh wave of erotic sensation washed over her as she felt it grow hard inside his mouth, pressing against his tongue.

Her hands came forward to his head, her fingers coursing through his black curls, gently guiding his face back and forth from one breast to the other as his tongue deliciously gathered in each firm, pink end with a lingering swirl, sinking into her deep and now very wet cleavage, then out again in a leisurely horizontal figure-eight pattern. She felt his hands gather her firm breasts together, decreasing the distance his flourishing tongue had to travel. All the while her hips moved faster and faster, pressing harder and harder; until finally she could feel what she wanted to feel—the soft nudge pressing lightly against her cervix with the intoxicating rhythm of her undulating hips. She preferred big men, strong sinewy men, men with hard bodies and smooth skin; and such was her hungrily feasting lover.

Her entire body had begun to lightly perspire again, despite the cool hush of the air conditioner in the room. An approaching pulse from deep between her thighs signaled the summit of erotic pleasure was rapidly about to be breached. With a sudden thrash, the billowing stimulation erupted inside her, every muscle momentarily paralyzed. In the same instant, her lover responded to her climax by drawing deeply on the erect nipple of her right breast, squeezing it between his front teeth hard enough to cause a slight burning pressure, but not to the point of pain; rather, an erogenous titillation that lusciously synergized with the pounding throbs of her orgasm, producing a combined sensation of exponential dimension that explosively blurred her vision and momentarily stole away her equilibrium. Her body involuntarily thrust forward against his chest, driving his head back; her chin buried in his moist, fragrant neck; her breath arrested in frantic waves of rhapsodic tremors. With a deep, sighing exhalation, she fell into limp repose.

Sabrina felt faint, barely conscious of his upper body laying back down on the bed, pulling her down with him, his arms tenderly embracing her. As her heart rate began to slow down, she became aware of his hips gently rocking beneath her. It sent more delicious chills up and down her spine. If he kept this up, it wouldn't take long for the orgasmic tide to rise once again—maybe more than once. She was about to try and push herself back up into a sitting position when both she and her lover rudely froze at the annoying intrusion of the telephone ringing on the nightstand two feet away.

Sabrina let out a sigh of disbelief, collapsing back onto his chest between the first and second ring. The steamy clouds of their passion evaporated with every urgent chirp of the electronic bell.

"Let it ring," he whispered in her ear. "They'll give up in a moment. Besides, if it's really important, they'll call back."

Sabrina propped herself up on one elbow in between the second and third ring. She looked into his dark brown eyes. "I told the desk not to disturb me unless it was an emergency."

His eyes conceded reluctantly. "Then I suppose you'd better get it."

Sabrina kissed the end of his nose and reached over for

the receiver, fumbling it off its cradle and awkwardly pulling it to her ear with a giggle. "Hello?"

She bit her bottom lip, eyes closed, as her lover's hips began to move again, pressing deep within her.

"Is this Sabrina Doucette?" It was a voice she didn't recognize. It sounded deep and very proper, with a slight trace of a British or Scottish accent.

"This is she," she said quickly, endeavoring not to give her mystery caller any idea of what she was occupied with at the time.

"Ms. Doucette, I'm sorry to bother you this evening," continued the deep male voice, "but I saw you race today and knew I had to give you a call and congratulate you."

Sabrina couldn't believe it. How did a fan get past the switchboard?

Her lover began to increase the speed of his hips; once again she could feel herself hardening against him. It was becoming very difficult to carry on a conversation. "Look, whoever you are. I don't know how you got this number, but I'm rather busy right now. I appreciate your call. Good night."

"Wait, Ms. Doucette," she heard the voice say as the receiver began its journey back to its cradle. "This is Roger Marks calling." The name pierced through the sensual delirium, the receiver jerking back to her ear.

"Who did you say?" she demanded.

The caller laughed. "This is Roger Marks. I'm sorry if I caught you at an awkward time. But my good friend Margaret Banks said I could reach you at this number. Do you have a moment to talk?"

Sabrina couldn't believe it. It couldn't be *the* Roger Marks of the Marks racing team. Two of his drivers already held Indy crowns. But the hotel operator would not have put him through if it was just a crank caller. She pushed herself back up into a sitting position, still straddling her lover. He smiled up at her, reaching around her hips and pulling her buttocks toward him. She slapped his stomach and shook her finger at him, demanding silence. He lay still beneath her with a look of bewildered dismay on his face.

"What can I do for you?" she asked hesitantly.

"Well, to get right to the point, Ms. Doucette," the voice stated flatly, "I'm calling to see if you might be interested in trying your hand at Formula-One racing."

"Are you serious?" She couldn't believe it.

The voice was quick to respond. "As serious as I'd like to see you come out to our facility in San Diego and try out some of our test models. I know your background is in stock cars, but I'm confident you'll find the transition fairly smooth and straightforward. And just between you and I, they're a hell of a lot of fun."

The hard-bodied young man began to rock again, which merited him another chastising look and a poke in the stomach with a rigid index finger. He winced as quietly as he could.

"I'm flattered. But why are you calling *me?*" Sabrina shook her head in amazement.

"Like I said," he answered, "I saw you race today. You're a national champion. I only want champion-caliber individuals on my team. And I like your style, cold as steel, right to the end. I'll be direct with you, Ms. Doucette, and I hope you'll be straightforward with me. If you have other commitments, I certainly understand. But if not, I would appreciate your coming out and looking us over before you decide one way or the other. Is that fair?"

Sabrina swallowed with great difficulty, her heart racing almost out of control. She steeled herself as best she could. "I think it would be an honor."

"Can I take that as a yes?" the voice asked.

After a more deep breath, she agreed, "Yes. I'd be happy to come out and have a look."

"Excellent." The voice sounded genuinely pleased. "I'll have my secretary get in touch with you in the next day or so to assist you in the arrangements. And thank you, Ms. Doucette. You won't regret this."

"Thank you for calling," she responded.

"Well, don't let me keep you. Good evening," the voice concluded.

"Good night." Sabrina returned the receiver to its plastic cradle in a mild state of shock. "Wow . . ." she muttered to the air.

"Who was it?" asked the dark-haired young man, tentatively pulling her toward him again.

This time she cooperated, though still distracted. "You wouldn't believe me if I told you."

"Try me," he challenged.

She looked down at him, her thoughts suddenly refocusing upon her lover in a teasing smile. "That was Roger Marks."

The young man sat bolt upright in the bed, looking her straight in the eye. "What?"

"Yep," she gloated, starting to seductively rock her hips again. "And he wants to know if I want to give Formula-One a try."

The young man flopped back down on the bed in despair. "You've got to be kidding."

She laughed with fiendish delight. "It's on to the big time now."

He slammed both fists down against the mattress, with arms stretched wide apart. "My big chance and I blew it! I knew I shouldn't have slowed down and let you get by me. I should have let you lock fenders and taken you with me into the wall."

Her eyes flashed. "Eugene Conner, I beat you fair and square, and you know it. Don't piss and moan about it!"

He rolled his eyes up toward the headboard. "No, you cheated, and you know it."

"How?" she demanded, moving her hips faster, the warm sensation beginning to grow.

He sat up again, looking deeply into her emerald-green eyes, his hips working in unison with hers, a smile blossoming from his lips. "By nearly driving me into a concrete wall at a hundred and ninety miles an hour. That's how."

She laughed again, playfully. "Racing's serious shit, son." Then she lifted her chin, striking a sarcastically melodramatic pose. "And whining like a spoiled brat doesn't become a true champion."

He huffed, thrusting deeper inside her, making her chin come down, her tongue delectably curled over her upper lip. "We'll see who's going to be whining in a few minutes here."

She rocked her head back, pumping harder and harder, her breath shortening. Her words came out in short pants, "Whining isn't the same as moaning. There's a distinct difference."

He laughed, beginning to run his tongue over her taut nipples once again. "We'll see," he mumbled.

She shook her blond locks from side to side behind her, the fires of ecstasy kindling hotter and hotter beneath her. Her words were now reduced to a mere whisper, "This time, if you bite, do it to the other one like you did before."

6

August 1974

Boston, Massachusetts

DR. ALLAN BARNHART PEERED OVER THE TOP OF HIS BLACK-framed glasses at the attractive dark-haired woman sitting in front of his desk. She was meticulously groomed in a conservative, dark blue business suit. Her tasteful silver jewelry spoke of cultured affluence. His eyes strayed back down to the folder in his hands, the résumé of Ms. Rebecca Danforth.

Rebecca watched him peruse the document for several moments in awkward silence, knowing she had to remain patient and not appear too eager; rather, make him want her—a useful skill she had developed to a very high degree. She would let him speak first and ask the questions.

Dr. Barnhart cleared his throat. "Miss Danforth, your educational background looks quite impressive, Radcliffe, Harvard Business."

"Thank you." Her smile was given in moderation.

He frowned, adjusting his glasses. "But I see here that you've only been in the industry for a year." He scratched his cheek with his index finger. "We were really looking for someone with at least five years under their belt for the position."

Rebecca willed her cheeks not to flush with emotion or anxiety; her resolve and control would prevail. "Dr. Barnhart, as you can see in my employment history, I went to work at Mercy Hospital in an entry-level administrative staff position. In the span of one year I became senior administrator of the entire medical complex, supervising a staff of over three hundred employees."

The balding medical consultant with a walrus moustache, looking somewhere in his mid- to late fifties, raised his eyebrows with interest. "Is that so?"

"I would encourage you to call Dr. Marcus Blanchard at Mercy and discuss my qualifications." Her voice was smooth and even, in complete control of the moment. "Dr. Blanchard is on the board of trustees, and can give you a good overview on my work habits and skills. He was directly responsible for my three promotions in a twelve-month period."

Rebecca's thoughts momentarily went back to the long, drawn face of Marcus Blanchard. His wife had never discovered their nine-month affair. She still saw him on occasion. He actually wasn't too bad for an older man. His years of experience paid rich rewards in patience and technique.

The older man grunted. "Marcus Blanchard, eh? I know Marcus. I think I'll do that, young lady."

"Please call me Rebecca," she requested courteously,

causing his eyes to blink with a trace of repentance, silently acknowledging her chastisement for being referred to as "young lady."

"Yes, Rebecca, very well." His eyes ran down the résumé again. "It says here you're twenty-seven years old. Is that correct?"

"Yes," she answered. "Is that a problem?"

He started to say something, but the look in her eye made him change his mind. She could see he was becoming very uncomfortable. He had that condescending look about him of an older generation that distrusted women in high positions of leadership, regardless of their qualifications or experience—especially young attractive women. He shook his head, cleaning a remnant of breakfast away from his eyetooth with his tongue, making a wet, squeaking sound. "No, I guess not."

"Dr. Barnhart," Rebecca offered, "I'm seeking this particular management position here at Secularian because I believe I can bring to bear a great deal of creativity and a strong sense of leadership to your sales and marketing team. I'm experienced in hospital administration, and I see your company's entrance into a burgeoning market as a very shrewd move at this point in time. I think together we can both mutually benefit a great deal."

Dr. Barnhart leaned back in his chair. "Miss Danforth, in case you don't know, Secularian is a small start-up corporation with only about a hundred and fifty employees. Our consortium of affiliate hospitals is struggling to compete in a vast and highly competitive marketplace. We're looking for solid plans and programs. We're not looking for a supervisor or personnel manager. We need ideas, ideas that will take this company to the forefront of the medical industry."

"And that's why I'm here," she declared confidently.

Dr. Barnhart shook his head. "Miss Danforth, your résumé doesn't indicate anything solid of that nature. What could you possibly bring to the table for us?"

Rebecca's mind was racing. Everything was going smoothly up to this point. Now she was being pinned down for specifics. She preferred the realm of inspiring generalities that lacked the haunting shadow of accountability. Dr. Barnhart was definitely positioning himself as a formidable obstacle. But she wanted this job, bad enough to resign a six-figure position at Mercy Hospital. Secularian Corporation had rated in the top three start-ups in the medical industry according to her independent market analysis. According to their 10-K report, Secularian was privately held by four corporate officers. She saw them as a ripe candidate for internal takeover by the right executive who knew how to play her cards. In five to ten years it could well be a multimillion-dollar, if not billion-dollar, enterprise. An aging medical consultant would not stand in her way.

She took a deep breath. "Well, Dr. Barnhart. My task, as your new product marketing director, would be to analyze your service base, compare that to all current competitive offerings, and devise a unique niche based marketing strategy to distinguish ourselves from all of the other offerings." She let out a breath, somewhat proud of her flag-waving, Marketing 101 answer.

Dr. Barnhart set her résumé down on his desk and leaned both elbows against the dark wooded barrier between them. "Of course, Miss Danforth, that's what we would expect any four-year marketing undergraduate to do. But that's not what we're looking for. We need ideas. The key to success at Secularian is solid market direction and innovation with real products and real services. Our new director of product marketing must play a key role in focusing our efforts toward the future, not merely lining up round pegs with round holes. If you have something distinctive, something creative, then say so. That's what we're looking for."

Several seconds passed while Rebecca furiously strained to organize her thoughts, not allowing her composure to falter for an instant. What revolutionary notion could possibly sway this bureaucrat in her direction? She decided to try and divert the issue. "Isn't Secularian doing any of its own research?"

"Not really," the older man answered, his voice becoming more gruff. "We buy what talent we need. Our main function is to affiliate the resources of numerous regional hospitals and eliminate redundant costs, thus opening up our margin potential."

Rebecca smiled politely. It was time to resume control of the conversation. "Yes, I know what a consortium is, Doctor."

He cleared his throat again. "As I said, Miss Danforth. You find us the cure for the common cold, heart disease, cancer, or acne pimples, and then we'll have something to discuss. Otherwise, I'm afraid there is not a great deal we would be able to offer you."

Rebecca could feel the door starting to close. That was unacceptable.

"Come now, Doctor," she challenged. "You need talented people on your team and we both know it. The fact that an existing product or idea isn't sitting here tied up neatly with a pretty ribbon shouldn't prohibit you from acquiring the best resources with the best potential to go out and get them for you. I have a Harvard degree in business, a proven track record of success, and the desire to go out and find whatever I need to make this corporation a leader in this industry. Where else are you going to find that?"

She could see in his eyes he was beginning to weaken, but he wasn't won yet. He sat back and looked at her for several awkward seconds, then gave her a faint smile. "You make quite a convincing case, Miss Danforth. That in and of itself may be of some value."

His words sounded more positive, but she could still see the hesitation in his face. She knew his type; on the one hand his mind told him that her facts were rational and solid, but on the other hand the testosterone in his system blindly protested, telling him that a human being without a full scrotum can't run a company. It was a distasteful reality, but fortunately, one she had learned to deal with over the past few years. She learned how to manipulate such arrogance to her advantage in college, and used that knowledge quite profitably in her early career. It was amazing what price a man was willing to pay, even to the point of putting his Neanderthal prejudices on the shelf, when the temptation of something he wanted was held just within his chubby little reach.

She gave him her most devastating smile, her eyes suddenly coy and coquettish. "Oh, I can be *more* than convincing, Dr. Barnhart. Much *more.*" The succulent voice of the temptress drew out the word "more." She lifted her chin and crossed her legs, intentionally letting her skirt ride up over her knee, exposing a shapely, well-toned, pair of legs. She saw him glance down over the edge of his desk, his thick eyebrows twitching in slight surprise. The fact that he didn't immediately look away or protest in any way assured her he was already predisposed to offer no resistance to her carnivorous web.

He inquisitively looked up into her eyes. "I beg your pardon?"

"Come now, Doctor. Your office door is closed. Let's be frank." The tone of her voice dropped, her smile still radiating. "I want this position. I know I'll do a good job in it. And I think you know that I will as well. You're in a position to give me this job. And I think it's only natural that if you are inclined to do something advantageous for me, I see no problem with doing something advantageous for you."

The atmosphere in the room was charged. His voice wavered slightly. "Exactly what are you suggesting?"

She leveled her gaze upon his, licking her full red lips once, her words dripping with sensuality, "Let's just say that I have a vast array of unique talents that don't appear on my résumé, but which I can, as you said, 'bring to the table.'" She glanced over her right shoulder to the small four-seat conference table in the corner of his office. "Like that table over there."

The doctor just stared blankly into her dark expression

for several awkward moments, then swallowed with difficulty. Rebecca could tell his mind was in the process of short-circuiting the rationality and common sense circuits. His eyes were roaming over the offer, inspecting the proposition from head to toe, while his libido was busy binding and gagging all of his seventeenth century morality. Finally, he sat back with a fat smile. "Well, I guess if we're going to be colleagues, it *would* be best for us to get to know one another better."

Rebecca just kept smiling with satisfaction. It was all too easy, requiring very little effort on her part. She pegged the good doctor for the type who would typically just settle for something quick and oral, just enough to get his rocks off without having to expend any effort himself. But that was satisfactory; she was not in the mood to put up with the hassle of having to get undressed and lie on a cold table. She'd rather just touch up her lipstick later. From the wide-eyed expression on his face, she knew he wouldn't take long. Besides, most men certainly didn't seem to mind fellatial treatment, especially in an office environment.

She was correct. Dr. Barnhart didn't mind.

7

October 1974

Boston, Massachusetts

THE LIBRARY WASN'T VERY CROWDED THAT SATURDAY, AND SINCE
the weather was nice, most of the New England population
was outside enjoying it. Beautiful days were a rarity in New
England; but if there was going to be one, it was usually in
the fall. The leaves were all turning into a collage of vibrant
hues; the temperature was in the high sixties to low seventies; the skies were clear; and the sunshine made everyone
squint. But like most Saturdays, Dr. Rae Taylor was sitting
in the Harvard library, one of the largest in the world,
gathering information for her research.

Rae's thoughts were lost in the abyss of articles in the *New
England Journal of Medicine.* With her face as illuminated
as her mind, she peered intently through her glasses at the
screen of the microfiche reader, jotting down notes and
scanning over to numerous cross-references. She suddenly
looked to her right, startled by the loud thump of a pile of
books dropped on the table just next to her. She looked up at
a pleasant-looking young man with short brown hair, smiling apologetically down at her.

"I'm sorry." He nodded, sitting down at the microfiche
machine next to hers and quickly going about his business.

Rae detected the familiar acknowledgment of her invisi-
bility. In the eyes of most other people, she was just one of
those plain, nameless, almost faceless individuals who blend
into crowds without distinction. She had convinced herself
that this provided her additional privacy to accomplish her

74

work. It was another one of the comforting axioms that held her mind together, and held at bay the tormenting demon of loneliness.

"Excuse me," came a timid sounding voice to Rae's right.

She turned to discover the pleasant-looking young man looking at her with a helpless smile. She raised her eyebrows. "Yes?"

"I'm sorry to bother you." He gestured toward the microfiche reader. "But I can't seem to get this thing to work."

Rae leaned over and looked at the machine. "Hmm." She pushed her glasses up on her nose and examined it carefully. In a few seconds she turned to him. "I think I see your problem."

"What's the matter?" he asked, moving his chair away from the table, allowing her to examine it more closely. "Bulb blown?"

She reached around the rear of the machine and lifted the power cord. "It appears someone's unplugged you."

He laughed. "That'll do it. Thanks. Sorry to interrupt you. I thought maybe I broke it or something."

"No trouble." She shrugged, and took her seat again. Out of the corner of her eye she watched the young man crawl under the heavy oak library table and plug in the microfiche machine. He bumped his head on the edge of the table as he attempted to crawl back out. Rae's fist came to her mouth, squelching a burst of laughter.

"Ow!" he moaned once, rubbing the back of his head. When he sat back in his chair, Rae saw him catch her looking at him again. He laughed louder this time. "I guess today isn't my day."

She quickly turned back toward her screen, a bit embarrassed to be caught looking.

The young man opened a large three-ring notebook and began to scribble down some notes from the article he was reviewing. A few moments later he reached over to pull out one of the books from the bottom of the tall stack he had placed on the table between himself and Rae, but inadvertently toppled the pile into Rae's lap. He jumped up with a look of horror on his face. "Oh, I'm so sorry. I really didn't . . . I mean . . . I . . ."

Rae was startled, but smiled sympathetically at the bumbling fellow as he did his best to collect the fallen volumes and restack them, many of which only slid back on the floor in the process. In a matter of seconds she was laughing to the point of wiping tears from her eyes. The young man finally gave up and sat back down, his face blushing.

He held up his upturned palms in a gesture of futility. "You probably wouldn't believe me if I told you I normally am quite adept at going to the library, eating, walking, chewing gum, dressing all by myself, and things like that."

That sent Rae into a fresh titter of laughter, which she tried to suppress in the wake of annoyed looks from other library patrons, which only intensified the hilarity of the moment. Soon her chest was in spasms as her diaphragm tried to force laughter past her clenched lips. It found a sniggering passage of escape through her nose.

"Well, I'm glad *one* of us is having a good time here," he whispered as loudly as he could.

Rae had to get some air. Actually, her laughter prompted her to go to the rest room. She returned a few minutes later, composed and relaxed. However, as she rounded the table and prepared to sit down, she took one look at the young man smiling at her and burst out laughing again. She sat down biting her bottom lip.

The young man leaned over, his head next to her shoulder. "You have no idea what you've done to my fragile male ego today." That made her shoulders and chest begin to quake again.

"I'm sorry." She could barely get the words out. "I don't know why you struck me so funny. I . . . I just can't seem to help it. You looked . . ." A fresh wave of chuckles overtook her. "You—You looked so helpless . . . against the avalanche of those books."

He leaned closer. "Yes, miss, that's my calling in life; to go forth each and every day and see pretty young women laugh their asses off at me." He sat back in his chair, wearily shaking his head.

The phrase "pretty young woman" captured Rae's attention, quenching the fires of her mirth. As her breathing quickly returned to normal, she timidly asked, "What are you working on?"

The brown-haired young man cocked his head at an angle. "I've got to have a thirty-page report done for my economics class by Monday."

"Oooh." Rae grimaced. "And you were only given two days to get it done?"

He looked embarrassed again. "Well," he half laughed, "actually I've had since the beginning of the semester, but I've sort of been busy."

Rae gave him a disapproving look. "Sounds like you've got a busy weekend in store, then."

"I know," he lamented with a forlorn sigh, setting his book back in the pile. Abruptly, he looked up at her. "Say. I've been here at the rock pile all morning, and I know I'm going to be stuck here probably till Monday. I think I could use a break right now. Since I've obviously ruined whatever train of thought you might have had, how's about letting me buy you a burger at the cafeteria downstairs?"

Rae felt flattered. She wasn't used to men being so warm and friendly. However, a dark thought went through her mind. He was probably one of those guys who looked for a studious-looking girl to charm into doing his work for him. He was too good-looking to just be friendly; he must want something. But just to be safe, she decided to let him know she'd take him up on a free lunch but abandon him afterward, and then see if he was still interested. "Sounds great. But as soon as we're done, I've got to go. I have plans this weekend. *All* weekend."

"Great!" His smile never faded. "Are you hungry?"

Rae's own smile returned as she walked with him down to

the cafeteria in the basement. Over a cheeseburger and fries, she found out his name was David Stratton, a business major at Harvard Business School. He was in his last year of an MBA program and was looking to go into business for himself. His only problem was a lack of direction. He knew he wanted to be involved in a service industry, but nothing really appealed to him thus far.

He was fascinated with Rae's long-winded dissertation on her cell research and the likelihood of perfecting the techniques for relief of major diseases. And never once did he look bored or anxious to leave. In fact, their conversation lasted for over two hours, long after the last few fries scattered in the red and white paper boat had grown cold and hard. David seemed to grow as excited about hearing of Rae's discoveries as she was in telling of them. He asked her numerous questions, and she was delighted to finally have someone other than another researcher to share it with. As a businessman, David asked her the same question as Cal Dominski regarding patents. She explained that she hadn't bothered to look into it yet, but had been meaning to call a friend who was a lawyer.

And much to Rae's surprise, when it was time to leave, David asked her if he could have her phone number and perhaps call her. She certainly didn't mind. And she was even more surprised when a few days later he called, asking her to dinner the following Saturday evening. Dr. Rae Taylor had not been on a single date in years. The only ones she had been on were usually blind dates or group affairs involving the chemists or medical technicians she worked with. But David Stratton had asked her out on a bonafide date. She couldn't sleep at all Friday night, and worried all Saturday that he would call at the last minute and cancel. He didn't. In fact, he arrived a few minutes early.

The dinner was superb. David took her to a nice restaurant off Beacon Street, near the Boston Commons. Once again they lost themselves in conversation for hours. After dinner they took a leisurely stroll around the Commons, then returned to her apartment. And like a perfect gentleman, he kissed her good-night and left. Rae couldn't go to sleep at all that night either.

Over the next few weeks Rae and David saw a great deal of each other. They discovered a mutual love for classical music, and subsequently made a regular habit of going to the symphony. Rae loved getting all dressed up and listening to the romantic strains of her favorite composers. And for the first time in her life, she wasn't going alone.

David always tenderly kissed her good-night, held her hand when they walked, and slung his arm around her shoulders when they sat on the couch late at night stuffing their faces with popcorn, watching Godzilla destroy Tokyo for the eleventeenth time. But he never made any overt advances toward her. In a way, she appreciated that; but in another context she wondered if perhaps there was something about her he *didn't* like. It kept her paranoid most of the time; but he kept calling, and he kept coming over. All in all, having David in her life made Rae's days take on a healthier air. She enjoyed her work more, her life more. But those ancient defense mechanisms buried deep inside kept her constantly wary that it all might disappear in an instant. Yet with each passing day, each time she saw him, a little more of the armor around her heart chipped away.

One afternoon as they sat at her small dinette table sharing what was left of a pint container of ice cream, David announced with great seriousness, "Rae, I've something very important to ask you."

Her heart skipped a beat.

"It's about your research," he stated flatly.

Her heart resumed its pace. "What about it?"

He stuffed a heaping spoon of the butter-pecan into his mouth, his words coming out mangled in the dessert, "I've been giving it some serious thought, and I have to tell you that you need to find a way to market your ideas."

"Market them?"

"That's right." His spoon dug around for a whole pecan.

"I know how much you've told me you want to see your discoveries help people in need. Well, you never will unless you have a vehicle to take it to the people."

This conversation sounded familiar to Rae. Cal Dominski's face came to mind. "And you have an idea?"

He smiled. "Well, I haven't worked out all the details yet. And you're probably going to think this sounds awfully presumptuous of me, but . . ."

"But what?" she prompted.

"Well," he said, pulling his next bite off the spoon, with his upper lip insulating his front teeth from the cold. "As you know, I'm about to graduate this semester, and I've been looking for a business idea in the service arena. And medicine is a service. . . ."

Rae's face brightened. "You mean you could possibly start a business using my techniques as a product?"

"Essentially," he continued hesitantly, obviously trying to gauge her reaction. "I pictured a kind of clinic, or a center. Not a hospital, sort of a fast-food niche market approach to specific diseases. Specifically, the diseases you know how to fix."

"Body shops!" She laughed.

His eyes crinkled with a chuckle, "I hadn't actually thought of it that way. But the central concept is there. However, I think we'd need to come up with a catchier name. I believe, officially, the auto mechanics, and unofficially, the brothel industry, have the copyrights to that one."

"True," she noted, her eyes growing serious, but her mouth still grinning. "So we'd have to think of something better."

David's eyes lit up. "So you think the idea isn't stupid?"

"No." She looked deeply into his eyes. "I think being partners with you would be wonderful."

"Rock and Roll!" he exclaimed, dropping his spoon in the ice cream container, grabbing Rae in a tight embrace, lifting her up off the floor and spinning her around.

She couldn't breathe until he set her back down. She could see the excitement in his face; his eyes were glowing. It was almost too wonderful to believe. Here was the chance to not only see her dream come to life, but have the chance to do it with the person she felt closest to in the whole world. What could be better?

He still held her in his arms, looking into her eyes. "Dr. Taylor, you won't regret this." His brow furrowed mischievously. "But you are taking a big risk, considering the unreliability, foolhardiness, and cavalier attitude of your prospective business partner."

She leaned forward, pressing her lips against his. "That's a chance I think I'm willing to take."

8

May 1990

Dallas, Texas

FRIDAY HAD NOT COME TOO SOON FOR NICOLE. THE FLIGHT FROM Boston to Dallas was uneventful, but the traffic from the DFW Airport to the North Dallas Women's Center was brutal. A jackknifed eighteen-wheeler turned out to be the cause of the problem, and it couldn't have happened at a worse location: the intersection of Loop 635 and Central Expressway. Traffic had been backed up for miles. By the time the white Mercedes limousine pulled beneath the massive stone archway of the Women's Center porte cochere, the bottle of Dom Pérignon was empty.

With a warm sensation coursing through her veins, a glassy expression, and a mischievous smile on her face, Nicole knocked twice on one of the polished walnut double doors of the executive office suite. A buzzing sound signaled her to enter. She gaily strode in with her black and gray ostrich-skin portfolio tucked under her arm. Dr. Rae Taylor swung around in her chair from the computer console on the credenza behind her desk.

"Nikki!" Rae's smile beamed as she stood from her desk and walked over to greet her friend.

Nicole embraced her warmly. "Hello, Rae. I appreciate you waiting for me this afternoon. I would have been here much sooner, but the traffic from the airport was dreadful. Some fool in a truck had the insensitivity to roll it over just before rush hour."

Rae assured her, "Oh, well there's nothing to worry about. I'm just glad you're here. I've been completely preoccupied with the new treatment schedule and staffing projections for next year."

"Good." Nicole nodded with a glassy grin, then added with coy hesitation, "I've got something for you." She walked to Rae's desk and unzipped the top of her portfolio.

Rae came up behind her, her eyes growing wide. "Is everything completed? So soon?"

Nicole giggled, handing Rae a stack of papers, "All ready for your signature. Just have Marsha and Alicia sign them where indicated, and you're ready to go."

Rae clapped her hands together. "Wonderful! That is absolutely wonderful! You have no idea how much this means to me."

Nicole's slightly inebriated smile faded into a serious look of concern. "Yes I do."

The two women just looked into each other's eyes for a thoughtful moment, both reminiscent of painful memories. Nicole couldn't believe how much her friend had changed over the last seventeen years. Her beautifully styled hair used to be so plain and straight; now her face was so elegant, her figure so graceful, her voice so polished and cultured. Even the opulence of her office was a superb testament of her power and influence. Everything around them, from the custom-designed furniture pieces, the two original van Goghs that adorned the walls, the select pieces of crystal, the adjacent private sauna, steam room, and exercise suite, the vaulted ceiling with glass-domed observatory—all of it spoke of a level of quality and excellence that few, if any, ever achieve.

Rae nodded, said with a note of sadness in her voice, "Yes, I suppose you do." She shook her head and forced her face to brighten. "But that's not today's worry. Have you got time to stay and visit? I can have tea brought in."

Nicole turned toward the door with a bouncing arch of her eyebrows. "If you don't object, I'd prefer to meet you for breakfast. With the traffic delays, I'm already behind schedule—*if* you know what I mean."

Rae laughed. "I understand." She turned to escort Nicole to her office door. "Well, I know I don't need to advise you to enjoy yourself. You seem to have developed quite a proficiency for that."

Nicole held the tip of her tongue between her teeth for a second and gloated, "Yes! It's true, it's true. My life is filled with lavish indulgence and erotic excess beyond measure—and it's all your fault, Dr. Taylor, and you know it."

"Guilty as charged, counselor." Rae smiled. "Shall I see you on the terrace at nine?"

"Nine." Nicole hugged Rae once more and strode from her office.

It didn't take more than three minutes to make her way out of the executive wing, through the gallery, past the reception area, up the brass-trimmed glass elevators, to her suite on the third floor. It was time for therapy; and, as usual, everything was meticulously prepared for her arrival. Only this time the relaxing classic strings of Pachelbel's Canon filled the air amid the humid burbling of the Jacuzzi. Sitting in the 107-degree water, sipping a flute of champagne, was Brett.

Nicole let out a giddy, Dom Pérignon inspired titter of laughter as she closed the suite's door with her foot, pulling the white sundress she wore over her head and tossing it over by the fireplace. "Hello, Brett."

He just smiled up at her, lifting his glass in a silent toast. Strong cheeks, a sculptured nose, and a cleft chin framed the warm, sweet mouth that Nicole often daydreamed about while opposing attorneys made closing remarks. His long, well-defined left arm was draped across the smooth marble rim of the tub. The bubbling and boiling waters frothed up against the smooth, stalwart muscles of his chest.

By the time Nicole reached the edge of the tub, her shoes, panty hose, panties, and jewelry trailed her in a straight line from the tile landing.

"Are you thirsty?" he asked.

"Always." She sat down on the edge of the hot tub, sliding her long legs into the steaming water. "Oooh, that's hot," she gasped.

"It's supposed to be." Brett reached over and pulled the bottle of champagne out of the silver ice bucket, filled the other crystal flute standing next to it, and handed it to Nicole. "You'll quickly get used to the heat."

"I hope not." She took the glass from his hand; condensation was already beading up along its stem and body. Her gaze stayed fixed on the deep blue eyes staring into hers. She sipped the sparkling wine as her body slipped hesitantly into the water, up to her shoulders, the heat scrumptiously enveloping her. The hot bubbling jets were already melting away her muscles, enhancing the euphoric feeling she brought with her from the limousine ride.

"I'll have you know I won the McDunough libel suit today, making me a much richer lady. And I mean *much* in the sense of filthy, gaudy, outrageous excess." She took another sip, licking her lips.

"That's wonderful." His eyes widened with sincere delight, then paused for a moment, looking deeply into her eyes with solemn appreciation. "I guess that's why you're the very best at what you do." He brightened. "In addition to being the most intoxicatingly beautiful woman I know, of course. I can only imagine how you must captivate judges and juries with your ruthless logic and that quick wit of yours. I wish I could have been there with you today."

Nicole drank in the compliment with a warm flush; it felt *so* good, a tonic for the soul. To Nicole, the verbal strokes were as gratifying as the physical ones, if not more so. She tilted her brow forward, looking from beneath her finely manicured eyebrows. "I wish you had been there too. But it's not too late to help me celebrate right now."

"I'd be delighted to." His even, gleaming teeth sparkled with anticipation.

"And what might our therapy theme be for today?" she asked playfully.

"Patience. The virtue of patience." Brett placed his glass on the marble edge of the tub, came across the hot, effervescent waters, and took Nicole into his arms. She closed her eyes as she felt his tender, full lips press against hers, her mouth willingly yielding to the nectarous penetration of his tongue.

Her hand carefully placed her glass on the hard surface behind her and wrapped her arms around his broad, brazen shoulders. His hands worked around her back, massaging and caressing, lifting her to him. She writhed forward, pressing her wet, glistening breasts against the well-knit musculature of his chest.

A moment later she gasped, her shocked eyes coming open, bursting into laughter, when she felt the icy chill of champagne landing on her upper chest, trickling down between her breasts. Brett leaned back and smiled at her, replacing her glass where she had originally put it. With a wave of bubbling heat from the Jacuzzi washing against her, she relished the feel of his mouth quickly moving to the center of her chest, nuzzling and tenderly licking away the white foam. A delicious swell of desire swept through her as she reached up and guided his face over her left breast, his swirling tongue sensuously encircling the circumference of her contracting areola.

Strong fingers served to quicken her breathing as she felt them part her legs beneath the turbulent waters, pushing the dark tufts of hair aside and exploring her delicate creases. The effect of the champagne, mixed with the sultry heat of the water, made her feel buoyant—floating along in a dreamlike state; the passionate sensations of rubbing, caressing, tasting, touching, and massaging ushering her deeper and deeper on her delightfully wet journey.

Moments later the warm wet hands lifted her slightly out of the water, arching her backward over the cool edge of the marble. She spread her dripping arms along the perimeter of the tub in both directions, lifting her legs until her knees emerged from the foaming waters. Her head rocked back, her eyes still blissfully closed, the enthralling symphony of his mouth and hands piquing her bodily appetite to ravenous dimensions. She was ready. She wanted to feel him please her, and please her deeply with no delay.

With her eyes still closed, listening to the pandemonious gurgle of the water jets and the melodious enchantment of the string orchestra, she could sense him lean back, standing up straight between her legs, his left hand still poised around her waist, gripping beneath the small of her back. His right hand moved between them, down past her inner thighs, stopping between his own sinewy legs. She drew in two long, seething breaths, knowing that any moment she would feel the fiery sensation of penetration plunging deeply and tenderly into her luscious folds.

But it didn't happen.

Her next conscious sensation was a light, toying touch, drawing long, deliberate ovals around her yearning orifice. A surge of voracious desire prompted an urgent, wistful moan—she didn't want mere external massage, she wanted to be filled, thoroughly, utterly, with complete abandon. Torturous moments of deprivation languished past—until her breathing abruptly stilled in an erotic jolt of unexpected ecstasy when she suddenly realized his lingering ovals were not the work of his finger.

Her whispering voice was filled with urgency, "I want you."

"Patience," was all he said. The teasing centrifugal force swelled in intensity, faster and faster, harder and harder— each brushing stroke sensitizing her passion more and more, each pass baiting her body and emotions beyond the limits of control. She could feel her own flesh pulsating between her legs with every pounding beat of her racing heart. She was about to scream.

His voice was low and even, taunting, "What's the magic word?"

"Now!" she screamed. "The word is *now!*"

"Close enough." He laughed, his words concurrent with his rapier entrance.

Her heels dug into his flexing buttocks as she detonated into rigid orgasm, her fingernails pressed white against the marble.

9

January 1982

Monte Carlo

AFTER A FULL WEEK, THE DEEP, PENETRATING RAYS OF THE MEDI-terranean sun had already turned Sabrina's well-oiled back to golden brown, her hair almost white. She lay facedown on a chaise lounge on the second-story rear deck of Roger Marks's 210-foot yacht, taking in the warm salt air in long, relaxing breaths. The strings of her white bikini top were untied and hanging off either side of the chaise lounge. Sitting a few feet away in a white deck chair was the legendary racing champion Roger Marks. Out of the corner of her half-closed eye Sabrina watched him looking intently at the thin black notebook filled with technical information provided by his engineers and technicians.

Roger took another sip of his martini and looked at Sabrina, the resonant British tone of his voice firm, but betraying a note of concern, "Sabrina, Troy tells me that the new front stabilizer will arrive this evening, and they're planning to work through the night to get it installed."

"They'd better," she said lazily, nuzzling her cheek against the long aquamarine beach towel beneath her. "The show's tomorrow."

Roger's face clouded. "I wish you would stop calling it a show. It's a grand prix, and not just any grand prix, but *the* Grand Prix. Sometimes I wonder if you're really taking this seriously."

She didn't move. "How did we do in Berlin?"

"You won—" he started to say.

"And Marseilles?" she interrupted.

"You won," he admitted.

"Then what could possibly make you think I'm not taking this seriously?" Her eyes were open now.

"I'm sorry," he apologized, closing his book and setting it on the white iron, glass-topped table next to him. "You ought to know me by now. I just get a bit jumpy before an important contest. It's of grave importance to me. You know that. We've got a great deal invested, time, money, preparation—"

"I know, Roger." She lifted her head. "Calm down. It'll be fine. I've been over the course all week. I know every turn, every straight. I know where I'll throttle in, and where to back off. I've even got attack slots identified to run the other bastards off the track."

Roger smiled. "All right, all right. I'm sorry. I get the picture."

Sabrina huffed, "You worry like an old woman."

He laughed. "Well, perhaps I *do* worry when it comes to a three-million-dollar investment sliding through flat hairpins and taking blind hills at nearly two hundred miles an hour."

Sabrina gave him a coy look. "Oh, admit it, Roger. You're worried about me."

Roger Marks looked out over the brilliant waves to the villas and shops built into the breathtaking hills. He was silent for a moment. "What if I *do* worry about you?"

Sabrina looked skeptically at the distinguished racing master, sitting there in his dark bathing trunks and a loose-fitting Ralph Lauren shirt. Could this be the same man who put her through four months of rigorous training, disciplining her like a drill sergeant? Was this the same man who left nothing to chance, going over every inch of the multimillion-dollar Formula-One racers with a staff of engineers that would rival NASA?

"What are you worried about?" she asked quietly, listening to the distant sound of shrieking gulls in flight and the waves lapping against the side of the boat. The afternoon breeze pushed the thin blond hair away from her right ear.

He didn't answer, just emptied his martini glass into his mouth, looked down at her briefly, then shook his head with a half laugh, appearing almost embarrassed. He stood up, walked to the wet bar underneath the deck cover, looked over his shoulder and asked, "Can I get you something?"

She didn't understand him, figuring him to be in another one of his "moods." She closed her eyes again, shrugging off his mysterious behavior. "Sure. Bring me a beer."

After Roger mixed himself a fresh martini, he reached into the small refrigerator, pulled out a long-necked bottle of beer, grabbed a bottle opener from the bar and popped the top. The rich white foam erupted onto the polished wood of the deck. He walked back toward her. "That's what I like about you, Sabrina. Simple tastes. Simple, inexpensive tastes. Oh, that all women could be so."

She giggled. "You haven't seen me eat, or spend an hour in a parts store."

He handed her the beer and sat back down, taking a neat sip of his drink. "Yes I have. And now that you mention it, I withdraw the compliment."

Sabrina propped herself up on her elbows and took a drink. As she tipped the bottle up with her right hand, she noticed Roger glancing down at her half-exposed chest. The thought of teasing came to mind, but she refrained. Roger had always been strictly professional with her in their year-long relationship. She liked him—a lot more than she was even willing to consciously admit to herself. And in his own subdued way, she suspected he cared for her too. He was in his early forties and treated her like a favorite daughter, with lots of admonitions, but in a fatherly, protective sort of way. He was so meticulous, so precise and orthodox in his manner. Often she wondered what he would do if she *did* try to seduce him. But each time, the potential risk of getting kicked off the team dissuaded her. However, it was still one of her favorite fantasies. With a polite smile she laid back down, setting the bottle on the deck next to her, and closed her eyes. "So what's the plan for the rest of the day?"

He yawned. "Just relax, I suppose. Soak up some sun. Enjoy ourselves. Whatever you'd like, really."

"Sounds wonderful," she commented. "Anything special in mind?"

His eyes looked at her again for a moment, then went back out to sea. "No." He cleared his throat. "But I do want you to know that I feel it is imperative that you be focused, relaxed, and fully prepared for tomorrow. There can't be any distractions. That race means a lot to me."

She coughed slightly. "It means a lot to me too."

"Yes . . ." he said, somewhat awkwardly. "But . . . what I'm trying to say . . ." He took another heavy breath. ". . . is that I fully understand you are a grown woman."

She opened her eyes and furrowed her brow. "I'm glad you think so."

He took a deep breath. "Sabrina, please don't take this the wrong way, for I don't mean to be rude, or insinuate anything improper . . ."

No, she thought, such a notion would be totally out of character. "What the hell are you talking about?" Her cheek was off the towel again, both arms folded beneath her chin.

He looked into her eyes; there was something there, something unspoken. "What I'm trying to say is, I realize that we've been training very hard for this race, and I understand that you may have certain *needs,* as a woman, that may need to be addressed—so as to ensure that you're not under any undue stress . . . or tension. . . ." His expression was already apologizing for that last word.

She bit her lips, suppressing a smile. So the gentleman was trying to be sensitive to her love life. Could he be serious? She wondered what he did for the male drivers on the team, Hookers? She could tell he was squirming to say what he had to say. This was starting to be fun.

"What kind of *tension* do you mean, Roger?" she asked coyly.

His expression grew serious again. "I think you know what I'm talking about. This is a bit difficult for me, as I'm sure you know. But you're an adult, and I'll be frank with you. If this isn't an issue with you, then fine. All the better. But if it is, then I would be happy to . . . arrange something for you."

She couldn't help her smile now. "Arrange something? Like what? Are you going to go into one of the casinos and hire some stud to come up and *service* me? You don't think I can attend to that *need* of my own accord, if I so desire?"

Roger was blushing and not looking her in the eye. He started to laugh. "Actually, you're the first woman I've had on the team, and I wasn't exactly sure how to broach this subject to you. The other lads usually appreciate it."

She cocked one eyebrow. "Well, perhaps I would too."

He snapped a half-shocked gaze upon her. The look on his face told her volumes. It was instantly obvious that she was supposed to have refused and he was supposed to have felt better by making sure that area was safely put out of his mind. That bit of information only made the game all the more fun.

"You would?" the disbelief was poorly hidden in his voice.

"Like you said." She played. "Women have needs. I certainly wouldn't want to climb in that cockpit tomorrow . . . frustrated."

His face betrayed his uncertainty over whether to take her seriously. The professional in him reluctantly decided he couldn't take the chance.

"As you wish," he said quietly, almost sad, in fact. "The ship has a crew of twenty. And from overhearing some of their conversations this past week, I can assure you any one of them would be more than delighted to assist you. They're all an exceptional lot, healthy and strong. If any one of them in particular has struck your fancy, let me know, and I'll promptly see to it that you're . . . accommodated. Discreetly of course."

He was so proper, it was unnerving—even in doing something that sounded sleazy. Sabrina did her absolute best not to burst out laughing. Her mind was toying with a bad pun concerning "seamen," but decided against it. No, it was time for some real fun, some real enjoyment; she knew what she really wanted. She wanted Roger Marks. And something deep inside her told her that this time she had to try. It felt right, and her instincts were rarely mistaken. She knew all she had to do was just let her mind and body flow in concert and the elusive prize fish would be caught. This time it would be worth the risk.

She propped herself up on her left elbow, rolling over on her left side, her temptatious breasts generously aimed directly at his line of sight. She leveled her enticing green eyes upon his. "Well, Roger, there is one man on this ship I have a desire for." She paused for effect; the tension of the moment was electric. "But he's not a member of the crew."

Another frozen moment in time held fast for several agonizing seconds. What was going through his mind? Shock? Outrage? Confusion? Embarrassment? Desire? A hunger to touch and taste what his eyes beheld? She couldn't exactly tell, he just sat there, motionless, staring.

The moment climaxed as his eyes widened with his smile. "Is that so?"

The hook was set; time to wind the reel. She sat up, facing him, massaging her fingers behind her neck, elbows lifted high, stretching the muscles in her back, bathing her face in the sun, giving him the full show. "Yes, that's so."

He took another drink of his martini and looked around the deck once more. The rear deck of his yacht was elevated above the rear compartments of the boat. They were completely secluded from any of the other crewmen or passengers aboard.

"Come here," she said.

He set his drink down and complied with no sign of resistance. He walked over and sat down beside her on the chaise. The silver streaks on his temples made him look so distinguished. His hazel eyes looked into hers expectantly. She reached up with her left hand and pulled his face to hers, pressing their lips together. His mouth was warm and sweet, patient and tender. She laced her fingers behind his neck and laid back on the lounger, pulling him slowly down on top of her.

He lifted his head and softly asked, "Wouldn't you feel more comfortable in your stateroom?"

"No," she answered. "I want you here."

He cleared his throat slightly. "Actually, I think I would feel more comfortable down below."

She could scarcely believe he was actually there, so close, touching her, about to make love to her. But the look of hesitation was back in his eyes. He wanted her, it was obvious; but she knew she had to push him a little further over the edge of inhibition. She took his right hand and covered her left breast with it. "No one will bother us here, Roger." She gave him an inquiring look. "Besides, I like the fresh air."

His hand obediently began to massage. He just smiled and leaned forward into her lips. And as his initial reluctance dissipated into an enthusiastic passion, she felt his mouth soon tasting her jawline, neck, shoulders, and breasts. Her hands reached down and untied the knots on the sides of her bikini bottoms, bidding him entrance.

She reached down, feeling for the edge of his shirt, intending to pull it up over his head; but surprisingly, he gently took her hands and moved them back to his neck. She didn't understand. And without explanation, he laid her back on the lounger, moved his face down her body, and was soon hungrily feeding between her slowly rocking thighs. As his tongue darted in and out, sending intense waves of pleasure throughout her entire body, she no longer cared what he did as long as he didn't stop. His titillating technique of the tongue displayed a mastery only excelled by his racing. The more her body reacted to the vigorous stimulation, the more relaxed she felt. Roger had been right; the bodily tensions were flowing out of her. But the very thought of the word "tension" instantly refocused her mind.

Tension. Suspension. Power. Acceleration. Speed.

In a moment her thoughts were stolen far away and she was conscious of the only pure form of exhilaration she knew—the thrill of sitting in an aerodynamic missile, precision balanced between four wide cylinders of high-performance synthetic rubber, while a rocket strapped to her back sent her hurtling at speeds that can kill, and will kill, if there's the slightest miscalculation of performance. The performance must be perfection—the dance of leather and steel, a thing of exquisite beauty, a true passion without flaw.

As Roger Marks patiently brought her to a short, sweet climax, her thoughts were still blurring by in the convoluted scenery of distorted memory and fluid imagination—at just over two hundred miles an hour.

10

December 1974

Boston, Massachusetts

THE MULTITUDE OF CHRISTMAS SHOPPERS THRONGING OUTSIDE IN the cold, trudging past the tall plate glass window of Cricket's oyster bar near Faneuil Hall, were invisible to Rebecca as she pulled her third morsel of escargo from its shell with a tiny pronged fork. Perry Como's version of "Let It Snow" droned in the background, blending behind the murmur of conversations and the occasional tinkle of glassware and cutlery.

Tracy Bonner, the vice-president of marketing at Secularian, sat across from Rebecca at the elegant private table by the plate-glass window, spreading caviar on a thin wafer. Rebecca had been eagerly anticipating this lunch for over a week. Tracy was one of the most powerful and politically astute officers at Secularian. She had been directly responsible for their nationwide modernization program the previous year, and was rumored to be next in line for the presidency. In fact, if you had any desire to advance at Secularian, you needed to know Tracy Bonner.

Tracy was Rebecca's boss' boss. It had taken a great deal of political maneuvering to discreetly schedule this meeting without Rebecca's superior, Jeffery Watkins, finding out.

Rebecca was direct. "Tracy, I asked you to lunch today because I want something you've got." She pulled the garlic sautéed delicacy off the fork with her lips, never taking her eyes off the stoic executive.

"And what might that be?" Tracy bit into the liberal layer

of caviar, chewing it slowly. Her short blond hair curled around her ears, behind two stunning diamond studs.

"Information." Rebecca's words had been carefully planned in advance. She didn't know if there would be another chance to make her move.

"Concerning?" The woman's bright blue eyes were intrigued.

"The direction of Secularian." Rebecca took a sip of her Chianti. "As you know, I support Jeff Watkins as director of product marketing, research division. I've approached Jeff on several occasions to provide input on growth segments over the next few years, but . . ." She smiled politely. "He's been reluctant to take any *decisive* action."

"And you feel compelled to go over his head and approach me directly?" Tracy leaned back, finishing her wafer and wiping the corners of her mouth with the burgundy linen napkin from her lap.

"Obviously." Rebecca knew not to back down. The executive would instinctively test and challenge to see how much moxy the rising star could generate. "And I know you wouldn't have accepted my invitation today if you didn't approve."

Tracy smiled, telling Rebecca she had passed an initial barrier. "I've been watching you, Rebecca. And I like what I've seen. You don't let anyone give you any shit. That's good." She took a sip of her Glenlivet and water. "But don't worry about Jeff. He's in a wrong position for his talents, and I may have to make some 'adjustments.' If you've got something worthwhile for me to hear, just let me know."

Rebecca smiled. "I appreciate you saying that. And that's why I asked you to join me today. I'm developing a program that needs some long-range direction. I think you can give me that direction."

"What's the idea?" Tracy leaned forward.

Rebecca hesitated with coy reservation, scoring another point. "It's not ready for discussion yet. What I need to know from you is where you see Secularian heading over the next three to five years. Then I'll know how to map my project along the proper path."

The vice-president was smiling again. "That's smart." She squared her shoulders. "All right. Here it is. The long-range plan for Secularian is to branch out into specialty care. We are specifically interested in women's health care, mammography, ob-gyn, that sort of thing. I have an advertising campaign and marketing strategy ready to put in place as soon as we identify all of the key products."

Rebecca's eyes grew wide. "That's what I was hoping you'd say. I had heard rumors, but I wanted to hear it from you."

Tracy looked skeptical. "Why? What have you got?"

Rebecca didn't miss a beat. "A proposal for you and the rest of the executive committee, defining an entire new product-development package. I guarantee it will revolutionize our total market penetration and increase revenues by at least fifteen percent per year for the next three years."

"Guaranteed?" Tracy's skepticism was starting to degenerate into disbelief. "That is quite a boast, Ms. Danforth. A boast that could make you look quite foolish for even mentioning it if you can't deliver."

The second challenge. Rebecca was ready. "And extremely rewarding when I do."

"When do I get to see this proposal?" Tracy Bonner pressed harder.

"I'll have it ready for you and the rest of the officers by the second to third week of January." The confidence in Rebecca's voice was dissolving some of the skepticism on her companion's face.

Tracy took a deep breath and shook her head. "Not the other officers. Just me. I want to see what you have the first week of January, finished or not."

Rebecca nodded with authority. "And *when* I deliver . . ." She paused a second to let her words have their greatest impact. ". . . I'd like the key to Jeff's office, along with his title on my business card."

The chill of electricity tingling through Rebecca's body was likewise discharging through the excited executive across the table. Tracy had not seen this kind of bold confidence in years. If this woman was solid, she would ensure her aggressiveness was well-rewarded. "Rebecca. If you deliver a package where I can see fifteen percent growth over the next three years, I'll see to it you get *my* job."

Rebecca's eyes were filled with energy. "I'm going to hold you to that."

11

December 1974

Boston, Massachusetts

THE TWISTING, HYPNOTIC FLAMES OF RED, YELLOW, AND BLUE crackling in the small fireplace held Rae's gaze transfixed long enough for the cup of herbal tea between her hands to have long since grown cold. The only other light in her small one-bedroom apartment came from the multicolored lights of the little twenty-four-inch, sparsely decorated Christmas tree next to the window, silently twinkling on and off. A yellow crocheted afghan hugged her shoulders, along with the comforting right arm of David Stratton. Her lazy eyes were about to drift off to sleep.

"Hey, sleepyhead," he whispered.

Rae looked up, her expression groggy. "Hmm?"

"Look what time it is." He pointed to the Big Ben alarm clock on an end table. Beneath the two oversized brass bells on top, the big hand was just past midnight.

"Merry Christmas." She smiled, her eyes glassy.

"Merry Christmas." David leaned over and pressed his

lips warmly against Rae's. She reached up and affectionately held his face to hers for several moments, relishing the tenderness of his mouth.

Rae was so happy to be spending Christmas with David. Day after day they were growing inseparable. She acted just like a puppy: whenever he was gone, she worried; whenever he returned, she was overjoyed. He had come to mean so much to her in the two short but wonderful months they had known each other.

David leaned back. "I know it's not Christmas morning in the sense of dawn and all that. But since it *is* technically Christmas, and since you're such a technical person . . ." He smiled. "I have something for you."

Rae started to wake up. "What'd you get me?"

With a big grin on his face, David rose from the small tattered couch and went over to where he had laid his coat when he arrived earlier that evening. Crumpled inside it was a drab yellow, legal-sized envelope. Rae watched him return and sit down beside her on the couch.

He looked at her for several moments, not saying a word.

"What is it?" she asked, her face growing puzzled.

He took a deep breath. "Rae, I've studied business and finance for a long time. And I've dreamed of one day doing something really great with my life. But until I met you, I never really knew what that great thing was."

She felt a loving chill sweep through her.

He continued, "And since, as of two weeks ago, I am an official, unemployed Harvard Business graduate; *and* since we *have* talked so much about our business ideas these last few weeks—"

"What did you do?" She was becoming impatient.

He opened the top seal of the envelope and reached inside. "Well, two things, really. One, I filed incorporation documents for Hope Corporation."

Rae's heart skipped a beat. That's what they called their fictitious company; but the dream was just one of those far-off fantasies on the distant horizon, too remote to ever realize.

She gasped. "You're kidding!"

His grin got bigger. "But there's more. I also took the liberty of contacting a lawyer, and I have the final papers here, ready to patent your discoveries so they'll always belong to Hope Corporation."

She squealed, throwing her arms around his neck. "David, you're wonderful!"

"Here." He pulled out a long legal folder from the envelope. "You just need to sign everywhere you see your name typed. Then you're off to being a rich and famous doctor."

She didn't let him go; her excitement was overflowing. "I can do that later. I just want to hold you now. David, I can't believe you did this! I know we'll be so successful together! I *know* we will."

He gently pushed her back, looking slightly embarrassed. "Rae, I'd really appreciate it if you'd look inside the folder. You're kind of blowing my big setup."

She looked at him with a long, questioning expression. *What was he up to?*

She took the long folder from his hands and opened it. As soon as the cover came fully back, her breathing stopped, her eyes welled with tears, her throat tightened, and her hands began to tremble. Taped to the inside of the folder with a two-inch-long, fingerprint-stained strip of Scotch tape, was a small gold ring with a very small diamond. Her chin began to quiver about the same time the rivulets of tears began to drip from it.

"I love you, Rae," he whispered. "Merry Christmas."

She could barely see him through the fountain pouring from her eyes. This was too incredible to believe. *Could this really be happening?*

She closed the folder, set it down on the well-marred coffee table, and pulled David's face to hers once again. The language of her mind couldn't embody or express what she felt at that moment. The only thing her inexperienced heart instructed her to do was to love, deeply and completely. She wanted to love him—forever.

Rae laid back on the couch, pulling David down over her, smothering him with her lips. He lifted his face from hers and stared deeply into her eyes, his grin still in place. "Rae, can I safely assume that you like my present?"

Her eyes drank in his. "David," she whispered, her heart pounding impulsively, "make love to me."

David's expression grew serious. The young man who had always been a perfect gentleman continued to look at her for several anxious seconds before he answered. "Are you sure?"

"As sure as I am that I love you too. And know that I want you to." She kissed him again. "Please?"

His smile returned. "It's me who should be saying please." He brushed her straight brown hair away from her eyes. "I've wanted to for a long time now, but I've never wanted to rush you. We've only known each other for a few weeks, and I—"

She covered his mouth with her finger. "No more words."

He nodded and kissed her again. She gratefully opened her mouth to receive the sweet exploration of his tongue. Rae had never wanted to be held and touched so much in her entire life. Her sexuality had been such a closed subject for so long, she had almost dismissed it. Now she wanted to explore it, and explore it deeply—with this man—more than anything in the world.

Without saying a word, as the golden fire sputtered and hissed, he patiently unbuttoned her faded blue work shirt— each touch of his lips against the white flesh of her upper chest a new exotic sensation. His hands pulling her shirttails apart was something no other person had ever done. A nervous chill tingled up her spine when his warm right hand cupped the gentle swell of her left breast. Though his hand was still outside the smooth white cloth of her bra, she suddenly longed to know what his hand felt like against her breast without it. She eagerly arched her back to accommodate his eager hands sliding beneath her back to unsnap it. When the two small hooks came away, her first feeling of apprehension struck.

What if what he sees, even in the dim crimson hues of the firelight, displeases him? She wasn't very big.

She didn't have time to entertain the thought before he had pushed the simple white garment up and was tenderly massaging both of them, his lips hungrily back upon hers. The sensation was like nothing she could ever have imagined. There was no physiological reason for the sensation of intense pleasure accompanying that particular area of skin, muscle, and glands; but it was incredible. Seconds later his lips moved down between her small breasts, gently kissing her breastbone. Her mind began to anticipate again, wondering what it would feel like when that warm, wet member of his mouth found one of the two ruby ends standing at eager attention on either side of his face. She felt the coarse stubble of his chin slide beneath the bottom edge of her left breast, her mind visualizing his mouth poised right above her erect nipple. She could feel each warm, sultry breath fall upon it, but the awaited sensation didn't come.

Instead, she felt his lips lightly land just to the right of it, then the wet pressure of his tongue gliding down the slight incline of her breast back to the center of her chest. Then his mouth returned, poised right over the budding peak, his warm respiration again flowing down upon it, followed by another light kiss, this time just to the left of it, his tongue trailing away toward her left arm. Next she felt his tongue drawing slow concentric circles, beginning at the base of the same breast. Yet with each lingering lap, the radius of the circle decreased—the hungry hunter, ascending the hill, stalking the object of its desire. As his tongue finally wound its way around her condensed areola, his left hand came up and covered her right breast, his thumb and forefinger playfully tweezing her protruding nipple. Rae suddenly felt a wet tug between her legs.

A desirous moan came forth from her throat, almost involuntarily. It seemed to cue him to close his lips over her yearning-to-be-tasted left nipple, tracing its contours inside his mouth with the tip of his tongue. It was the most intensely erotic thrill Rae had ever experienced. Her breathing became more labored. Even in the cool chill of her badly heated apartment, Rae's body was beginning to perspire lightly.

Where did he learn how to do all of this? Her whirling mind didn't care, as long as it was here at this moment for her.

While his left hand and mouth continued to stimulate her breasts, she felt his right hand reach down and unsnap her blue jeans, his fingers patiently working the zipper down. She bit her bottom lip, pulling in her abdominal muscles to allow his fingers to delicately work their way inside, under the elastic band on her panties, through the soft brown hair beneath, to their warm, moist destination. A second pang of apprehension seized her. No man had ever done that.

What if something was wrong? What if . . .

His forefinger and ring finger meticulously separated her pubic hair from the tender cleft, allowing his middle finger to gently caress her, softly curling near the top—giving rise to an erotogenic sensation that caused her whole body to tremble uncontrollably. He steadfastly continued the undulating massage between her legs as he planted his lingering kisses at a variety of key pleasure points around her body. An ember in the fire popped, casting a few moments of brighter light in the room, swelling in concert with Rae's burning desires, melting away all her apprehensions and fears. She no longer doubted. This was the man who had chosen her, declared his love to her, proved his love with commitment and a plan for the future. This was the man to give all of herself to, not withholding anything.

She sighed with pleasure as she felt him slide her pants and panties down her legs, pushing them onto the floor. She sensed him stand up next to the couch. The clinking sound of his opening belt buckle invited her eyes to open. He had already pulled the heavy cable-knit sweater over his head with several crisp, crackling pops of static electricity, and he was now sliding his pants down to the floor. The fire was to his back and she couldn't see everything completely, but what she saw was beautiful. The deep yellow and orange hues of the fire cast a soft aura down the entire left side of his body. She could see he was aroused, a bit bigger than she had anticipated. Another pang of timid apprehension tried to force its way in, but she was now determined—this night belonged to her and the man who would be her lover. This was her moment, and his.

She heard him whisper softly, "Rae. Are you really sure?"

She looked up to his face, but it was hidden in shadow. She sat up on the couch and pulled her open shirt and bra off, tossing them down on the floor with David's clothes and her pants. "Yes, I'm sure. I want all of you. And I want you to have all of me."

He stepped toward her. She didn't really know exactly what to do, so she just let her body move on instinct and desire. She reached around his smooth, cool buttocks and pulled him closer, her lips finding the soft end of his erection. She ran her tongue lightly over it, along the top side of it to the tangled nest of dark brown hair on his body. Above her, she heard a labored sigh.

David took Rae's hands from behind him and knelt down on the floor in front of her. He looked into her eyes again as he spread her knees, coaxing her to scoot to the edge of the couch. The low sofa positioned their hips at a convenient height.

She blushed, then said awkwardly, "David. There's something I want you to know. You're the first man I will have ever . . . been with, and—" She couldn't finish the sentence.

At first he didn't understand. Then a look of surprise washed over his face. "Really?" Then somewhat amazed. "Wow. Well, I guess that's about the most precious Christmas present I could ever have wanted. You, Rae. Just you."

She reached out and pulled him to her, wrapping her legs around him, kissing him again. She felt him push her back once more, his compassionate eyes inches from hers.

"Rae. This really is very important." He looked sincere. "I want you to know that no matter how much I want to make love to you at this moment, or you to me, I would understand if you wanted to wait."

Her heart was about to pound out of her chest. "I don't want to wait. I can't wait. It'll be all right."

He looked at her skeptically. "Are you sure?"

Her eyes smoldered like the light in the room. "You've asked that question too many times tonight."

He fell into her arms. She relished the sensation of his lips quickly returning to the delightful banquet of her body. A few moments later she felt him reach down and begin to massage her again, this time letting his finger explore within. It sent a delightful tremor through her, foreshadowing something wonderful to follow. Soon he had two fingers inside her, pushing firmly, deeper and deeper. Her body was demanding he delay no further before joining himself to her.

"Make love to me now, David," she whispered in his ear.

He kept massaging, spreading his fingers as he went. "Not just yet. You'll enjoy it a lot more if you just give it time. The first time can be a little . . . uncomfortable, unless you—"

She giggled. "I know, I'm a doctor. Remember? Please?"

He softly chuckled. "All right."

David reached down with his right hand and guided himself to her. Rae lifted her knees and spread her thighs as wide as she could. The academic side of her brain knew that when this day finally arrived, it could be quite painful. But pain was not an issue right now. To give her love to David Stratton was all that mattered, any pain would be worth it. She wanted it—to the point of sweet desperation.

He began gradually, patiently, with such delicate care there was very little initial discomfort. As he barely moved inside her, she felt herself gasp slightly. It was happening! It was finally happening!

He continued to kiss her and caress her, not rushing, not forcing. The delicious new sensations radiating from within quickly dissolved any trace of discomfort, and Rae began to instinctively rock her hips ever so slightly, urging him on, wanting to feel more, craving it with each passing second.

He pushed in a little farther, causing her to become aware of a slight burning sensation, fostering a reluctant grimace on her face. Sensing her irritation, he began to withdraw.

"No," she panted in his ear. "Don't stop. I'm fine."

After a considerate pause, he pushed back in slightly, whispering sympathetically, "This may hurt a little."

She nodded, holding her bottom lip between her teeth.

Patiently and deliberately, he pushed forward with an even, steady force until he was completely inside her. She didn't cry out, but grit her teeth tightly as the burning sensation gave way. A dull soreness throbbed between her legs, but it didn't matter. He was there, where he was supposed to be, joined as one.

"Now just try to relax," he whispered between kisses. "Let me please you."

He tenderly rocked his hips against her, methodically arousing such a wealth of intense pleasure within her that within the span of five minutes any remaining discomfort had been replaced with an entirely different sensation, almost ticklish, a sensation of need and ungratified desire that invited her to push her body against him all the more, yearning to be satisfied. Soon he was gliding in and out comfortably, and the succulent euphoria was growing beyond anything she had ever dreamed. How could she have lived for twenty-four years and never known this feeling?

Sweet, tender minutes of quiet, steady lovemaking passed. But something else was beginning to happen to Rae that she wasn't expecting. A feeling of great urgency seemed to consume her emotions in concert with the passions of her body, prompting her to wrap her hands around David's back and pull him inside her faster and faster. A deep, fiery pleasure from within fed the sensation with an appetite that demanded more as it received more, spiraling rapidly into a whirlpool of passions that no musician or poet had ever, or could ever, adequately describe. Her lover held her tightly, his hands pushing firmly against the small of her back, sensing her desire, increasing the frequency of his long, firm thrusts, kindling the conflagration of pleasure to a roaring inferno.

What was happening?

Understanding no longer mattered; knowledge was an illusion—reality consisted only of heat, speed, and rock-hard pressure against one unique spot. Rae's fingernails dug eight fine red scratches across David's deltoids as her breathing accelerated to a bated pant.

All at once her body locked around his as the sensual tidal wave abruptly swelled to its towering height, crested in the stillness of her breath, and crashed within her, clamping her entire being into a constriction of pure paradox—pleasure and pain, mixed in a single thunderous explosion. Every neuron in the young doctor's body fired in the same rapturous moment of frozen ecstasy. And then, like a great wave ebbing back out to sea, the molten tide of sweet sensation gracefully abated. Rae's chin fell forward, suspended on David's shoulder, her chest heaving.

"Are you okay?" David asked softly.

"I don't think so." She could barely breathe. Her heart was furiously pounding, every limb shuddered, her thoughts confused and jumbled, all her emotions laid utterly bare. She was starting to cry again. "Oh, David, I love you so much. I've never felt anything so wonderful, so precious, in all my life." A few more heavy breaths later, "You were so, so . . ."

He laughed softly. "Just relax, Rae. Just relax and enjoy."

As David began moving his hips again, picking up speed rapidly, Rae felt the warm sensation returning inside her. It was welcome. She wanted to feel it again. But unexpectedly, there came an ardent pulsation deep within her. She felt every muscle in David's body become taught and hard, though his rocking hips continued their frantic pace. A moment later she felt it—the hot, wet series of explosions within her. It was a beautiful sensation, as enjoyable as all the rest she had discovered that precious night. She pulled him against her even closer as the firm throbs grew weaker and weaker. His hips didn't slow down until many seconds after the wet pulses had ceased.

She continued to hold him tight, feeling the firm presence deep within her fading away. The experience was all so perfect, so glorious, beyond anything she ever could have imagined lovemaking to be. She felt like a real woman, a loved woman, a complete woman, filled and fulfilled. This may have been her first time, but she knew in her heart it was definitely only to be the first of many times. And the thought of waiting till dawn for the next time was utterly out of the question.

12

May 1990

Dallas, Texas

THE THICK LAYERS OF GAUZE ON EMELIA TRAVAIN'S RIGHT HAND retracted in the wake of the surgical scissors, snipping from the tip of her middle finger down to her wrist. When the bandage was cut free, Dr. Alicia Brighton carefully pulled the white strips away from her patient's hand and tossed them into the stainless steel basin on the table beside her. Next she clipped the four strips of adhesive tape that held the steel carpal brace contoured along her palm and extending six inches up her forearm. The brace was the primary support that had held the world-renowned concert pianist's wrist immobile for the past seven days.

The gaunt-looking young woman with straight black hair twisted into a long braid behind her head spoke with an eastern European monotone as dark and morose as the expression on her face. "Dr. Brighton, I feel like this is all a very great waste of your time. They have told me this damage to the nerves of my hand is not a temporary thing."

Alicia's face grew chastising, still holding the long, pale hand in her own. "Emelia. You promised me you would let the medication have time to work before you gave up." She gave the dark woman her best smile. "And I won't let you give up. Now sit still a minute and let me do my job."

The young woman took a deep breath of despair, filled with the recurrent anguish of past disappointments. "It's no use. It will never be as before. Before, I play five hours every day, two, three concerts a week. Even now, to move my fingers brings the burning."

Alicia pushed her wire-rimmed bifocals up on her nose, looking down through the bottom lenses. "That was true a week ago, my dear. Perhaps not today. I'm going to give you one more treatment right now, and I think you are going to be quite surprised."

"You mock me." The dark eyes of the musician challenged her. "Many doctors have done many things, and nothing. You have put needles in my hand every day for seven days, and nothing."

"Nothing?" Alicia tossed her short, gray-streaked black hair back with a smile. "Make a fist for me."

Emelia Travain hesitated.

"Go on," Alicia prompted patiently.

The twenty-nine-year-old prodigy looked into Alicia's eyes with growing disdain. Her face clouded. After an awkward stillness, she suddenly clenched her fist, steeling herself, eyes crushed shut against the expected pain that had ended her illustrious career as one of the world's most celebrated classical musicians.

Nothing happened.

"Well?" Alicia asked hopefully.

Emelia suddenly began to take in short excited gulps of air. Her eyes came open, her gaze transfixed upon her trembling hand.

There was no pain.

With a slight gasp and a single sob, she flexed her hand,

opening and closing it again and again, faster and faster. She began to laugh as thin, silver streaks of tears ran down her face.

Alicia began to laugh too, a triumphant feeling of satisfaction washing over her. "That doesn't look too painful to me, Ms. Travain."

Emelia stopped flexing her hand and looked through tearstained eyes at Alicia. "How have you done this magic?"

Alicia stood up from the examination table, walked over to the antique oak armoire, pulled the heavy door open and retrieved a syringe. "It's not magic, Emelia. It's medicine. The nerves, tendons, and ligatures that were damaged in your hand just needed to be told what they were supposed to look like to be well. At least that's the way I understand it. The medicine you have been given made that happen." She walked over to a small refrigerator and pulled out a small, clear vial and began to fill the syringe. "Now I want you to understand, the process in your hand isn't complete yet. That's why we need to give you one more treatment today, and then possibly one more the day after tomorrow."

Emelia stood up from the table and practically ran across the room to throw her arms around Alicia's neck and hug her tightly. "Dr. Brighton, I have no words to tell you my heart. I cannot thank you so much enough. I—I—"

Alicia walked Emelia back over to the round kitchen table of examination room five. "Oh, it's all right, dear. But I'm not the one you ought to thank. This treatment is available because of Dr. Taylor."

"I must see her," Emelia exclaimed.

Alicia set the syringe down on the table and examined the pianist's hand very carefully. "You can't right now, dear. She's away on business, but will return by the weekend. By that time she'll want to see *you.*" Alicia looked into the pianist's dark, glassy eyes. "But I think, more than anything, she'd like to hear you play. She tells me she's a big fan of yours."

Emelia gasped. "I may play? When?"

Alicia couldn't help but chuckle. "We're having the

Steinway Grand from the main ballroom delivered to your suite in three days. You may begin practicing at that time." Alicia held up an admonishing finger at the pianist's euphoric look of shock. "And not before. No more than one hour per day the first week. Two hours the second week, and perhaps a little longer in about three weeks. Is that understood?"

Alicia felt the firm grip of Emelia's arms around her neck again, and a wet cheek nodding against her own. Alicia's words came out half choking, "Of course, we will expect to hear you entertain next month at the Director's Ball."

"Yes! Certainly! Certainly." Emelia sat back, her face aglow, allowing Alicia to administer the injection.

"There." Alicia set the empty syringe back down on the table, then looked into Emelia's face with a mischievous smile. "As your doctor, I suggest you just relax for the next couple of days and give your medication more time to do its job. A few quiet evenings of relaxation with your therapist are highly recommended."

Emelia blushed. "Oh, yes. The therapy, as you call it, has been most wonderful. My gentleman, Jonathan, is so kind. Today I go horse riding with him."

"Wonderful." Alicia beamed. "Just be careful with the hand now that the brace is off. Let him use *his* hands. Understand?"

Emelia blushed again with a toothsome grin, and gave Alicia a shy little nod.

13

May 1984

Indianapolis, Indiana

MEMORIAL DAY. THE INDIANAPOLIS MOTOR SPEEDWAY.

The long awaited day had finally arrived. The carnival atmosphere was intoxicated with the wine of celebration, amidst the screaming thunder of high-performance engines, charged with the voracious energy of pure competition, craving satisfaction. Every nerve of every racer lay raw and exposed.

An hour earlier the sea of humanity had cheered when the racing marshal had announced over the public address system, *"Lady,* and gentlemen, start your engines." And from the moment the elaborately decorated Chevrolet Corvette pace car had pulled into the pits and the green flag waved, Sabrina Doucette's Formula-One racer, representing the Roger Marks team, had stayed within four car lengths of the leaders. Early in the race she had dropped to seventh position, but by the two hundredth lap she worked her way back up to third position, looking for an opening to overtake Bobby Unser in second and Mario Andretti, racing in first. This was her chance to realize the dream of a lifetime. Lap after lap she came closer and closer, the taste of victory already in her mouth. Each time she roared past the grandstand, she replayed her fantasy. There she was, standing by her car in the winner's circle, the champagne flowing, the crowd screaming, her arms lifted high in triumph. It was going to be glorious—and nothing was going to stand in the way.

ANTICIPATION

The sensation of movement in a Formula-One racer, averaging between 190 and 200 mph, is similar to flight. The g-force evens out to a surrealistic calm, the scenery flows by on all sides in a fluid current. The only objects that appear to be in the same physical dimension are the other racers, winding their way in and around the slower moving cars, moving high into the turns, diving down low against the infield, accelerating out of the turns and throttling hard on the straights. As the unrelenting minutes turn into hours, the racer's raw concentration becomes more instinctive, a function of reflex and pattern. Consequently, the mind often has time to become a passive spectator to the whole blurred panorama of sight and sound. And in those moments, Sabrina's mind reflected a great deal about where she was and the awesome realization of what she was doing. But most of all her thoughts were on Roger Marks.

For the last two years they had grown very close, ever since that sensuous day in Monte Carlo. Sabrina had never experienced what she thought of as a *serious* relationship with a man. For her, most men were just sources of amusement. But Roger was different. There was a caring side of him, a thoughtfulness she had never experienced from anyone else. But there was also "the problem."

Ever since that warm, sensual day on the deck of his yacht, Roger enjoyed a great deal of intimacy with Sabrina, but he had never allowed her to see him without wearing his shirt and pants, nor would he allow her to sleep with him in the same bed. At first it had bothered her a great deal; she wanted to be close to him. He would take her to bed and please her completely, but his only tools were his hands and his mouth. When he was finished, he would always kiss her good-night and mysteriously leave. On several occasions she had tried to touch him, but he then patiently took her hands away and quietly asked her to refrain. She had been afraid to confront him openly about the situation for over two months, speculating that he was just overly sensitive about some physical shortcoming. She didn't find out the truth until a few days after arriving in Rome.

They had been staying in adjoining suites at the Michelangelo Hotel near the Vatican. One evening, in the mood for a little romantic intimacy, Sabrina had taken it upon herself to undress, slip into Roger's bed, and wait for him to finish taking a shower. Emerging from his bath, Roger walked into the room, still completely naked, and stopped at his dresser to find his nightclothes. He didn't notice Sabrina lying behind him with a look of shock on her face. What Sabrina saw made her stomach tighten. All along his back were thin scars and light pink patches that looked like old burns. One long straight scar going from his waistline up the small of his back, at least ten inches long, appeared to be an incision from an operation. When he noticed her in the mirror, he spun around, his expression livid, and screamed at her to leave. Now, almost two years later, she couldn't remember any of his ranting words from that night—she only remembered the sight. In that horrible moment, her eyes had been locked on the discolorations on the front of his body. The slightly raised red patches were all across his stomach, spreading down the tops of his thighs.

Sabrina had jumped out of the bed, her thoughts a mixture of fear, sorrow, and horror, hastily retreating to the sanctuary of her own room. She remained there, sitting in an overstuffed chair, crying through the remainder of that night, mortally afraid to knock on the door and talk to the man she realized she deeply cared for. He didn't speak to her for almost a full week. And when he did, it was one of the most painful conversations she had ever endured.

It happened in an outdoor café, sitting along a riverbank of humanity flowing by on the streets and sidewalks of Rome, near the ruins of the Roman Forum. In an ominous-sounding tone, Roger had asked to speak with her. She suspected, and dreaded, he was going to remove her from the team with no explanation or occasion for appeal. But instead, as he sipped a small glass of red wine, he told her a sordid tale of pain and bitter disappointment.

"Sabrina, I want to apologize for my behavior last week,"

he began; much to her surprise, in his very proper British way. "And really for the last few months, for that matter."

She didn't say a word, but just stared into his pained eyes, seeing how difficult it was for him to say what he had to say.

"It happened about five years ago, actually," he continued, somewhat abruptly. "I was racing in Sidney. Masters competition. Seven-figure purse. It was quite simple, really. I came 'round a turn and hit a patch of oil. It hadn't been there on the previous lap. It was still quite fresh. The only thing I can still remember is an uncomfortable moment of vertigo as the car tumbled over the side rail. They told me afterward the car flipped seven times before it hit the wall of a commerce building. But I can't tell you that's true. All I know is that when I woke up in an Australian hospital a week later, I was broken, bruised, burned . . ." He took an awkward breath, looking down at the table. ". . . and greatly afraid. From that moment until now, I've never been behind the wheel of a racer."

Sabrina could still remember how tight her chest and stomach felt listening to Roger's words. The memory itself was chilling. A racer's greatest fear is not hitting the wall and being gone, but hitting it and waking up only half alive.

Roger had placed his hand on top of hers, sitting at the wrought-iron table for two in the spring morning air amidst the tumultuous traffic noises, swarms of tourists, and buzzing throng of restaurant patrons. She could still picture his sad hazel eyes looking into hers. His words still rang in her ears. "Sabrina, I'm almost old enough to be your father. I've told myself that it doesn't matter. Furthermore, in getting to know you, indeed, I've discovered you to be quite a mature young woman. But—" He took a pained breath. "I've come to realize that I've been utterly unfair. I know I can never be the kind of man in your life that you need—that you deserve."

She didn't know what to say. What could she say?

He had laughed, trying to make light of his pain and ease the tension in the air. "You see, my sweet, ever since the accident, I've tried to be with a woman on several occasions. And much to my dismay, and the ladies' as well . . . How do I say it?" His eyes had fastened on hers again. "It was a most *disappointing* event."

Sabrina remembered finding her voice. "It's all right, Roger. That's not what's important."

He had patted her hand with a note of thanks. "It is important, my love. To be sure, it certainly can't be the sole foundation of a relationship, but its absence will be sorely missed, and an occasion for a pain I have no desire to see you endure. You're spending entirely too much time with an old man who can never be everything I should be for you."

She remembered how his words stirred up heartrending emotions inside her, prompting words she never thought she would ever hear herself tell a man. "Roger, I care about you. More than I want to admit, even to myself. And I *want* to have a relationship with you—a good relationship. I can understand your fear." She raised her voice. "God, Roger, *I'm* afraid everytime I climb behind that wheel that *this* may be the time I come back without an arm or a leg or in much worse shape than you're in. Dammit, every racer feels that way! It's what we live with. It's what makes the winning mean something! How in the world could you not expect me to understand that?"

She remembered the way he sat quietly for so long, then lifted her hand to his lips. "You are a special lady, Sabrina." Then his face darkened. "But I know what I am now. I don't want sympathy for a freak."

She snatched her hand away. "And you'll get none from me. But what you will get is a woman who thinks you're very special, perhaps the most special person I've ever known; a woman who's very thankful for a man who gave her a chance to become a true world-class champion when few others even noticed I was alive." Her voice cracked with emotion. "A woman who only recently realized she's in love with a man she's afraid doesn't want to be close to her."

"You're wrong," he had whispered, shaking his head in desperate protest. "I do want to be close to you." His next words came out hard, rash. "But I can't take away what's hideous."

Sabrina had given him her best smile, her eyes glistening with a faint film of tears. "Won't you let me try?"

For the past two years there had been no real "happily ever after," but there had been a great deal of understanding and compassion. After many frustrating months Roger had finally let Sabrina sleep with him, but he still wore long pajamas to mask his scars. He still made love to her, but in his limited way. As time passed, what frustrated her more and more was the knowledge that each time he took her in his arms, she was denied the pleasure of seeing him fulfilled. It made her feel selfish. She had never felt that way in any of her many backseat romances, but with Roger it was different. There was a subtle torture in watching him perform for her each time, then modestly retiring.

A sudden clunking noise disturbed her flow of thought as she flew around the track at Indianapolis. A quick glance down at the instrument panel thrust an unexpected bolt of horror through her heart. The oil pressure gauge was slowly diminishing, sinking along with all her hopes and dreams of victory that day.

"Oh, shit . . ." She instinctively knew there would be a dark plume of smoke following her. The rhythmic clunking sound became louder and louder as her car began to lose speed. Her trained mechanic's mind could picture a scored piston tearing against the wall of the engine block. As the high-viscosity oil quickly burned away, leaving metal rubbing against metal, the heat would cause the engine to literally weld itself into one useless mass of metal in a matter of seconds. Indeed, this was not going to be the day—no champagne, no flowers, no trophy.

Sabrina had already climbed out of the crimson wing car and thrown her helmet in the seat in disgust by the time the yellow emergency van arrived in the grassy infield where her smoking car came to a smoldering stop. The racing announcer was expressing his condolences on her behalf to the thousands gathered at the raceway and the millions watching on national television. She didn't say a word as she rode back to the hotel after leaving the track, amid the disappointed looks from her crew. She had only nodded mournfully at Roger as she went back into her hotel room and took a long, lethargic bath. A depression as black as death had seeped through her skin, threatening to suck the marrow from her bones.

Roger came in an hour later and had to physically drag her out of the tub and make her get dressed. He was being entirely too cheerful for someone who had just lost a multimillion-dollar investment. With a great deal of coaxing, he got her to agree to go out with him and get blithering drunk.

Two hours later they sat across from each other in a booth at one of the more elite dance clubs in Indianapolis, drenched in pounding music and orbiting lights. Sabrina knew Roger was trying to cheer her up as best he could, but not even the promises of "next year" could take away the dull ache enveloping her heart.

This was supposed to have been the day.

She was so close, *so close.* Even with five beers and two shots of tequila in her and another one on order, her senses were still too coherent to cope. All she wanted to do was go back to the hotel, climb in bed, and not get up till next year. The last place in the world she wanted to be was in some stupid bar, swilling beer, and watching other people have a good time.

"Would you like to dance?" Roger looked hopeful.

"Are you out of your fucking mind?" she asked sweetly, took another sip of her beer, crossed her arms defiantly and leaned back in her chair, surveying the silly people gyrating on the dance floor. Look at them, she thought. The women were all disco bimbos with moussed hair, dressed like sluts, meat in a meat market; the men, all cheap bastards hoping to get laid if they told enough lies and flashed enough money.

Roger laughed. "Quite possibly," he said, answering her

previous question. "Come on, Sabrina, I thought we were going to have a little fun."

She forced another stony smile. "Oh, whatever makes you think I'm not having fun?"

Roger leaned over and touched her elbow. "If you get that 'March to Bataan' look off your face, I'll tell you a secret."

She looked at him quizzically, leaning away from the aroma of the five martinis on his breath. "What secret?" she demanded flatly.

"Not good enough," he chided. "I need to see those pearly whites, come on, just start with a little upturn around the corners of your mouth." He put his fingers on either side of his mouth. "It's very simple, babies can do it. Go ahead. Try, like this."

He looked so ridiculous, miming his own instructions, she couldn't help but start to smile, then reluctantly percolate into a giggle.

"There we are," he applauded confidently. "You see, the world isn't such a terrible place."

Her smile faded. "Yes it is."

He chuckled, then leaned closer to her ear. "You know, I spoke with Peter Gustoff yesterday."

"Who the hell's Peter Gustoff?" Her tone was patronizing again.

Roger leaned back with an I-know-something-you-don't-know look on his face. "You know, that's part of your problem, Sabrina. Your experience lies only in American cars." He looked at his fingernails nonchalantly.

"What's that supposed to mean?" she demanded.

Roger cleared his throat. "Peter Gustoff is a design engineer who has had a distinguished and illustrious career with BMW. I trust you have heard of the M1?"

"Right, their speed wagon. Cute as a razor blade, world records, lots of neat shit like that." Sabrina gulped down the rest of the beer in her glass and handed it to the waitress as a new one was set down in front of her. "So what?"

"Well," Roger was enjoying beating around the bush entirely too much, "as you may know, the M1 is one of the most powerful six-cylinder engines in the world, used in many racers as well as competition racing boats."

"Enough history, Roger. Make your point." She was getting exasperated with him.

"Peter Gustoff is one of three men who originally designed the M1 engine. And he has some very unique theories on Formula-One racing. In fact, he published an article, which I read recently, that caught my attention. So I called him." Roger looked like he was finished.

Sabrina just stared at him, waiting for something else. "That's it? You called him. That's great, Rog, how's he doing?"

Roger smiled, oblivious to her sarcasm. "He's quite well in fact, thank you." He took another sip of his martini. "And he'll be arriving next week to start working for Marks Racing, Incorporated."

"What?" Sabrina was shocked. "You hired a German engineer?"

Roger suddenly became very excited, leaning close to Sabrina's ear again. "Not just any engineer. *The* engineer. Peter is going to build us an engine for next year's race that will surpass anything that's ever been run at Indy—an engine more powerful, more durable, than anything that's *ever* been built."

Sabrina was becoming intrigued. Some of the darkness within her was starting to get faint glimpses of the dawn. "He can do that?"

Roger looked confident, finishing off his drink and setting the glass down with a firm thump. "Sabrina, today you had an opportunity to get the feel of the track. Valuable experience, to be sure. Next year, with our new engine, you will be in poll-position number one when you get the green flag on Memorial Day, and will be first across the finish line five hundred miles later under the checkered flag. I'd be willing to guarantee it."

A fresh current of energy was rapidly reviving Sabrina's dead batteries. Her smile was genuine. "Next year?"

"Next year." He gave her a half-inebriated nod.

"Come on." She grabbed his hand and stood up. "I feel like dancing."

14

January 1975

Boston, Massachusetts

IT HADN'T SNOWED IN ALMOST TWO WEEKS, LEAVING THE HEAPS OF plowed and salted slush and ice along Cambridge Street stained a dismal brown and gray by the residue of cars, buses, and trucks. The depressing overcast canopy of gray above continued to isolate the huddled community below from the inspiring light and warmth of the sun, continually threatening to wrap its wintery shroud tighter and tighter as each new cold front marched in. Pedestrians wrapped their scarves closer to their eyes and hunched their shoulders at more acute angles to stave off the bitter winds. But in each shop or home, fires, heaters, boilers, and the like, all glowed with the same effusion of warmth as the myriad conversations of the inhabitants huddled beside them. Sitting on the hard plastic seat of the McDonald's restaurant, as far away from the icy blasts of the opening and closing door as possible, Rae took another sip of her coffee.

"You *know* I'm very happy for you," Nikki advised. "But what you did, Rae, was really stupid. And you know it. I don't care how much in love you think you are."

Rae just smiled. "I don't think so." She set her plastic cup down. "Besides, it was only a day or so after I finished my period. It was safe."

Nikki Thompson looked at her friend in shock. "Rae, you know biology. For God's sake you're a medical puke. You should *know* better. What would you have done if you'd gotten pregnant?"

Rae just looked out the window at the gray day. "Been happy, I guess. We *are* getting married, you know."

Nikki glanced down at Rae's left hand again. Her friend was so proud of the tiny little diamond ring. Nikki vividly remembered the incoherent phone call she received on Christmas Day from a very excited young biochemist. She had been so happy for Rae. She had cried with her on the phone. She screamed and hugged Rae when she came over later that afternoon. And she accepted the hasty appointment as Rae's maid of honor. But what she didn't like was Rae being so smitten she took foolish chances, risking her future on things that were not "done deals" yet.

"So you're ready for a family right away?" Nikki chastised.

"Lighten up, Nick." Rae sat back. "Look, I know. You're right. I should have been more careful. And ever since that first night, we've been taking proper precautions. So you can put your mind at ease."

"What kind of precautions?" Nikki demanded, like a well-meaning, but bluntly tactless mother.

"He bought some condoms," Rae whispered, blushing behind her thick-framed glasses, glancing around the restaurant to ensure that no one overheard her. Rae's right shoulder thrust forward with her chin, pointedly accenting her words, "Is that okay, Mom?"

Nikki looked out the window at the gray world, still not satisfied. "They're not a hundred percent effective, you know. You ought to see your gynecologist and get on the pill. What happens when your boyfriend conveniently runs out of them, and then things get hot and heavy, and then you just do it anyway, and then—"

"And then I get pregnant." Rae interrupted in the same rapid-fire cadence as her friend. "And then out comes this baby, and then the country goes into hyperinflation, and then they declare war, and then the earth explodes." Rae made a crude explosion noise, illustrating it with her hands, fluttering into a mushroom cloud.

Nikki gave her a stern look. "Funny. Real funny. Go ahead, make fun of me. I just think you'd better get your head on straight before you end up in trouble. I've seen too many of these college romances fizzle out and some poor girl is either stuck with a small mouth to feed or lying on her back in some butcher's office."

Rae's expression grew serious. "Nikki, I know you mean well. But you're going to have to believe me. I love David. He loves me—deeply. We're going to share our lives together. And we're starting a family business together that's going to give me the opportunity to see a whole lot of women helped in ways that have never existed before."

Nikki softened her tone, "I'm sorry. I just worry so much about you."

"Why?" Rae looked puzzled.

Nikki shrugged. "I don't know. Maybe I just like you and I want to see everything go all right for you." She was unwilling to admit, even to herself, the real reason for her concern for Rae, her underlying fear of seeing a close friend end up facing what she herself faced every day in her own home.

"Everything is going all right," Rae insisted. "We shouldn't be here arguing. We should be celebrating. You passed the bar exam this week, and last week I got engaged. What in the world do we have to be complaining about?"

"I'm not complaining," Nikki contended. "Like I said, I'd just like to see you to take things slow and easy. Give this guy some time to level out. You've only known him for three months."

Rae squared her shoulders. "I don't have any doubts about David. He's the nicest, most loving man I've ever met.

Nikki, he's already moved out of his dorm into my apartment, and we're very, very happy together. You're married. I thought you'd understand."

"All right," Nikki conceded, seeing the resolve in her friend's expression. She did understand, all too well. She popped the last french fry in her mouth, weary of the current subject. "Let's go back over to your place. I want to get my Elton John eight-track back."

"You need it back already?" Rae looked surprised. She pushed her glasses back up on her nose and complained, "I haven't even got a chance to listen to it yet."

Nikki gave Rae an incredulous look. "Rae, I gave you that tape the week before Christmas."

Rae blushed again with a smile. "I've been kind of busy."

The walk back to Rae's apartment took almost twenty minutes. Neither woman spoke much along the way, their words often repeated through the heavy scarves wrapped around their faces. Both women shuddered in unison as they closed Rae's apartment door behind them, laboriously extracting themselves from gloves, hats, scarves, overcoats, and wet snow boots.

"How about some more coffee?" Rae asked, heading into the small kitchen and pulling open a cabinet.

"Sure, anything warm." Nikki walked over by the television and looked at an empty shelf on Rae's bookshelf where a layer of dust bordered a clean rectangle. "Rae, where'd your stereo go?"

Rae called back from the kitchen. "What do you mean?"

Nikki raised her voice above the sound of a percolator being filled at the sink. "I mean, where is that cute Panasonic stereo you got David for Christmas? Did he move it to the bedroom or something?"

The water stopped. Nikki heard the sound of the percolator lid being replaced. Rae walked into the room and over to the empty bookshelf with a puzzled look on her face. She muttered, "That's weird. It was there this morning."

A look of shock swept across Nikki's face. "Oh my God,

Rae, you've been robbed!" She grabbed Rae's shoulders, looking into her bewildered eyes. "I'll call the police. Don't touch anything, but go around and see if anything else is missing."

Rae's breathing accelerated as a wave of panic came over her.

Robbery?

The thirteen-inch portable television was still there. She raced into the bedroom and opened her top drawer, her heart beating faster. Her camera was still there. She opened her closet to see if her tennis racquet was still in place.

"Operator, I'd like you to get me the police." Nikki spoke evenly into the receiver. After three rings and an apathetic greeting, the desk officer's voice was abruptly cut off in mid-sentence with a click. Nikki jerked her attention to the wall-mounted phone. Rae's hand was holding the switch hook down. She screamed, "Dammit, Rae, what are you doing?"

Rae's face was ashen, her eyes empty. "Don't. There was no robbery."

Nikki didn't understand. She dropped the receiver, letting it bang against the linoleum tiles, and walked through the apartment. When she arrived at the bedroom, the closet door was still open. Rae's clothes were still hanging bunched together along the left side of the closet. The right side was empty. Only a few wire hangers dangled askew, as barren as the branches on the trees outside. The weight of realization slammed into Nikki with enough force to make her choke, a nauseating wave of revulsion welling up inside. She flew to Rae in the next instant.

Rae was still in the kitchen, standing mutely by the telephone. The phone-off-hook alarm beeped its obnoxious interval of shrill tones up from the beige plastic receiver laying on the floor. Rae just stood there, staring at the tall silver percolator. The first light-brown bubbles of coffee had just started to hurl themselves against the round glass knob on the lid. Nikki replaced the receiver back on its hook, then quietly wrapped her arms around her motionless friend. Rae put up no resistance when Nikki silently led her into the living room and sat her down on the couch.

Nikki kept trying to think of something to say, but nothing sounded the least bit appropriate or comforting. She couldn't suggest they try to find him. She couldn't say that it probably wasn't as bad as it seemed. It was too obvious to be a wrong assumption. The bastard had moved out, without so much as a good-bye. Or did he? A troubling thought occurred to her.

"Wait here," Nikki whispered to Rae as she stood, walking back into the bedroom. If indeed Rae had been as abruptly dumped as it appeared, the jerk would have at least left a note or something. She wanted to find it before Rae did, in case there was more insult to add to injury.

There was nothing in the bedroom, bathroom, or kitchen. Nikki opened the door to the small second bedroom Rae used for an office and stopped short in the doorway.

"Rae!" Nikki couldn't stop from yelling with bloodcurdling urgency. "Get in here!"

A moment later the dazed biochemist walked down the hall and absently looked inside her office. The once heavily cluttered room filled with small metal bookshelves bulging with three-ring binders and piles of boxes overflowing with over five years' worth of research and documentation—was completely bare. Not a scrap of paper remained.

Nikki turned and looked at Rae with a fury she had never felt in her life. *"Now* I'm calling the police. You *have* been robbed!"

Rae never heard those words. She was barely conscious of Nikki's instructions to sit on the couch, much less her request to come to the study; her body had obeyed of its own volition, devoid of thought. A whirlpool of horror had swallowed her from the moment she saw the empty wire hangers, her head spinning as she felt all at once like her insides had been savagely torn out and trodden upon. Her limbs trembled; her mouth went dry; a dull ringing filled her ears. All Rae's sensation blurred into a numbness that knew no reality, no relevance. She faded into unconsciousness, her body dropping to the hardwood floor of her office in a heap.

Rae Taylor's pain certainly had no relevance a mere three miles away in a lavish high-rise apartment near North Station, where the raunchy electric strains of Aerosmith playing "Walk This Way" from their new *Toys in the Attic* album thundered from a new Pioneer turntable. Her loss was of no importance to the pleasure of a woman with long black hair, kneeling in her bed, her entire body damp with perspiration, her knees slightly apart, her hands gripping the smooth varnished spindles of the her headboard as her lover knelt behind her, making furious love to her from the rear—pounding and pounding, his thighs slapping against her backside, moving ever faster as the intensity of their passion kindled. His surging pelvis thrust in a steady rhythmic pace, accented by the squeak of the antique walnut bed frame keeping time.

She felt him lean forward, pressing his lips between her shoulder blades, his hands sliding from her waist to her breasts, kneading them. Her mouth was almost completely dry from her short, frantic pants. She pulled her pelvic muscle inward as hard as possible to increase the pressure on the penetrating movement inside her. The tremors of pleasure were building, she could feel it approaching; her back arched down to increase the angle of sensation—but it wasn't enough. Her right hand released the headboard spindle, instinctively moving down between her legs, her fingers pressing firmly against the one remaining spot not in violent contact with her lover, massaging in concert with the erotic movement within.

When the molten eruption of her orgasm overflowed, her perspiring left hand slipped from the remaining spindle. She fell onto the satin-cased pillows, her body convulsing beneath her toppled lover, who finished seconds later in warm invigorating throbs. A moment of stillness held them motionless as she felt the frenzied pulsation wane.

She stiffly straightened her legs with a sigh of relief, her lover still panting in her right ear, fresh perspiration rapidly condensing between her back and his heaving chest. She felt his dead weight on top of her for several minutes as their respiration rates both slowed back to normal. His wet, limp organ finally slipped out onto the black satin sheets. With a gentle nudge of her left shoulder, she rolled him off to her right.

She turned over with an exhausted moan, gathered the shiny thin sheet around her, suddenly feeling a chill in the air. A glance at the clock radio next to the phone confirmed that she was late in making her promised call. Fortunately, it wasn't too late. Her lover had taken a great deal longer than originally anticipated; but she wasn't complaining. She picked up the stereo remote control, lowered the volume, then reached for the princess telephone on the nightstand to her right.

"Hello. Tracy Bonner, please," she said evenly into the receiver.

A voice picked up on the third ring after the call was transferred. "This is Tracy."

"Tracy, this is Rebecca." She took a quick breath, feeling the excitement building within her.

"Hello, Rebecca. I've been anticipating your call." Indeed, Tracy's voice sounded eager. "Is everything ready?"

"The presentation will be ready to go by ten o'clock tomorrow morning." Rebecca glanced down at the hand probing under the sheets, gliding up her thigh, finding the sensitive spot between her legs and softly caressing it. She licked her lips beneath a furrowed brow.

"That's excellent, Rebecca," came Tracy's voice. "And I haven't forgotten. I keep my promises. If you deliver, that key to Jeff's office will be waiting for you."

Rebecca's eyes narrowed. "I'll deliver. I have the product in hand as we speak."

"That's incredible," came the reply. "How did you do it so soon? Doesn't legal have to get involved in negotiations?"

Rebecca glanced over at the warm blue eyes next to her.

"Oh, that's all been taken care of. Actually, I have a very capable research assistant, who I've promised a major promotion if he brought me a breakthrough on schedule. We have the patent acquisition signed, in hand, and are ready to proceed with development."

"Rebecca, if what you showed me on Monday is solid, you'll be able to give him your old job." Tracy Bonner's enthusiasm was rising along with Rebecca's. "Who is he?"

Rebecca smiled down at the matted brown curls now moving over her left breast. "Stratton, from over in marketing analysis. Handpicked for the assignment a few months ago."

"David Stratton?" came Tracy's voice with a note of surprise. "That's wonderful. You made a good choice. I hired David myself a little over two years ago. He's a good man. Use him well."

"Oh, I have." Rebecca's voice was sinking into a whisper; the tongue encircling her left nipple was making it harder to concentrate. She welcomed the feel of her lover's reviving erection against the side of her leg. "And you're right. He's very good."

15

June 1990

Dallas, Texas

THE STACCATO RIPPLE OF METICULOUS FINGERING TECHNIQUE
cascaded down the keyboard in rapturous eloquence, building toward the finale. Each tendon in both hands energeti-
cally commanded a fluid cadence against the precision
balanced weights of white ivory and raised ebony. The
instrument sang a song of triumph, a symphony lavished
forth with such moving and explosive passion the audience
sat transfixed, breathless, an electric sense of anticipation
growing in the air as it approached its final strains. The
master pianist's eyes were focused upon the stately silver
candelabra elegantly perched atop the glossy black grand
piano; but she could only see the blur of its flickering lights
through the tears of euphoria welling in her eyes and
coursing down her cheeks.

Before the music stopped, while the final chords thundered across the vast expanse of the Fortunato Ballroom at
the North Dallas Women's Center, the assembled group of
more than two hundred women, plus their escorts, were
already on their feet rendering a thunderous ovation. And
sitting at the head table closest to the stage, clapping the
loudest, was Dr. Rae Taylor. To her left stood Marsha
Collins, and on her right, Dr. Alicia Brighton. With the
applause still ringing through the hall, Emelia Travain
stood, took an abbreviated bow, and ran over to embrace
Alicia and Rae. Marsha presented her with two dozen
long-stemmed red roses. Admiring patrons pressed in to

obtain autographs, shake her hand, politely kiss her cheeks, or take a moment to heap adulation and praise upon the brilliant musician.

The Director's Ball was an incredible success. All of the most powerful and elegant clients of the elite Women's Center were in attendance; and attention to detail was spared no expense. Beneath the glittering chandeliers, the air was filled with the joyous melodies of a sixty-four-piece string orchestra. Champagne flowed by the case. Liver pâté, baked Brie, marinated shrimp and crab delicacies, plus three distinct varieties of imported caviar, *never* allowed to go empty, splendorously graced every table, all sumptuously surrounding an ice sculpture centerpiece flanked by a wreath of black orchids.

The duck à l'orange was magnificent, but many guests chose the lobster Fontaine, the chef's specialty, some guests opting for portions of both. Each dish, down to the cherries jubilee, exotic pastries, brandy, cognac, or Irish coffee, was served by the delightfully attentive staff, ensuring a satisfied smile on the lips of every guest. The dazzling array of original evening gowns, tailored tuxedoes, custom-designed jewelry, diamonds, furs, and precious gems was a spectacle unto itself. Rae, stunningly dressed in a full-length, strapless, black sequined gown, an original Rosinni, was very pleased with what she saw. With a subtle gesture of her chin pointing toward the door, she turned and discreetly departed, quickly followed by Marsha and Alicia.

Marsha closed the door to Rae's office as Rae sat down behind her desk, removed her long, black opera gloves, and tossed them down in front of her. Marsha looked a bit confused. "Don't you think we should be out hobnobbing with the guests?"

Rae didn't answer.

Alicia took a seat in a large wing-backed chair in the sitting group by Rae's office fireplace. "What is it, Rae?"

Rae took a long thoughtful breath. "It's good news. I had to tell you both right away. I've spoken with Nikki again, tonight, just before the performance. That's why I was a few minutes late." Her gaze went back and forth to the two anxious expressions. "The prospectus is final. The SEC gave us the rating."

Alicia gasped.

Marsha took a seat on the sofa near Alicia. "That's wonderful. I told you it would all work out."

"You did at that," Rae conceded. "But, you know, I never really knew until tonight just how well it was all going to turn out. Everything was magnificent! It's all just like we envisioned it, every detail, every ingredient. It's all here. It's perfect."

Alicia turned to Marsha. "Well, I believe we've still many things to attend to before we declare any state of perfection. You haven't got all of the cash together yet, have you?"

Marsha batted at the air. "Oh, don't worry about that. It will all be in hand when the time comes. In the meantime, you just keep doing what you're doing. I was most impressed with the results of your work this evening."

Alicia laughed. "Don't look over here. All I did was play nurse and give injections. You can thank Dr. Taylor over there for the results."

"Yes, I suppose that's true," Marsha agreed. "It really was a miracle, Rae."

Rae was beaming, her thoughts still filled with the sounds of the beautiful symphony, the image of the delighted young girl's tears of joy burned into her memory forever. But a pang of unfinished business tugged at her heart. "The entire portfolio of treatments is still not complete. We have to have it all to be successful."

Marsha stood. "We will, Rae. And *soon*. A lot sooner than you think."

Rae stood up, walked over to her marble wet bar and lifted the top from a tall crystal decanter. "I know. I can wait. I'm just eager to see that same look on so many women's faces—the same one I saw on Emelia's tonight."

"That's what it's all about," Alicia stated profoundly.

Rae nodded, pouring three small glasses of sherry and

handing two of them to her associates. "A toast, my friends."

Marsha and Alicia joined her, taking their glasses and holding them aloft with Rae's. Marsha looked at Rae. "To what?"

"To hope," Rae whispered elliptically.

"To hope," the two other women repeated, and sipped their drinks.

Rae stared into the bottom of her empty glass.

16

March 1975

Boston, Massachusetts

THE OVERWORKED STEAM HEATERS IN THE COURTROOM HISSED softly amid the occasional murmur of the few individuals gathered in the gallery, making an unbearable situation excruciating. The dark woods, broad beams, ornate moldings, milled rails, hardwood flooring, and heavy chairs had witnessed the parade of justice since the days of the colonial government. Faded portraits of long-forgotten jurists leaned forward from the framed paneling, still imposing stern looks of judgment and scrutiny. The amber shafts of the afternoon sun illuminated the suspended motes of dust, connecting the tall, paned windows on the west wall to the floor. A uniformed bailiff carried on a hushed conversation with the court recorder, ever so often chuckling loud enough to draw the attention of the others in the room.

Nikki Thompson sat at the plaintiff's table next to her client, Dr. Rae Taylor. It was her first case as an attorney at law in the Commonwealth of Massachusetts. Actually, it wasn't really a trial yet, merely the preliminary hearing before Judge Olivia Browning, an elderly black woman, reputed to be extremely strict in her interpretation of the law. Preliminary motions had been filed earlier in the week, and her ruling was anticipated during the current proceeding. Judge Browning had yet to make her appearance.

At the defense table sat Daniel O'Hara, attorney for Secularian Corporation, a ruddy, heavyset man in his early fifties. He looked at ease, as bored as the rest of the assembly, ambivalently perusing briefs from his overstuffed satchel. Nikki glanced again at Rae, whose eyes remained fixed on the door to the judge's chambers, as they had for the last hour.

The past two months had been an utter nightmare. Nikki remembered staying with Rae for almost thirty-six hours without sleep, fearing what she might do in her state of mind. Hours after Rae had regained consciousness from her faint, the tears had come, tears and the racking sobs of a soul torn and discarded. Nikki had never seen such anguish in another human being, and the sight of it brought tears of her own for her friend. When there were no more tears to cry, with Rae's face swollen, red, and rubbed raw by her clenched fists, she would slip into a semicatatonic state of numbness, staring into empty space, oblivious to all external sensation. And after a few hours the crying would resume, in a vicious cycle of despair.

When Rae did finally collapse in exhaustion, Nikki had put her to bed and called another friend to come and sit with her. She had no intention of leaving Rae alone. Fortunately, Rae slept for almost twenty-four hours, and when she awoke, much of the storm, at least on the surface, appeared to have past. However, Rae didn't eat for almost a week, and what little she did get down quickly came back up with frightening bouts of dry heaves.

During that horrible week, Nikki took it upon herself to do some investigation. It wasn't long before she had located the missing Mr. David Stratton, discovered his place of employment, and learned the devastating truth about his true intentions toward Dr. Rae Taylor. With unusual irony, the revelation of Rebecca Danforth as the instigator of the crime was the very piece of information that brought Rae back to reality. Nikki could still picture that awful conversation, telling Rae the sordid details of Rebecca's intention to steal her discoveries for her own gain. It was then that Rae's broken heart began to weld itself back together with the heat of outrage and anger. Foolish conversations took place, some humorous, some chilling, ranging from murder to several sadistic forms of torture. But in the end the rational mind of the scientist acquiesced to the plea of the lawyer to properly punish Rebecca Danforth in the hallowed halls of justice.

The Secularian Corporation was being sued for conspiracy, fraud, and patent infringement. Rebecca Danforth was being held libel for alienation of affection, conspiracy, and embezzlement from Hope Corporation. David Stratton was accused of misrepresentation, fraud, and conspiracy. If Judge Browning approved all of the pretrial motions, *Taylor* v. *Secularian* would begin a jury trial in the next sixty days. If they prevailed, there was the potential of a fifty-million-dollar judgment; at least, that's how much they were seeking. Nikki speculated the civil case would precipitate a grand jury investigation and, hopefully, a criminal indictment against Rebecca and David Stratton. This case had the potential to be quite sensational. Nikki hoped she could generate a great deal of negative sentiment against Secularian in the press. For a first case, this one would be unforgettable. Her fee to Rae had been set at ten dollars.

"All rise," came the apathetic charge from the bailiff as the judge's chamber door swung open. Judge Browning climbed behind the tall wooden facade and laid several thick folders down on her desk. With a rap of her gavel, everyone in the courtroom reclaimed their seats.

"This court is in session," came her raspy voice. "Mrs. Thompson and Mr. O'Hara, would you please approach the bench." It wasn't a question.

Nikki squeezed Rae's shoulder as she stood, then walked

before the jurist. Judge Browning looked at O'Hara for a moment, then at Nikki, her expression betraying a sincere frustration mixed with a note of sadness. "I'm sorry, Mrs. Thompson, but I'm afraid I have no choice but to recommend this case not go to trial."

Nikki's heart sank. It took a few seconds for the statement to fully register. "I beg your pardon, Your Honor?"

O'Hara continued to stand there, apathetically listening to the judge as though he had heard this information many times before.

Judge Browning opened the first folder on her desk. "Mrs. Thompson, all of the patented materials in question here, originally the property of Dr. Taylor, became the sole property of Hope Corporation on December 25, 1974. You're fully aware of that?"

"Yes, but—" Nikki started to protest.

The judge went on, "And Dr. Taylor assigned ownership of all rights and privileges, per standard engineering, research, and development language in this contract I have before me, as an employee of Hope Corporation. Is that not so?"

"Your Honor," Nikki began. "Those discoveries were stolen, coerced by David Stratton, a Secularian employee."

"Dr. Taylor?" Judge Browning called over Nikki's shoulder to the stoic-faced yet trembling young woman with dark brown glasses, who sat at the plaintiff's table. "Dr. Taylor, can you tell me if you signed these documents of your own free will or under some type of duress?"

Rae didn't answer.

"Dr. Taylor?" the judge prompted.

Nikki turned around, her heart still pounding, and looked into her friend's pained expression.

"I signed them," Rae whispered.

The judge looked back at Nikki. "I'm sorry, counselor. The facts are that Hope Corporation is comprised of privately held stock, all shares legally in the possession of Secularian Investment Corporation as of the date of incorporation."

"But, Your Honor!" Nikki's voice was growing frantic. "Dr. Taylor never knew *any* of that. She was *cheated!*"

Judge Browning raised a wrinkled hand. "I know, Mrs. Thompson, I know." Her voice grew grave and scolding. "But the fact remains, you would have done Dr. Taylor a great deal more good had you read these contracts before she signed them, and preferably counseled her against it. Mrs. Thompson, Dr. Taylor is an employee of Hope Corporation, legally. And Hope Corporation is the property of Secularian Corporation, legally. They have ownership of all of Dr. Taylor's research concerning cancer therapy. She's a young woman, and obviously did something very foolish, being led by her heart instead of her head. But I can't change the law, no matter how much sympathy I feel for the circumstances of a plaintiff."

Nikki's voice broke, "But, Your Honor, they've stolen her whole life! Everything she's worked for, everything she's dreamed about."

Judge Browning took a deep breath and glanced back at Rae for several pensive moments. "Mrs. Thompson, you'd have had a much better case if you'd pressed charges against Mr. Stratton for rape. I don't like what I've seen here, and I hate what I have to do. But the law is the law. She gave away her property of her own free will." She looked back at Nikki, her eyes filled with compassion. "I'm sorry, Mrs. Thompson. Perhaps Dr. Taylor will have a prosperous career at Secularian. She *is* still an employee."

"No, Your Honor—" Nikki was on her tiptoes, her hands raised in frustrated fists.

"Case dismissed." The gavel banged simultaneously with the judge's words. Then the judge rose awkwardly and made a hasty departure from the court chamber. O'Hara obliviously plodded back to his table and began gathering his things.

Nikki spun around in shock. This couldn't be happening. Sitting behind the empty defense table in the spectator's gallery was Rebecca Danforth. Next to her sat David Stratton. Nikki refused to watch them hug and kiss, celebrating their wretched crime. She walked over to Rae, who was still sitting at the plaintiff's table, the ashen look of shock still on her face.

"Is it over?" Rae asked politely.

"I'm sorry, Rae." Nikki felt like she wanted to cry. "I don't know what to say."

"They got away with it, didn't they?" Rae's voice was slipping back into that catatonic daze.

Nikki's silence answered her question.

Rae's voice was hushed, pained, "It's all gone." She stood up, her head feeling light. "All of it. All my work. I found the answer and the slut took it, just like she said."

"Don't be bitter, Rae." From a few feet away the icy, cutting voice of Rebecca Danforth brought Rae's mind back into focus. Rebecca had the gall to walk over behind Rae to gloat. "You made an error in judgment. You just forgot to read the *fine print,* my dear. Perhaps you'll learn a little lesson from your unfortunate experience."

Rae slowly turned around to face Rebecca with all the dignity she had left. An unusual calm filled her as she bore down on the single object of a smoldering rage, preparing to explode, but held in check by a keenly disciplined mind. "This isn't over, Rebecca."

"Isn't it?" Rebecca taunted. "I don't expect to see you again, Dr. Taylor. In case you haven't received your notice in writing, you've been terminated at Secularian, by order of your superior, Mr. Stratton."

Rae glanced over Rebecca's shoulder and at the man she now loathed with the same degree of passion she once loved. But she couldn't stop her words. "Why, David? Why?"

He smirked, his expression callous. "It's just business, Rae. Someday you'll understand. It was never meant to be anything personal."

Rae felt a wave of nausea well up within her, but it was quickly suppressed by the boiling ire within her, honing every thought, every emotion, every action, every word to a lethal edge—sharper than diamond, colder than the endless void of space. She glared back at Rebecca's frigid, dark eyes;

her voice dropping low, menacing, blood-chilling, seething with a vehemence so uncharacteristic of the frail young woman, it frightened Nikki, who stood a few feet away. Rae raised a dagger of a trembling finger in Rebecca's face. "Listen to me very carefully, you diseased cunt. Now it's *you* that needs to watch your back. The day will come when I'll see you suffer, make you suffer, and suffer indeed. Wait and watch, Rebecca, wait and watch."

Rebecca stared at Rae's enraged eyes, speechless, for several moments. The painful tension broke when she forced a mocking laugh, her torturing tongue lashing back to full strength. "Grow up, little bitch. I told you once, and apparently you never learned your lesson. There's nothing you have I can't possess, nothing of value you prize that I can't make mine."

Unflinching, Rae continued to stare at the cold, dark eyes. Rebecca expected a vulgar retort, but grew more agitated when it didn't come. The young doctor's eyes were not the eyes of a human being any longer, but of an animal pushed to the point of self-preservation or death. It made her feel good. There was a helplessness about Rae that affirmed the measure of her own power and influence. It made twisting the knife in the moment of victory irresistible.

Rebecca leaned toward Rae and whispered, "You ought to be thanking me, Rae. I finally got you laid. But just between us girls, Rae dear, David says you're a limp lay, even for a cherry. He told me he much prefers a real woman that knows how to please him. In the future you might try a little more aggressiveness—if you ever find a real man of your own."

Rebecca's smile faded when Rae didn't explode, or scream, or rant, or take another swing at her—Rae's expression just faded into a polite smile, and she deliberately turned away, toward her attorney. "Let's go, Nikki."

"Come on, David," Rebecca said with a laugh, more to Rae than David. "Let's get out of here. It's time to celebrate. I'm in the mood for something wet and hot."

Rae watched Rebecca take David's arm and strut out of

the courtroom in a pompous parade of triumph, followed by the waddling counselor, Daniel O'Hara. She felt Nikki's hand on her arm again.

"Rae, I'm going to make this up to you somehow." There was a thin film of moisture around Nikki's eyes.

Rae patted Nikki's arm, her mind strangely at ease, focused and alert. "Don't be silly. None of this is your fault, Nikki. There's nothing to make up."

"Yes there is," she insisted. "I let you down. You're right, they got away with it, and I didn't do anything to stop it."

Rae shrugged. "The damage is done. And they have their moment to gloat for today." Her eyes brightened. "But there *will* be a tomorrow. I know that now."

Nikki looked astonished. "You're amazing. I'd be stone-dead drunk by now if I were you."

Rae laughed. "Now there's a thought. Okay, you can start making it up to me by taking me out and getting us stone-dead drunk."

"My pleasure." Nikki threw her arm around Rae's shoulders and walked her out of the courtroom.

17

May 1985

Indianapolis, Indiana

LIGHT RAIN HAD THREATENED TO CANCEL THE RACE ON MEMORIAL Day, but a break in the clouds two hours before the scheduled start time had only produced a minor delay before getting under way. The umbrellas and rain slickers of the thousands gathered in the grandstand and infield were put away to witness the racing pinnacle of the year. The damp track had already dashed three racers' hopes for victory, two of them in spectacular crashes. One was seriously injured, but fortunately there were no fatalities. Ten racers had dropped out with various mechanical failures. Each time the yellow flag came out, the cars slowly wound around the track in single file. When the green flag emerged, they immediately roared back into thundering motion. With only four laps remaining in the race, two cars held a two-lap lead on the rest of the field. In first place, Bobby Unser; and a car length behind, representing the Roger Marks team, Sabrina Doucette.

The Gustoff engine delivered more horsepower than any other vehicle ever run at Indy. And unlike last year's race, each lap had been a fluid work of art, flowing around the track, drafting behind the leaders to conserve fuel and avoid traffic—waiting for the right moment to push the pedal all the way down on the final stretch. However, Unser's team was also boasting of an experimental engine, which delivered a respectable performance against the Gustoff design. But Sabrina sat in the cockpit with an uncanny sense of calm, knowing that nothing, not even the son of the world-famous racing champion, a world champion in his own right, was going to stand in her way today.

When the white flag came out on the final lap, her front air dam was inches behind Unser's rear tires. She followed him through turn number one, down the straight and into turn number two. But on the far side a wave of energy surged through every cell of her body. It was time for dreams to come true.

"Base One. Base One. Tell Roger," she said calmly into her headset. "It's showtime."

"Bring it on in, sweetheart," came the electronic sound of Roger Marks's voice in her earpiece, instead of the grandstand spotter. Her heart began to pound again, the excitement building to a finale that had been so long coming.

Sabrina swung her wheel slightly to the right, gliding her crimson wing car up high against the outer rail, staying in Unser's right blind spot. The racing announcer noticed the move with frenzied enthusiasm, the thousands of spectators on their feet, most screaming their lungs out.

Now.

Sabrina pushed the accelerator flat against the metal firewall, genuinely startled by the radical surge of power still left in the engine. She sailed past the dark blue wing car and Unser's shocked expression. The fresh wave of g-force pressed Sabrina back into the leather seat as turn number three loomed ahead. A disquieting thought leapt to her mind. Would the car hold the turn at this speed on a slightly damp track? She had to be moving at well over two hundred miles per hour. Instinct pulled her hands to the left, dropping in low ahead of Unser, but her foot defensively came off the accelerator as she entered the turn. The chilling whine of rubber in her ears sent a jolt of alarm through her, but she held on, steeling herself against any temptation of panic. The car slid sideways about three yards, but the smooth high-performance racing tires gripped the pavement and surged forward.

With do-or-die courage Sabrina pressed the pedal down again and soared out of the turn, widening her lead by four car lengths. That space gave her enough room to comfortably throttle down into turn number four and accelerate again before Unser even reached the high bank. When the crimson fury, piloted by a blond-haired, green-eyed champion, launched out of turn number four headed for the checkered flag, over a hundred thousand people, and millions across the world, were cheering, clapping, stomping, and shouting in a triumph that would humble a Caesar. Racing officials clocked the Marks entry at the finish line moving at 214 miles per hour, with an average speed of 198 for the entire five hundred miles.

After a tear-filled victory lap, the Marks crew lifted the 1985 Indianapolis 500 champion out of the Formula-One racer the moment it came to a stop on the checkerboard pavement of the winner's circle. It was jammed with flashing cameras, members of the press, television crews, racing officials, and jubilantly squirming fans. Jim McKay from

ABC Television's "Wide World of Sports" pushed his way through the throng, followed by a remote camera crew desperately attempting to pull their tangled array of cables and equipment into the proper position for a postrace interview.

"Sabrina," Jim tried to call above the cheering mass, pushing his foam-covered microphone bearing the ABC logo near the beautiful racer as she pulled the black crash helmet off her head, along with the fire hood. As the oil-stained, sweat-soaked fire hood snapped off her head, her long blond hair dumped out on her shoulders. McKay managed to wrestle his way up next to her. "Sabrina, congratulations! Tell us how it feels to be the first woman driver to ever win at Indianapolis."

The pandemonium erupting all around Sabrina was beyond anything she could have ever imagined. How did she feel? There were no words to express the elation. How do you tell the whole world that you came, you saw, and you kicked everyone's ass, and still sound gracious? She was about to say something innocuous when geysers of champagne exploded in the hands of her exuberant crew; the fountains of bubbling white foam showering herself, the television crew, and all the bystanders. Sabrina erupted in laughter, grabbing one of the bottles, shaking it up and spraying it back at her delirious comrades. McKay had the wisdom to step back a pace and wait before securing his interview, joking with his colleagues up in the broadcast booth. When Sabrina did make her way over to the ABC correspondent, her face was glowing with an excitement that warmed the heart of an entire nation watching from coast to coast. Tears of joy had cut streaks through the black racing film around her eyes unprotected by the fire hood.

"Jim," she sobbed freely, endearing millions all the more, "this is the greatest moment of my life!" She wiped her eyes with the bright red sleeve on her forearm. "And I wouldn't be here if it wasn't for two very special men in my life."

"And who might that be?" McKay asked, as if he didn't know.

"First, Peter Gustoff, for building the best racing machine in the sport today." A round of applause and a hearty cheer went up from the crew. "But mostly, to Roger, who believed in me, and gave me the chance to show the world what I could do."

Jim McKay turned to the camera. "Ms. Doucette is of course referring to Roger Marks, the owner and general manager of the Marks Racing team." He turned back to Sabrina. "Sabrina, the gossip tabloids all say you and Roger Marks are quite close. Any truth to those stories?"

Sabrina looked toward the grandstand sky box where she knew Roger was still standing. She could almost picture his smile beaming down at her. "We're as close as we need to be," she replied.

The lasting memory of that incredible day faded in Sabrina's mind as she looked at her own smiling face, pictured on the cover of *Time* magazine, standing next to her candy-apple-red wing car, holding the tall silver-plated trophy. The copy lay on the coffee table in Roger Marks's private jet. The image was forever memorialized, the ultimate consummation of her life's dream. It had only been two weeks since the race, but for a twenty-five-year-old racing champion, what was next? Roger and Peter had already answered that question. They sat on the sofa of the jet as they winged their way back to San Diego, looking at blueprints of next year's design. The watchword was: repeat.

The notion of back-to-back championships was intriguing, but a little frightening. It wouldn't be long before other teams discovered the same mechanical design secrets they had used, and soon the competition would be much more keen, and much more dangerous. Sabrina voiced her opinion loud and long, personally convinced that the stress factors introduced by more powerful engines would be far and away in excess of what the physical structure of the car could endure. Both Roger and Peter had assured her that all of those factors were fully taken into account and her worries were unfounded. She wasn't convinced.

Sabrina watched Roger's eyes as they went back and forth

from the blueprints in his lap to Peter Gustoff's excited expression. Amid their intensely technical discussion, while Peter did his best to remember the English words for all of his ideas, Roger would steal a glance at Sabrina. In the instant their eyes made contact, there was always a twinkle of recognition. Sabrina was genuinely undecided which was a greater experience, Memorial Day 1985, or Memorial night.

After the race, Roger had promised to take her out on the town for dining and dancing, which he did. But when they returned to the hotel, still drunk with the triumph of the day, she was quick to inform him that he was not in a position to refuse her anything she desired. She remembered emerging from the elevator on the Concierge Floor of the Crown Plaza Hotel.

"Roger, I want to thank you again for all you've done for me." She stopped at the door to their suite, grabbing his dark maroon tie and pulling him toward her.

He took her in his arms and kissed her, his lips warm and full, the fragrance of his Aramis cologne filling her with desire. He leaned back and looked into her eyes. "It's me that should be thanking you. You've made me a much richer man today."

She opened the door to the suite with the plastic card key. "Well, you *can* thank me. There's something I want you to do—something just for me. Something *very* special."

Roger tossed his jacket on the back of the overstuffed sofa and walked over to the wet bar to mix a martini. "And what might that be?"

She followed him over to the bar, kicking off her shoes as she came. "Tonight," she said tentatively, "I want you to make love to me."

Roger smiled. "That's an everyday request. How is that special?"

She reached over and brushed the tips of her fingers across the back of his hand, still holding his gaze. "I don't mean like before. I mean, *really* make love to me."

Roger's face clouded; he looked down into his glass.

"Please, Sabrina," he said in a low voice, "I'm not in the mood to discuss this right now. I've told you before that if you're dissatisfied—"

"Shut up!" she scolded. "I don't want to hear that anymore." She walked around the bar, reached up and put her arms around his shoulders. "You're a beautiful man. A very beautiful man. I don't care what you think. I mean it. Beautiful. Inside and out."

He wouldn't look at her. The air grew tense.

She took him by the hand. "Come here. I'll show you."

"Sabrina, don't do this." He tossed his head from side to side, reluctantly following her, continuing to protest as she led him into the bedroom. "I've told you before, I've tried. Believe me, I've tried. You're only going to be disappointed. We've had a great day. The best day. Let's not ruin it."

She smiled playfully. "You, sir, as a mere mortal, have no right to refuse to go to bed with the sexiest, most desirable world champion on the face of the earth. If word of this hit the papers, you would instantly be declared mentally incompetent, and all your millions would be confiscated by the government."

Roger laughed. The tension in the air eased considerably. He took her in his arms again and said patiently, "Sabrina. I'm warning you. You won't like this. And I'll only feel embarrassed. Please don't do this to me."

"Sorry," she retorted. "Come along willingly or prepare to be raped. It's up to you."

He laughed again, looking up at the ceiling. "Would you at least turn out the lights?"

"Of course," she whispered. She slipped out of his arms and went over to the light switch, hastily extinguishing the two bedside lamps it controlled. Roger closed the bedroom door, plunging them both into complete darkness.

"Now come here," she commanded, sensing him walk up in front of her. She could still smell the arousing fragrance of his cologne and the scent of gin on his breath. "Undress me."

He obediently complied, unbuttoning the black blouse

146

she wore. While his hands found the top button and zipper of her acid-washed jeans, she reached up, removed his tie, and began to unbutton his shirt. They both giggled as their arms entangled, trying to remove each other's shirts. He found the front closure of her bra after a quick and unfruitful search around her back. In the dark, with trembling hands, he managed to get it open. Sabrina reached up and pulled the straps over her creamy smooth shoulders, letting it fall behind her to the floor.

She unbuckled his belt, his pants button, and slid his zipper down with her left hand. Her right hand slid inside his briefs, through the knotted curls to the flaccid mound of flesh below; at the same time, she used her elbows to gather her breasts together, gently rubbing them across his bare chest. This technique had never failed to inspire any man. Unfortunately, all she sensed were his muscles growing tense. The air was becoming more uncomfortable again. However, Sabrina was determined to prevail.

She took Roger by the hands and silently made him lay down on the bed, pulling off his shoes, socks, trousers, and briefs. She slid her pants off and laid down on the bed beside him to his left, running her fingers up and down his body from his chest down to his uncooperative genitals. On each pass the tips of her fingers could feel the slightly raised areas of marred flesh on his torso. But in the dark they were just variations in the topology, nothing hideous, nothing at all to be ashamed of.

"Roger," she whispered. "I think you have a beautiful body."

He just took a deep breath and let it out with an uncomfortable sigh.

"I know you don't believe me," she continued with as much sincerity as she could put in her voice. "But it's true. Actually, I think you're the one that doesn't know how handsome you are."

"I appreciate you saying that—" he began.

She cut him off. "Don't say anything. Just lay there and don't think of anything, but what you feel." She pressed a little harder against the taut muscles of his chest and abdomen. "Do you feel my fingers running up and down? All I feel are little bumps and valleys along the way. Nothing more. I just feel you. And what I feel, feels good. Doesn't it feel good?"

He didn't answer. But she also noticed he didn't protest. She felt a twinge as she realized she was leaning uncomfortably on her right breast. She adjusted her position, rolling over against his side. "Every time we've been together, you've always taken care of me. Well, tonight I just want you to lie still and let me see what I can do for you."

He remained silent.

She pressed her lips against his collarbone, the center of his chest, and trailed over to find the tiny nipple, running her tongue over it the way she liked it done to her. She felt him trembling.

"Roger, relax. It's just me." She looked toward his face, though she couldn't see anything in the darkened room. "Look, if nothing happens, nothing happens. It's not going to make me love you any less."

She heard his head rise from the pillow, tilting toward her. He whispered, "You really think you love me?"

She slid up and ardently pressed her lips against his, humming an affirmative reply. He wrapped his arms around her and kissed her deeply, with great fervor. When he tried to roll her over and proceed in his usual routine of caressing and oral stimulation, she stopped him. "No, Roger. Lie back. Tonight we do it my way."

He obediently complied again, except without as much reluctance.

Once again her lips and tongue danced about on his chest. She heard him gasp slightly when her tongue ran over one of the patches of scar tissue on the right side of his abdomen, but he seemed to relax when she deliberately displayed no reaction of repulsion or any sign of hesitation. Sabrina continued to kiss him without regard to what she felt with her lips or tongue. It didn't really feel that different. His skin was smooth and soft, devoid of any small hairs; but nothing to cause any sense of alarm. She put the image of the dark red and brown discolorations out of her mind. Instead, she focused on arousing a man she wanted to make love to. It was but another challenge to be met and conquered.

He started to protest when her tongue weaved down his body, through the dense jungle of pubic hair, but refrained when Sabrina lifted her head and scolded, "Roger, lay still. It's what I want to do. If you don't have sense enough to just relax and enjoy it, it's your loss, not mine."

With a growing hunger inside of her, she lowered her head, kissing, tasting, and toying, never lingering in one spot more than a few seconds. Her teasing streak instinctively knew to slowly work up to the more pleasurable sensations for maximum effect, letting the greatest sex organ, the brain, heighten the sensation of pleasure in anticipation.

She moved her entire body down the bed, lifting his knees apart to face him directly. Her hands slid up the outside of his thighs, cupping her fingers over the tops of his legs, and softly pulled his knees farther apart. She could feel the slightly raised scars on the tops of his legs. But rather than succumb to any sense of repulsion, she began to massage the long, sinewy muscles beneath. That seemed to help him relax all the more.

With deliberate patience she continued to methodically kiss and nuzzle, letting her tongue trace every delicate contour. Some encouraging sighs from up above prompted her on. She felt his fingers run through her hair and begin to massage the back of her scalp. A tingle ran up her spine. She tenderly resumed her oral stimulation, maintaining the leg massage for quite some time. To her dismay, there was still no sign of life.

"Doesn't that feel good, Roger?" Her sultry voice was hushed, the words matted between lingering kisses and toying licks.

He just moaned, "Yes . . ." His hands continued to course through her hair.

With no intent of retreat, Sabrina increased the flourishing sweeps of her lips and tongue. She thought his timid flesh felt slightly fuller, but it was hard to tell. It could have been her imagination, or muted success, but it certainly didn't feel as spongy as it did a moment ago; and it was noticeably warmer. In any event, it was encouraging; so much so, she could feel the wetness between her own legs tugging at her libido, yearning to be fed. It was time to bring in the heavy artillery.

Sabrina took him completely into her mouth and drew with a steady, undulating pressure from her tongue and cheeks. At the same time, she pulled herself toward him, sliding forward, tilting her chin down, careful to keep her lips where they were, until she felt her breasts make contact with the edge of his testicles. With a little maneuvering, she was able to squeeze them against her generous cleavage; and swaying methodically, she began to lightly massage the tender mound with one of her erect nipples. If this wasn't getting through to him, it was certainly having its impact on her. She didn't know how long she could keep this up before her own desires overcame patience. His moaning was growing louder.

"Do you feel that, Roger?" Her words were understandably garbled. She lifted her head, allowing him to slide out of her mouth, then leaned forward, pressing her right nipple firmly up against him. "Can you tell what that is?"

She felt his left hand move down her ear, cheek, and neck, locating the firm swell of her breast, his index finger tracing the nipple up against his soft flesh. He let out a pleasurable moan of discovery. She could tell his head was tilted back, teeth clenched. There was no mistaking it now, there was definitely some activity between his legs. He was elongating slightly, but was still far from aroused. But it was progress, and it sent a wave of excitement through her. She knew she was going to prevail.

Sabrina also knew not to lose any momentum. She leaned down and kissed him once again, then lifted her head and teased, "Roger, I want you to try and picture in your mind what you're about to feel. Imagine it as vividly as you can."

She moved her body up a little farther, pushing his legs

down flat on the bed, lifting his uncooperative member faceup. She covered it with her breasts, tucking it firmly into her cleavage. She could feel his coarse pubic hair brushing against the inside edges of her breasts as she rocked forward and backward, smoothly sliding over the thin film of her own saliva and perspiration. He slowly began to rock his hips as his breathing accelerated. She could feel the warm flesh between her breasts thickening and elongating a bit more. It inspired the same rush of excitement she experienced coming out of turn number four that afternoon for the last time. Success was in sight; she could feel it.

She slid her graceful body back down, taking his semierect organ into her mouth once again. Her own excitement continued to build as she could actually feel the mushrooming sensation of growth. This was incredible! It was working! Her thighs twitched together impatiently. This was definitely going to be worth the wait. But rather than get overconfident, she vowed to continue to act and respond on instinct, letting her body tell her what had to happen next. She mused that even if he exploded in the next instant, it would have been worth it. She would have proven to Roger Marks that his impediments weren't a function of his accident, but a casualty of his mind.

It took almost twenty minutes before Sabrina was satisfied that he was fully aroused. Without saying a word, she climbed up, straddling him, carefully inserting the fragile development inside her. The initial warmth of the penetration, after so long a wait, thrust her to the brink of climax almost instantaneously. With labored breaths Sabrina rocked her hips forward and backward, snapping her back like a whip. Roger's fingers were interlaced with hers, their arms spread between them. She could hear his seething breaths.

He didn't last half a minute. But when it happened, it didn't need to go any further. The moment she heard his breathing still, felt every muscle in his relaxed body go rigid, his fingers clamping into the backs of her hands to the point of pain, then the hot explosions deep inside her—her own body followed in kind, constricting in euphoric spasms, with waves of pure pleasure radiating to the tips of her swollen fingers. When her breathing and pounding heart subsided, she was surprised to hear a totally unexpected sound.

Roger Marks was crying.

18

May 1975

Boston, Massachusetts

THE CREDIT FOR BABALOO MANDEL AND THE "HAPPY DAYS" theme song played over Henry Winkler's frozen expression of "cool" as Nikki Thompson rose from her sofa and walked into the kitchen to refill her soda glass. Her husband Steve remained on the sofa with his feet lazily propped on the coffee table, eagerly awaiting the start of "Laverne and Shirley" following the obnoxious series of advertisements. The tint on the small color television always had an annoying abundance of pink and red, prompting Steve to vainly promise at least three times a week to invest in a new one very soon. That had been the case for over two years, almost as long as they had been married. Their third anniversary was just two months away. Nikki didn't envision it as an especially joyous occasion.

"Honey," Steve called after his wife, not breaking his gaze from an extremely important cat food commercial. "Would you grab me another beer while you're in there?"

Nikki stood at the refrigerator door for several moments, debating whether to comply with her husband's request. That's all he needed, she thought to herself, another beer.

His belly had distended over the last year to unsightly proportions. It was no wonder. Steve wasn't nearly as active as he used to be when he was working on the job sites himself—far from it. Now, as a general contractor, he spent most of his time carrying around a clipboard and rolled-up plans, shouting orders and pointing, instead of wearing his tool belt and putting in long, sweaty hours as in the old days. Sure, more money was coming in, but the changes in Steve resulting from his mediocre advancement had not been for the better. However, the thought of his irritation and clamming up in front of the television for the remainder of the night prompted her to pull open the refrigerator door and pull out another can of Budweiser.

"I still can't believe all that's happened to Rae." Nikki shook her head as she sat back down on the sofa next to her husband, handing him his beer.

He nodded, fizzing open the pull tab, his eyes still fixed on the television screen. "Yeah, really sucks, from what you said."

She turned toward him, not interested in the advertiser's probing question of how one spells relief. "She hasn't been able to find a job for two months."

Steve took a long sip of his beer, belched, and adjusted the crotch in his trousers. "How come? I thought she was supposed to be some hot shit scientist."

"She is. It's just that that bitch Rebecca Danforth got away with five years' worth of her work, and now she has to start all over again from scratch." Even after two months, Nikki still couldn't believe the tragedy, nor was she able to shake the feeling of direct responsibility in her impotence to prevail on Rae's behalf. The system she believed in had let her down.

"Hell." Steve set his beer can between his legs. "Why can't she just get some research job for one of those high-tech companies out on Route 128?"

Nikki looked at her husband, as appalled at his ignorance as she was at his appearance. He used to be so attractive, each muscle toned with a skilled tradesman's labor, his skin always dark from working outside every day. Now he looked older, his arms and legs heavier and flabby, in harmony with the degeneration of his personality. He'd just as soon spend each evening vegetating on the couch in front of the tube than having any real fun with her, like they used to.

Her tone was chastising, "It's not that easy. She's in a very specialized career field. Opportunities aren't that plentiful for her skills."

He gave her an apathetic shrug. "Then maybe she should find a new line of work."

"Right," she answered sarcastically. "Well, she better find something soon. She told me yesterday her savings are almost gone, and she doesn't want to have to call her mother again. Her mom's been in the hospital and isn't doing very well."

"Sounds to me like she's hinting for a loan," Steve noted with callous indignation.

Nikki's irritation swelled to a head. "No! It's not like that at all. I just happen to know her situation. She'd never ask anybody for money. Rae may be quiet, but she's fiercely independent. She'll make her own way somehow, or starve to death trying."

Steve nodded. "Well, that's good, 'cause we ain't got any extra right now. You remember that. Till you start making some big bucks from your expensive law degree, things are still gonna be check to check. The winter was pretty slow, if you still remember."

"I remember," Nikki conceded. She felt restless—very restless. The thought of watching "Laverne and Shirley" and then "Barney Miller" had no appeal whatsoever. It was like this almost every night, and she was getting sick of it. A thought came to mind; her face brightened. "Hey, babe. Why don't we get our shoes on and head down around the Commons for a drink and maybe a little action on the dance floor? Then we can come back and I'll let you have your way with me. You know? Like we used to do?"

Steve looked at her skeptically. "Nikki, I ain't in the

mood for no dancing. Never did like it that much. We got plenty of beer here. And if you want to mess around, we got all night for that. Jeez honey, my show's coming on in a little while."

Nikki was sincerely offended. "You mean you'd rather sit around watching TV than go out with me?"

"What's your problem?" he lashed at her. "I just want to spend a relaxing evening at home. Is that okay with you?" He proceeded to probe his left nostril for an obstruction.

Nikki stood up from the couch. "Yeah, that's just fine with me."

He didn't say anything as she went into the bedroom, put on her shoes, and grabbed her coat. She stopped by the door and picked up her car keys from the small table next to the hall closet. The jingling sound broke Steve's attention from the opening credits of Cindy Williams and Penny Marshall hopping down a concrete flight of stairs.

"Where are you going?" he demanded.

"Out," she snapped in reply, opening the front door.

"Where?" he demanded again.

"I'll know when I get there." She slammed the door closed behind her and walked down to her car. She stopped by the car door, waiting a moment to see if Steve would emerge from the apartment door to stop her. He didn't. Obviously Lenny and Squiggy had more clout with him than she did. With a disgusted huff she climbed into her rusting Chevy Nova and pulled out of the parking lot.

An hour and a half later she sat alone at the bar of the Ace Club near the Plaza, looking at the silent television over the bar; a hockey game was in progress. She didn't care for hockey. The jukebox was playing "Philadelphia Freedom" by Elton John. She had made that selection herself; she liked Elton John. Her third gin and tonic was almost empty. Being a Tuesday night, and only nine o'clock, the place was nearly deserted. A nod to the bartender was all that was necessary to summon him to refill her glass. She looked around the bar, dimly reflected in the wide mirror against the wall. There were only about a dozen other patrons, seated in ones and twos, and like her, silently sipping drinks or carrying on muted conversations.

"Hi," came a friendly voice to her left.

She hadn't seen the smiling young man walk up.

He sat down on the bar stool to her left and asked, "Aren't you Nikki Thompson?"

She didn't recognize the dark-haired man wearing a Boston College sweatshirt underneath a brown leather bomber jacket. "Do I know you?"

"Probably not." He smiled, setting a half-empty mug of beer on the bar. "I work for Foster and Finnman, a little law firm near South Station. I was in a class with you at Harvard about a year ago."

"Really?" Nikki brightened. She was thankful to have a little conversation. It kept her mind off the unpleasantness at home. "Forgive me for saying this, but I don't think I remember you."

The man's thick eyebrows arched in concert with his smile as he extended his hand. "Completely understandable. We were in Professor Tomlin's Corporate Contracts class, with two hundred other students. I sat high up in the back, when I showed up. My name's Allen Binotti."

Nikki smiled, taking his hand. "Hello, Allen Binotti, pleased to meet you." She noticed the flicker of his eyes to the plain gold wedding band on her left hand, which was still holding onto her glass. For an awkward moment she wished it wasn't there.

"So where are you working?" he asked, looking her in the eye.

She shrugged. "Nowhere really. I've had one case since I passed the bar, and it was a disaster. How about you?"

The man looked a little embarrassed. "Oh, I'm just a junior attorney at F and F. They have me doing more research and writing briefs than anything else. It'll probably be a year or more before I ever see the inside of a courtroom."

Nikki took another sip of her drink. The warm liquid flowing through her had done wonders to quell the simmering anger she had felt for the first hour, and it had given her a dangerous sense of confidence. "Actually, I know I should start looking for a placement pretty soon, but I just haven't been in the mood."

That was true, she reflected; more true than she realized. In fact, until that moment it hadn't really occurred to her how much she had progressively drifted further and further away from the burning desire she once had to be Boston's greatest barrister. In a small way, seeing an old classmate seemed to revive a faint hint of that feeling again.

"Really?" He sounded genuinely surprised. "I thought you would have landed one of the better slots right off. That's why I remembered you. You were always the one asking all the probing questions and keeping Tomlin on his toes, and the rest of us entertained."

Nikki really needed to hear that. She laughed. "That was a fun class."

Allen cleared his throat and asked an awkward question, "So you're, like, married?"

A wave of uneasiness flooded over her. The image of her beer-bellied husband loomed in her mind. Steve didn't care anymore, she was convinced of that. And the more she thought about it, she realized she didn't either. Her words came out almost of their own accord, "More or less."

The man's face looked quizzical. "What *exactly* does that mean?"

She leaned closer to him. "It means that, yes, I have a husband, but I make my own schedule."

Allen took another sip of beer, glancing around the bar. "Is he joining you later?"

"I hope not," she huffed, then shook her head apologetically. "I'm sorry. I shouldn't have said that." She scratched her right brow. "Actually, I think by now he's totally engrossed in the 'Mystery Movie of the Week.'"

Allen gave her a devastating smile that made her heart

pick up its pace. "Bad move on his part. If I was married to a woman as bright, beautiful, and energetic as you, I wouldn't waste an evening with a damned television."

A warm sensation spread across her chest. "What would you be doing?"

He moved a little closer. "I'd probably be dancing, or getting something good to eat, taking in a show, cruising through the Commons, or whatever else came to mind."

Nikki looked around the bar once again with a twinge of felon's guilt. "That sounds great. Too bad I've already eaten."

Allen laughed, putting his right hand on her shoulder, his index finger twirling through her auburn hair. "Not for me. It's more economical."

She didn't react to his hand on her shoulder; rather, she gave him an inviting smile, saying, "I like that, a pragmatist." She made an impulsive decision, dictated by a deep desire, a desire impervious to resistance or objection. "So take me dancing, Allen Binotti. And I'll think about the whatever later."

Nikki couldn't believe what she was doing, but her actions moved her forward, with her sense of guilt rapidly fading into an insatiable craving for adventure. She walked with the handsome gentleman across the alley to a disco and danced with him for hours, absorbing many more gin and tonics. He was a good dancer; he knew how to rotate his hips and move his feet much better than the assortment of disco hounds in earth shoes, velvet bell bottoms, and nylon shirts with oversized collars and puffed sleeves. He laughed with her, told her genuinely funny jokes, reminisced about college days, and sincerely showed her a wonderful time. They were both delighted to be sitting together at the small round table, growing more and more joyously inebriated, and laughing hysterically at the more bizarrely attired patrons of the dance establishment.

When the lazy arpeggio of the introduction to "Color My World" by Chicago was played, she let him drag her out on the lighted dance floor and hold her close—very close, their feet slowly fading from side to side. She couldn't remember the last time she had just been held; it was magical. She felt his lips gently pressed against the side of her neck, just above her shoulder. His warm breath whispered across her gently perspiring skin, raising cool tingles of delight up and down her spine. She wondered if he could tell she wasn't wearing a bra underneath her loose sweater. She felt his hands massage up and down her back, certain he was checking. The relaxing sensation of the movement, mixed with the alcohol and the exhaustion of the evening, drew her cheek down to his shoulder. Even beneath the layer of leather and cloth, she could feel the firm strength. He pulled her closer.

"Let's get out of here," he whispered in her ear.

Nikki walked into her own bedroom at just before three o'clock in the morning. Steve was snoring away in the queen-sized bed. The burning waves of guilt washed over her again.

What have I done?

She slipped into the bathroom and looked at her face in the mirror; her makeup was smudged and her auburn hair was askew. She knew she needed to take a shower; she must smell of smoke, alcohol—and him. Even as the near-scalding rivulets of water pelted her skin, it couldn't wash away the memory of that night, nor did she really want it to, no matter how much her conscience was berating her.

She couldn't believe she had actually been necking in the backseat of a car, as she used to do back in high school; French kissing, having her breasts groped, fondled, and kissed. But it had felt so good, so exciting, so exhilarating. He was all over her, and she wanted it, all of it, even though it didn't actually last very long—no, there was far too much impatience on the part of both parties for endurance. Standing in the heat of the shower, she vividly remembered how much she had shivered when her bare skin touched the vinyl seat of her own car.

It had not been great sex from a sheer physical standpoint;

rather, it was more animalistic, sweat-laden, and furious; but it accomplished its basic purpose—and more, much more. It rekindled a flame within her that she now knew had grown dim, almost extinguished, over the past couple of years. There was a part of her that she now told herself she wasn't willing to live without, even if that meant Steve would not be a part of it. She rationalized that all along it had always been his choice to meet her needs and help maintain the vitality of their relationship. But that wasn't very high on his agenda these days, nor had it been for a very long time. The very concept of the kind of fervent passion she knew she wanted, and needed, was an oxymoron when put in the same context with Steve.

Nikki dried herself, slipped into a nightgown, and quietly laid down beside her husband. He groaned wearily and rolled toward her as she pulled the blanket up to her chin. Her movement had awakened him; he had always been a very light sleeper. She felt a rough hand slip over her arm and cup her breast.

His raspy voice croaked, "Glad you made it back. Come here, I need some lovin'."

Nikki felt nauseous. She coldly rolled away from him, away from his intruding touch, toward the wall. "Don't. I don't feel like it tonight."

"Umm," he groaned with no evidence of concern, rolled over, and within minutes was snoring again.

The burning memory of white-hot passion replayed in Nikki's mind again and again until she drifted off to sleep.

19

June 1990

Dallas, Texas

THE CRYSTAL CLEAR WATER WAS EXACTLY SEVENTY DEGREES, brisk, and invigorating, lap after lap. With one final scissor kick, Emelia Travain broke the surface in a sparkling shower, diffusing the afternoon sunlight, and was instantly embraced by the ninety-seven degree heat of a cloudless Texas afternoon. She grabbed the smooth ceramic tiles surrounding the edge of her private lap pool on her terrace, her fingers instantly recoiling from the intense heat absorbed from the afternoon sun. As she rose carefully from the cool water, she let the dripping excess from her long black hair create a dark pool on the tile, a pool of water cool enough to sit on without being burned. She rose from the water, turned around, and took her seat on the edge of the pool with her legs still lingering in the water. As her chest heaved from the mile-long swim, she leaned back and lifted her chin, letting the relaxing rays of the sun penetrate her face and body.

"Tired?" The Familiar voice behind her was Jonathan's, always enthusiastic and caring. Jonathan was her therapist. He was sitting beneath the royal-blue awning, sipping a chilled glass of Chardonnay.

Emelia took a long, languid breath and stretched her back, arms spread wide. "Winded more than tired, I think."

"Can I get you anything?" he asked.

She lifted her legs from the water and spun around on her seat to face him, her dripping feet leaving an arc of water on

161

the stone decking by the pool. She glanced at him, asking in her clipped Slavic accent, "You can bring me a towel. Yes?"

Jonathan set his glass down, grabbed one of the oversized yellow terry towels and walked over to her. She took his hand and rose. A delightful shudder went through her body as he wrapped her in the towel and began to dry her off. She loved the feel of his strong hands briskly moving over her limbs and torso; he did it so well, and so often. He leaned near her ear as he dried her back. "Emelia, I have to tell you again, I was most impressed with your playing at the Director's Ball the other evening. You were incredible."

"Do you really think so?" She turned around and looked into his brown eyes. His answer meant a great deal to her.

"Yes." He nodded, but then furrowed his brow. "But I have to admit, just between you and me, I could tell you were holding something back."

She looked away, moving past him, and laid down on one of the two padded loungers on the terrace. "I did my best," she whispered.

Jonathan walked over and sat down on the edge of the lounger beside her. "I know you did. But don't forget, I've been listening to you play for years. I've heard you play with such passion, such force, it can bring tears to my eyes."

She looked in his eyes again. "And the other evening you had no such tears?"

She watched his eyes measure her expression with a sincere look of concern; his hands took hold of hers. "Emelia, what I heard was beautiful. It only lacked one thing—something I first heard on your Carnegie Hall album."

Her heart began to pound. She wasn't sure if she really wanted to hear this, but knew she must. Jonathan had always told her what she really needed to hear. Ever since she arrived at the center over two months ago, he had been so patient and careful to encourage her, and never let her persist in a state of depression while her treatments were ongoing. Even now he steadfastly refused to let her settle for anything less than complete commitment to her success. She asked tentatively, "What was this one thing?"

His face wrinkled as he searched for the right words to say. "I've been trying to find the right word for it, and until I do, I can only express it as a form of confidence, or aggressiveness, or perhaps it's just an attitude, an attitude of courage. Something like that." He stopped and focused his gaze upon hers. "You're afraid. Aren't you?"

How could he see so clearly into her heart? She never could understand that. How did he sense her fear? After the damage to her hand was treated, would she ever be able to create the majestic rapture that had catapulted her to fame as a child? How could he know the turmoil she fought every time she touched the keys, unsure if the sounds that came forth were truly of the caliber she had once produced?

She looked over the smooth aquamarine surface of the thirty-foot-long and six-foot-wide pool. "I had hoped it was not so . . . how do you say . . . obvious?"

She felt his lips press against her fingers. He said softly, "It isn't obvious to everyone. Perhaps only to those who care the most."

A warm pang in her stomach pulled her gaze to his. "You are a good friend, Jonathan. You are very true with me, ever since I have come to this place for treatment. You are also very special to me."

"I'm glad to hear you say that." He set her hands down in her lap again. "I consider you a very special friend of mine as well. In fact, I was very excited to hear you had chosen me when you came here. I can promise you, there were many others who wanted the job."

A dull, apprehensive tightness pressed against her lungs. This man seemed to care so much, yet there remained a great barrier that kept the entire experience of the Women's Center from being absolutely perfect. Jonathan was an employee, and she was a client. She looked at him seriously. "Jonathan, I want you to tell me something."

"Anything," he replied.

"You are my friend because they pay you here? Or are you my friend because you *want* to be my friend?" She knew his answer would be gracious and supportive, but she was listening for something more—looking for something that would let her know that the affections, the support, the encouragement, weren't just the polished performance of a paid professional; but rather, authentic gestures of compassion and concern from someone who genuinely saw value in a person who was struggling to feel valuable once more.

Jonathan gave her a warm smile; his voice lowered as though he didn't wish to be overheard. "Emelia, I won't lie to you. I took this job here at the center to help pay my way through school. In fact, with the exception of the guys who came here from Houston, almost all of the guys are like me, working their way through school. And believe me, it's a great job." He shrugged. "But after graduation, I plan to move out to California and start a life." His eyes spoke to her as if no one else in the world existed in that moment save themselves. "But one thing I can promise you. Though it was this job that gave me the opportunity to meet you, long after we both leave this place, I'll always be your friend. No matter what. If you ever need me for anything, I'll be there."

Emelia reached out, wrapping her arms tightly around his neck and pulling his cheek against hers. She had seen in his eyes what she had hoped to see, something much deeper than the patient-therapist relationship. "Thank you," she whispered, her eyes becoming misty, her throat tightening. "But tell me one more thing." She felt his lips on her neck, gently pressing. She had to know.

"Yes?" he asked.

"Does it happen so much that the clients here at the center fall in love with therapists?" She knew he must feel her heart beating against her breastbone. Inside she prayed he knew what she was really asking, and that the answer was yes.

He laughed softly. "Occasionally. They tell me in the past two years since this place has been in business, there've only been three weddings. However, a number of the guys have gone into full-time employment with some of their clients, if you know what I mean."

Emelia leaned back and chuckled with him. "I can imagine this."

His eyes grew serious, piercing into hers. "But for some of us, it's very difficult. We have to constantly remind ourselves of our professional relationship; because we know that one day the client might be gone. And if we let ourselves violate that professional relationship, and get emotionally involved, it can be quite painful." His voice dropped to a whisper. "Sometimes too painful."

For a long, awkward moment she stared into his eyes, saying nothing. His eyes said that he loved her, but he hadn't said it with his lips. She wanted to tell him what her heart was crying out to say, but the timidity, the shyness, the reserved shell that had grown in place shortly after the burning sensation had appeared in her hand years ago, forbid it. Instead she embraced him again and whispered into his ear, "Perhaps, after my hand is well, I will need much more treatments to bring me this aggressive confidence you say."

He held her close. "I'd say much more, in my professional opinion."

She pressed her lips just beneath his jawline. "Perhaps I must talk to Marsha Collins about getting my own full-time therapist to come back with me to my home in California."

She felt his chest heave with excitement. He leaned back and looked at her again. "You'd do that? For me?"

"I don't want to not see you never again." As her heart pounded, her English suffered for it. "I mean to say," she corrected herself, "I want to see you always. You will come, yes?"

His face beamed. "You couldn't keep me away."

She wanted to see him—every day, for the rest of her life; she wanted it more than anything, every sunset, every sunrise. And the more she realized she wanted it, the more she wanted to make love to him again, immediately, and often. A new excitement was building inside her, a swelling emotion beyond anything she had ever experienced. A burning desire to be much closer to this man was ravenously consuming her every thought and feeling. She gave him a playful smile. "Of course, you must show me what this more aggressive therapy is. I don't know if I like it yet. Maybe it makes me sad? Yes?"

"Well, you'll have to tell me if it does." His mouth was as sweet as it ever was, the delicious hint of Chardonnay remained as his lips closed over hers, his tongue exploring the inner recess of her mouth. He lifted his face from hers, his voice filled with expectancy, "Actually, I think you should try it right now. Here, without waiting another second. What do you think?"

Emelia's body yearned to be touched, held, caressed, pleased like never before. Her voice was impatient, filled with sensual urgency. "Yes. Tell me what I must do."

"All right." His eyes brightened with an energy that sent a chill up her spine. "You must listen very carefully, and open up your thoughts and feelings to what I'm about to tell you."

"I will." She nodded, her dark eyes impatient.

"Emelia, you must learn to take, not merely receive," he advised. "You must decide what you want—and you must *take* it. You cannot lie still and be passive, as in the past, but be much more aggressive and forceful. Become aware of the hunger inside you, craving its complete fulfillment."

"So . . . you are saying I must do everything?" she asked timidly, the initial thought a bit frightening, but the pulsating warmth growing beneath her swimsuit urging her on, despite her inhibitions.

He shook his head. "Not at all. I'll do everything within my power to please you, as always. But this time *you* must be dominant, and let your confidence grow. Unleash your passion and explore every fantasy you've ever dreamed of. Allow all your talents of melody and harmony to be expressed by your entire body, instead of just your hands. Feel the music. Taste the music. Feed on it. Try to think of me as your instrument, my body the object of your expression. Play it. Feel it. And later, when you play the piano, and you feel the smooth keys beneath your touch, you must think of them as me. Let the heat within you, the heat I know is there, boil up and overflow until it consumes us both."

All of Emelia's shyness and icy timidity melted in the heat of Jonathan's words, as they painted surreal images more seductive than she could stand, lustily building and erotically coaxing her passions to fever pitch. She couldn't sit still. In mid-sentence she cut him off, pulling his face to hers, feeding on his mouth, burrowing her tongue into the honey beneath his own. Her hands coursed up the firm flesh of his stomach and chest, ravenously groping against the muscles beneath. Taking his cheeks in her hands, she guided him down to her right onto the lounger, laying him down on his back. With an impetuous mount, she swung her long, thin leg across his waist, sitting up straight, straddling him.

"You mean like this?" she teased, her tongue licking her lips in savory anticipation.

He sat up, his arms going around her back. "Uh-huh. But more. More! Take, Emelia! Take what you want!"

"Then you must do as I say." Her voice was giddy, prepared to play. She grabbed the material of her black bathing-suit top at the point where it was gathered over her sternum between her small breasts, and pulled it out about an inch. "Take this in your teeth," she commanded.

Jonathan eagerly obeyed, clamping his teeth into the thin, satiny material, his dark brown eyes wide with desire.

"Now tear it off," Emelia ordered. She braced her back ramrod straight as he strained backward with his neck muscles, giving it his best effort.

"Pull!" she shouted, giggling at the sight of him tugging and growling like a terrier, the tendons on his neck standing out, his face flushing red, his eyes bulging to see below her tan line the delectable morsels hidden inside. The garment just stretched forward about six inches with no sign of tearing. However, Emelia burst into peals of laughter as she reached back, unclasped the hook in the rear, and watched the strapless lycra snap across his brow, knocking him prone against the stuffed lounger pad in a huff.

He laughed through a mouthful of wadded bathing suit. "Cute," came his muffled voice, spitting out the shiny black cloth.

"Aggressive?" she asked, running her hands up her tanned torso, cupping her small, firm, orchid-white breasts, weighing them, eagerly displaying them like an open-market produce peddler for his approval.

Jonathan tossed the black bathing top aside, a look of delighted amazement pasted on his face. "You're definitely a quick study."

Emelia seductively leaned forward, welcoming the hot sensation of a swelling hardness rising up between her legs against her bathing suit. She took his cheeks in her hands once again and temptingly traced Jonathan's moist lips with her rock-hard right nipple. "Actually, in my country they say I was a prodigy."

20

May 1975

Boston, Massachusetts

ALMOST ALL OF THE BOXES WERE PACKED IN THE FRUGAL TWO-bedroom apartment in Cambridge. Rae had all of the windows open, enjoying one of the few nice days New England offered during the year. A light breeze made the work of packing up all of her belongings for the three-day drive to Houston, Texas, much more bearable. Nikki had helped her pack for most of the day, still bewildered by the continual downturn of events that plagued her friend. It had only been two days since she received another tearful phone call from Rae, this time announcing the tragic news that her mother had passed away at St. Matthew's Hospital in Houston, finally losing her long battle with cancer. Today Rae had been quietly somber. Nikki felt awkward, doing her best to be comforting.

"It's not like it wasn't expected." Rae tried to sound pleasant, her eyes still red and puffy. She folded a heavy sweater and stuffed it into one of the cardboard boxes she rescued from a Dumpster behind a 7-Eleven. "We both knew the cancer was going to take its toll sooner or later."

Nikki picked the contents out of a dresser drawer and piled them in a box of her own. "She had ovarian cancer, didn't she?"

"Yes," Rae said softly. "She had a hysterectomy about six or seven years ago, but the doctors told her there was always the possibility of cancer spreading to other places before they got it. They had her on chemotherapy for the last few years."

Nikki closed the drawer. "Well, you said she passed peacefully. Right?"

Rae shrugged. "That's what they told me." For several tense moments she stared out the open window at cars going by, then slapped the lid of the box in anger. "Nikki, it isn't fair! She didn't even tell me it was this bad this time. The last time I talked to her, she said she was going in for some more tests. That's all! And the next thing I hear is her doctor calling me, telling how *sorry* he is! I should have *been* there!"

Nikki walked over to her friend's side. "Hey, don't get all worked up again. There was nothing you could do."

Rae glared up at her. "Yes there was—but not anymore."

Nikki's memory replayed Rebecca's gloating look as she strutted out of the courtroom with the legal rights to Rae's experimental cancer therapy. The guilt of her loss in court weighed down heavily upon her again. It never really occurred to her until that moment why Rae felt so strongly about finding a cure to that specific disease. She put her arm around Rae's shoulders and gave her a hug. "It'll all work out, Rae. You have to believe that. No matter what."

"Yeah, I'm sure it will." Rae's voice was soaked with despair. "Well, I'm nowhere near rich, but my mama left me a twenty-five-thousand-dollar life insurance policy and a paid-for house in Pasadena. I guess good ol' fate will show me what happens next."

Nikki didn't like Rae's fatalistic comment. "Don't you have any plans?"

Rae shrugged again. "Not really. I'm going home to the house where I grew up. And when I get there, I expect it to be very empty. I never had any brothers or sisters, and I told you about my dad."

"Yeah." Nikki remembered. "You said he passed away when you were little."

"Yeah, he had heart problems." Rae mused, "You know, I don't even remember what he looked like. I've got some old pictures of him, but no real memories."

Nikki took a deep breath and admonished, "Well, if I were you, I'd sell the house, get yourself a nice apartment, and make a fresh start. Sit down, make a plan, get some solid goals, and move on. That old house will just drag you down in a pit of unpleasant memories. And then I'll see your picture in the paper with the caption: 'Biochemist hangs herself with stethoscope.'"

That made Rae laugh, but Nikki was half serious. Rae squeezed Nikki's arm and smiled. "Thanks for the shoulder. It's about the only thing I think I'm going to miss about New England."

"Anytime." Nikki returned the smile.

Rae deliberately changed the subject to break the tension in the air. "So how are things going with you and Steve? Any better?"

Nikki rolled her eyes. "Don't ask. It's nonstop arguing now. And to be quite honest, I don't think I can take much more."

Rae looked concerned. "Are you guys thinking of splitting up?"

testament to the affluent simplicity of life. The feel of the deck rocking peacefully beneath him was the antithesis of the high-tech craze mesmerizing the rest of the nation. Donald couldn't believe the report he read in the *Boston Globe* that morning of people standing in line for eight hours to see some new science-fiction movie called *Star Wars*. No, this was the life. He took a seat in the deck-mounted deep sea fishing chair, resting his feet on the wide metal foot brace.

"Donald, we're out of ice." It came from behind him, a woman's irritated voice from below deck.

Donald smiled. A perfect addition to a perfect weekend at sea—a beautiful woman. "Just wait a while," he called over his shoulder, still entranced by the hypnotic lull of the waves. "The ice maker takes forever."

Rebecca Danforth walked out on the rear deck and leaned against the side rail holding a Bloody Mary in her hand. "These taste terrible with no ice."

Donald turned and looked at his weekend guest. She was attired in a bright red jogging suit with Adidas printed in slanted white lettering on both jacket and pants. Her long black hair was tied in a ponytail. He gave her a frown of concern. "Aren't you cold?"

Rebecca took a deep breath of the sea air. "No. It's too hot down below. I need some air." Rebecca set her drink down on the side of the boat and looked back at the sixty-two-year-old executive. His hair was completely white, but his angular features were still quite distinguished and striking. He wore a heavy navy-blue sweater and white deck slacks. His accommodating smile prompted her to finally bring up the subject that had been on her mind for several weeks. "Besides, I want to talk to you. It's important."

The chairman of the board of directors at Secularian turned to face his senior vice-president of marketing. "What about?"

Rebecca walked around the fighting chair to the stern of the boat and leaned against the wide edge. "Business. We both know that over the past fourteen months the new women's treatment campaign, all via my Hope Corporation acquisition, has been an incredible success."

"Yes," Donald agreed. "Loomis, over in finance, tells me we've seen a twenty-seven percent increase in market share since it was first announced. Splendid work, Rebecca. The whole board is most pleased. I've told you that before."

Rebecca looked him in the eye. "Well, to be quite frank, Donald, despite the fact that my contributions have made some of the most significant advances in our industry, let alone the enormous impact to our company's bottom line— personally, I'm concerned about my career."

Donald chuckled with a genuine note of surprise. "How's that? For God's sake, woman, you own almost ten percent of the outstanding shares of common stock. What more could you want?"

Rebecca leaned back over the stern, locking her fingers around the thin chrome railing, intentionally accentuating her bustline in the morning sun. Her voice was measured, calculated for effect, "First, I want you to get the board to move us out of the northeast. The whole headquarters operation. I'm sick to death of cold weather."

Donald frowned. "You want to relocate? Where?"

Rebecca seductively unzipped the Adidas jacket down to the middle of her stomach, watching his eyes travel down with the metal tab. She held her shoulders still, allowing the jacket to part just enough to reveal her lack of any other garment on beneath it. The cool of the morning had already succeeded in bringing to attention the two other prominent elements of her advertising campaign. "I want to move somewhere warm, where I don't have to wear all these heavy clothes all the time. Somewhere I can lie in the sun and turn coconut-brown—without any tan lines. Wouldn't that be nice?"

She could see his chest expand with excitement. This wasn't going to be difficult. He looked at her expectantly. "Now that you put it that way, it might not be a bad idea to find a little more suitable working conditions. Did you have any particular place in mind?"

"Dallas," she stated flatly, then hit him rapid-fire with the barrage of facts she had compiled. "It's centrally located in the U.S., decreasing our time-zone loss nationwide. It's got a brand new international airport bigger than O'Hare. Real estate is cheap. Office space is plentiful. We can liquidate the existing campus in Braintree, relocate all personnel, and still have in excess of $750,000 in cash left over as a dividend." She measured his genuinely impressed expression, evaluated the impact, and iced the sale with a smile. "Besides, I think the Texas sun is just what I need for my complexion."

Donald Bennet's eyes were still darting between her eyes and the inviting cleavage below. "That sounds tempting. I'll look into it. Give me all you've put together on Monday." He chuckled to himself. "You know, my wife's family is from Texas. Moving down there would be a lot easier than you might think." He suddenly looked puzzled. "So you think moving to Texas is really going to further your career?"

"Yes." Rebecca walked forward from the rail and put her hands on Bennet's knees, parting them slightly. Her dark eyes took deadly aim. "Because I want you to leave Tracy Bonner here in Boston. We'll maintain an R and D division here. Put her in charge of that. And if we make it a wholly-owned subsidiary, she can even keep her title."

Bennet looked a little shocked. "Rebecca, Tracy Bonner is one of the most capable presidents this company has ever had."

Rebecca reached for the buckle of Donald Bennet's cloth belt and opened it. "You're right. She's a fine woman. But she wouldn't *be* a president if it hadn't been for me. She lacks vision, Donald. Can't you see that? You know my credentials. You know what I can do. That job belongs to me, and I want it. It was *my* vision that moved us ahead twenty-seven percent. And it's *my* vision that will move us ahead into the 1980s. Isn't that what you want for the company?"

Donald's eyes looked down to her hands, unbuttoning his white slacks and unzipping his zipper. "Rebecca, my dear. You know I'd do almost anything for you, but I don't know about this." He made no move to stop her hands.

Rebecca kept her eyes on his while her right hand slid inside his boxer shorts. He was already hard. She knew he would be. "Donald, if your wife should ever discover that you've been spending so much time alone with me, wouldn't it appear more proper for you to be working hand in hand with your company president rather than just a V.P. of marketing?" When she said the word "hand," she gripped his organ and pulled it out into the cool air. A quick glance down told her he was in no position to refuse her anything. Men were so weak, she thought with disgust.

Bennet's voice was down to an eager whisper. "You're right. That would appear more natural." His face clouded with indecision. "But I don't know. Tracy will be crushed. There's no justification. I—I—"

Rebecca knelt down on the pivoting metal foot brace and devoured him, squelching his babbling hesitation, her head slowly bobbing up and down. She heard his breathing become labored, and felt the muscles in his legs tensing with pleasure. She increased the speed of her neck, her inner cheeks and tongue drawing harder and harder for several sustained minutes, until she sensed him about to explode.

Abruptly she stopped and looked up into his deprived expression. She tortured him further with a riddle. "Donald, do you know what the difference between V.P. and president is?"

"What?" he gasped, his question blurted out more in a state of confusion than in any intelligible response, his hands quickly moving to the back of her head, desperately prompting her to complete the task at hand.

She smiled at him. "A V.P. only does a part of the job." She playfully licked the end of his palpitating organ once again, her eyes growing wide, "But a president makes sure all the job gets done. Even if she has to swallow whatever comes along."

Donald Bennet cleared his throat with great difficulty. Rebecca could see it in his eyes—the extent of his loyalty to Tracy Bonner was only about as long as the length of her tongue. The white-haired senior executive creased his eyes with a salacious grin, his voice urgent. "Well, don't let me keep you from finishing your job, Madame President."

She finished—about ten seconds later—reveling in the white-hot sensation of invincibility and omnipotence, relishing the gratification of raw power, intoxicated by her ability to manipulate and utterly dominate. It was all too easy.

22

May 1986

Indianapolis, Indiana

THE DRONE OF THE POWERFUL FORMULA-ONE ENGINE SHIELDED the roar of the thousands upon thousands of cheering fans watching Sabrina Doucette flying toward her second Indianapolis 500 championship, an unheard-of back-to-back victory. The new Gustoff engine was putting out more horsepower than she dreamed, rocketing around the track for more than two grueling hours, at speeds in excess of 210 miles per hour. The second- and third-place racers were both a full lap down, furiously battling it out for second place.

Another jarring vibration, rattling down the sidewall of the crimson racer's fuselage, frightened her foot off the accelerator a bit. The disquieting shudders of the car's body, frame, and stabilizer struts were happening more often. At first it only occurred when she pressed the velocity envelope beyond 220 miles an hour, but now it was happening in the 210 to 215 range. She didn't like it at all. The new production engine for the car had only been finished and installed three weeks before the race. It performed well enough in the time trials to warrant a first-place poll position at the start, as Roger had promised; but she knew she had yet to push the pedal all the way down to see what it could really do. An ominous feeling came over her every time she felt the sudden vibrations. A sour ache down in her gut told her that she was strapped to more engine than car.

The race as a whole had gone smoothly thus far, with only two yellow flags the entire day. Watching their champion dominate the race all afternoon, the euphoric pit crew screamed and yelled each time Sabrina flew in and out of the pits. The sports commentators had run out of superlative adjectives to laud upon her, and consequently spent much of the last forty-five minutes analyzing the second- and third-place competitors. Five and a half more laps and Sabrina would be in the record books again.

A flashing red light tore her gaze from the track to the small instrument gauges mounted above the steering column. It wasn't the oil light, thank God. But it was cause for alarm. The fuel light was blinking. The high-performance engine used considerably more fuel than last year's edition. Their calculations for pit stops had to be adjusted on the fly all afternoon. A desperate dilemma seized her. If she stopped, her fragile one-lap lead would evaporate. If she kept going, the odds were she'd come up almost a full lap short. It didn't take long to make a decision. If she stopped, she was still in the race and might lose. Running out of fuel meant definitely losing.

"What the hell are you doing!" came the furious voice of Roger Marks over her headset as her car bore left into the pit lane.

"I won't make it!" She screamed back into her microphone as her car screeched up to the near-panicked expressions of her crew. "The damn fuel light's on. I'm not dropping out stranded on the backstretch!"

"Shit!" crackled the voice in her ear.

The flexible hose splashed the nitro-alcohol mixture down the side of the racer as the crew fought to preserve every precious second.

"It's enough!" she yelled at the pit chief. "I've only got five laps!"

The pit-crew chief dropped his clipboard, grabbed the hose out of the fuel spout, pushed the fuel technician out of the way, and slammed the cover back down, screaming, "Clear!"

Sabrina's foot launched into the pedal, tires screaming all the way out of the pits. Her car sailed back out on the track three car lengths down from the new first- and second-place racers. The 100,000-plus crowd was on its feet. The commentators were ecstatic. Suddenly it was a race again.

"Dammit, Sabrina," came Roger Marks's enraged voice in her earpiece. "If you fuck this up, you're history. You got that! You're bloody history!"

A pang of fear gripped her heart. How could those words come from the man who held her in his arms every night and tenderly loved her more than she ever dreamed a man could love? Was the race really the most important thing in the world to him? Is that all that mattered?

Her foot pressed down harder on the accelerator. In seconds she was right on the tail of the two leaders. With one masterful maneuver, she overtook the second-place racer and was bearing down on the leader from the Andretti team.

No, she thought, he's just upset. He always got upset when it actually came to the races. He was jumpy and irritable before the races, and an absolute basket case until it was over. It was always that way. Roger was a passionate man—God, was he ever; and his passion was part of his racing. She knew that. She couldn't allow his fears, his underlying concern for her, or even his temper, to blemish what she sincerely believed about him. He loved her. He had told her so on so many occasions. No, it was time for the real champion in her to come forth and show the man she loved, and the entire world for that matter, that she had what it took to win. Her foot pressed harder.

The Andretti racer fought her off, staying in front of her, pushing his machine to its limits. Round and round the track they went, under the white flag and into the final four turns. Flying into turn number four for the last time, Sabrina knew what she had to do to win. The leader would enter the turn high and drop in low for a sprint to the finish. She would follow him into the turn, then stay high, trusting the genius of Peter Gustoff and the traction of Goodyear to hold the turn and bring her to victory along the outside of the track.

True to form, the Andretti racer made his move, gliding into the turn at 197 miles an hour and diving in low. Sabrina held the wheel firm and planted her foot against the accelerator. The Gustoff power came to life, gripping hard into the high-banked turn. She exited the final turn at 205 miles per hour according to the gauge in front of her. The two cars ran parallel accelerating to 210 . . . 215 . . . 220 . . . 225 . . . The Andretti racing machine was holding its own down the last quarter mile, to the shock of both Roger Marks and Peter Gustoff, standing against the glass in their private sky box. The crowd was on its feet, all 100,000 plus holding their breath.

As Sabrina saw her speedometer pass 230, her heart sank—the vibration was starting again. She could see the tremor in the sidewalls and shimmies in the front struts. Her car took the lead by inches.

"You got it, baby! You got it!" came the familiar screaming voice in her earpiece. "Come on! Come on! You can do it!" With a sob of confidence, teeth clenched with raw determination, Sabrina held the pedal solidly to the floor.

The Roger Marks entry officially took the checkered flag half a car length ahead of the second-place finisher, clocked by racing officials at 237 miles per hour. Sabrina never knew it. She lost consciousness after a momentary sensation of vertigo and the racking shock of an explosion.

ANTICIPATION

Her car had not cleared the finish line by twenty yards before the ecstatic cheers of the frenzied spectators turned into screams of ghastly horror as the crimson wing car disintegrated with half a tank of fuel on board. The body of the car flipped end over end, ripping along the outside wall in a spectacular shower of sparks and flying metal and fiberglass. A thunderous conflagration of red and yellow tongues of nitrous heat blasted down the raceway amid the black billows of smoke. Pieces of the car showered the grandstand as terrified bystanders fled back in panic, trampling many underfoot.

A single Goodyear high-performance racing tire rolled into turn number one and completed almost a quarter of Sabrina's victory lap.

Part II

NEW BEGINNINGS

Of the passions that stir the heart, there is one
which makes the sexes necessary to each other, and
is extremely ardent and impetuous; a terrible
passion that braves danger, surmounts all obstacles,
and in its transports seems calculated to bring
destruction on the human race which it is really
destined to preserve. What must become of those
who are left to this brutal and boundless rage,
without modesty, without shame, and daily
upholding their amours at the price of their blood?

—Jean Jacques Rousseau
A Discourse on the Origin of Inequality

23

March 1977

Boston, Massachusetts

IT WAS THE SAME COURTROOM NIKKI HAD STOOD IN TWO YEARS
earlier with her client, Dr. Rae Taylor; the same dark woods,
broad beams, ornate moldings, milled rails, hardwood
flooring, and heavy chairs. The faded portraits leaning
forward from the framed paneling still kept their silent vigil.
Even the sunlight falling through the tall glass windows
elicited an uncanny sense of déjà vu. Except this time there
were two distinct differences: a different judge, and a gallery
crowded with people. The judge was Walter Gallimore, a
well-respected jurist in his late thirties. The standing room
only crowd pressed in to see a trial that had received much
public attention in recent weeks. On trial, Dr. Samuel
O'Brien, a thoracic surgeon of Secularian Hospital in Boston, and also Secularian Corporation itself. The plaintiff
was a young man named Mark Hoffman, the husband of the
late Julia Hoffman.

Nikki, now asking people to call her by her given name,
Nicole—it sounded more formal in court—was taking
great delight in representing the grieving widower in his
attempt to obtain a ten-million-dollar judgment against
Secularian for malpractice and criminal negligence. Eight

months prior, Mrs. Hoffman had been badly injured in an automobile accident. Witnesses had testified in Judge Gallimore's court that after Mrs. Hoffman was brought to Secularian's emergency room, she was examined by Dr. O'Brien, one of the attending physicians on call. Dr. O'Brien had reviewed initial X rays, vital statistics, and made the preliminary examination. He determined that her injuries did not warrant surgery, but simply a night of observation. Julia Hoffman died three hours after admittance of an internal hemorrhage.

"Dr. Davidson," Nicole asked the young trauma specialist on the witness stand. "Isn't it true that you advised Dr. O'Brien on the evening of July 23, 1976, that initial tests showed Julia Hoffman's blood pressure unstable and dropping between the time the emergency medical team arrived at the accident location and the time she arrived at Secularian?"

"Yes," the tall, thin, clean-cut physician reluctantly replied.

"And what was Dr. O'Brien's reaction to that information?" she asked, matter-of-fact.

Dr. Davidson looked over to the Secularian attorney for help.

"Dr. Davidson?" Nicole stepped in front of the witness, intentionally obscuring his view.

He looked at her with a helpless expression. "He didn't say anything."

Nicole looked skeptical. "He didn't say anything? Do you mean to tell this court that after you informed the attending physician of a dangerous patient status, he just ignored you?"

"Objection." Timothy Cranston, lead counsel for Secularian was on his feet. "The witness has already answered the question."

"Sustained," came Gallimore's stoic reply.

"I'll rephrase, Your Honor." In fact, the question itself was all Nicole wanted the jury to hear. "What precisely did Dr. O'Brien do for Mrs. Hoffman that you're aware of?"

Dr. Davidson's face wrinkled with frustration. "You have to understand. The E.R.'s a zoo some nights. That night was no exception. All that happened was Doc O'Brien looked at the charts and had to make some tough calls. We had two patients that night with gunshot wounds, plus a lady in labor."

Nicole did her best to look shocked. "Are you saying that Dr. O'Brien had too many things distracting him to adequately attend to Mrs. Hoffman's needs?"

"Objection. Calls for a conclusion," droned Cranston.

"Withdrawn," Nicole amended before the judge had a chance to rule. "Could you tell us *this,* Dr. Davidson. In *your* opinion, was the emergency room understaffed that night to meet the needs of the patients present?"

Davidson squirmed in his seat. "Hey, it's not like they can schedule who's going to shoot who on a given night. We do the best we can."

"Tell that to Mr. Hoffman," she said coldly, pointing back at her client. She let a pregnant pause burn her comment into the jury's mind.

"Do you have any further questions for this witness, Ms. Prescott?" Gallimore asked. Nicole had gone back to using her maiden name after her divorce a year earlier.

"I do, Your Honor." She turned to face Dr. Davidson. "Doctor, in your professional opinion, was there conclusive evidence presented to Dr. O'Brien the night of July twenty-third, the night that Julia Hoffman died of internal bleeding, that exploratory surgery *was* needed, that in fact exploratory surgery could have *easily* discovered a severed artery near her liver, and that had such surgery been performed, Julia Hoffman would be alive today?"

"That's hard to say," Davidson said softly. "You never know."

"I beg your pardon?" Nicole glared at the witness in utter disbelief. "Doctor, did you or did you not testify to this court that Julia Hoffman died of internal bleeding caused by trauma to the abdominal aorta?"

"Yes." He glanced at the jury.

"Would not this injury have been detected in a routine exploratory operation?" Nicole's heart was pounding. Her logic was already three moves ahead of her questions.

"It's highly likely," he offered lamely.

"Highly likely?" Nicole walked to the jury rail. "Doctor, if the abdominal aorta was ruptured, even a little bit, and the patient's heart was still beating, wouldn't a fountain of blood be able to be seen squirting several feet into the air?"

"Yes," he conceded.

"Good!" Nicole spun around and faced him again. "So could we then safely assume that in an exploratory operation a qualified surgeon might conclude that something was amiss when he saw the fountain?"

The gallery burst into laughter. Nicole was cutting the defense's witness to shreds in her cross-examination, and the people loved it—almost as much as she did. Cranston had the good sense not to object. Judge Gallimore rapped his gavel twice to hush the murmurs.

Nicole didn't wait for Davidson to answer. "Tell me this, Dr. Davidson. Was the vital-statistic information given by you to Dr. O'Brien sufficient to warrant surgery?"

"That was for Dr. O'Brien to decide." Davidson looked pleased with his evasion.

Nicole didn't let him off the hook. "I'm not asking him, I'm asking you."

"Objection, Your Honor," Cranston interrupted. Nicole bristled, as she sensed the power of the moment fading. It was obvious that's exactly what Cranston wanted. He noted again, "The witness has answered the question."

"Your Honor," Nicole interjected before Gallimore had time to speak. "We're not talking about a subjective observation here. There are sound laws of physiology and accepted medical practice to which both Dr. Davidson and Dr. O'Brien have been trained and licensed by this state to perform. I don't think it's inappropriate to get one of them to stop hiding behind their situational ethics and give this court a straight answer."

Gallimore gave Nicole a stern look. "Ms. Prescott, you

can save your plea for the jury." Nicole was taken aback, but brightened when she heard Gallimore say, "Objection overruled. The witness will answer the question."

It was as if every eye and ear in the room was poised with anticipation. The room grew deathly still. Davidson's eyes roamed back and forth from Nicole to Cranston, to the judge, to the jury, to the spectators in the gallery. He looked back coldly into Nicole's eyes. "It was warranted."

"No further questions." Nicole spun around and headed for the plaintiff's table amid the buzz of excitement erupting through the room. Two newspaper reporters dashed from the courtroom.

Closing arguments took the remainder of the afternoon, but the jury took only two hours to come back with a favorable verdict for the plaintiff. Both Nicole and Mark Hoffman took it as good news, but Nicole was not satisfied. The jury found Dr. Samuel O'Brien guilty of malpractice and awarded Mark Hoffman a $1.3 million judgment. But it found Secularian not criminally libel for any of Dr. O'Brien's actions. She knew their insurance company would pick up O'Brien's tab, but she wanted to see them pay, at least on paper. The way it stood, they would be absolved in the press, and O'Brien alone was their scapegoat. The jury had believed her argument about O'Brien's hasty decision costing a woman her life, but they failed to grasp the testimony she presented demonstrating the cost-cutting policies at Secularian that resulted in understaffing and poor overall patient care.

In any event, the win was viewed by the law partners of Foster and Finnman as a superb performance by one of their junior attorneys. The senior partners had used her in court for over six months, and each case she tried improved her skills. Nicole had an inherent knack for persuasive argument and debate. It flowed effortlessly from her personality. And it didn't take long for the senior attorneys to recognize its value. Nicole hoped *Hoffman* v. *Secularian* would be momentous enough to earn her a junior partnership in the firm. If she had won a judgment from Secularian directly, she estimated her chances were much higher. But now she really wasn't sure. Regardless, a win was a win, and that meant it was time to celebrate.

Six hours later, in the bathroom of the Riviera Club downtown, Nicole stood in front of a smudged mirror, carefully freshening her makeup. One of her legal associates, Marian Pitts, a slightly overweight brunette, stood at the next mirror trying to get an uncooperative curl to stay in place. Cindy Monahan, a stockbroker and close friend, had met them for drinks two hours ago to help celebrate Nicole's win. Cindy was still out at the small table, keeping her eyes on the coats and the good-looking men. Two hours' worth of cocktails had given the trio a glassy-eyed bravado and a terminal case of the giggles.

Marian wet her finger at the sink and rubbed it against her hair. "Shit! It won't stay."

Nicole sputtered into laughter, wiping a thin line of mascara on the top of her eyelid. "Oh, great. Look what you made me do."

Marian burst into laughter. "Don't worry. It's too dark out there for the guys to notice."

"Then what the hell am I doing this for?" Nicole looked over at her friend with mock agitation.

Marian shrugged. "Tradition."

Nicole nodded as though she understood, or more likely it was the six scotch and waters that professed to understand. "That makes sense." She went on to complete the task with the thin black bristle brush.

"Say, are you still dating Allen Binotti over in the litigation department?" Marian looked over at Nicole, temporarily forgetting about her hair. The door to the ladies room came open as another patron entered, letting in the thumping rhythm and electric howl of the live band on the dance floor. She waited till the door closed to answer. With the door shut, the deafening music was reduced to a dull roar.

"No, didn't you hear?" Nicole screwed the mascara

applicator back into its tube. "He took that job out in L.A. He left two months ago."

Marian walked toward the door, following Nicole. "Do you ever hear from him?"

Nicole shrugged and pulled open the door, raising her voice over the intruding thunder of the band, "He's called a couple of times. I don't worry about it. There's a lot here to keep me busy."

"Is there ever." Marian delightfully surveyed the sea of humanity wedged en masse. The two women emerged from the rest room into the pounding atmosphere of the crowded club, doing their best to squeeze through the throng of gyrating humans, laboring to retrace their steps back to Cindy and their coats.

The local Boston band performing at the club had recently released an album which was being received very well around the nation. One of its songs was already in the top ten of Casey Casem's "America's Top Forty." The band took its name from the city itself, Boston. The crowd cheered when the blasting distortion ebbed into the beautifully melodic introduction of a song called "More Than a Feeling."

Nicole squeezed into her seat next to Cindy. Marian sat across from her. Two fresh drinks awaited them. A half-empty glass sat in front of Cindy, a bubbly redhead with a spray of freckles across her cheeks and upper chest.

Cindy lifted her glass in a toast and shouted above the roar of the electric guitars, "To winning!"

"Here, here." Marian tapped her glass against her comrades' glasses and took a deep sip.

Cindy leaned over to Nicole's ear to be heard. "So you wanna get out of here and find someplace where we can hear ourselves think?"

Nicole looked past her to a handsome young man standing a few feet away against a pillar, looking at her with an inviting smile. "No. Not yet. I think things are just about to get fun."

Cindy looked at her with a puzzled frown, then turned to see what was in Nicole's line of sight. She spotted the young man. He was dressed in a dark suit with a red power tie. His short blond hair swept back from his temples with a gentle wave, styled and neat. His smile blended well with the energy in his bright blue eyes. "Oooh," Cindy moaned. "That could work."

"I'll let you know." Nicole stood up and edged her way around the table, walking directly up to the smiling young man.

"Hi," he yelled above the band.

"Hello." Nicole took another sip of her drink, then playfully chastised, "I caught you staring. It's impolite, you know."

He shrugged. "I'm sorry. I couldn't help myself. I liked what I saw."

Six and a half scotch and waters did the talking. "There's a lot more to see."

The young man set his drink on a nearby table and nodded. "Oh, I'm sure of that. Would you like to dance?"

Nicole set her drink down next to his. "No. That's not the *first* thing that comes to mind."

The song ended and the volume of the club dropped down to a comfortable level. The lead singer of the band announced a short break. The blond young man laughed. "You're very direct. You're a lawyer? Right?"

Nicole looked down at her dress. "Does it show?"

The man shrugged. "Only in the newspapers, Ms. Prescott."

A hot flush of embarrassment washed over her. "You know who I am?"

He stepped closer to her. "Will my answer affect the first thing that came to your mind?"

Her composure revived into a coy smile. "Perhaps. I value discretion."

"And I insist on it," he stated flatly.

She grinned. "Good answer. Let's get out of here."

Nicole waved at Cindy and Marian as she left, chuckling, as both of them shook their bewildered heads at her. The nameless young man took her to the Plaza Ritz Hotel and paid for an executive king suite. The room was plush and comfortable, and that's about where the excitement ended.

The young man was impetuous and rough. There was an initial exhilaration in pulling each other's clothes off and wrestling around on the bed, kissing, touching, and fondling. But he forced his way inside her too soon. The six scotches didn't eliminate the burning sensation she felt as he entered, it only took away her concern about it. She just laid there on her back, her head swirling in the mist of Cutty Sark, pulling strained breaths in under the frantically pumping young man's dead weight. He was finished in less than five minutes.

Nicole woke up the next morning in the king-sized bed alone. The dim red digital readout on the clock radio said it was almost ten A.M. She had slept for nine hours. Not even a long, hot shower could wash away the throbbing ache in her temples and the agitated sense of frustration in her heart. She always felt that way afterward; each time it was a little worse.

Nameless bodies taking their turns with her were far too common an occurrence over the past six months. She didn't want to admit it, but it was true. For the first six months, after her difficult divorce from Steve, she had seen Allen Binotti on a regular basis, and had started to grow quite attached to him—until she showed up at his apartment one afternoon and found him in bed with Gloria, the receptionist at Foster and Finnman. It had been a mutual decision to "see other people." Not long after that he was conveniently offered a job on the West Coast and hastily took it.

From that point there never seemed to be any time to cultivate anything close to a serious relationship. Instead there had been a regrettable stream of friendly smiles, fast hands, and sweating bodies. Part of her said she needed to prove to herself that men still wanted her and found her desirable. Another part of her just wanted to be close to someone. But then there was that part of her she didn't fully understand, a part that rose up like a nocturnal beast, hungry for its prey. It defied objection when it was feeding, but produced the most remorse on the mornings after. All she *could* understand was that the beast was a part of her, a necessary part, the part that enabled her to win. When unleashed in a courtroom, it captivated judges and juries alike, ruthlessly analyzed facts and figures till the naked truth became decisively clear and persuasively swayed all concerned to her position, no matter what it took.

Nicole dressed and opened the door of the hotel room. Outside the door, lying on the hall floor, was the morning edition of the *Boston Globe*. Her own face was staring up at her, pictured standing next to Mark Hoffman. The caption read, "Hoffman awarded $1.3 million by virtue of brilliant performance by Prescott."

Nicole silently leaned down and picked up the paper. She would clip out the headline and put it in her scrapbook. Right now the words "virtue" and "brilliant" were words she desperately needed to hear, and desperately wanted to believe were true.

24

June 1978

Dallas, Texas

AT MIDNIGHT THE TEMPERATURE WAS STILL IN THE LOW NINETIES, with the possibility of dropping into the mid-eighties before dawn. All the cars leaving the swank dinner party thrown for all the Secularian executives and senior managers had their windows rolled up and their air conditioners on. An impressive display of limousines, Mercedes sedans, BMWs, Cadillacs, and a few Italian sports cars wound their way down the long circular drive, leaving Rebecca Danforth's Highland Park mansion. The red-jacketed valets scurried to retrieve the vehicles of the few remaining guests.

Donald Bennet closed the door of his Mercedes 500 Series sedan for his wife, walked around the driver's side of the car and climbed in the car. He had no sooner put the transmission into gear when his wife turned to him with a chilling glare.

"You made me look like a fool tonight, Donald." She crossed her arms and pressed her back firmly into the wide leather seat.

Donald Bennet started the engine. "Don't be ridiculous. I'm sorry if you felt ignored. This party was for our best managers. I have a responsibility to be supportive and keep them all enthusiastic."

She bristled. "Is that what you call what you were doing? You don't think I saw you groping that woman by the piano?"

Donald rolled his eyes. "Of, for God's sake, it was all in

fun. I harmlessly flirt with all the women we employ, and try to make a point to put an arm on the shoulder of all the men as well. They like it. It lets them all know I care. You're blowing something very innocent entirely out of proportion."

"I know what I saw," she retorted.

"Look, sweetheart. Rebecca Danforth is the president of Secularian, and it's very important for her to be received well by all the other managers. That was the purpose of this party. Remember?" Donald took a corner faster than usual, causing the tires to squeal on the hot asphalt.

"I'm not a fool, Donald." She stared out the front window. "I didn't mind coming back to Texas, but I hope you realize I left a great deal of longtime patients and a healthy practice in Boston to come here for you. That decision was not made lightly. I have no seniority here at Baylor Medical, despite my credentials, and I don't like it." She turned back toward him. "And it never really hit me until tonight that you made all this happen just to accommodate *that woman.*"

Donald raised his voice, "Who said anything was done to accommodate one individual? There were a number of significant reasons why we relocated the firm. And much of our stock dividend this year will bear that out quite handsomely, thank you."

"I shouldn't have come here," she muttered absently, pushing a lock of her short black hair out of her eyes. "It was a mistake."

"Alicia, don't be ridiculous." Donald tried to sound reasonable, but came across condescending. "You're a brilliant surgeon. You're published all over the nation. Think about it. There are just as many people in need of a good cosmetic surgeon in Texas as there are in Massachusetts. Who knows, probably more. You're just feeling the pain of the transition. I'm going through it too. We all left our roots back East." He softened his tone to the point of near sincerity. "Come on, honey. Try to look at all of this as a fresh start, a new beginning."

Alicia Bennet felt a little unsure. Did she really see what she thought she saw at the party? Was her husband constantly glancing to the dark eyes of that Danforth woman? Did she really see him casually putting his arm around her while talking to the other guests, occasionally letting his hand roam down her emerald-green evening gown across her buttocks? Could it all be an innocent exaggeration? Her mind didn't know what to think. After twenty-six years of marriage, three grown children, and two careers, the thought of someone else standing at Donald's side was repulsive. Not even the pleasant sound of starting over fresh in a new place with new challenges could completely take that subliminal revulsion away. A new beginning? A beginning of what?

25

September 1978

Houston, Texas

A THOUSAND PEOPLE WERE GATHERED IN THE CONFERENCE HALL at the Houston Convention Center, most of them women. The conference chairman was droning on about changes in Texas usury laws affecting loan assumptions and property foreclosure. The air-conditioning was barely adequate, prompting many in the audience to fan themselves with their program brochures. The nagging doubts questioning Rae's judgment of why she was there steadfastly refused to go away. With bored disinterest in the speaker's monotone commentary, her thoughts were far away, struggling to accept the endless sequence of treacherous pitfalls she encountered every day.

Rae's first year back in Houston had been the most difficult, trudging through the anguish of the funeral, the endless tedium of settling her mother's affairs, and the constant stress of getting readjusted to a new place. She thought it would be different, a welcome feeling, like coming home. It was the same house and the same neighborhood she left after high school, but Pasadena was a different place in 1978. Most of her old neighbors and friends had all moved away. She also discovered that Nikki had been right. The old house depressed her every time she came through the door. The kitchen was too empty with no mother in it baking or washing something, like she was supposed to. The small, three-bedroom house sold for forty thousand dollars. Rae now lived in a two-bedroom apartment on the west side of Houston. She had been there for the last two years.

"I'm sorry, Dr. Taylor." The words of the university administrator still rang in her memory. "Your grant request has been denied due to legal liability regarding patent infringement."

Six months after her mother's death, Rae had applied for a research grant at Rice University to pick up the pieces of her life and continue her work. But even across the country, Rebecca Danforth's treachery still haunted her. The law now prohibited her from doing any work in the area of gene therapy and cancer research using any of her own discoveries and techniques.

Eight months later, with her savings almost gone, she recognized the necessity of getting a job, doing something—anything. A Sunday newspaper ad promised an exciting and financially rewarding career in real estate, with flexible hours and free training. At that point in her life she wasn't in a position to be very particular. She could still remember her interview with a fast talking real estate broker in a hideous red blazer who managed to convince her to give it a try. The training had been very academic and extremely boring. Three-fourths of her colleagues were middle-class housewives who wore too much makeup, cheap perfume, and didn't care whether they made any sales or not.

Fortunately for Rae, most of her clients liked her simple approach and matter-of-fact presentation. She had one of the better sales records in her branch. In less than a year she was a member of the "Million Dollar Club." Her earnings just barely covered the bills.

Six weeks prior to the conference she was presently attending, her broker, fast-talking Don Blasky, encouraged her to attend the conference to improve her sales skills. He gave her an animated pitch about self-esteem and projecting a positive image, which she subsequently let go in one ear and out the other. Don had no credibility. He was an insatiable flirt who always had the smell of beer or cigar smoke about him. None of the women at the office took him seriously, with the exception of Bernice Rawlins, a longtime salesperson with a beehive hairdo and cat-eyed glasses. Don and Bernice were the richest source of gossip around the office. Rae found it an amusing distraction. And with no viable argument against attending the seminar, she conceded to go.

The speaker concluded his remarks to a halfhearted, polite round of applause. He introduced the next scheduled guest, the keynote speaker, a woman by the name of Marsha Collins. The name caught Rae's attention. She had seen it on several motivational books stacked on the display tables outside the convention hall. The audience awoke with a hearty ovation as a tall, elegant woman with dark red hair, neatly folded back in a French braid, ascended the platform and stood behind the podium.

The clapping died down as the woman smiled and surveyed the entire congregation from left to right. "Thank you all very much for that warm welcome. It's my privilege to be asked to address the Greater Houston Board of Realtors, distinguished guests, and colleagues."

Rae was impressed with the gracious style of the woman; it was captivating. Marsha Collins looked across the crowd with a serious expression. "Ladies and gentlemen, some of you out there have big dreams of success in the marketplace today. You have goals that yearn to be achieved. And yet day after day you don't find yourself any closer to achieving those goals as you were the day before." Her expression grew grave. "Or worse yet, you find obstacles along the way that dash your hopes and aspirations at every turn. Have you ever felt like that?" She stopped to allow the majority of the crowd to nod in assent.

"I have too," she continued, stepping away from the podium, a wireless microphone attached to the lapel of her dark business suit. Her long legs opened the pleats in her skirt as she stepped toward the center of the stage. "I've been where many of you are today. I was married, with a beautiful son and a daughter. I was studying broadcast journalism, with the aspiration of being a famous news personality one day. But as life would turn out, I found myself at the age of thirty-one." She smiled. "And I won't tell you how long ago that was . . ." The audience laughed. "I found myself in a single day a widow with two elementary school children, no job, no savings, and no plan for what I was going to do."

The audience grew still.

Marsha spoke evenly, with a polished sense of control. "I can still remember the phone call. My husband worked at one of the local refineries. It was a job-related accident, they said. Naturally, I was completely devastated. I didn't know what to do. I had no one to turn to. I had no plan. So what did I do?"

Everyone in the room sincerely wanted to know.

"I did what you'd do. I cried. I prayed. I talked to well-meaning family and friends." The air was growing tense. "And then I did something revolutionary, something that many of you haven't done. I didn't quit. I didn't give up. I fought back."

A chill of excitement ran through Rae. Every word she heard soaked into her soul like a healing balm.

Marsha stood straight, confident. "And I won. Over the past many years, as some of you may know, I have developed one of the largest real estate development corporations in America. I don't say this to boast, but to let you know that it's possible. I enjoy a standard of living I never dreamed of when I first got married." She took a step to her left and pointed at the crowd. "But I can see your faces. I know what you're thinking. You're thinking, sure, that's simplistic, just change your attitude and you can become a multimillionaire. Am I right?"

A few chuckles were heard.

She pointed to the crowd and nodded. "And you're right. That *is* simplistic. And if you'll give me your undivided attention, I plan to spend the next half an hour or so giving you some concrete tools for you to use to win your battles as well. Is that fair?"

The audience applauded.

"Good." She walked back over to the podium and looked at her notes for a second. "The first thing I want every one of you to do is say with me, 'I am a businessperson.'"

The crowded room repeated the phrase in unison.

Marsha prompted, "Say, 'I am in business to succeed.'"

They all did, Rae chanting along, mesmerized by what she was hearing.

"Good. And to succeed you have to know where you're going," Marsha admonished. "Think about it. When you go on vacation you don't just go to the airport and say, 'Sell me a ticket to anywhere.' No, you make a plan. You set an itinerary. And that's rule number one. A journey toward success has a map. You rarely, if ever, will find success by accident. Success is achieved. It's earned. It goes to those who build it."

Rae felt a pang in her heart. Or to those that steal it, she thought.

Marsha took a deep breath. "And I'll let you in on a little secret." The room became still again. "You can't cross bridges that aren't there." She paused for effect. "Isn't that profound? You don't understand?" She laughed. "What I mean by that is, so many of you go out into the marketplace and think that you're going to find someone to buy what you have to sell. That's not the way it's done. It's completely backward. You have to sell what people want to buy—and learn what not to sell. Sometimes the greater wisdom of the successful businessperson is to recognize what needs to be avoided in lieu of what needs to be approached. Do you hear what I'm saying?"

More nods came from all over the hall.

Marsha leaned toward the audience. "Don't just sell them what you have. Sell them what they want *in addition* to what you have. Oh, I know what you're thinking now. How the hell do you do that? Simple. By adding Market Based Value."

Many people squirmed in their seats.

"Yes, write that down." Marsha mimed the act of scribbling. "I know it's business jargon to most of you, but it's critically important. Market Based Value, MBV, is what you get when you find out what motivates a person to buy, and then you ensure that it's a key part of your sale. That's really all it is. But it's a powerful tool. For example, in Texas we all know how hot it gets, and down here in Houston the humidity only makes it worse. Is it hard to sell a house with a swimming pool here in Texas? Of course not. A Texas house without a pool is seen as deficient. So if you're trying to move a house without a pool, see if you can get the owner to consider installing one to encourage the sale. But sometimes the dollars don't make that feasible. Right? What about a hot tub? What about a wet bar? What about season tickets to see the Astros play?"

She mocked the looks of surprise on everyone's face. "That's right, tickets to a baseball game. Or what about tickets to the symphony? Who says a sales incentive has to have anything to do with the product itself? The whole nature of an incentive is to appeal to the specific needs of your customer. I promise you, if you can find out what your customers really want, really need, really *desire*—and can satisfy that need economically, you'll make a sale. I guarantee it."

A ripple of excitement and a buzz of side conversations erupted.

"You like that idea." Marsha laughed. "Good. And the extent of your success will be measured by the depth of your imagination to meet the real needs of those you wish to do business with. Remember that. MBV. Market Based Value. Give them what they *want . . ."* She cocked her eyebrow with a sly pause. ". . . or what they *think* they want—and the cash will start to flow in your direction."

Marsha went on to explain to the group several other key marketing strategies that had contributed to her multimillion-dollar empire. She concluded with an announcement regarding several workshops she was giving over the three-day conference detailing more on creative financing, how to help your clients avoid down payments and credit hassles, plus how to manipulate lending institutions.

Rae was mesmerized by every word she heard. And over the next three days she attended every workshop Marsha gave. On the final day of the conference, Rae found the courage to go up and thank Marsha for the powerful impact she had made in such a short period of time.

"Ms. Collins?" Rae asked timidly at the speaker's lectern in the small breakout room of the convention center. Most of the other attendees had departed.

"Please, it's just Marsha," she answered, finishing an autograph of one of her books for one more grinning fan. "And you are . . . ?"

"Rae Taylor." Rae held out her hand.

Marsha took it in her right hand and warmly covered it with her left. "Hello, Rae."

"I just wanted to come up and tell you how much I've enjoyed hearing you speak during the conference. It's meant a great deal to me." Her heart was beating faster, terrified that she might say something stupid.

Marsha smiled. "Thank you very much, Rae. I've noticed you in all the workshops. You were very attentive. I really appreciate that."

"You're welcome," was all Rae could think of to say.

Marsha looked at the plain young girl in front of her. Something about her, nothing she could specifically put her finger on, but *something* in her eyes, genuinely intrigued her. "So why did this conference mean so much to you, Rae?"

Rae blushed, shaking her head to dismiss the comment. "It's a long story. Mostly, I really needed to hear your speech the other day on starting over and winning. I was beginning to wonder if anyone knew it was possible."

Marsha took Rae by the arm and walked toward the door. "Well, I happen to be very partial to long stories. Could I impose upon you to join me for lunch? I think I'd like to hear yours."

Rae was stunned. She stammered as best she could, "Is that all right? Don't you have to be somewhere?"

Marsha gave her a reassuring smile. "No. I've all afternoon free."

Their conversation took most of the afternoon, long after the coffee had grown cold and the dishes cleared away. Marsha was both repulsed and intrigued by the story she heard from the young biochemist. But the more she heard, the more she was convinced that the young girl she had found was the one she had been looking for.

Collins Enterprises needed to expand, but Marsha felt strongly that expansion had to come from fresh ideas and fresh motivation. She had interviewed scores of MBAs and business executives who littered her office with proposals of tried-and-true methods of corporate development. She didn't like any of it. Marsha was looking for someone intelligent, creative, compassionate—and hungry. She wanted someone on the bleeding edge of life that would give more than her forty hours to be successful—the way that she herself had been in the early years. By the end of the conversation, she was convinced that person was Dr. Rae Taylor.

Rae was too much in a state of shock to fully appreciate the unexpected offer of employment that Marsha made her. But that small voice inside her had the good sense to accept the apprentice position, working as executive assistant to Marsha Collins at Collins Enterprises, Inc. With hope again rekindled, at last, Rae felt as if a door had opened and now her life might begin again.

26

July 1986

Los Angeles, California

THE FIRST REAL SENSATIONS WERE THE INDISTINGUISHABLE sounds of movement, blurred human voices, the steady beeping of something electronic. All sense of touch lethargically oscillated between a dull ache and a cold numbness. The smell of clinical antiseptics were not enough to mask the odors of dried blood and healing wounds. The bitter taste of iron was mixed with the acrid flavor of a plastic feeding tube uncomfortably lodged in the throat. The eyes were still too weary to open, aimlessly flirting back and forth behind their lids. The sound of footsteps pierced through the fog in her mind.

"She's awake . . ." came an echoing voice, as though it were deep in a cavern. More movement followed as the blackness swallowed her once again into the netherworld of the unconscious.

A warm sensation moved across her chest with a faint tingle of energy. She had no idea it was two days after she first awoke. And she didn't initially believe the doctor who later told her she had been lying in a Los Angeles intensive care unit for over two months.

"Sabrina," came an unfamiliar voice. "Sabrina, can you hear me?"

She did her best to lift her heavy eyelids, but couldn't. She sensed someone standing by her bed. She tried to turn her head, but her neck wouldn't move. All that came out of her mouth was a feeble moan, before all sensation slipped away once again.

For the next three days Sabrina incoherently lapsed in and out of consciousness, barely aware of muted voices, disjointed electronic sounds, and many more footsteps.

With little concept of how much time had passed, she awoke with a start, gagging, feeling like she was choking to death. A calming voice near her urgently admonished, "Don't try to move. Don't try to swallow. It's all right. Just relax. Your neck is in a brace, and you've got a feeding tube down your throat. We'll be disconnecting it later today and put you on an IV from now on. I think you'll find that much more comfortable."

As Sabrina's mind swam up from the black depths of endless sleep, a disquieting state of confusion and fear swept over her. Where was she? What had happened? What was going on? Why couldn't she see? She became visibly agitated.

She sensed someone come over next to her and sit down on the edge of the bed. "It's okay. Settle down. Everything's fine. You made it, Sabrina. We were all worried about you for quite a while, but you made it. And you're going to be all right. Lie still. Don't try to move. Your legs are in casts, so don't worry about moving them. So are your arms. There are bandages over your eyes, so don't worry about not being able to see. They'll all be coming off in a few days."

Some of the panic raging within abated into the calming tone of the mysterious voice beside her. She felt something touch her shoulder. It was the first new sensation she could recall. "Sabrina, I'll be back to talk to you after you have a chance to rest a bit more. Everything will be fully explained to you concerning your condition after you've had a chance to regain a little strength. That may take a few days. But don't worry. You're going to be fine."

Sabrina drifted back into unconsciousness. When she

awoke, she vainly tried to move an arm and a leg. No motor function obeyed any of her commands. As her mind became more lucid, her instincts told her plainly that she was injured very badly. Hour after hour she concentrated on taking deep breaths and focusing her attention, becoming a little more alert as the time passed. The task was near impossible, as she fought not only her injuries, but the powerful narcotics in her system stemming the pain.

Between vignettes of unconsciousness, she heard other voices come to her room to innocuously chat. In those moments part of her desperately wanted to know what had happened, but another part just wanted to sleep. The voice she had originally heard introduced himself as Dr. Hyrum Stevens. He introduced two other doctors, but she initially didn't catch their names. As promised, the feeding tube had been removed, but the raw, burning sensation lingering in the back of her throat kept her from trying to talk.

From what she was able to comprehend, the three doctors were very kind and supportive in their preliminary visits, but they were evasive in describing her actual physical condition for several days. They always arrived together, giving her unrelated bits of encouraging information, then politely left.

Seven days after she awoke, the bandages were removed from her eyes, and the darkness was replaced by blurred images. By the tenth day, the fuzzy shapes in her room took on definition and a semblance of clarity. But Sabrina's mind still wandered in a frightened fog. Shortly thereafter she was finally able to match faces with familiar voices. After two weeks her three physicians came to tell her what she had been so eager to know but dreaded to hear.

"Sabrina," said Dr. Stevens, a tall man with dark hair, as he stood by the foot of her bed. "Dr. Burton, Dr. Everet, and I have been greatly encouraged by your progress these last few days. And we've all agreed that it's time we brought you up to date on what you've been through over the last two months. In case you don't remember, you are in the Los Angeles County Crisis Center's intensive care unit. You've been in a coma since you were brought here. Do you remember me telling you this the other day?"

Sabrina shook her head slightly. Her voice was still too weak to reply.

Dr. Stevens looked at his two colleagues. They nodded for him to continue. "Sabrina, do you feel up to hearing this?"

She nodded slightly, her eyes pleading. Her mind was clearing, and everything within her yearned to know exactly what had happened and the true extent of her injuries.

Dr. Stevens gave her a warm smile. "You were transferred here from Indianapolis about two weeks after your injuries stabilized."

She gave him a questioning look, but he understood her expression.

"The reason you're here is because we're specially equipped to deal with cases as severe as yours." Her green eyes grew wide. "But please don't let me frighten you. We all want you to know that before we give you any details regarding the treatments you've received, or that are pending, that you know that your body will be completely restored. You aren't missing any limbs. You've got all your fingers and toes, and every one of them is going to work, though they may be a bit reluctant at present. A physical therapist will help you in that regard."

Dr. Stevens could see she was relaxing a bit. "Of course you'll have to be patient. I'll be honest with you. It's a miracle you're alive. There were very few bones in your body that weren't broken. You've got enough pins and artificial ligaments in you to set off the metal detector in every airport you visit for the rest of your life."

Sabrina tried to smile, but her cheeks wouldn't comply.

Dr. Stevens opened a long metal chart and took a deep breath. "Dr. Burton here is a staff psychologist here at the facility. His job is to help you through some tough times we know you may encounter in the near future."

Dr. Burton spoke up. He was a short, balding man with a well-trimmed beard. "Yes, Ms. Doucette. We want to be forthright with you from the outset, and assure you that we are fully aware that the damage your body has endured will naturally produce all manner of concern on your part. Some of it is physical, some emotional. Our desire is that you work through your recovery to a healthy conclusion."

Sabrina's eyes went back to Dr. Stevens as he interrupted, "Much of Dr. Burton's work will be in conjunction with Dr. Everet." Stevens gestured toward the third man. Dr. Everet looked uncomfortably at Stevens and Burton. He knew it was his cue, and his reluctance to speak caused Sabrina even more concern.

Everet looked into Sabrina's eyes. "Ms. Doucette. Since you've been here, I've operated on you six times. You were very fortunate to have been wearing your fire suit; but unfortunately, it was badly torn in several places and we've had to do some significant skin grafts."

Sabrina's eyes flew wide with recognition as her mind rapidly sobered. Her memory jolted back to something she learned years ago. L.A. County Crisis Center was known nationally for its burn ward.

Dr. Everet could see the recognition in her eyes. He swallowed with difficulty. "Yes, Sabrina, I'm a burn specialist. But listen to me. The one fact I want you to bear in mind, above all else, no matter how difficult the days ahead may be—is that you're alive. Do you understand that?"

She nodded faintly, her heart racing.

"Good." Everet looked back at his colleagues with a note of relief. "Sabrina, you're going to discover that most of your body is bandaged. There will be some light scarring on your arms and legs and a thin line around the small of your back where your fire suit separated."

Sabrina kept her attention on the doctor. It was obvious he had more to say—something he didn't want to say.

He looked at her with all the professional detachment he could muster. "I'm afraid, however, that the damage inflicted to your face, up around your eyes, where the fire hood is open, will be our greatest challenge. Your helmet practically melted off your head. The burns were third degree, and I'm afraid that even after multiple grafts, there will still be a great deal of scarring. We're at a loss to explain how your vision remained intact. You're not going to like what you see, and that's why Dr. Burton is here to help you. I'm sorry Ms. Doucette. I promise you we'll do everything within our power to help you. Please believe that."

Sabrina could feel her chest begin to heave with a surge of adrenaline. How bad was it? She felt the sudden impulse to get up and run, but none of her limbs were responsive to any of her commands.

She watched Dr. Burton walk up next to her bed and insert a syringe in the IV tube attached to her right arm. He gave her a compassionate smile. "Sabrina, I'm going to give you a mild sedative now. I know this information is shocking, and you have every right to be as upset as you wish to be. This is natural. As time passes, we will work through this together. And we *will* get through it. This I can promise you."

Dr. Stevens spoke up from the end of the bed. "Sabrina, we'll let you get some rest now. But before you fall asleep, there's someone out in the waiting area who has asked to see you."

The three physicians awkwardly filed out of the room as the heavy door slipped closed behind them. A few moments later it opened again. Sabrina's eyes welled up with tears when she saw Roger Marks's face. He was carrying an oversized bouquet of flowers.

"Hi, baby," he whispered softly, set the flowers down on the nightstand beside her bed, leaned over, and tenderly kissed her bandaged forehead. She could barely feel the pressure of his lips, but it was greatly appreciated. "I told them to call me as soon as you woke up, but they said I couldn't see you until today." He looked back toward the door. "God, Sabrina, I've been sick with worry about you. I'm a total wreck." He suddenly looked chagrined, realizing his clumsy use of the word "wreck." He quickly apologized, "Sorry. Bad choice of words."

She gave him a helpless sigh. She had no memory of a wreck. The last thing she knew was flying down a racetrack, and the next moment waking up immobilized in a hospital bed two thousand miles away. She could see his eyes carefully surveying every inch of her face. By now she was aware that it was wrapped tightly with bandages over every area except her eyes. The thought of looking like a mummy occurred to her and made her smile.

"What is it?" he asked, then shook his head. "Well, you couldn't tell me if you wanted to. They've got you mummified enough."

She smiled again. He patted her shoulder. "I suppose no one's congratulated you yet, but in case you didn't know, you *did* win the race. You're in the history books again. Not just as the first woman, but the first racer ever to win back-to-back championships at Indianapolis. It was incredible. And something I know you and I both will be proud of for the rest of our lives." An uncomfortable tension seized the air. The comment was embarrassingly inappropriate. Roger cleared his throat with difficulty. "But don't you worry. They're going to get you all fixed up. I told them to spare no expense." He lowered his voice and tried to smile, "Besides, we're insured."

Her eyes brightened in the light of his humor. It helped a great deal. But something was wrong. She could feel it. Something was very wrong. There was a distance between them, as though none of the closeness they had shared ever existed. As she watched his eyes, she could tell he was carefully trying to see beneath the edges of her bandages at the area around her eyes. Her brow furrowed with obvious concern.

Roger Marks's voice became very serious, almost whispering. "Sabrina, I'm so sorry about what happened. Please believe me. You warned us. You tried to make us see, but neither Peter nor I listened." His voice cracked with remorse, "And look what we've done to you. How can I ever expect you to forgive me?"

She was crying on the inside, though her body laid in limp resignation to the medication in her system.

"All right," he said awkwardly, with a note of finality.

"You do what the doctors tell you. They're going to do everything they can to fix your body and give you a new face. They promised me that."

That comment alarmed her. How bad *was* her face?

He wouldn't look her in the eye anymore. "You see, my dear, I'm afraid I'm going to be out of pocket for a bit. The team and I are planning to head for Europe next week to prepare for the fall Grand Prix circuit. Supposed to be keen competition this year." He forced a laugh. "You know, I really hate to compete with you not out there winning for me. But we all have to move on with our lives. Right?"

She didn't like the sound of that at all, no matter how innocent he tried to make it all sound. Roger sat, silently staring at the door for several moments.

"And please, Sabrina." He stood, his chin starting to quiver. "Do like they say, and let them fix you up. Like I said, I'm sorry." He closed his eyes tightly for a moment. "So very, very sorry. We all are." Without another word, without saying he loved her, without saying good-bye, Roger leaned forward and kissed her forehead again, then hastily left the room.

Sabrina's heart was thundering in confusion, her temples pounding in syncopated rhythm. What did he mean by the "we all have to move on" comment? The medication was beckoning her to return to the twilight limbo of semiconsciousness where all sensations blur into surrealistic haze, and her faculties were reluctantly accepting the invitation, despite her frenzy of emotions raging within.

Yet the truth was plain. It was undeniable. There was no empirical evidence to prove it, but she heard the voice within, and it was telling her the truth. A haunting voice from deep within the pit of her stomach plainly told her she had just seen Roger Marks for the last time.

27

January 1979

Keystone Ski Resort, Colorado

THE RESIDUE OF THE DAY'S FRESH POWDER MELTED IN THE FIRE-warmed heat, the silver drops lightly dripping from the precision Rossignol sport skis hanging in the entryway, puddling onto the Spanish tiles below. The enchanting fragrance of the white oak crackling in the fireplace filled the two-story, luxury condominium at the base of the mountain near River Run Plaza. The lavish Spanish-style villa was just over two thousand square feet, complete with a vaulted loft, spiral staircase, a full kitchen and dining room, three bedrooms, a game room, and a master bath rivaling the Medici Palace in Florence.

As the penetrating steam rose from the effervescent water of a twelve-foot, inlaid-marble Jacuzzi, Rebecca Danforth rose halfway out of the turbulent waters and reached over to a silver platter garnished with refreshments. In the center of the platter lay a wide crystal bowl filled with cut fruit. In a smaller bowl next to it sat an artistically served portion of whipped cream. A stack of serving dishes and spoons graced the other side of the fruit bowl. Rebecca glanced across the steaming waters to Donald Bennet, lying on one of the contoured ledges, the burbling water up to his chin. His eyes were closed as he relaxed after the long, taxing day on the slopes. Rebecca bit her tongue with a naughty notion of inspiration. It was time to play.

She took one of the small silver serving spoons and scooped up a heaping portion of whipped cream. With mischievous care, so as not to attract any premature attention, she spread the cool, white topping over both of her glistening wet nipples. She then leaned back over the edge of the hot tub, keeping gravity in her favor, and garnished each white mound with a small strawberry half. The left one started to slide off as her body reacted beneath the chilled spread, but she was able to repair it. Rebecca knew she had to move quickly. The heat would reduce the whipped topping to milk in a few seconds.

"Donald," she asked innocently. "Some desert?"

He opened his eyes and burst into laughter. However, he didn't have to be asked twice, nor did the whipped topping have an opportunity to melt. He came across the tub and took her into his arms, his mouth quickly accepting the scrumptiously served morsels, sending titillating tingles of pleasure up and down her spine with each languid lap of his tongue. Rebecca laced her fingers behind his neck and lifted her knees out of the water. She felt the warm contact beneath the water as he stood straight, wrapping his arms around her waist, pulling her to him.

"I want you." Her words dripped from her mouth with the same sultry vapor as the 105-degree water rising into the air.

Donald took a deep breath. "Rebecca, dear. We skied for almost seven hours today. I don't know how much energy I've got left."

Her eyes burned into his. "You just stand there. Let me and the water do the work."

Without waiting for a reply she reached under the churning currents, her hand descending between them, quickly locating his half-interested member. With a little coaxing it rose to attention. She splashed toward him with a wave of pleasure, carefully inserted it, allowing gravity to pull her pelvis forward, filling her fully.

Rebecca reached up and laced her fingers behind his neck, taking advantage of the water's buoyancy to keep her up. With Donald standing in the center of the tub, the bubbling water came up to the base of his chest. The depth allowed

Rebecca to kick her legs out straight from the knee with strong, deliberate upward strokes, which served to slowly raise her pelvis away from him. Then she relaxed, letting gravity pull her back down. As a former high school and collegiate swimmer, she knew exactly what she was doing. An assistant swimming coach had showed her the delightful technique after practice one afternoon long ago, and helped her refine it over the period of a year.

Donald tilted his head back and began to moan with each penetrating stroke about two to three seconds apart, slow and easy, building in intensity. Each time her legs thrust forward, her thigh muscles flexed inward, tenderly squeezing him as he withdrew. When she relaxed, he effortlessly slid back inside her, deeply and completely. In and out, riding up and down, as the heat of the water melted every muscle, every tension, stroke after stroke.

Rebecca continued her steady pace for fifteen minutes, aware of the growing sensation within her about to ignite. She closed her eyes, increasing her pace, splashing the boiling water against his chest, moving closer and changing her technique, working more with her arms instead of her legs. Donald remained ramrod still, gasping in humid gulps of air through clenched teeth. Rebecca could feel the pre-shocks of the approaching quake, preparing for imminent impact. Like an approaching army, hungry for conquest, it drew closer. Her body and emotions welcomed it, invited it, drew it closer with every labored thrust. She could tell it was going to be good—very good.

Donald apparently sensed the approaching erotic cataclysm and reacted instinctively. She felt his hands slide from her waist to her buttocks, his arms falling into pace with the stabbing rhythm between them. Seconds later the orgasmic deluge hit full force, rocking her head back in a long guttural moan of undiluted ecstasy, her hands unconsciously unlocking from his neck, her fingernails raking over his shoulders as she slipped back into the torrid effervescence, the heat instantly enveloping her for a moment, only to be lifted back into the cool air by Donald's strong arms. Her entire body constricted in waves of euphoria, violently splashing water out of the tub along the length of the pastel-tiled walls of the master bath. As her own wet passion ebbed, Rebecca let her entire body relax around the sweet pressure of his rigid surging deep inside her. He arrived at the same explosive destination as she, just a few strained seconds behind her.

Panting like a marathon runner, Donald carried Rebecca back through the bubbles, over to the edge of the tub and set her down. With a trembling hand he retrieved the chilled bottle of champagne from the ice bucket next to the silver fruit platter and poured a glass. "You're going to kill me if you're not careful," he stammered. "I'm not eighteen anymore, you know."

She slid behind him, kissing his shoulder. "No. *You* know what you're doing. Teenagers are only good for crude athletic events."

Donald turned around and handed her the half-filled glass. She took it, watching him pour another, and complimented him, "Thank you, my love. That was exquisite."

He held his glass up in a silent toast. "Indeed. And what else may I do for your pleasure this evening?"

She measured his gaze, while her heart rate continued to drum its feverish cadence. He looked ready. It was time to press him. "You can tell me when I get a seat on the board of directors."

Donald frowned. "Rebecca, let's not talk business. We came up here to get away from business."

"I thought we told everyone this was a business trip," she teased innocently.

He shook his head, humoring her. "So you figure you have to get in one or two agenda items to keep everything legal and aboveboard?"

She playfully looked at him with mock affront. "Of course. I wouldn't want anyone to accuse me of an ethics violation."

"You're insane." Donald laughed and sipped his champagne.

"Perhaps." Her voice dropped back to its seductive

whisper. "But I want you to answer my question. When do I get on the board? I have enough stock. Don't I?"

Donald shook his head, reluctantly resigned to address the issue. "You only have twelve percent, dear. You need at least twenty for a board nomination."

Rebecca stuck out a pouting lip. "Well, how much do you have?"

Donald hesitated before answering. "Thirty-nine percent."

A flash of energy ignited inside Rebecca. The plan would work. "All right," she conceded. "Enough of business. Let's talk about us."

Donald seemed relieved the business discussion was ended. "What about us?"

Rebecca looked slightly offended. "I mean, when are you going to make up your mind to make our relationship public and stop all this silly sneaking around. I hate it."

Donald set his glass down. "Rebecca, I'm a married man. You know that. I may be an infidel, but at least I'm a discreet infidel."

It was time to spring the trap. She gave him her best sigh of displeasure. "Well, what if I don't like the arrangement? I don't think it's right. It's not fair to me, nor your wife. We shouldn't have to share you."

"What are you suggesting?" Donald looked deeply into her eyes. "Do you want to terminate our relationship?"

She moved up next to him, deliberately rubbing her breasts against his chest. "Not at all. I think it would be to your advantage to decide who you would rather spend the rest of your years with. Alicia, with her petty jealousies and criticism; or me, an aggressive partner who knows what she wants and knows how to make it happen."

His expression grew skeptical. "And I'm what *you* want? Come now, Rebecca. This has all been quite entertaining. But you're suggesting a very serious move here."

"That's right," she agreed, her tone boldly asserting her refusal to be denied. "And you're what I want. I want you to choose, Donald. Think about it. You trade in your car when a superior model comes along. You're an intelligent man. You make hard decisions every day." She covered his lips with her finger as he was about to say something. "Don't answer now. Take some time. Just understand that you're what I want. If I'm what you want, then all you have to do is say so."

Donald took a deep breath, kissed her finger, then took her hand in his. "It's not quite that easy. I can't just leave Alicia."

Rebecca's tone was even, almost callous, "Why not? It happens every day in America." She took another sip of her champagne. "Think about it. We could build Secularian by day, and swim deeply into uncharted waters of passion every night. For the rest of your life."

An hour after they had emerged from the tub, showered, and dressed, Donald came over by the fireplace where Rebecca was sitting, and advised her that when they returned to Dallas he had decided to consult a lawyer. She made love to him again on the thick fur rug in front of the fireplace, reveling in the knowledge that very soon she would ultimately control fifty-one percent of Secularian's stock. Finally, it would all be hers.

28

July 1990

Dallas, Texas

THE BRILLIANT MULTICOLORED ARRAY OF HOT-AIR BALLOONS from the annual Plano balloon festival drifted over the treetops, heading west out of the rising sun. All shapes and sizes, round ones, traditional inverted teardrops, some resembling sausages and wristwatches, others defying description, almost a hundred in all, rose lazily into the early morning sky with each deep thrust of propane flames blasting up from the tiny gondolas secured below.

As the balloonists rose to an altitude of seven hundred feet, the panorama of the Texas plain was breathtaking. To the south, the civilized network of concrete, glass, and steel. To the east and west, endless fields of tree-lined suburbia. To the north, sprawling farmland. Yet the most striking sight capturing everyone's attention lay to the northeast, silhouetted by the morning sunlight reflecting off Lake Lavon. Situated on the lake's striking north shore could be seen a manicured golf course, aquamarine swimming pools, terraced bungalows, and a massive main complex. And even at this early hour, a long, white limousine made its way up the winding drive past the sculptured gardens to the entrance.

Phillip opened the door of the Mercedes limousine, allowing the uniformed doorman to escort Nicole Prescott into the entrance of the North Dallas Women's Center. Stephanie was on duty at the reception desk.

"Ms. Prescott." Stephanie beamed. "We're so glad you made it. We were expecting you last evening."

Nicole nodded. "I know. I got tied up in Boston and couldn't get out till early this morning."

Stephanie laughed. "Well, everything is ready for your pleasure. I'll notify Brett you're here. Welcome back to Dallas."

Nicole put her palm on the edge of the reception desk with a note of urgency. "Thank you, Stephanie. But first I need to see Rae and Marsha."

"They might still be on the tennis court, but I'd check Dr. Taylor's exercise suite first. They ought to be finished playing by now. You can usually find them there every morning between eight and nine getting their morning rubdowns after their game." Stephanie suddenly held up an interrupting finger and looked at her computer console. "Yes, this is the front desk. Right away, Ms. Halliran. I'm sure we can find him."

Nicole marched past the reception desk, through the great room, and down the administrative corridor to Rae's office.

"Hello?" Nicole called tentatively as she opened the door to Rae's private exercise room. The room was larger than her office. The vaulted ceiling and outside wall were made of smoked privacy glass, but enough of the sun filtered in to give it a warm, comfortable feeling of openness. Along the edge of the room stood various pieces of exercise equipment. Two long, leather-upholstered massage tables were positioned parallel in the center of the room.

As Nicole entered she observed Rae and Marsha in mid-conversation, receiving their morning rubdowns. The sight of the two nude women lying on their stomachs, being caressed and kneaded by two of the most exceptionally attractive young men at the center, made her decide to keep this conversation extremely brief. As usual, Keith was massaging Rae, and Rick was attending to Marsha.

Both women looked up as Nicole came in. Rae's face lit up joyfully. "Nikki! You made it."

"Hi." Nicole closed the door behind her. "I didn't think I was ever going to get out of Boston. I couldn't get out till five A.M. this morning."

Marsha propped herself up on her elbows. "Well, we're glad you're here. What's the latest?"

Nicole took a seat on one of the exercise benches. "Everything's proceeding as planned. I've hired a local stockbroker here in Dallas to handle the transaction, a senior arbitrage man named Malcolm Bodell. He understands everything that's expected, and my sources say he's supposed to be trustworthy."

Rae looked at Marsha. "What if he screws up?"

Marsha shook her head. "He can't without going to jail."

"That's right," Nicole added. "Women's Center stock will go public as soon as he releases the share notices."

"When will that be?" Rae asked with a moan as Keith's hands kneaded into her lower back.

Nicole watched the two athletic men work, increasing her desire to promptly finish this conversation and leave. Brett would be waiting for her in her suite. She deliberately looked Rae in the eye. "Probably not for several weeks. Marsha, you've still got to come through with the cash ratio. The prospectus will be suspect if you don't have a big enough kitty."

"Let me worry about that," Marsha admonished. "What about the advertising campaign?"

Nicole crossed her legs. It made her feel better. "I've hired a New York firm. They're good. They handle most of the Fortune one hundred. They say they'll put together a media blitz for the stock as well as detailed brochures for the medical treatments. It's all slated to be released by year's end. Some advance feelers will be placed in most of the business magazines, the *Wall Street Journal, Barron's,* and the other trade rags in a month or so."

Rae looked concerned. "Will that give us enough exposure before the stock offering?"

Nicole smiled as she stood. "Everyone who needs to see the ads will see them. Even if we have to resort to direct mailings. I can guarantee it. Don't worry."

"That's wonderful," Marsha commended, pulling her

dark red hair away from the back of her neck to accommodate Rick's swirling fingers. "You've done well, Nikki."

"Thank you." Nicole smiled with a gracious nod.

"Time to turn over," Keith politely whispered to Rae.

Rae rolled over on her back and looked affectionately into the warm eyes above her. "You know, you're getting really good at this. Brett taught you well."

Keith laughed. "But I'm still not as good as Brett. Right?" He folded his arms, awaiting her answer to continue.

"Oh, no." She grinned. "You're much better."

"Right answer." Keith lifted Rae's arm and began to massage her wrist and fingers.

Nicole was surprised to see Rae undressed; she hadn't in years. She never remembered her being so busty or well-toned back in college. But at the mention of Brett's name she rose and headed back toward the door. "If you'll excuse me, I've got a massage of my own waiting to loosen me up before my golf match."

Marsha gave her a cupped-hand wave. "So don't let us keep you another moment. Go enjoy."

Nicole winked as she opened the office door. "I intend to."

After the door closed, Marsha turned to Rae. "I like Nicole, Rae. I really do. She's an amazing woman."

Rae shook her head in amazement. "Yes she is. I worried about her after I left Boston. She had a bad marriage and an ugly divorce. And from what she tells me, after her divorce she did some pretty wild and crazy things trying to figure out what she wanted. I'm really glad she's with Brett. He's definitely helped settle her down." She grinned. "She seems so happy now. Couldn't you see it in her eyes?"

Marsha nodded. "It looks like Brett's tender charms have certainly been good for her."

Rae giggled. "Brett's *good* for anything that ails you." Her remark merited a chastising glare from Keith.

29

February 1979

Houston, Texas

THE NEW POSITION AT COLLINS ENTERPRISES TURNED WHAT RAE anticipated to be a very depressing holiday season into a most enjoyable experience. Marsha Collins sponsored no less than seven major social affairs from mid-December through New Year's Day, with Rae assisting her in every minute detail. Rae didn't mind spending her days doing more catering than business. At least it was fun. It put her in contact with many interesting people, places, and delightful events.

It was obvious from the first week Rae spent with Marsha Collins that Marsha had taken an instant liking to the reticent ex-biochemist. Objective number one on Marsha's agenda was to take Rae down to the Galleria and outfit her with a new wardrobe, at company expense, naturally. Spending a full day at Neiman Marcus and various boutiques was a mystifying experience for Rae, but one to which she readily acclimated. Marsha insisted that Rae "dress for success."

Over several extended luncheons, Marsha relentlessly hammered the concepts of self-image, positive appearance, and decisive confidence into Rae's head. Marsha even went so far as to take Rae to an optician, disposing once and for all of her heavy brown-framed glasses. Rae was fitted with a pair of tinted contact lenses which brightened her blue eyes all the more.

Rae didn't mind the homework either; it kept her mind

occupied, and that was refreshing in and of itself. For the first few weeks, Marsha directed Rae to read a veritable library of books, some of which she had authored herself, and Rae genuinely enjoyed them. They ranged from business keys to success, to personal development and growth. Some of the ideas they presented were completely foreign to her thinking, but most of what she read opened her mind to a marketplace where it was painfully obvious that only the strong and shrewd survived. Marsha was a survivor, and took great delight in playing mentor to her younger apprentice.

When the stately black Lincoln limousine arrived at Rae's apartment to pick her up early on Saturday morning, she was surprised to find the chauffeur's instructions were to take her to Shady Oaks County Club instead of the tall glass office building in Bellaire. Marsha had mentioned the day before that she wanted to start training Rae on sales strategy that weekend. This made no sense. Rae knew about Shady Oaks, but only from its longstanding reputation. Everyone in the greater Houston area knew it required some serious money, strong political clout, and usually intercession by the Pope to even be seen by the membership committee. Acceptance by the committee was an even greater feat, accomplished by only a handful in recent years. Marsha Collins was a member.

When the limo stopped in front of the sculptured archway leading into the clubhouse, it was met by a smiling, uniformed doorman. Rae liked that. It made her feel more than welcome; she felt special. With a breath of eager anticipation, she entered the august facility to find her wise master of the affluent arts. A friendly receptionist confirmed her guest status on a clipboard and directed an escort to take Dr. Taylor to the ladies' facility.

The country club had common facilities for men and women, including the golf course, health club, and racquet courts. But there were also segregated wings for specialized beauty treatment, massages, dressing and shower rooms, lockers, saunas, steambaths, and tanning spas. It was incredible. Rae tried not to gape at the lavish surroundings as she followed the escort to the beauty salon on the second floor.

"Rae, there you are," came Marsha's uplifting voice, but Rae didn't see her.

Several women seated in salon chairs were being fussed over by multiple attendants, some styling hair, some doing nails, some feet, others faces. Rae finally realized that one of the women lying back in a salon chair, draped with a satin wrap, her hair wrapped tightly in a towel, her face completely covered with jade facial mud, was Marsha.

"Is that you under there?" Rae asked with a grin.

"Yes, dear, and you will be too in a moment." Marsha tried not to smile and crack the mask.

Rae felt a jolt of excitement run through her. She had read about this kind of thing in fashion magazines, but never dreamed of experiencing it herself in her lifetime. She walked over next to Marsha. "I thought we were going to discuss sales strategies today."

"We are," Marsha agreed. "But we're going to enjoy ourselves while we do. Besides, there's some unique training you require that you can only receive here."

Rae gave Marsha a puzzled look. "What kind of training?"

"You'll find out." Marsha displayed a great deal of satisfaction in her elliptical answer.

Rae looked up as a young lady in a pastel-blue smock approached her. "Miss, will you please come with me?"

Rae followed the young lady to a dressing area where she was instructed to disrobe and put on a royal-blue satin robe hanging in the dressing cubicle. She closed the louvered door and complied, feeling more like she was at her gynecologist's office than a beauty shop. When she emerged, the young lady was waiting for her. She took Rae's clothes and advised her they would be placed in safe keeping and returned to her later. Another attendant appeared unexpectedly and brought Rae back into the main salon area. The attendant was a handsome young man who instructed her to sit in a reclining salon chair. He covered her with a cloth similar to the one covering Marsha and tilted her chair back until her neck rested in the recessed edge of the sink basin behind her. She heard the sudden rush of water blasting out of a flexible hose as the attendant adjusted the temperature.

"Is the water temperature to your liking?" he asked politely.

Rae smiled up at him. "It's fine." This was wonderful. Rae couldn't ever remember being pampered like this in her life. The young man proceeded to wash her straight brown hair, massaging her scalp with the thick foamy lather. His fingers worked down the back of her neck, relaxing her to the point where she started to fall asleep.

"You may sit up now," the young man advised.

Rae was startled. "Oh, yes, thank you." She blushed as she sat up, letting the young man wrap her head with a towel.

"Henri"—which he pronounced On-*ree*—"Will be with you in a moment." The young man bowed politely and disappeared.

Rae looked over at Marsha. "This is exquisite," she said.

"Isn't it?" Marsha sat up and looked at Rae. "Get used to it."

A few minutes later an effeminate-looking man with a long ponytail emerged from a back room and went to work on Rae's hair. He gave her a deluxe perm, producing a veritable cascading fountain of beautiful curls, which totally transformed her appearance. But that was only the beginning. Marsha treated Rae to a facial, a manicure, a pedicure, and finally, hours later, escorted her to the massage center.

As they walked through the door with their wraps clung about them, Marsha asked, "Rae, have you ever had a full body massage?"

Rae trembled at the sound of that. "No." She hesitated at the door. "What exactly do you mean by 'full body'?"

Marsha laughed. "Something that you'll learn to enjoy in

no time whatsoever. Come along. And don't be shy. I'm counting on you."

Rae obediently followed Marsha into a reception area where they were met by another smiling attendant, a young woman with long blond hair. "You're right on time, Ms. Collins. Right this way."

The attendant took the women down a long hall, through a heavy privacy door, to a spacious room with a wide skylight filled with plants along its edge. Four long tables stood regimented in two rows and two columns near the center of the room. From an archway in the back, two young men emerged dressed in white trousers and white collared sport shirts. Rae thought they looked like ambulance attendants.

"Enjoy yourselves," the blond attendant commented with a nod as she turned and left, closing the heavy door behind her.

"Ms. Collins?" One of the masseurs held out his hand to Marsha.

Rae was a little embarrassed when she saw Marsha nonchalantly remove her robe and lie facedown, completely nude, on one of the tables near her. The other young man walked up to her and held out his hand. Rae just stood there for several seconds, not knowing what to do. The thought of standing naked in front of two men she didn't know and a woman she only knew briefly was out of the question.

Marsha looked up at her. "What's the matter, Rae?"

Rae looked around, then back. "Marsha, I don't know about this."

Marsha looked at the young man next to Rae. "It's all right. It's her first time. Be gentle with her."

Rae looked into the piercing blue eyes of the young man and gave him a half laugh. She read his name embroidered in royal-blue cursive script on his shirt. It said *Brett*.

Brett smiled at her, his voice calm and reassuring. "It's all right, miss. Just think of it like a medical treatment. We're professionals. Everyone is a bit shy at first."

"Oh, for Pete's sake, Rae. You're a doctor," Marsha said in a chastising tone. "Lie down and have a good time. He's not going to hurt you. And I can assure you, everyone in this room has seen a woman unclothed."

Rae didn't want to disappoint Marsha. She reluctantly turned around with her back to Marsha and Marsha's masseur and allowed Brett to remove her robe. She quickly laid down on the table on her stomach to modestly cover the majority of her vital interests. When Brett's hands touched her shoulder, she was surprised to feel how warm and strong they were. In a matter of seconds they were moving in delicate circles up and down her spine, warmly causing every muscle to relax in their path.

Marsha called over to her, "Isn't that nice?"

Rae had to agree, despite her misgivings. "Yes, definitely."

"A little lower, Rick," Marsha instructed her masseur, then turned her attention back to Rae. "Rae, tell me something honestly."

"All right." Rae looked over at Marsha while she relished the skilled touches coursing up and down her legs.

"How did you feel today coming here?" Marsha folded her arms under her cheek.

Rae beamed. "It's wonderful!"

"And I suppose you realize that most women won't ever get the opportunity to enjoy the special comforts and benefits you've seen today. Right?" Marsha was leading up to something. Rae could tell.

Rae nodded. "Right."

"Well, today I've decided to let you in on part of my secret to success." Marsha's eyes were widening with excitement.

Rae could feel the energy herself. "I take it that this is something not covered in any of your books?"

Marsha laughed. "Hardly. But some of my theories were certainly derived from what I've experienced in practice. You see, Rae, what I discovered as I began to build my fortune in real estate is that you can't be a generalist. If you try to please everyone, you end up pleasing no one."

Rae stared with eager interest, still intimately aware of Brett's stimulating touch.

Marsha continued amid pleasurable moans each time Rick hit a spot she especially liked. "You have to specialize to some extent. You need to identify a target market that you can address in a focused manner, superior to all the competition. Does that make sense?"

Rae nodded.

"Good." Marsha went on, "Now tell me this. Does it necessarily take any more or less time to sell a fifty-thousand-dollar house as it does a five-hundred-thousand-dollar house?"

Rae shrugged. "Technically, no. But there aren't as many people out there buying half-million-dollar homes."

"That's where you're wrong." Marsha was on a roll. "They're there. The problem is the average middle-class housewife out there supplementing her husband's meager income hustling real estate doesn't know how to find them. She doesn't move in their circles, know their needs."

Rae was intrigued. "And you do."

"Naturally." Marsha looked matter-of-fact. "Rae, when you're paid on a fixed-commission percentage, it's more beneficial to sell big-ticket items than it is to sell nickel-dime. That's obvious. The key, as you made general reference to a moment ago, is to maintain a high increment of sale. That's the goal."

Brett's fingers firmly probed into her shoulder blades, slurring Rae's words, "So your niche is the rich and famous?"

Marsha smiled. "Close. Actually, it's more specific than merely the rich and famous. I specialize primarily in wealthy women. Women of substantial means, who can naturally afford the big-ticket sales. Primarily, I look for strongly independent women, most of them single by choice or circumstance. Some married, but to husbands obsessed with career or other women. I understand their needs. What I look for, *specifically,* are women with a great deal of money, a sense of their own destiny, and little time for serious love interests. That's how I qualify an account."

Rae was confused. "Why?"

Marsha hesitated before answering. "Think about it, Rae. If you were a rich powerful woman with little opportunity to meet men or carry on an active social life; or if you were a widow, past the flower of your youth; or a divorcée unacquainted with the protocol of social circulation—what common denominator, what specific need, would you think is of special concern to such women?"

Rae blushed. "You mean sex?"

Both of the masseurs laughed, making Rae blush even more.

Marsha joined them. "It's a tried and true strategy that Madison Avenue has employed for decades. Sex sells. Trust me."

Rae was slightly repulsed. For some reason the image of Rebecca Danforth came to mind, spreading her legs for everything she ever got. "I don't like that, Marsha. It sounds degrading."

Marsha propped her head up with one hand. "I'm not talking about having to compromise yourself for advancement. That's the way a man thinks. I'm talking about meeting a woman's needs in a way she finds both desirable and well-suited for her lifestyle. In return, she buys my product. Is there anything degrading in that?"

Rae shook her head in disbelief. This was too much to grasp. "So what do you do to make this happen?"

"Various things." Marsha laid her head back down. "For example, some women like personal valets, masseurs, chauffeurs, or gardeners. If a house has a pool, the pool man comes at least once or twice a week. You just have to use your imagination. And you'd be surprised at how eager some of these ladies are to sign a contract, at the asking price, when you inform them that the sales price includes one year of personal valet service from the man who has just finished massaging her, here at Shady Oaks, of course."

Rae gasped. "You work from here?"

Marsha nodded. "Almost always. I'm sure you'll agree it's much more comfortable than an austere office environment."

"And this works?" Rae was incredulous.

"Rae, I have amassed over fifty million dollars in cash and liquid securities in less than ten years." She wasn't boasting, just stating facts. "You tell me."

Rae swallowed with difficulty. "I don't know, Marsha. It all sounds so bizarre. I can't envision how all these women you talk about can just treat their sex lives so casually. I don't think I could ever sleep with a man I wasn't in love with." Her thoughts painfully paged back to the memory of David Stratton and a tender Christmas Eve.

"That's your decision, Rae, of course," Marsha quickly agreed. "It's every woman's prerogative to do as she pleases when it comes to her sexuality. But remember. Your body belongs to you. You use it as *you* see fit. It's your property, no one else's. As you grow older, your attitudes may change. Perhaps a lot sooner than you think."

Rae shrugged. "Perhaps."

Brett patted Rae on the rear. "It's time to turn over."

A wave of alarm went through her. She looked over her shoulder as her heart began to pound. "I beg your pardon?"

Brett gave her a warm, disarming smile. "Come on. It's the best part. You'll love it."

Rae looked back to Marsha, who just wiggled her eyebrows, then discreetly turned her head toward the far wall. Rae looked timidly back to Brett without moving.

"Hang on a second." He went over to the wall and pulled a tall three-sectioned teakwood dressing screen with gossamer panels between the two massage tables and unfolded it. The screen provided a modest amount of privacy between the two tables. His deep blue eyes calmly looked into hers. "There. Better?"

After a moment of indecision, still afraid of offending Marsha, Rae hesitantly turned over, hoping the handsome young man didn't burst into laughter or say something rude. He didn't. He continued to look into her eyes with a caring she hadn't seen in a very long time.

His hands lifted her arms one at a time, placing her hand against his smooth cheek, and worked each muscle with the virtuoso precision of a harpist. She closed her eyes as the warm fingers and palms worked over her shoulders, down her sides, over her legs and hips. She was almost completely relaxed when she involuntarily gasped as his hands warmly cupped her near-nonexistent breasts. Her eyes came open, but she relaxed again when she saw his expression, Brett passively going about his task with no sense of alarm or undue concern.

He looked down at her with a warm smile. "Do you like that?"

She nodded before her mind could stop her.

"Good." He smiled. "I'll stop if it bothers you."

Again her head was involuntarily shaking from side to side. "Don't stop." She couldn't believe those words came out of her mouth. Yet with each touch, each caress, inhibition after inhibition melted away.

His hands continued to knead her chest, slide down her stomach, and burrow into her thighs. Her eyes drifted shut again as she felt him part her knees slightly and caress her inner thighs. She became aware of a slight wetness between her legs. Something inside her suddenly wanted him to touch her. When his finger absently came in contact with the edge of her pubic hair, the momentary tickle it elicited rippled up and down her spine, involuntarily stimulating her back into a gentle arch.

From the other side of the screen Marsha's voice cut through the dreamlike trance into which Rae had fallen. "So Rae, if I told you that Brett came with the house you were going to buy from me, would you sign a contract here and now?"

Again Rae's mouth spoke of its own accord. "In a heartbeat."

The two young men chuckled. Marsha giggled. "I thought so."

A few minutes later Brett leaned down and whispered in her ear, "Dr. Taylor, if you have no objection, I'd really like to see you later this evening. You don't have to accept. It's not part of the Shady Oaks service or anything."

Rae's heart began to pound. She looked into his sincere eyes and whispered back to him, "Is Marsha paying you to do that?"

"No," he answered emphatically. "She paid me for the massage, and told me it was all right to ask you out if I wanted to. And I want to—if that's all right with you."

Rae was simultaneously flabbergasted and extremely flattered. She hadn't been on a date in years—not since David. And lying there stark naked before the man who had just spent the last fifteen minutes touching virtually every square inch of her body made the situation somewhat awkward, to say the least. A strange courage appeared within her. She smiled at the handsome young man, keeping her voice hushed. "There's not much more of me to see."

"Yes there is." His eyes already answered her next question.

Many hours later, as she lay in her own bed beneath a man she had only met that very day, Rae's perspective on her own sexuality had radically altered. It felt good to be told she was beautiful. And it was true, she was beautiful. She felt beautiful. It felt so good to be treated like a queen and pampered. It felt good to be held and caressed. She never wanted it to stop. So much of the darkness of the last three years faded around her in a single day as she explored the mysterious and sensual world of Marsha Collins. Her legs started to tremble again. It was about to happen for the fifth time in the long, exotic hour Brett had been tenderly making love to her.

She could feel the sensation swelling and building within her. It was *nothing* like her elementary experiences with David Stratton. Brett was so patient and steady, sensitive to what pleased her, and aroused her to each delicious peak. Her hands delighted to explore each taut sinew and muscle of his firm body, drawing him into her with a hunger she never knew was there. As the sexual tension rose within her, her breathing became heavier, labored, frantic. Brett sensed it and quickened the pace of his rigorous penetration, moving his hands beneath her, increasing the direct pressure and intensifying her pleasure.

After Rae convulsed into the heat of her fifth violent climax, her body wringing with perspiration, her new curls matted against her forehead. She threw her head back against her pillow, gasping for air, her vision blurred, her head spinning. "Brett." Another dizzying gasp of air. "I can't go on anymore," she lied, amid two more desperate pants. "I'm about to die."

He laughed. "No you're not." Then he sensuously whispered in her ear, "We've just barely started. We've the whole night ahead of us."

She laughed in exhaustion. "My God, how can you keep doing this? I'm getting sore."

"All right," he conceded, laying his head on her shoulder, nuzzling her neck with his lips. "Just relax."

After a few more moments of gentle lovemaking, Rae felt his entire body tighten; a few seconds later she felt the warm sensation of his consummation.

Brett stayed the night and made love to her three more times. Rae didn't have the strength to go to work in the morning. She told Brett she'd call Marsha and explain what happened sometime next week when she finally made it out of bed. That made Brett laugh. Still dozing, she heard him shower and dress. Her head was still in a daze. She didn't think nights like that existed—but now knew she wanted more of them.

Before he left, Brett kissed her tenderly once again and told her, "I'd like to see you again, if that's all right."

Rae felt a little surprised. How could anyone make love like this man and think that it was just an incidental interlude? She was tempted to lock him up and never let him leave the house. This one was definitely worth keeping—at least for the time being. Her mind began to fantasize. Were there others out there like Brett, as exciting, or as passionate?

"Certainly." Rae smiled at him through tired, glassy eyes. She giggled. "I could always use another massage."

Brett rose from the edge of the bed and walked to her bedroom door. "It would be my pleasure. I'll drop by tonight and bring my hot-oil machine. It's different. But I think you'll like it."

30

December 1987

Catalina Island, California

THE WAVES CARESSED THE STONY SHORE WITH EACH PULSATING rush of the sea's energy. The sun had almost slipped beyond the horizon, casting its dull red pall between the dark blue hues of the Pacific and the gently fading light of the cloudless evening sky. Gulls winged overhead with random shrieks, waiting for the night feast on the waters. The air was sweetly cool and wet; a gentle breeze whispered in off the waves, its salty fragrance renewed with each crash of the surf. Sabrina stood at the redwood rail of the cantilevered deck of her private villa, admiring the quiet splendor of the sea. As she beheld the hypnotic undulation of the waves, letting the refreshing rush of the wind blowing in off the water course through her long blond hair, she pondered again the living death that had become her existence.

Eighteen months had passed since she left the Los Angeles County Crisis Center. The doctors had been right about her body. Only a trained eye could detect the hairline scars on her arms, legs, and torso. But her face was altogether a different matter. When the bandages first came off, she had actually vomited at the sight of her own reflection. In an almost perfect oval, tracing the outline of what had been the opening in her fire hood, were dark red and black scars, hideous beyond anything she could have imagined. The skin actually appeared to be permanently bubbled and torn. Skin graft after skin graft refused to adhere to the tissues, leaving weeping lesions that took weeks to heal, producing even more scars.

Sabrina tried to be strong, teasing the doctors by calling herself the "Phantom of the Racetrack." She adapted the moniker from the black harlequin-styled mask she used to cover her injuries. The doctors were kind enough to treat her like any other patient. But she never failed to notice the instantaneous look of shock displayed by each physician on his initial observation. Everyone reacted that way. She didn't blame them. She felt that way herself.

For almost eighteen months now Sabrina lived in the four-bedroom villa she had purchased on Catalina in self-imposed exile from humanity. Two female servants attended to her every need, and visitors were not welcome. She had tried to go out in public once or twice, but the mask she wore drew as many stares as her scars, minus the repulsion, naturally. For a year and a half she had never held a steering wheel in her hand, or felt the touch of a man.

The notion of suicide was never far from her thoughts, but something inside her would never let her seriously entertain it. She didn't know if it was her champion's spirit to survive, or just cowardice of death. In any case she resolved to pass her days in mute resignation to her fate, bearing a pain in her soul which even the regular consumption of a case of vodka a month couldn't diminish.

Just offshore a speedboat roared by, pulling two skiers dressed in wet suits. The driver of the boat waved at her. Sabrina had no desire to see people enjoying life. She turned around, swallowed the warm remains of her vodka, walked back inside the house and turned on her stereo. The gentle strains of a classical pianist filled the room.

After her accident Sabrina threw out all of her rock and roll albums, from Boy George, to George Michael, to Michael Jackson. The spirited music reminded her too much of what it was like to live with people who were still alive. She resigned herself to another age, another era, where music was sensitive and soothing, passionate and abstract. In fact, she had developed a sincere appreciation for classical orchestras, symphonies, and the works of the great composers. Her favorite performing artist was a pianist from Czechoslovakia named Emelia Travain. On the back of her favorite album, *Emelia: Live at Carnegie Hall*, it had printed her real last name. It had more letters in it than a food preservative. She was wise to choose a stage name, Sabrina thought.

And in eighteen months Roger Marks had never called once. He sent a few light, chatty letters the first few months, briefly advising her of his Grand Prix wins in Europe, but contained nothing about how he felt about her or when he might come to see her. And then the letters stopped. It didn't make any sense, but then in a twisted way it did. He, of all people, should have understood. He knew firsthand how she felt. Yet until the accident, she never really knew what it felt like to value yourself less than what you were—to have that sick, helpless feeling of hopelessness and worthlessness hanging around your neck day and night, choking the life out, day after day. But there was a difference between them, a difference she couldn't overlook.

She had been willing to face *his* tragedy and help him regain his confidence and self-esteem. Roger Marks was unwilling to reciprocate. Or worse, he ran away from her, looking on her now as the symbol of everything he once hated about himself. She had many other speculations. And all of them hurt—sometimes more than she felt she could bear.

"Signora," came the voice of Gabriella, one of her servants.

Sabrina turned and looked at the portly maid with her hands folded. "Yes?"

"Dr. Burton is on the telephone again." Gabriella gestured politely toward the kitchen.

Sabrina turned back toward the stereo. "Tell him I'm asleep." She held out her empty glass. "And get me another drink."

31

November 1980

Boston, Massachusetts

THE AFTERNOON SUN OVER CAPE COD RAISED THE AIR TEMPERAture inside the greenhouse to just over eighty degrees, although outside the November breeze gusting in over Wellfleet Harbor was in the low sixties. The twenty-by-fifty-foot greenhouse was filled with all of Nicole's favorite plants: ferns of every description, gloxinias, ivies, philodendrons, ficus, rubber trees, elephant ears, wooded avocadoes, and a colorful array of flowers of every sort, all in bloom. The fresh fragrances mixed to produce an intoxicating atmosphere of life and growth. Green leaves and budding blooms completely camouflaged each and every table and shelf lining the glass room—with the exception of the long wooden worktable in the center, where Nicole lay looking up at the fogged panes of glass overhead while her lover stood at the foot of the table, rocking against her.

The heat of the room had been too sweet to resist. Nicole's latest boyfriend, Brian Hughes, a stockbroker from Manhattan, had been suggesting ideas of how to decorate her new Cape Cod estate, a steal at only two million. The sultry warmth of the room had inspired her to pull her blouse off and boldly invite him to take her in the open air and sunshine. Brian's lips were busy tasting her creamy flesh in the next instant, and she relished the feel of her nipples inside his mouth. He eagerly nursed them like an infant, which she had earlier told him drove her wild. Moments later she had discarded the rest of her clothes in a pile and fell back across the hard surface of the worktable, pulling him to her, impatiently opening his belt and zipper.

Brian had dropped his pants to his knees and spread his legs enough to maneuver himself to the proper height to enter her. Nicole felt no resistance when he plunged inside, only the honeyed movement, probing deeper and deeper within. When his hands took hold of her ankles and lifted, she accommodated by extending her long legs upward toward the sun, knees slightly bent, resting her heels on his shoulders. The table squeaked and creaked with each of her lover's forceful pelvic thrusts. Nicole licked her lips, running her fingers up through her hair as the heat between her legs kindled.

Her eyes popped open as a totally new sensation imminently threatened to mercilessly throw her over the precipice of orgasm—she sensed the moist recess of his mouth, tongue, and lips closing over her toes, one at a time, sucking on them individually, tickling the tender crevasses between them with the flicking tip of his tongue. Concurrently, his hands massaged her heels, ankles, knees, thighs, and hips. The explosion was about to happen at any second.

She felt him part her legs again and wrap them around him as he leaned over, weighing her breasts in his hands, momentarily pausing his rhythmic penetration to taste the twin peaks again. Her fingers laced behind his neck, pulling him down as she arched her back, lifting her breast into his nursing lips—the sensation was incredible. Her mouth was going dry. She made an effort to try and keep her gaping mouth closed and breathe through her nose before she started choking.

After each breast had been given individual attention for

several delicious minutes, Nicole felt Brian sliding away. To her momentary dismay, the welcome firmness inside her faded, but was soon replaced by the savory intrusion of his darting tongue. A glance down her body confirmed he had knelt down on the soft earth covering the floor of the greenhouse. She loved that—as much if not more than anything else. The sweet throbbing was starting again, and he was teasingly curling his tongue against the right spot, just like he was supposed to, plunging inside for a moment, then retreating to where it pleased most. The sky above was starting to blur. Bolts of erotic energy radiated spasms of raw carnal power through every cell of her body, swelling in intensity, building in force. Her lungs' frenzy for oxygen announced the impending resolution of her desire. It was a matter of seconds now, perhaps less. With the snap of Brian's neck, his tongue pierced deeply inside her seven times in rapid succession. It had started by the third.

Some faint voice in the background of her mind warned her his skull might be instantly crushed between the viselike grip of her thighs, but she didn't care. All that mattered in the orgasmic rush was to hang on and ride it to the end. Her body was doing all the work now by itself, her heart pumping torrents of blood to the sensuously throbbing tissues within her in exchange for waves and waves of the soul-enslaving pleasure.

And then came the lull, the eye of the storm, the gentle quietness that follows such frenzied exertion. Brian stood back up and reentered her. Nicole winced slightly as he pressed his way in, her tender flesh now highly sensitized. In a few seconds the rhythmic pushing was welcome again. She felt the hot intrusion of his climax a few minutes later, in the languid wake of her own blissful fatigue.

An hour later, sitting in her sunken conversation pit with a glass of brandy in her hand, dressed in a full-length, white terry-cloth robe, Nicole raised a toast. "Here's to another verdict for the good guys!"

Brian joined her in the pit, still wearing only a towel from their intimate shower together. "What did you win?"

"Conservation International versus Petron Chemical." Nicole set her glass down on the edge of the circular coffee table in the center of the conversation pit. "Four point three million in favor of the environmentalists, escrowed for a three-year cleanup campaign."

Brian looked impressed. "Wow. What did they do?"

Nicole smirked. "Just dumped a few million gallons of toxic shit in Boston Harbor, impacting local drinking water." She sipped her brandy. "So it wasn't just the ducks and the fish we were fighting for."

Brian smiled and moved closer to Nicole, sitting on her right, playfully reaching inside her terry-cloth robe and cupping her left breast in his right hand, gently massaging her nipple with his thumb. He kept looking her in the eye as though nothing was going on. "So I guess that makes you a pretty hot property right now at the firm."

She smiled, trying to pretend what he was doing didn't feel as good as it did. "Hot enough to offer me a full partnership."

Nicole watched Brian push back the thick white cloth of her robe, lean over and kiss the erect bud he had aroused. "That's great." He licked it with the tip of his tongue. "Seems like every time you win, your free agent status goes up." His lips closed over it fully, his tongue slowly encircling the sensitized spot inside his mouth.

Nicole felt the wet tug in her thighs again. She did her best to maintain her concentration. "So are you going to stay in New York?"

"Umm-hmm," he affirmed, without interrupting his treat.

Nicole was disappointed. Brian seemed like a genuinely nice guy; and they were rare. With the endless string of losers who had crossed her path over the last three years, the idea of finding someone who had a little sensitivity and care for her needs was refreshing. While it was true that her suitors had progressively come from higher and higher stratas of the social scale, the lot of them were primarily interested in a relationship consisting of a few minutes of lifeless humping—and no strings, little conversation, and low priority.

Nicole wanted much more than that; she felt she deserved more than that. Brian seemed to be what she was looking for; but he had a thriving business in New York, and didn't see the necessity of allowing his relationship with her to interfere with it. She saw him once or twice a month at most, whenever she could coax him to catch the Eastern Airlines' shuttle and make the forty-minute flight to Boston. That little voice inside told her, though he was definitely a cut above the rest, he was just a temporary, like them all.

Brian kissed the middle of her chest and sat up. "Nikki, you know what you should do?"

"What?" She was feeling depressed.

"I think you should run for office." He was excited. "You know, Congress, maybe even the Senate."

She huffed, "You're crazy. I don't have any desire to get tangled up in politics." But inside, she was glowing in the light of the compliment.

"I don't know," he observed. "Some of those senators have some pretty decent perks. Besides, I think you'd like it."

"Right." She smiled politely, filing that notion under ideas for a rainy day. It was a silly notion, but a caring notion. *That* mattered. "Next subject?"

Brian pulled his towel off and tossed it on the glass-topped coffee table. Nicole glanced down at his firm erection, taking that as a compliment too. She shivered when he seductively ran his fingers through her hair and massaged the back of her neck.

"See anything you want?" he asked.

She gave him a coy grin, her momentary depression quickly eclipsed by a fresh libidinal urge from within, and the small voice inside reassuring her it was better to enjoy what you have—while you have it. She heard him gasp as she leaned down and closed her lips over the torrid length of flesh.

32

September 1979

Houston, Texas

THE ENCHANTING RESONANCE OF THE LONDON SYMPHONY ORchestra's rendition of the first movement of the William Tell Overture filtered down through the chlorine-spiced air above the Olympic-sized indoor pool at Shady Oaks. Rae stopped at the end of her lap, pensively looking through the broad plate-glass window overlooking the putting green on the grassy terrace. She liked the look of the terrace. It had a certain majesty to it. Several golfers, most of them elderly men, tapped their shots into the small metal recesses as they awaited their tee times.

Marsha Collins swam up beside her. "Are you ready for lunch?" she asked, wiping the water from her eyes.

Rae turned to her. "Yes, I'm famished."

The two women emerged from the sparkling water, dried themselves with heavy towels provided by the club, and took a seat beneath one of the straw and bamboo cabanas on the wide stone patio, just outside the pool area. Marsha summoned an attendant and directed him to prepare their meal to be served outside. With towels wrapped over their wet suits, they lethargically reclined in the eighty-five-degree fall weather around a low glass table, sipping chilled wine, and snacking on imported cheeses and sliced fruit.

"I'm very proud of you, Rae." Marsha meant that. She was genuinely amazed at how fast Rae had progressed in less than a year. Actually, in just under eight months Rae had developed an entire subsidiary real estate brokerage under

Collins Enterprises and was becoming quite wealthy—not to mention contributing favorably to Marsha's bottom line. "You've exceeded my expectations a hundredfold."

Rae nodded once. "Thank you. I've had a good teacher."

Marsha laughed, her voice singsong, but chiding, "Ah, but you're holding out on me." She shook a chastising finger in jest. "You've added a few twists to the techniques that I never thought of. Come on, admit it."

Rae blushed. "Well, not really twists. I try to think of it more as . . . quality of merchandise."

"That sounds clever." Marsha was intrigued. "Explain."

Rae popped a seedless red grape in her mouth, squeezing the last remnant of water from her damp curls, letting it drip on the multicolored Fiesta Stone beside her chair. "Well, having spent most of my life in academic circles, I realized that your technique could be used to solve more than one problem simultaneously, taking advantage of more than one pool of felt needs. Two birds with one stone, you might say? It concerns . . . how do I say it . . . recruitment."

Marsha brightened. "Ah, you found a plentiful supply of young men?"

"Not just quantity." Rae's eyes narrowed. "But quality. *Motivated* quality."

"Tell." Marsha was getting excited again.

Rae swallowed another grape and took a sip of wine. "Okay, it's like this. Rather than hiring professional masseurs, gardeners, handymen, like we've done in the past, I went to the local universities and shopped around at the frat houses, sports clubs, that sort of thing."

"Oooh," Marsha cooed, a delightful shiver going up her spine. "Young, firm ones."

"Young, firm, and *poor* ones," Rae appended. "I was surprised to discover what some young men will do to earn their degrees."

Marsha was surprised. "Well, what do you tell them? I don't expect you just come right out and tell them the truth."

"Yes, I do," Rae stated flatly. "I make them a simple business proposition. And they like that. It's direct, and it's honest. The deal is, they can get all their educational expenses paid for, plus in many cases room and board. Term of employment is until graduation. In return, they merely have to take care of my clients. I don't have to explain that. If the position is mutually acceptable to client and employee, they are free to make longer-term arrangements after graduation of their own accord. They understand. It's a simple system. Very little additional explanation is necessary."

"That's amazing," Marsha commented. "That was always the most difficult part for me, the recruiting, that is. I always depended on word of mouth, friends, that sort of thing." She frowned. "What happens if you get a dud? Sinewy, well-tanned beauty isn't the only criteria."

Rae gave Marsha a surreptitious glance with one eyebrow cocked. "That can't happen. I'm in charge of quality control."

Marsha's mouth went agape as she burst into wide-eyed laughter. "Rae Taylor, you're terrible! A genius, but terrible!"

Rae gave Marsha a mock stare of gravity. "Ms. Collins, it was *you* who wrote that your job should be your pleasure, not your burden. I believe that. Even if it's not doing exactly what you thought you'd be doing."

Marsha composed herself. "I'm jealous. And you know the minute we leave here, I'm going to steal your idea."

Rae's face clouded.

Marsha saw it, and instantly realized her blunder, her face going red with embarrassment. She reached out for Rae's arm. "I'm sorry, that's not what I meant. That was a stupid thing to say . . . I wasn't thinking."

Rae smiled, refusing to let her mind conjure up the image of the dark-haired bitch. "It's okay. I know what you meant, and I *want* you to use the idea. It works well. Perhaps we can find a way to use it together."

The instantaneous tension in the air eased back to a comfortable level. Marsha was relieved. "Thank you, Rae. So tell me more about your college men."

Rae brightened, the dark memory of Rebecca now pushed out of her mind. "There *is* one more thing I didn't mention. Like I said, it has to do with product quality. I have each of the young men enroll in a six-week training program."

Marsha looked at Rae with unabashed wonder. "A training program?"

"Yes, it's something new I just put in place a couple of months back." Rae poured herself another glass of wine from the carafe on the table. "I hired Brett away from the club here to give masseur lessons to all my trainees. That's fundamental number one. Plus he also gives a few weekly academic 'how-to' type of classes on how to *properly* treat a lady. And believe me, he's qualified to teach."

Marsha leveled a searching gaze at Rae. "So how *are* you and Brett getting along? Aren't you still seeing him?"

Rae shrugged. "Not really." She quickly added, in light of Marsha's look of surprise, "I like Brett a lot. He's a good friend."

"A good *friend?*" Marsha looked skeptical. "That's *all?*"

Rae batted at the air, admitting, "It's not like you think."

"What do I think?" Marsha probed.

Rae's eyes softened. "Brett's very special to me. I can't deny that. He's probably the most tender and gentle man I've ever met. He helped me discover a special part of myself I didn't know was there. And I'll always be thankful to him for that." She rolled her eyes. "Yes, it's true, at first I really thought *this* was the guy I wanted to hang on to for a long time. And I'm sure you remember how much time we spent together last spring. But after a while, I guess we both knew that the chemistry just wasn't right."

"Chemistry?" Marsha's skepticism was even more pronounced.

"That's right," Rae insisted. "It wasn't anything tragic. We're just good friends. *Very* good friends. That's all. When I finally meet someone I really want to have a long-term relationship with, I'll know. But for now, I'm having fun and enjoying my prospects. And Brett seems to really enjoy teaching. It's just one of his *other* talents." She laughed. "It isn't hard to get the trainees to show up for his lectures."

"So Brett's teaching is the extent of your training program?" Marsha picked up another slice of Gouda cheese and delicately bit into it.

Rae dropped her voice to a confidential whisper and she covertly glanced around the cabana. "No. Just between you and me, I supervise all the lab work."

Marsha started to choke on the piece of cheese, her face turning bright red. Rae covered her mouth with her fist, laughing at her mentor's plight.

"Marsha! Marsha Collins!" called a voice from across the patio.

Rae looked toward the main building and saw an older woman with short black hair and wire-rimmed glasses approaching, waving enthusiastically.

Marsha did her best to collect herself and swallow her bite with a sip of wine. She looked at Rae and whispered, "Here comes someone I want you to meet. We'll finish this conversation later. Count on it."

The other woman cheerfully walked up as Marsha rose to greet her with a friendly hug. "Alicia, you look lovely today. Come sit down and join us for a little refreshment." Marsha turned to Rae. "Rae, I'd like you to meet my doctor. This is Dr. Alicia Bennet."

"Brighton," Alicia corrected stoically, pushing her bifocals up on her nose.

Marsha gave Alicia a puzzled look.

Alicia held up her bare left hand. "I'm a single lady again."

Rae could tell by the woman's awkward tone she was doing her best to sound pleasant about something very painful. Rae graciously extended her hand, easing the moment. "Pleased to meet you, Alicia."

Alicia gratefully accepted Rae's hand and joined the two ladies at their table.

Marsha's face was still grave, "I'm so sorry. What happened between you and Donald? Is this recent?"

Alicia looked flustered. "Oh, my divorce has only been final for about two months now. It was just one of those things, I guess. Apparently Donald finally hit his mid-life crisis and became enamored by the affections of one of his employees and decided to 'pursue other interests,' as they say in the business world. But I'm fine, Marsha. Really."

Neither Rae nor Marsha believed that. Marsha looked repulsed. "That bastard! After you relocated your practice to Texas? After you gave up all your clients?" Abruptly, Marsha looked at Rae, aware of the need to lighten the moment. "I'm sorry, Rae. You see, I've known Alicia for years. She's a brilliant cosmetic surgeon. I won't go to anyone else. Two years ago I flew all the way up to Boston just for my boob job."

"Breast augmentation," Alicia corrected with a roll of her eyes.

"Whatever." Marsha tossed her shoulders back and forth. "Doesn't she do good work, Rae?"

Rae looked at Marsha's chest. Her breasts were definitely full and shapely, a good solid C-cup in Rae's estimation. Rae mused how thankful she'd be just to be a B. "I'll take your word for it. I've never seen you otherwise."

Marsha laughed, tossing her fingers at Rae, then turned back to Alicia. "So what are you doing now?"

Alicia looked noticeably uncomfortable, obviously wishing to go on to another subject. "It's not as bad as you might think. I had a good attorney. Donald had to part with just over fourteen million, plus attorney's fees, to see me go."

"Wow," Rae exclaimed. "That's incredible."

Alicia looked at Rae. "It's enough to tide me over for the time being."

Marsha laughed again. "I think you'll manage to eke by. So what are your plans?"

Alicia turned back to Marsha. "Well, that's why I called you. I've decided to move back to Houston. Most of my family lives here. Since I didn't have much time to get established in Dallas, I'm not really leaving anything behind. And personally, I have no desire to stay there." Her tone became terse, "Besides, I don't want to run into Donald and his *whore* at any social functions."

Rae and Marsha made eye contact, silently acknowledging the woman's understandable bitterness. When Alicia called and asked to meet for lunch, Marsha had no idea that her visit was anything more than a social call. The notion of Alicia and Donald Bennet splitting up was preposterous, and she wouldn't have believed it if she hadn't heard it from Alicia herself. She couldn't possibly imagine what, or who, could have come between them.

Alicia continued, "In time, I plan to reestablish a practice here in the Houston area. I've got the cash. But first priority is to find a good place to live. And that's your department."

Marsha finished her glass of wine. "Wonderful. But actually, Alicia, I think you really need to talk to Rae here. She has the best leads on the best places. Plus she has some deals, which, I can promise you, you'll feel good about."

"How wonderful." Alicia turned her smile back to Rae. "Do you think you can help me?"

Rae gave the older woman a look of genuine concern. "Oh, yes. In more ways than you could ever imagine."

33

September 1979

Dallas, Texas

THE STEAM WAS SO DENSE, REBECCA COULDN'T SEE THE GLASS door fifteen feet away, dripping with condensation. The smooth, wet tiles beneath her were new, installed in her Highland Park mansion only two weeks ago. She ran her fingers through her saturated hair, lifting it from her neck, letting the penetrating clouds work into her skin. Rivulets of perspiration beaded up over every inch of her body. Every muscle was marvelously relaxed, but her mind was filled with anticipation.

Her new husband, Donald Bennet, was in Boston for the week on business. She knew he was really seeing Tracy Bonner. It was no secret she had been his mistress during his first marriage. Why should it be any different now? There was no other reason why Tracy hadn't resigned after being demoted and left out to pasture in New England when the corporation pulled up stakes and moved south. Donald was taking good care of Tracy, in his fatherly way. Rebecca didn't care. Donald was somewhat repulsive, and as far as she was concerned, Tracy could have him. Besides, she was expecting a visitor any moment, someone she wanted to see. Her new vice-president of marketing was due to arrive any second.

"Rebecca?" came a hesitant voice through the fog.

Rebecca could feel the sudden change in temperature when the door opened. "Come in, David."

David Stratton slipped into the steambath and pulled the

glass door closed behind him. Rebecca could faintly see he was already undressed. That was good, she was growing impatient.

"Where are you?" David called.

"Why don't you feel your way around?" she replied.

His silhouette approached, his right hand finding her left knee. Rebecca's steambath was fifteen-by-fifteen feet square, with completely tiled walls, ceiling, and floor. Two wide ledges stair-stepped up to the back wall. Rebecca sat on the upper ledge, leaning against the back wall, her legs extending down on the lower ledge. David made a satisfied sound at locating her. "There you are."

"You're late," she scolded.

"I'm sorry," David apologized. "The traffic on Central Expressway coming out of town was murder. The radio said some asshole rear-ended some other asshole just before Mockingbird. Cars were backed up for miles. I managed to get off and come up Greenville Avenue." He softened his tone to a suggestive whisper, "Isn't there some way I can make it up to you?"

Rebecca put her hands on his shoulders and pulled him onto the lower ledge, kneeling. She wrapped her legs around his waist and squeezed him tight. "I'm sure you'll find a way. You always do."

He smiled. "Well, Mrs. Bennet, I was hoping you'd say that."

"That's Mrs. Danforth-Bennet, sir," she corrected.

"Excuse me," he said sarcastically, then leaned into her, his lips pressing into hers.

His mouth tasted warm and sweet, moving in and around her lips, his teeth gently nibbling her bottom lip, pulling it out and playfully releasing it. She probed his mouth with her tongue, and he reciprocated. The two lingual members thrust and parried within their locked lips. Amid the constant hiss of live steam a few feet away, rivulets of perspiration continued to run down Rebecca's face as she hungrily devoured his mouth. When she felt her hands starting to slip against the wetness clinging to his shoulders, she slid her fingers up to his neck, intertwining them in his hair.

David apparently took that as a signal to redirect his kisses and lashing tongue to her cheeks and jawline, stopping to nibble her earlobe, then moving down the firm tendon in her neck, tracing circles on her shoulder. The superheated wet air was growing more difficult to breathe. She leaned forward and locked her mouth on his shoulder. Its taste was already seasoned with the salt of his sweat. She massaged the back of his scalp, eliciting an urgent moan of pleasure from him.

Rebecca took a deep, humid breath, shivering from the ecstatic sensation of his lips and tongue kissing their way down to her breasts, tracing the full curvature of her body from her arms to her sternum and back again, teasing the nipples with brief brushes as his mouth passed by. She became more aroused with every wet, savory sound that proceeded up from the contact of his face with her sweat-laden body. A drop of perspiration fell from her chin and landed in her cleavage. His tongue was quick to mop it up with a ravenous flourish.

Rebecca felt his hands part her knees, his fingers weaving up her damp thighs. While still enjoying the gratifying stimulation of her breasts, she writhed forward, pressing her body against him as she felt the warm sensation of his fingers stroking and separating the entrance to her pleasure. With a gentle twist, she felt his index finger disappear inside. Her breath stilled. Then, with increased desire, she pulled his head into her chest with even greater force.

She lowered her right shoulder to allow her hand to extend down between them, checking to see if he was ready; she knew *she* was ready. Her fingers negotiated through the coarse brown pubic hair down to the object of her search. It rose in her hand, responsive to her touch. As she lifted it up, sliding her fingers to the end, she guided the hot mushrooming flesh against her. She slid her hips forward on the ledge, allowing him to begin his eagerly anticipated penetration at any second. But to her surprise, David leaned back, his hands gently pushing her shoulders against the warm tile wall behind her. Her fingers released him, accepting the gentle push. She knew enough to trust David. He always knew what to do to please her.

David allowed himself to barely enter her, rocking his hips forward and backward with brisk, teasing strokes, stimulating the opening alone. Her desire to feel all of him was overwhelming, and it was obvious he sensed it. With no warning, she felt him plunge into her fully, eliciting a seething gasp of the sultry steam—but only once. He quickly withdrew, but not completely, and resumed his teasing dabs. David kept this routine up for several minutes, coaxing her desire to the point of desperation, then giving her what she wanted—but not as much as she wanted—only to continue the sensational torture. She loved it. She hated it. She wanted all of it.

Whenever Rebecca sensed his inward thrust, she would wrap her legs tightly around his back and squeeze, endeavoring to immobilize him. But she would soon feel his hands against her hips, pushing her away. And all the while he never diminished his feast on her glistening wet breasts. Amid humid pants, she swallowed the excess saliva that collected in her mouth. The eruption of an eight-point Richter scale orgasm was pursuing her with a vengeance. Her body was racing to meet it.

She was getting dangerously close, but not quite there yet, letting a wistful moan ease past her lips as her fingernails raked deeply across David's back, not caring if they drew blood. Without warning, she knew she had to have him completely. The teasing had to stop. It was painful now. No more torture, no more waiting, no more delay. The quaking in her legs and rapid acceleration of her breathing apparently was the signal her lover was waiting for. She felt his hands slide around her wet hips, and *finally*—he pierced into her deeply and completely, sensuously impelling his pelvic bone directly against her own taut protrusion with rapacious pressure, quickly followed by a feverish barrage of deep, swift, devastating thrusts. His hips rocked wildly, accelerating the erotic impact, zealously stabbing and stabbing with wrenching animalistic fury.

"Yes!" she screamed at the top of her lungs through the stifling steam. "Yes!" It was exactly what she wanted. With each cataclysmic penetration, her climax constricted and convulsed in harmonious unison. She could no longer breathe, her diaphragm was going into spasms, her vision blurred, a loud ringing filled her ears, her hands pressed against the sweat of her lover's back, her rigid fingers trembling—until she suddenly sensed his pace begin to diminish. *No!* A wave of panic flashed through her. Her words instinctively commanded with abrasive harshness, "Don't stop! Oh, for God's sake, don't stop!"

She felt him obediently accelerate his debauching penetration to its former wanton intensity, faster and faster, sweetly harder and harder, wringing every ounce of delirious orgasm out of her utterly ravished frame. Then, as though a great switch was thrown inside her, her entire body flopped limp against the tiles, her lungs heaving for want of precious oxygen. Her equilibrium spun in nauseous circles, prompting her hands to grip the tiled ledge for support. Trembling aftershocks quaked through her arms and legs. Even her toes randomly wriggled from the ravaging effect.

"Are you all right?" David asked with a chuckle.

She looked up at him through dazed eyes. "Don't ever do that to me again . . ." Then smiled in an unsteady stupor. ". . . until next time."

She saw him wince in pain. He said timidly, "I need to sit down. This tile is hell. My knees are about to fall off."

Rebecca summoned all the strength she had left to sit up and guide her lover down to the floor. It was much cooler down by the drain. She felt like she could breathe again. She laid David on his back and straddled him, leaning forward slightly to let him position himself for reentry. When she sensed the firm tip touch her in the right place, she sat back, shivering again at the feel of the fullness sliding within. She gently rocked her hips back and forth, sweet and easy, for several minutes as she caught her breath, allowed her vision to clear, and gave her mind time to refocus.

She looked down at him. "I do think you're getting better at this, Mr. Stratton. Who taught you to do that?"

He innocently grinned. "I read a lot."

She huffed, "I'll bet." Her eyes narrowed. "You know if I found out some other woman had stolen your affections, I would be most displeased."

David laced his fingers behind his head. "Well, I certainly wouldn't want to see that happen."

Without interrupting her lovemaking, Rebecca's mind shifted gears. She gave him a stern look. "David, I need your help again."

He smiled, arching his back a bit to increase the pressure beneath Rebecca. "Anything. Just ask."

As her hips kept up the heat of their undulating rhythm, her eyes grew cold and dark. "I want you to help me get rid of Donald."

David Stratton's expression grew serious. "What exactly do you mean by 'get rid of'?"

Rebecca's dark eyes remained fixed, but the speed of her hips increased. "Donald made me CEO of Secularian, but he still refuses to let me sit on the board of directors. I don't like that. And I'm not used to being told no. It's very simple, really. He has something I want. Combined, our total stock holdings exceed fifty percent. That's all I need to take full control of Secularian."

David looked puzzled. "But Texas is a community-property state. If you divorce him, you'll only end up with half. That's not enough for full control."

Rebecca's eyes flashed, she could sense another devastating orgasm on the way, rising up from a dark recess within her. "Who said anything about divorce? A widow inherits it all."

David stared into her eyes for several moments, then swallowed with great difficulty. Rebecca could feel him begin to fade inside her. He spoke softly, "Rebecca, you don't know what you're asking. You're scaring me. This is serious shit. Tell me you're just kidding."

Rebecca reached behind her, taking David's testicles in her hand. "Come on, David. You've got the balls for it." She squeezed them, her voice dropping low and malevolent. "You just get me what I need, and I'll take care of the rest."

"What . . . exactly . . . do you need?" he asked, a fearful look growing on his face. Rebecca relished the sight. It made her feel strong. She released him.

"You have friends in chemical research." Her words flowed with excited cadence. "Get me something liquid, odorless, tasteless. Something that affects the heart. And leaves no traces."

David's eyes widened in alarm. "You're serious. Aren't you?"

"As serious as a heart attack," she mocked.

David awkwardly propped himself up on his elbows. "Rebecca, you'd better think about this. I don't know. This sounds pretty crazy to me."

Rebecca pushed him back down on the floor, a surge of power rippling up her body. Her hips jolted forward with pounding force. "You don't have much choice, Mr. Vice-President." She squeezed his withering member inside her by tightly flexing the muscles of her perineum, forcing him back to attention with steady pressure and motion. Her words were staggered between thrusts, "If you complete this assignment, there'll be an available CEO office with your name freshly painted on the door." She squeezed harder. "If you fail me, you'll be collecting unemployment for a long time." She smiled. "Or worse. Do we understand each other?"

David closed his eyes and took a deep breath, having no desire to discover what "or worse" meant. He laid silently on the floor for almost a full minute. "I'll see what I can do."

Rebecca smiled with satisfaction. "Good. Now why don't you just relax and enjoy yourself. Don't think about this discussion any further. You're going to need all your strength this week while Donald's gone."

A blank expression swept over David's face, the same expression Rebecca remembered seeing when he faced Rae Taylor in a Boston courtroom years ago. She didn't reasonably expect him not to have concerns about her request, but she could see by the detached look on his face, he had at least resolved the conflict within himself in regard to his actions. He spoke flatly, "I won't let you down."

"I know, David," she replied, her words tapered to an abbreviated hush as the rush of power, mixed with the aphrodisia of her body, pushed her over the edge of another brief orgasmic seizure, a small one, not thoroughly satisfying. The nearness of her triumph occasioned a much more acute spectacle of gratifying passion. She looked down at him, hungrily licking her lips. "Get a towel to put under your knees."

34

February 1988

Catalina Island, California

DR. BURTON, THE PSYCHOLOGIST FROM THE L.A. COUNTY CRISIS Center, sat on one end of Sabrina's couch in her self-imposed island prison. Sabrina sat on the other end, wearing a faded sweat suit—and her black harlequin mask. The soothing strains of Emelia Travain's concerto played on the stereo. Gabriella brought in a tray of tea and quietly placed it on the coffee table.

"Thank you, Gabriella," Sabrina nodded at the polite woman.

"Sabrina, you have to come with me to the city," Dr. Burton insisted. "You have to get out around people, around life."

"I don't *have* to do shit, Doctor," Sabrina snapped. "And you're not my father, and you don't order me around."

Dr. Burton raised his hands defensively. "Please believe me. I'm not trying to manipulate you. I'm just trying to get you to see that you are going to die here by yourself. You have to get out. You have to live your life."

"Why?" Sabrina spat the word at him. "Maybe I don't want to go on living."

The doctor's tone grew stern. "Now that's the talk I don't want to hear. Sabrina, you are still a young woman. What are you, twenty-eight, twenty-nine? You have your whole life ahead of you. What? Are you just going to roam the halls of this house until you grow old and die?"

"You don't understand how I feel." She turned away from him. "No one can understand how I feel." She knew that wasn't true. There was one person who could, but he chose not to. And that pain went deeper than the scars on her face.

Dr. Burton softened his tone. "Sabrina. You have a disfigurement. This is a fact. But your disfigurement is not all of Sabrina Doucette. You may not want to hear this, but I'm going to tell you. And mostly I tell you this because it's true. You are a very beautiful woman."

She glared at him.

"It's true," he insisted. "I saw your picture on the cover of *Time* magazine years ago and I thought you were perhaps one of the most beautiful women in the world."

Her voice was cutting, "But not anymore. Right?" She got up and walked out on the deck, facing the sea.

"Wrong." He followed her. "Your injuries comprise less than two percent of your body. Can't you accept the fact that ninety-eight percent of you is the same as it ever was?"

Sabrina stopped at the rail and shook her head, her eyes fixed on the white-crested waves. "It doesn't work that way, Doc. Are you telling me if I took my pocketknife and only made a two-percent hole in a priceless painting, it would still be ninety-eight percent valuable? What fucking planet are you from?"

The doctor didn't answer her, just silently leaned against the rail next to her and folded his arms. He knew she had to get the pain out, express it, vent it. That's why he was there. But this wasn't progressing as well as he had hoped.

A cool breeze blew across her face, pushing her blond hair back. She turned her head and stared at the doctor for several awkward moments, measuring his frustrated expression. In a way, she felt sorry for him. The poor bastard was only doing his job—but he couldn't *begin* to address the pain she felt, the ache of loneliness and the bitter sting of abandonment.

"I'm sorry, Sabrina." The doctor lowered his gaze. "Bad example. But my heart still tells me what's true. And the truth is, you're a beautiful woman."

A rage was beginning to boil within her. He just felt sorry for her. He pitied her. He had no *right* to pity her. The words of Roger Marks spoken in a Roman café came back to her. She wanted no sympathy for a *freak*. She faced him directly. Her hand maliciously came up and ripped the mask off her face. She saw Burton's eyes go wide.

"You *still* think I'm beautiful, Doc?" she shouted. "Take a good look."

The only sound was the gentle rush of the sea caressing the shore in the distance.

When the cutting tension of the moment seemed to pass, Dr. Burton took a deep breath and moved closer to her. His words were firm and sure, seasoned with a quiet air of respect and dignity. "Yes, I think you're beautiful."

Sabrina was surprised to see him lift his hand and stroke her cheek. It felt wonderful. Her heart was pounding. *What was he doing?* She so much wanted to lean into his arms and be held, but a revulsion within her, a revulsion of herself, made her turn away. *No!* It couldn't be. Tears trickled down her blemished cheeks. "Don't. Please."

"Why?" Burton asked. "Do you find *me* distasteful?"

Sabrina fixed her eyes on the horizon, gripping the cedar rail with both hands. "You would want something that looks like me? Like I am?"

"I must make a confession to you. You see, for many years I have had a crush on the queen of racing. I have dreamed about meeting you for a long time." He gave her a bashful laugh. "I am a medical man. My specialty is the mind. In all my years, I have learned that physical problems are much easier to deal with than the human psyche, much easier." He tapped his temple with his index finger. "It is your mind that causes me much greater concern than your face."

Sabrina leaned over and kissed Dr. Burton's jovial cheek, just above his well-trimmed beard. "Thank you. That means a lot." She leaned back and tried to smile. "You know, you're kinda sweet for a shrink."

Dr. Burton shrugged. "We each have a unique bedside manner."

The thought flashed through her mind for a moment, but she couldn't. She knew she just couldn't. Not now, not yet. She patted the doctor on the hand and sincerely thanked him for coming to see her. He graciously accepted her invitation to come again and see her another day, and escorted her back inside the villa.

Before leaving, he opened his leather notebook and pulled out a business card. "Oh, I meant to give you this."

"What is it?" she asked.

He held the card to his shoulder before handing it to her. "First, let me say I don't want you to get your hopes up or anything. It's just that I know you had a bad time in the past with the surgeons who tried to help you with your face."

"And?" she prompted.

He smiled. "And . . . I recently got a recommendation from a colleague of mine concerning a surgeon in Texas. It may be a worthless lead. I don't know. It's up to you whether you even want to look into it. I didn't know how you would feel about going through any more medical treatments."

Sabrina could feel the depression surrounding her again. Treatments meant more pain and disappointment.

Burton went on, "But what my friend says is that this woman is supposed to be very good. She's been working with some other doctor on some experimental treatments. He says they're looking for volunteers."

Sabrina felt some hesitation, but she had to ask. "What kind of treatments?"

Burton shrugged. "I don't know. Nonsurgical, from what I understand. Think about it. Maybe give them a call and get more information. Like I said, don't get your hopes up. But who knows? Maybe this lady has come up with something that can help a little."

Sabrina took the card, thanked Dr. Burton once again, and saw him to the door. Burton hadn't made it to the end of the walk before the telephone was in Sabrina's hand dialing the 713 area code. She read the card as she dialed: Brighton, Taylor and Associates.

35

October 1979

Houston, Texas

THE BOTANICAL GARDENS IN MEMORIAL PARK WERE RADIANT IN the fall. Winding trails leisurely weaved through the grandeur of nature's beauty. The view was very serene and tranquil. At midweek there were only a few lovers quietly strolling arm in arm. A few preschool children darted in and around the trees, tossing bits of popcorn or bread to the oversized carp drifting in the lily ponds. Across the pond a maintenance man turned on a sprinkler to shower a section of ferns. Rae Taylor sat admiring the quiet splendor with Alicia Brighton in the outdoor restaurant overlooking the floral expanse.

"Did you like the house?" Rae asked innocently.

Alicia nodded. "It was beautiful. However, it's a bit larger than I think I require." She took her glasses off and laid them on the table, rubbing the bridge of her nose between her thumb and forefinger.

Rae folded her napkin and set it next to her plate. The blackened red snapper had been exquisite. "Well, you have to understand, King's Heights is one of the most exclusive areas in Houston. While it's convenient to shopping and downtown, it also offers a quiet serenity and security very similar to the gardens here."

Alicia looked around and took a deep breath, savoring the ambrosial fragrances. "I appreciate that, Rae, but the home has over six thousand square feet. I live alone. What am I going to do with all that room?"

Rae looked surprised. Over the past year the technique had been well-polished. "Oh, didn't I mention it? One of the rooms will naturally be used by your personal valet. I'm sure he'll want to use one of the other rooms as a private exercise and massage therapy room for you—"

"Hold on," Alicia interrupted. "What valet? I don't have any servants."

Rae acted forgetful. "I'm sorry, Alicia. I must be slipping. Do you recall our visit to Shady Oaks last week?"

Alicia's face brightened. "Oh, yes. I wouldn't forget it. Marsha definitely knows how to treat her friends to a good time. It was positively sinful."

Rae shared her smile. "Do you remember the young man who gave you your massage? I believe his name was Charles."

Alicia blushed. "Oh, yes." She leaned over discreetly. "Rae, even as a medical professional, I have to tell you, confidentially, nudity is not something that concerns me, normally, not even my own. But I have to tell you, I was positively terrified." She leaned back, closed her eyes with rapturous remembrance. "However, by the end, I was praying I didn't have to leave. If Donald had known how to touch me like that man did, I probably would have fought to keep him."

Rae laughed. "Well, that's what I was getting to. Charles only works part-time at Shady Oaks. He's transferring his employment to Collins Enterprises. Marsha and I have a subsidiary corporation for domestic services." Rae's brow creased as though she was trying to remember something important. "I was sure we had that written on the information sheet about the King's Heights estate." She smiled at Alicia as she dropped the bomb. "In any case, it doesn't matter. The fact is, our properties come with staff included. If you decide to purchase the estate, Charles's personal services, for a period of one year, are included in the sales price. He's there full-time to attend to your needs as you see fit."

Alicia sat dumbfounded. "Are you serious?"

Rae didn't answer her question immediately. Her eyes sparkled. "And I mean your *every* need."

Alicia furtively glanced around the outdoor restaurant to see if anyone else was listening. "Rae, you're teasing me. Aren't you?"

Rae sat back, speaking philosophically, "Alicia, Marsha showed me how wonderful life can be if you only know how to enjoy it. You're a woman of substantial means. You can *afford* to enjoy it. Imagine waking up every morning to a brisk massage, a dip in your pool, breakfast in your own private garden, a hot-oil rubdown before retiring each evening. And every moment you desire spent with a gorgeous companion who is ultimately attentive to your every desire, your every whim."

Alicia continued to stare, almost trancelike.

Rae locked her eyes on Alicia's. "Alicia, you've experienced a devastating turn-around in your life. I know what that's like. I got sidetracked myself—involuntarily." She let out a sigh. "But in the process of putting my life back together, I learned very quickly how good it feels to be treated like someone of great value. To be told what I really need to hear, when I needed to hear it most. To be touched with warm sensitivity when I want to be touched. To feel alive again. To feel like a complete woman again. To feel good again. That's what I'm offering you today."

Alicia sat there for several moments, staring at her half-eaten plate of food. What Rae just described sounded too good to be true—and too tempting to pass up. She finally looked up at Rae with a reluctant grin. "I think I could get used to six thousand square feet."

Rae beamed. "I thought you might." She paused for a second, then added, "And as an added bonus, I can arrange for Charles to come by your hotel and give you a ride to my office in the morning to sign the papers. You wouldn't mind if he's a little early, would you?"

"How early?" Alicia's eyes were more eager.

Rae discreetly lowered her voice, "Say around seven this evening?"

Alicia blushed and arched her eyebrows. "That would be wonderful." She absently brushed her short black hair behind her ear, picked up her glasses and slipped them back on. "But tell me, Rae. I have to know. Marsha says that you're a doctor yourself. How in the world did you get involved in selling homes with her?"

"It's a long story." Rae batted at the air to dismiss the saga of her tragedy, not at all in the mood to retell it. She just made another $120,000 in commissions; it was time for celebration, not remembering wounds from the past.

"Oh, come on," Alicia prompted with her infectious smile, her eyes slightly magnified through her bifocals. "What's your field?"

Rae reluctantly gave in. "Biochemistry. I was involved at MIT in doing some of the original work in cell mapping, gene therapy, and specialized cancer treatment."

"Really?" Alicia looked impressed. "I'm familiar with

that. My husband—" She stopped herself. ". . . make that *ex*-husband, used to talk about it a great deal."

Rae looked surprised. "Are you sure? It was highly experimental. The only people who know about it were with the corporation that developed it, and the *bitch* who stole it from me and gave it to them." Rae shook her head. "I'm sorry, I didn't mean to say that. I've worked very hard not to hang on to any bitterness. I can't say I've entirely succeeded in that area."

"It's all right, dear." Alicia patted Rae's hand. "Like you said, I know how you feel." She took a sip from her water glass. "But to answer your question, my husband's company was working very hard to bring cell mapping to the marketplace. They had some spectacular results with clinical trials in treating breast cancer, cervical cancer, ovarian cancer, and the like."

"You're kidding." Rae shook her head. "That's amazing. I really thought I'd cornered the market in that area. I guess I was wrong. My old professor told me lots of folks were working on the same ideas." Rae's brow furrowed. "But how did they get around Secularian's patent rights? I couldn't figure out how to do it. Wasn't there any infringement?"

Alicia laughed. "Rae, my ex-husband is the chairman of the board of Secularian Corporation."

Rae gagged. "What?"

Alicia's face clouded. Rae's earlier comment suddenly registered in her mind. "I'm sorry, Rae, did you say their product was a stolen discovery of *yours?*"

The old anger was rising again. It couldn't be stopped. Rae's mind was reeling. "That's right."

Alicia shook her head in confusion. "That can't be, dear. Donald told me those treatments were the work of a subsidiary corporation they acquired three or four years ago."

"Called Hope Corporation?" Rae asked harshly.

Alicia blinked behind her thick lenses. "Well, yes, as a matter of fact. But it was my understanding it was the work of my husband's chief executive officer." Her face scowled. "Which incidentally turned out to be the direct cause of my divorce."

"Hope Corporation caused your divorce?" Now Rae was confused.

"No, *she* did. His CEO," Alicia stated flatly. "The harlot who turned Donald's head."

A forboding chord struck in Rae's soul. "What was her name?"

"Danforth," Alicia said with disgust. "Rebecca Danforth. Why? Do you know her?"

36

July 1990

Dallas, Texas

At four in the afternoon, the blistering Texas heat had long since driven the mercury into triple digits. Very few golfers had ventured out on the course that afternoon, but Nicole had been anticipating it all week, and wouldn't be denied. She was playing a round with Brett, and having an extremely difficult time keeping her mind on the game. Brett had come dressed only in a pair of neon-green swim trunks, a loosely slung black tank top, and sandals. His polished muscles rippled with seductive strength every time he moved. Nicole couldn't keep her eyes off of him, nor did she fail to notice his alluring glances toward her most of the afternoon. She knew he was as eager to finish the game as she was.

On the fourteenth hole her ball landed just shy of the

water trap, a two-acre, tree-lined pond that barred the green. A few mallards paddled around the still waters.

Nicole sat in the shade of the golf cart, looking over at her ball. "What do you suggest for this one?"

Brett got out of the cart, walked around to the golf bags stowed in the rear, and extracted a nine iron from her bag. "Lots of height and not much distance."

Nicole set her half-empty long-neck Lone Star beer in the cup holder and got out of the cart. She was dressed in cool summer shorts, a matching tube top, white ball cap, and was barefoot. Dark sweat stains stood out on her tube top under her arms, between her breasts, and across the middle of her back. Her face was flushed and covered with perspiration. "Right, Arnold Palmer. Watch me hit a worm burner right in the water."

He laughed at her. "No you won't. Come on. I'll show you."

Nicole obediently trudged over to her ball, where Brett was standing.

"Here." He handed her the club. "Now address the ball."

"Hi, ball," she lethargically joked as she took the club and stood ready to take a swipe at the helpless, dimpled sphere.

Brett laughed again. "Now lean over it a bit." He walked up behind her and put his arms around hers. "You've got to swing down into it, and get *under* it."

Nicole felt his chest press solidly into her back. It was wet. She could smell the dark, haunting fragrance of his body, a natural smell of a man covered in sweat—and she liked it. "Get . . . under it?"

"That's right." He put his wet cheek against hers. "Practice it one time with me. Pull the club way back." She turned her upper body with his. "Then swoop in low, cutting underneath it." He slowly turned her through a practice follow-through, gently swiping the ground with the head of the club.

She felt his hips press against hers. "Show me that again."

He smiled. "Okay, easy drawback." He turned her body

slowly to the right. "Then a hard, firm, thrust down. Follow-through deep and easy."

Her thigh muscles loosened at the sound of those words. Her heart was beating faster. The idea of playing three more holes of golf quickly became ludicrous. She turned around and faced him.

"What's the matter?" he asked innocently.

Nicole grabbed the front of his tank top and backed away toward the pond with Brett in tow. "I've decided golf is out. Swimming is in."

He brightened. "Oh? Is that right?"

She stopped at the mossy edge of the water and pulled her tube top over her head. "Yes, that's right." Topless, she reached over and yanked his tank top off. The thin material easily tore in her hands. "But no swim wear allowed in my pond."

"Hey, careful," he protested with a grin, "that's one of my best shirts."

Nicole was urgently pulling his shorts down to his knees, her eyes growing wide with her delightful discovery underneath. "I'll buy you the factory that makes them."

Brett laughed, stepped out of his shorts, kicked off his sandals, and stood there nude, helping Nicole get her shorts and panties off. With a peal of laughter he scooped her up in his arms and threw her headlong into the water. The cool embrace of the pond was delicious. Nicole emerged from the deep water, treading away from the shore just in time to see Brett dive in. The turbid water grew still. A moment later she burst into laughter as tickling fingers raced up her legs, probed into her ribs, and arced across her back. Brett's head splashed out of the water, and with a snap of his neck he threw his wet hair out of his face.

His deep blue eyes blinked at her. "Has anyone ever told you you were impulsive?"

"Never." She swam forward into his arms, devouring his lips. Her arms came up under his, embracing his back. With two swift kicks she maneuvered them over to shallow water where her feet could feel the cool mud squishing between her toes. Brett's lips continued to voraciously consume her own.

Nicole opened her eyes when a wave of water violently splashed against the side of her face. Brett pushed himself away and playful splashed her again; this time the water painfully went up her nose. Naturally, that meant war.

Nicole furiously swam after him, laughing with each splashing stroke, racing to the other side of the pond, following him into water only waist deep. They both stopped and stood still, panting, dripping, and giggling. She stood ready to pounce if he made a move. Suddenly, he made a frantic attempt to splash her again, but she was ready. She dove toward him, knocking him back in the water with a thunderous slosh. Brett retreated toward the shore, swimming and crawling backward as best he could; but he wasn't fast enough for her pursuit. She pinned him down in the soft mud on the far bank. From his chest down, his body lay half submerged in the shallow water.

Nicole sat across his lap, straddling him, looking down at her panting prize. "Gotcha."

He smiled up at her. "Yep. I'm your prisoner, ma'am. Do with me as you will."

Nicole reached into the water on either side of him and scooped up two handfuls of dripping black mud. "I intend to."

Brett gasped as she rubbed the wet mire across his massive chest, smearing it down his washboard stomach. She willingly held her arms out straight to either side when he delightfully reciprocated. The cool, slimy earth felt wonderful as his hands massaged it into her breasts, beneath them, and around her ribs. With her eyes closed, she reached directly behind her, beneath the shallow water, to find what she wanted. It wasn't difficult to locate. Her knees sank deeper into the mud as she rose up to allow him to enter. The penetrating fullness made her quiver as she sat back down.

The shallow water just covering his stomach splashed forward onto his chest with each forward rock of her hips, washing away the fresh mud. Brett continued to scoop up the slippery black ooze and paint it over her body till she was completely covered from her neck down. She heard it squish through his fingers as he lusciously kneaded it into each breast, as he had done on many occasions with coconut-scented oil. Each gooey handful molded against her body drew away the oppressive heat of the afternoon. It was invigorating and delightful, almost chilling. When she sensed him sit up, she wrapped her mud-caked arms around his head, pulling his face between her muddy breasts. He rotated his face in a circular motion, increasing the exotic stimulation. She let go when she heard him sputtering.

Nicole opened her eyes and looked down at her lover's mud-streaked face, which sent her into a fresh wave of laughter. Brett just wet his hand and wiped his mouth, spitting to his left. He took another cupped handful of water and poured it over her right breast. The soft coral hue of her areola and erect nipple appeared from the blackness. He covered it with his mouth and began to gently suck it, massaging the end with his tongue. She couldn't see his tongue, but she could certainly feel what it was doing, and loved it.

The water seemed to be getting deeper, but in reality the motion of her hips was driving them both deeper and deeper into the soft mud. Nicole held Brett's head tightly to her bosom as the climactic waves of pleasure approached. To her surprise, when the orgasm arrived, it wasn't violent, or delightfully exhausting; rather, close, and gentle, like the cool water and soft mud embracing them. It lasted for several sweetly stimulating seconds, almost patient, but nonetheless completely satisfying.

And for some strange reason it made her start to cry. She didn't know why. It just felt right to cry. Not sobs of sadness, just a wet release of deep emotion from within. Everything was so wonderful at the Women's Center. The fact that Rae Taylor had given her a free membership as an enticement to join still boggled her mind. She'd have paid any price for what she felt in her heart at that moment—or for the fire in her soul she carried back to Boston every week.

The North Dallas Women's Center had become a touchstone of power for her. Its enigmatic magic fed her, nurtured her, set her face like a flint toward victory and achievement in every dimension. She couldn't accept all that for nothing. She had argued with Rae about it on several occasions, but Rae insisted that she just pass the word around to her influential friends. Rae kept assuring her that if she wanted to give money, that time would come, but not now.

Nicole didn't know why. And as Brett was applying another thick, oozing coat of mud to her upper body, and with the fires of pleasure heating up again between her legs—it ceased to be important.

37

December 1980

Houston, Texas

THE BOYS CHOIR FROM ST. AGATHA'S CHURCH STOOD ON THE stage and sang "Silent Night" to the delight of all the guests at Marsha Collins's gala Christmas party. It was the grandest social event on the Texas calendar. But then, all of Marsha's parties were like that.

The ballroom at Shady Oaks was ornately decorated with live holly and garland. Four hundred poinsettias lined the stage area. In the back corner was a twenty-five-foot Christmas tree which towered to the top of the hall, magnificently covered with a rich display of ornaments from around the world, almost a thousand in all. Banquet tables were covered with every culinary treat the chefs of Shady Oaks could imagine or import. Over twelve hundred people thronged in and out, buzzing with the social elite from around the country. Many famous sport stars, movie personalities, and other celebrities glittered among the crowd. Everyone was dressed in dazzling original gowns, suits, and winter apparel. Marsha had the club management turn the air conditioner down to sixty-five degrees to make it feel a little bit like Christmas. It was still seventy-eight degrees outdoors, humid and sticky, unseasonably warm, even for Houston.

Marsha was undeniably stunning, arrayed in a silver lamé gown that had been designed and sewn for her by her personal couturier in Paris. She told Rae it attracted more compliments than cat hair. The dress had arrived only two days before the affair, driving Marsha to near panic, prompting dozens of overseas calls before she was fully satisfied it was on its way. But once she put it on and saw how elegantly it clung to her long, graceful frame, and blended so regally with the $600,000 diamond choker and matching earrings, she knew the wait had been worth it. Marsha didn't care how tired her legs became that night, she refused to sit down and wrinkle her dress. On one of her rounds through the clamorous throng, she found Rae and Alicia sitting at a table in a far corner, buzzing in their own private conversation.

"Rae Taylor," she scolded. "Why aren't you out there looking beautiful and collecting sales leads? You don't get this much money in one room but once a year."

Rae laughed. "I will in a minute. Alicia and I are discussing business."

Marsha looked temporarily placated. "Very well. As long as it's business."

Rae and Alicia both put their heads together in muffled laughter as Marsha sauntered away to chat with the governor. Alicia's eyes grew serious again. "Now tell me again. Your technique actually uses DNA to manipulate cell regeneration?"

"Right." Rae nodded. "The chromosome pattern contains the map for each cell location and the instructions for normal development. All I have to do is take cancerous cells, synthesize the DNA pattern structure with healthy cells, then grow them in a culture. When I have a sufficient catalyst culture, I inject the serum into the cancerous tissue, and the DNA patterns are exchanged with the mutant cells. On the subsequent regeneration cycles, the cancerous cells ccase to reproduce because they're not in the pattern. Then the normal cancer-fighting cells can destroy them."

"That's amazing," Alicia sighed. "I never really understood it until you just now explained it. But I can tell you, Secularian made a lot of money doing that very thing. It's a shame you don't still have the patent. I can think of many other uses for that technique."

Rae was intrigued. "Like what?"

"Well, like in my field," Alicia noted. "If I could affect cell regeneration in cosmetic surgery, I could repair damaged tissue, perhaps heal muscles and torn ligaments, get rid of age spots, scars—who knows, perhaps even reverse the aging process itself."

Rae was getting excited. "I never thought of the process being used in any other capacity but to fight cancer."

"Well, it's worth thinking about." Alicia looked back at the murmuring multitude. "I'm getting ready to open up shop here in Houston. And right now I could really use something radical and distinctive to attract a healthy practice."

"Well, even if this was it," Rae said mournfully, "Rebecca Danforth and your ex-hubby would sue us blind."

Alicia crossed her arms thoughtfully. "What exactly was the scope of your patent? Did it cover the technique itself in *any* application, or was it merely confined to cancer treatment?"

Rae felt foolish. "I don't know. David drew up all the paperwork, and I just assumed that all of my work became the property of Hope Corporation, and subsequently Secularian. I can't tell you."

"Who could?" Alicia sounded like she had a plan.

Rae thought a moment. "Nikki might."

"Who's Nikki?" Alicia leaned closer.

"She was my lawyer in the nonlawsuit against Secularian. She's an old college friend who still lives in Boston, I think. I haven't seen her in five years. We haven't kept in touch like we promised we would." Rae shook her head in disbelief. "She may still have some records from back then. I know she did a great deal of research regarding the patent, but at the time, our attention was on the issue of ownership, not application."

Alicia sat back. "It could make a big difference. And if you find out that it was only for the cancer therapy, I'd be in a position to make you a very attractive business proposition."

Rae's heart jumped. She'd give anything to be back in her chosen field. She sincerely enjoyed Marsha's world, but it wasn't complete. Rae wanted to be able to do so much more than she was doing. The mere thought of possibly working with her own discoveries again was electrifying. Alicia couldn't know how much her suggestion meant to Rae. Rae had only known this woman for a few months, but in that short time they had grown extremely close, as close, if not more so, than Rae and Marsha. Alicia was almost twice Rae's age, but it didn't matter. They had become like sisters almost overnight. Rae and Alicia shared a common bond—and a common enemy.

"I'll call Nikki." Rae promised. "Tonight if I can. And if she confirms what you say, I'd be willing to talk to you very seriously about that business proposition."

Alicia lifted her champagne glass from the table. "To Taylor, Brighton, and Associates."

Rae laughed. "Madame, it's you who's going to have to bankroll the majority of any would-be enterprise. I only made my first million this year." She lifted her glass next to Alicia's. "To Brighton, Taylor, and Associates."

The glasses touched once with a delicate crystal ring.

38

June 1980

Dallas, Texas

THE CHAUFFEUR CLOSED THE DOOR OF THE LONG, BLACK CADIL-
lac limousine behind David Stratton as he took his seat next
to the bereaved widow, Mrs. Rebecca Danforth-Bennet. The
funeral had been small, but tasteful. All of Secularian's
executive staff and a few of Donald's friends from the Dallas
area managed to attend. Most of the employees were still in
a state of shock after hearing of the elder executive's heart
failure. The emergency medical crews and police officers
had found his body lying peacefully in his own bathtub.
Rebecca told the authorities how he had eaten a quiet
dinner at home with her and retired to a hot bath to relax.
Rebecca also told the investigators how he had been complaining of chest pains for several weeks and was meaning to
see a physician. They had commented on how typical that
was for men of Donald Bennet's age. Donald Bennet passed
away with little notice at the age of sixty-five.

Rebecca sat quietly while the chauffeur pulled away from
the grave site, proceeding at a respectful speed back toward
Highland Park. As soon as Rebecca raised the privacy glass
between the chauffeur's compartment and the rear of the
car, she tore her black veil off and threw it on the floor.

She grabbed David's cheeks and kissed him. "We did it,
David! It's mine now! All of it! Over seven hundred million
dollars' worth! All mine!"

David said softly, "Congratulations."

Rebecca looked put out. "Oh, David, don't be so con-

275

trary. What's done is done. You're a chief executive officer now. So act like it. That means you sometimes have to make the tough calls. And don't forget, I'm now the chairman of the board." She kicked her shoes off and reclined on the luxurious leather seat. "I think I'll go into semiretirement, travel around the Caribbean for a few years and work on my tan. You can run the empire and be my general. I'll check in from time to time for progress reports and to see how you're taking care of things. In the meantime, I think I'll look around and see what other nice little enterprises there are out there, ripe for acquisition. I'd like to elevate my status from millionaire to billionaire in the very near future."

"Don't you ever get tired?" David asked in amazement.

"Tired of what?" She didn't understand the question.

David looked uncomfortable. "Tired of building, and taking, and scheming, and all that shit."

She stared at him for a moment, then laughed. "No. Why?" Her voice became sarcastically patronizing. "Are you having a little conscience attack?" She shook her finger at him. "That's not like you, David. You're my man of steel, iron nerves, conqueror of battles, and spoiler of helpless virgins."

David laughed. "Right. Where would we be today without helpless virgins?"

Rebecca winked at him. "I don't know. I haven't been one in so long, I forgot what it's like."

"I'm not surprised." David looked out the window as the limousine pulled onto the highway.

"Aren't you?" Rebecca tried to sound offended. "Well, be glad I'm not. My hyperlibido tendencies have been an instrumental part of my success, as I'm sure you're aware. But look how far I've come. I'm a thirty-two-year-old multimillionaire—and your boss." She aggressively leaned over and slipped her hand up firmly between his legs, squeezing the soft mount of flesh in her palm. She suddenly felt like doing something crazy, and forbidden. "So if I were you, I'd shut up and take my clothes off. The mourning period is officially over." Her voice seductively dripped with urgency, "We've got at least twenty minutes to kill, and I know how I want to do it."

David swallowed with a frown. "Rebecca, come on. Here? In a funeral limousine? For God's sake we just left the graveyard of your dead husband. Show a little respect. That's morbid."

Rebecca leaned down into David's lap and began opening his black trousers. "Sure I can't change your mind?" She unzipped his zipper and reached inside, pulling his limp organ out and devouring it. She felt it come to life almost immediately. She lifted her head. "I see at least part of you is interested."

David looked toward the front of the car. "Can he see us?"

"No," Rebecca lied. The glass was transparent and only stopped sound. She didn't care what the chauffeur saw in his rearview mirror as long as he didn't hit any inopportune bumps.

"Well . . ." David pressed his lips together tightly. "Let's go real fast."

Amid Rebecca's triumphant laughter, David roughly lifted her black dress over her head and tossed it on the rear-facing bench seat. Rebecca pulled her slip and undergarments off as David unbuckled his pants and slipped his trousers down to his knees. Rebecca sat in the center of the backseat and pulled her knees apart, exposing herself fully to him. She hoped it looked shocking; she wanted to shock him. If he gasped, it would be fantastic. She saw David's eyes grow wide with desire as he looked down and eagerly leaned into her. She grew impatient.

"Come on," she ordered. "Give it to me. Now!"

She felt his fingers run through her dense pubic hair, then he looked at her with concern. "You're not ready yet. It'll hurt."

"I'm ready enough," she demanded. "Make it hurt." She winced with a fiendish sense of power as he sliced into her like a hot lance. He had been correct, the proper juices had not been given adequate time to prepare, but his obedience was worth the discomfort.

"Push!" she ordered.

David complied, his pants flapping back and forth as he made love to Rebecca in the rear of the limo, pumping as fast as he could go, as fast as she made him go—and it wasn't enough for her.

"Harder!" she demanded.

Rebecca reeled with delight, sensing him increase his pace as instructed, relishing the hot, juicy sensation working its way into her. He dared not refuse her anything. She'd make him pay dearly for any sign of insubordination.

For the next ten minutes David frantically rutted between Rebecca's open thighs, bringing her to a fiery orgasm, but she wouldn't let him stop. She was far from satisfied. She pushed him back and turned around, kneeling in the wide floorboard and leaning over the backseat, making him do it to her from the rear until she came again. Finally she sat him down in the rear-facing seat directly behind the chauffeur, and straddled him facing forward. As they entered Highland Park, she deemed it an appropriate time for the finale.

Rebecca pulled David's hands off her breasts and wrapped them behind her back. As she bounced against his pelvic bone with ever-increasing fury, she smeared her breasts over his face, dodging her shoulders from side to side, not letting his open mouth lock onto the firm ruby ends. Then, with her palms placed firmly over his ears, she held his face still, flogging his nose and eyes from side to side with her nipples. She watched him with torturous glee as he helplessly sat back and endured the erotic thrashing. But as the heat built below her, her pounding pelvis jarred the seat hard enough to get the chauffeur's shocked attention.

The unsuspecting young man driving the car practically swerved into a parked car as he watched the dark-haired lady's face in his rearview mirror suddenly contort into a silent grimace of ecstasy behind the privacy glass. He strained to pay attention to traffic as his eyes continued to dart back to the mirror. He couldn't believe it. For God's sake, he was driving back from a funeral—the funeral of this lady's *husband!* Part of him felt repulsed at the thought of what was happening in the context of the afternoon's occasion; but another part of him wanted to climb into the backseat and join the party. He was still watching when he saw her open her eyes and catch him looking. He steeled his gaze back on the stately tree-lined lane ahead in morbid embarrassment.

A few moments later he chanced another glance and was again stunned when he saw her seductively blow him a kiss.

39

May 1982

Boston, Massachusetts

JUDGE GALLIMORE LOOKED AT THE FOREMAN OF THE JURY. "Mr. Foreman, how does the jury find?"

An elderly man with thick horn-rimmed glasses cleared his throat and said, "Your Honor, we the jury, find for the plaintiff."

A thunderous explosion of cheers and applause went up in the packed courtroom, quickly squelched by Judge Gallimore's impatiently rapping gavel. "Order in this courtroom! Order! These proceedings are not concluded." When silence resumed, he asked, "Mr. Foreman?"

The bespectacled man continued, "Your Honor, this court elects to award Ms. Pollard a punitive judgment from her former employer, Bankston Commodities, the sum of $375,000, to be paid in one lump sum."

The courtroom exploded again, but the judge was quick

to bang his worn wooden mallet down three times in quick succession, bringing the crowd to order once again. "Thank you, Mr. Foreman, and ladies and gentlemen of the jury, for your service to this court, and to the community." He banged his gavel once again. "This court is adjourned."

The spectators' gallery thundered with applause as Nicole Prescott stood and embraced Katy Pollard, a former mid-level manager with a commodities trading house in Boston. Katy had been promoted to a department-head position, but at a third less compensation than her male counterparts. When she raised the issue with her superiors concerning equivalent compensation for her position, she had been terminated.

To Nicole, the judgment was only worth $125,000 to her, one of her smallest commissions in recent years, but she took the case more on principle than money. With two years of brilliant wins under her belt, her clientele had grown to astronomical proportions. Enough so to prompt her to leave Foster and Finnman and open her own firm, Prescott and Associates, the hottest law firm in Boston. However, this case gave her a chance to fight for something she believed in.

Nicole stood before the massive collection of microphones piled together for the press conference outside the courthouse. Reporters crammed close amid flashing cameras and television crews to hear her post-trial remarks. "Ladies and gentleman of the press, I want you to know what was accomplished in this courtroom today. A woman didn't just win a great deal of money. She sent a message to corporate America about fairness and discrimination. Our case was built on a simple premise, that is, equal performance in equal responsibility means equal compensation."

Another salvo of camera flashes ignited across the crowd of journalists and spectators.

Nicole shuddered with excitement, doing her best to appear calm and in control. "In our case we openly recognized the fact that different people have different skill sets and different levels of contribution. We freely acknowledge the exceptional performer who should be rewarded in an extraordinary manner. But we told a jury of citizens, like yourselves, that when a precedent is set by a corporation for compensation in a particular identified task, then each employee of that corporation who performs that task should be entitled to that same level of compensation—with no regard to their gender, race, creed, or national origin."

The reporters all broke into spontaneous applause.

"And the jury agreed with us," Nicole continued, with great pathos in her voice. "We set the standard in this case for all businesses. We established the fact that when, not one, which could be an exception, not two, which could be a coincidence, but three employees are doing the same task for the same pay, which establishes *policy*, then that policy should be the norm for all. Ladies and gentlemen of the press, this landmark decision opens the doors of industry for millions of women across this nation to be rewarded for their contributions to this society fairly, equally, and justly."

The crowd clapped again enthusiastically.

"Thank you all for coming today. This concludes our statement." Nicole hastily escorted Katy down the courthouse steps away from the feeding frenzy of questions. Katy had asked for Nicole to keep the reporters away from her and cancel the press conference altogether; but Nicole had convinced her of the importance of a brief formal statement concerning their accomplishment.

When they had climbed into Nicole's two-seat Mercedes coupe and pulled out of the parking lot, she looked over at Katy's somber frown and asked, "Hey, what's with you? You should be ecstatic."

"Yeah, right," Katy huffed out the passenger-side window, absently gazing at traffic.

Nicole frowned. "What's wrong? You were just awarded a lot of money. And made a little history."

Katy looked at her in frustration. "Ms. Prescott, you know they'll appeal that verdict, sure as shit."

"Sure as shit," Nicole agreed. "So is that it? Are you upset because you might have to wait longer to get your money?"

Nicole turned up Massachusetts Avenue by the Commons and headed toward her office.

"It's not just that." Katy sounded depressed. "Money's part of it. I've been living off what little I saved for the last three months since they let me go. But there's more to it than that. I'm screwed."

Nicole shook her head. "I don't understand."

"Ms. Prescott, who's going to hire me? Huh?" Katy demanded. "I'm the bitch that blew the whistle. Yeah, it's great a lot of other girls may now have a hammer to go after their bosses and get a raise. But no one's going to let me in the door. No way. I'm the friggin' sacrifice lamb in this one. If I ever get to see any of that money, it's going to have to last me a good long time. Like I said, I'm screwed."

Nicole took a deep breath. "No you're not." She reached down and turned on the radio. The car was too quiet. The crooning voice of Boy George cut through the car. She stabbed at another preset button and got a classical station. She liked classical music, especially Chopin.

Katy was getting more upset. "Lady, you don't know what it's like to have to fight for a job out there with only a four-year degree, and especially being a woman. God help the ones that don't have a decent education. You probably think it's easy, strolling in and out of court, collecting big money, and driving around in your fancy cars. It's *easy* to look down from the top. You don't know what it's like to look from the bottom up."

Nicole felt horrible for Katy. Everything she said had a ring of desperation to it. But she wasn't right about her situation. "No, you're wrong. I *do* know what it's like to live in a tiny apartment wondering if I have enough cash to make the electric bill, the water bill, the department store credit cards, the car loan, the rent, and perhaps enough left to pay everyone else in the pile of unpaid bills. The difference between now and then, which wasn't that long ago, came from the fact that I figured out what I wanted to do, how to get there, and then got off my ass and got busy."

"You think I haven't tried?" the frustrated young woman challenged.

"I'm not saying that," Nicole retorted. "I'm saying maybe you just haven't looked in the right places. Maybe you haven't hitched your wagon to the right team of horses, as an old college friend of mine from Texas used to say."

"Maybe you're right." Katy shrugged. "But, like I say, with my face in all the papers, who's going to hire me?"

Nicole had an inspiration. "What's your degree in?"

"Business and finance," Katy replied.

"Have you had any experience in personnel supervision?" Nicole turned the radio down to carry on her conversation with less distraction.

"Yes. My department, prior to my termination, had thirty-five people in it." Katy looked at Nicole with uncertainty. "Why do you ask?"

"Do you think you could supervise ten law clerks and two junior attorneys?" Nicole gave Katy a warm smile.

"Are you serious?" Katy stopped breathing.

"Completely." Nicole stopped her candy-apple-red Mercedes 380 SL at a traffic light. "As you know, I just opened up my own firm this year, and I've yet to hire an office manager. The caseload has grown faster than I had anticipated, and I really need the help. I can start you off at about forty-five thousand a year, plus medical, and a group life policy. Interested?"

Katy beamed. "When can I start?"

"You just did." The light turned green, and Nicole drove her new employee back to her building to show her her new office. Katy cried the whole way there.

Nicole felt great—for the moment. Everything seemed to be coming in line as she had hoped, and much of it faster than expected. Except she still lived alone in her Cape Cod estate. She didn't like being alone. And there was precious little time left in the day to consider establishing any serious relationships. She longed for some exotic escape that could remove her from the hustle and bustle of law practice, even if only for a day or two. That's all it would take. She had so much passion pent up inside her, and no outlet to release it. Some of it seeped out in the courtroom, but it was not what she really craved. She wanted a place to go where she could be free to express all that was in her, a place with people who cared about her, and listened to her, and were sensitive to her needs and desires. Unfortunately, no such place existed in 1982.

Nicole had told Katy the truth, the caseload had indeed grown beyond what she could handle, or could shuffle down to her two junior associates. Soon she would be hiring more partners in the firm; she had no choice. But that meant more rewards of battle. And that was acceptable, even desirable. Winning was a part of her blood now. It had become a professional tradition. And another of her honored traditions was to go out that evening to celebrate her victory. Katy was her guest of honor. With one phone call she arranged escorts for herself and her new office manager. They were both ready for something exciting.

The music in the dance club was energetic, and the place was filled to capacity with gyrating bodies. Katy's escort kept her on the lighted floor most of the evening. Nicole was content to sit and sip a cocktail, chatting politely with her date. On one of her trips back from the ladies room, she heard a voice she hadn't heard in many years.

"Nikki! Nikki! Over here." It was Steve's voice. Her stomach sank.

She turned around and saw him leaning against the bar. He had lost a little weight, and his hair had a hint of gray in it. She felt an obligation to go over and say hello.

"Hey!" he greeted her cheerfully, and awkwardly attempted to hug her.

"Hello, Steve," she said flatly, not wishing to belabor this encounter any more than necessary. Their divorce had been a mutual decision, but it had gone back and forth with numerous violent arguments, unkind words, and foolish threats. In the end they had separated peacefully, vainly promising to keep in touch. This was the first time she'd seen him in six years.

He lifted his beer mug to her in a silent toast. "I saw you on the news tonight. Sounds like you're really going places."

"That's right, Steve." She wasn't in the mood for this. This was a victory day. *Bastard.* Why did he have to come along and spoil it?

"You know," he volunteered. "The business is really doing well these days. I got jobs lined up clear through to next year."

Nicole smiled politely. "That's wonderful. I'm very happy for you."

His face took on a serious air. "Nikki, are you happy in what you're doing these days?"

"Very." She looked back over to her table. Katy and her escort had returned between songs.

"I gotta tell you, honey." Steve touched Nicole's elbow. "I've been meanin' to call you. I thought . . . maybe . . . we might try to see each other sometime. You know, like old times?"

Nicole looked at him with a wave of revulsion. "I don't think so. We live in different worlds now, Steve. And I like it that way. Understand?"

"Come on, baby," he pleaded. "Give me a chance. I've changed. I really have. I'm like a totally new guy."

"Really?" she arched her eyebrows. "You don't sit around in your apartment watching Scooby-Doo on Saturday mornings, drinking beer, and farting?"

Steve gave her a forced laugh. "Nikki, come on. Can't we at least be friends?"

She sighed. "Sure, Steve. Friends. Look, I have some people who are waiting for me. It was nice seeing you again." Nicole nodded curtly and turned away, walking back toward her table.

Steve followed after her. "Nikki, wait. Come back."

She didn't want a scene. This was going to be difficult. She knew he was right behind her.

"Nikki, let's talk some more. I'm serious. You don't know what you're missing." His voice was embarrassingly loud.

Nicole stopped at her table, with Steve trailing behind, and turned around to face him one last time. "Yes I *do* know, and that's the way I like it."

"Nicole, is there a problem?" Nicole's escort rose from his chair, a distinguished-looking man in a tailored blue suit.

She turned around with a polite smile. "Not at all." She stepped back so Steve could see her date. "Steve, this is Senator Thomas Wellford from New Hampshire."

The senator extended his hand. "Hi. Call me Tom."

"Steve Thompson." Steve shook his hand as his face blushed. "Pleased to meet you, sir. I'm sorry to interrupt. Excuse me." Nicole watched with burning satisfaction as he turned around with his tail between his legs and walked away.

"Who was that?" Senator Wellford asked as they sat back down.

Nicole rolled her eyes. "My ex-husband."

"Oh, I'm sorry. I didn't realize you had been married before," the senator said with genuine interest.

"It's nothing to apologize for. It's just a brief part of my life I've tried to forget." Nicole looked back toward the bar. Steve was still staring at her. That's right, mister, she thought. Take a good look. If you hadn't had such a bad case of cranial rectitis, it might be you sitting at this table today. You don't know what *you're* missing. Who knows? Maybe he did know. If so, the thought made her feel better.

40

July 1990

Dallas, Texas

"Welcome to the North Dallas Women's Center, madame." The smiling, uniformed doorman held the rear door of the black Cadillac limousine and extended his hand to its passenger. From the gaudy interior of the car emerged an elegantly dressed woman in her early forties, attired in a Parisian-styled sleeveless black dress. Dark glasses covered her eyes. Her dark hair was twisted in a bun behind her head. She briefly touched the doorman's hand as she gracefully rose from the car and marched past him without any further acknowledgment of his presence. The woman stopped at the reception desk, looking past Stephanie into the grandeur of the great room.

"Hello, ma'am." Stephanie smiled. "How may I help you today?"

"I'd like to see whoever's in charge here," the woman demanded.

Stephanie frowned. "That would be Ms. Collins, ma'am. Do you have an appointment?"

The woman slowly pulled down her dark glasses to the end of her nose, peering over the top of them with a note of indignation, her dark eyes pressing into Stephanie. "I don't make appointments, little girl. Notify her immediately that Rebecca Danforth has arrived and wishes to speak with her. I assume you have a lounge here?"

Stephanie nodded. "Yes, ma'am. Several. One moment, please." She pressed a button on her computer console.

"Mark, this is Stephanie out front. Could you furnish an attendant right away? Yes, that's right."

Stephanie looked up at Rebecca's cold stare. "Ms. Danforth, one of our escorts will show you to the Montressor Salon. They're serving a champagne brunch right now. You're welcome to enjoy yourself there till we can locate Ms. Collins for you."

Rebecca looked pleased. She liked superior service. "Very good."

A few moments later a handsome young man came and offered Rebecca his arm. She arched her eyebrows skeptically, hesitantly taking his arm as he led her into the great room and toward the refreshment salons.

Stephanie punched her intercom. "Rick? Is Marsha back there with you?" She paused a few moments. "Marsha, it's Stephanie. She's here. Rebecca Danforth. No she didn't call first. She's just here. I know, I sent her to the Montressor Salon for brunch. Is Rae with you? Good."

Marsha placed the receiver back in its cradle and stared at it for several seconds. She looked across the exercise room to Rae coming out of the dressing room. Marsha didn't know how Rae would react to the news. She was almost afraid to say what she had to. Rick had just finished cleaning up the massage tables. He noticed the look of concern on Marsha's face, and graciously left the two women alone to talk.

Rae caught her pensive stare. "What is it, Marsha?"

Marsha watched Rae finish buttoning her blouse. "That was Stephanie. Rebecca Danforth is here."

Rae's hands froze. "What do we do?"

"Let me handle it," Marsha admonished. "You've trusted me this far. You can trust me the rest of the way. This was unexpected, but it doesn't matter. Everything will be fine."

Rae's expression grew cold. "I'll be in my office if you need me."

"All right." Marsha looked in the mirror to ensure her dark red hair was neatly in place, then made her way through the center to the Montressor Salon.

ANTICIPATION

The salon was decorated in French Renaissance decor, according to Marsha's tastes. Ornate moldings lined high ceilings. White furniture with delicate lines neatly formed various sitting groups. Lace and finery dripped from every quarter. Portraits of Renaissance composers, writers, and philosophers adorned the walls. A few women were buzzing around the buffet tables, sampling the delicacies and sipping their mimosas. A dark woman in a black dress sat by herself at one of the rear tables.

Marsha walked up to Rebecca's table. "Ms. Danforth?"

"Yes?" Rebecca looked up.

"I'm Marsha Collins." Marsha extended her hand.

Rebecca took it, but didn't rise. "Pleased to meet you, Marsha. I think I've heard of you. Sit down. We need to talk."

"Certainly." Marsha politely sat down at the table, curbing her urge to have the woman removed from the premises for her insolence. "How may I help you?"

"Tell me about this operation," Rebecca ordered.

"I'm sorry?" Marsha looked a little indignant. "Do you need information regarding membership? If so, I'll need to know who your sponsor is. We accept no new memberships without a sponsor, that is, a member in good standing."

"Cut the horse shit, Marsha." Rebecca glared. "I'm not a trifling peon from the valley. I'm Rebecca Danforth, chairman of Secularian Corporation, and president of the whole damned Chamber of Commerce for that matter. Don't act like you don't know who I am. I came here because my good friend Louise Halliran gave me the rundown on what you've got going out here. It sounded preposterous, but it intrigued me enough to come out here and see for myself. I want information."

Marsha forced a smile. "Louise recommended you? Well, that's certainly different. But I must tell you, Ms. Danforth, despite your financial status, or social status in the community, this is a private club. You still have to apply for membership like anyone else."

"I'm sure," Rebecca cut her off. "So let's dispense with the pleasantries, shall we? Can I get straight answers out of you, or is there someone else I need to be talking to?"

It took everything inside Marsha not to reach over and slap that arrogant expression right off the bitch's face. Rae had told her time and time again what Rebecca Danforth was like, but in less than two minutes Marsha realized Rae had not even covered the half of it. She forced another smile. "You're direct, Ms. Danforth. I can appreciate that. So I'll be candid with you. My time is valuable. What exactly do you want to know?"

"I want to know about this place." Rebecca gave Marsha her own dark smile, feeling in control of the conversation. "Louise tells me of exotic services, leisure activities, exquisite dining, relaxation—and sexual favors that sound very illegal."

Marsha didn't flinch. "I can assure you, every service offered by the North Dallas Women's Center is state licensed and approved. We offer a premium retreat service for our clients for general relaxation purposes, or for recovering patients who come here for cosmetic surgery, or some of our other specialized medical treatments."

"What kind of treatments?" Rebecca probed. "I'm in the medical business myself, you know. I'd be interested to find out what you offer."

"It's quite a long list." Marsha kept her eyes locked on Rebecca's. "I'll have my secretary get you a brochure."

"Thank you." Rebecca's smile almost looked pleasant. "And your *other* services?"

Marsha folded her hands on her knee. "Sexual therapy?" She absently tossed a hand in the air, dismissing the subject as trivial. "It's an approved medical practice under the supervision of our two attending physicians. Most of our clients seem to enjoy it."

"Come now, Marsha," Rebecca huffed. "Louise tells me of gorgeous young men pampering her day and night, acting out lusty fantasies and carrying on like she'd died and gone to heaven. What kind of brothel are you running here?"

Marsha straightened her back. "I'll ask you to refrain from such derogatory insinuations, Ms. Danforth. We're very proud of the services provided here at the center, and our distinguished clientele is a testament to its caliber of quality and overall satisfaction to our customers."

Rebecca raised her hand. "Calm down. I wasn't *insinuating* anything. I'm telling you that I was somewhat surprised to find out such a delicious concept for an establishment existed in my city without my knowledge. I've lived in Dallas for thirteen years and I've made it my business to know every significant business concern in the area. And I want to know about yours."

"I'm afraid I don't know what else to tell you, Ms. Danforth." Marsha shrugged innocently. "You are welcome to take a tour of our facilities this afternoon, and stay for dinner as my guest. But that's about all I have to offer. If a woman in your position could benefit from our services, I'd be glad to furnish you with an information package with all the appropriate membership applications."

Rebecca sat quietly for a moment. She wasn't satisfied. Louise had made such a fuss about this place at their lunch the previous week at Willow Bend Country Club, she had to see if any of it was true. She tilted her head back and furrowed her brow. "I'd be delighted to take your tour. But before I do, tell me a few more things."

"Such as?" Marsha was growing weary of the interview.

"How long have you been in business here?" Rebecca's mind was recording every fact.

"Almost two years," Marsha answered matter-of-factly.

"Didn't this used to be the Durango Country Club?" Rebecca leaned forward, her memory piecing every detail together.

"That's right." Marsha leaned back in her chair, realizing she might be there for a while. "The previous owners went belly up. The property was ideal for our purposes. The golf course was already in place. With a considerable amount of renovation, some new construction, and almost a year's worth of landscaping, we have what you see."

Rebecca nodded. "You said 'we.' You have partners in this deal?"

"Yes." Marsha was waiting for this moment. "The two physicians who administer the medical and therapeutic treatments."

"Who are they?" Rebecca demanded. "Serious players?"

"Very serious." Marsha's expression grew grave. It was the moment she had been waiting for. "Dr. Alicia Brighton and Dr. Rae Taylor."

Rebecca's face went pale. Her words came out hushed. *"What?* Alicia and Rae? In my town?"

Marsha could see Rebecca had suddenly become very uncomfortable. "Yes. Why? Do you know them?"

Rebecca looked around the salon nervously, no longer looking Marsha in the eye. "I knew them both a long time ago."

"That's strange," Marsha lied. "They've never mentioned you."

Rebecca pursed her lips and nodded. "Really? Well, I'd like to see Dr. Taylor, if I may. For old time's sake. Renew old acquaintances. You understand, I'm sure."

Marsha looked doubtful. "Oh, I don't know if that's possible. She's very busy today. And it's often quite difficult to get on Dr. Taylor's calendar. She's a very important lady, extremely powerful and influential. I could try to make an appointment for you, but I can't promise anything."

Rebecca's eyes grew dark. "She'll see me. Tell her I'm here."

"I don't think that's advisable, Ms. Danforth." Marsha smiled again, enjoying every moment now. "But I'll tell you what I can do. I'll arrange your tour of the facility. We'll get one of the charming young men to show you around. And when you're done, I'll see if Dr. Taylor has a moment for you."

Rebecca started to object, but her instincts told her to play this woman's game for the time being. The inconsequential delay would give her time to get the lay of the land. "Very well, Marsha. Tell Rae I would sincerely *appreciate* her indulgence."

Marsha rose. "I will. Please feel free to enjoy your brunch while you wait." Without waiting for a reply, she turned around and went directly to Rae's office.

Rae was seated behind her desk. Keith was standing behind her chair massaging her shoulders. She looked up when Marsha came in. "What happened?"

Marsha closed the office door behind her, laughing. "It was great. She was devastated to hear that you and Alicia are behind all of this."

"Thank you, Keith." She nodded up to the handsome beau behind her. "If you'll excuse us, I need to talk to Marsha."

"I'll be in the lab." He leaned down, softly kissed her cheek, and left the room.

Marsha came over and sat down on the edge of Rae's desk, mockingly driving her fist into the palm of her other hand. "She *demanded* to see you."

Rae looked alarmed. "Is she coming in?"

Marsha huffed, "No, no. I sent her on the tour with Mark. I want her to sweat a little before you talk to her."

"Does Alicia know she's here?" Rae asked.

Marsha shook her head. "I think she was visiting all her patients today. You know, Emelia is going back to California this afternoon."

Rae nodded. "I know. She's taking Jonathan with her. He'll be missed."

"They'll both be missed." Marsha sighed. "But they do make a cute couple. Don't they?"

"Yes." Rae leaned back in her chair, her thoughts not on the departing pianist.

Marsha gave Rae a concerned look. "Are you going to be able to handle this meeting?"

"I have to. Don't I?" Rae stood up.

"We could do this another day." Marsha stood as well. "I can easily send her away. She knows where to find us."

"No," Rae insisted. "It's time to get this over with."

"As you wish." Marsha gave Rae a motherly smile and left the office.

Rae sat in her office chair for two hours, just staring out over the lake, her thoughts miles away, across the vast expanse of fifteen years, to a dark time, a horrible time. She thought about calling Keith, but she felt the need to be alone. When her intercom buzzed at four-thirty that afternoon, her nerves were frazzled but her mind was focused and alert. She would once again see the one person in the whole world she despised more than words could describe.

Marsha's voice came over the intercom. "Dr. Taylor. Are you available to see Ms. Danforth?"

Marsha's pretentious formality made Rae smile. She needed that. "Send her in." Rae spun around in her high-backed chair with her back facing the door and pretended to be busy with some papers on her credenza. She heard the door open behind her and then the sound of footsteps. Her heart was pounding. She didn't know if she would be able to speak.

Rae heard Marsha's voice. "Rae. This is Rebecca Danforth. She tells me you two have already met."

"Rae?" came Rebecca's sultry voice. It didn't sound as threatening or intimidating as Rae remembered it. Rae held up a hand, signaling not to be interrupted while she finished pretending to do something important. She felt the urge to giggle, hiding behind her high-backed chair. If she was going to go through with this, she might as well do it right.

Marsha took the sign. "Dr. Taylor will be with you in a moment. Please take a seat."

With a deep breath Rae forced a stoic, poker-faced expression to her face and slowly swiveled her chair around. She felt as if at any moment she might go into cardiac arrest. "Hello, Rebecca."

Rebecca was seated in one of the two white wing-backed chairs in front of Rae's desk. Marsha sat in the other one. Rebecca leaned forward in genuine amazement, staring at Rae.

"Rae Taylor! Look at you!" Rebecca's mouth fell agape. "Girl, you have *blossomed* in fifteen years. I never would have recognized you."

Rae leaned back in her chair, not smiling. "Marsha said you asked to see me?"

Rebecca leaned back and smiled. "Well, Rae, it looks like we've both done very well for ourselves over the years. Haven't we?"

Rae didn't answer.

Rebecca turned toward Marsha. "I have to tell you both, I was most impressed with what you've done to the old country club. This place is exquisite. I think I'm going to enjoy visiting you often."

"How's that?" Rae asked coldly. "This is a private club. It's for members only."

Rebecca glared at her, then forced her smile to return. "I realize that. And I am considering applying for membership."

Rae furrowed her brow. "I don't think you'd really like it out here, Rebecca. We're very choosy about our clients. They have to be human."

Marsha shot Rae a chastising look. Rae kept her eyes on Rebecca's.

Rebecca laughed. "Bitterness doesn't suit you, Rae. It never did. And since you've obviously become a successful businesswoman, I think you know better."

"Don't lecture me," Rae snapped. "You're on *my* property now. I don't think it would be very seemly for the newspapers to discover that the president of the Chamber of Commerce was arrested for trespassing on private property."

Rebecca laughed again. "Very good, Rae. You have learned a lot in fifteen years. You've got heart. That's good. If you had that much savvy fifteen years ago, we probably wouldn't have gone our separate ways under such adverse circumstances."

Rae felt a certain confidence rising up within her. She was

no longer afraid. Her heartbeat was settling down. "You're probably right."

Rebecca crossed her legs casually and folded her hands on her knees. "But as I was saying, I am very impressed with this little operation. You must be pulling in some serious coins to keep a ship like this afloat."

Rae smiled. "It turns a dollar."

"I'll bet it does." Rebecca's eyes flashed. "I'll bet it does. I can smell it. There's a quality here I really like. It appeals to one's finer tastes."

"That was the intention." Rae looked at Marsha, who still had a "be careful" look on her face.

Rebecca looked out of Rae's wall-sized window at the lake. "My, what a spectacular view. You must love it."

Rae's tone became terse, "Rebecca, did you stop by to chitchat, or do you have something on your mind you'd like to discuss?"

Rebecca feigned a shocked expression. "Rae Taylor. Is that any way to talk to a prospective client?"

Rae shook her head. "I told you, Rebecca. This is my operation. You wouldn't like it here. And just for old time's sake, between you and me, you're not welcome here."

Rebecca's smile faded. "Now, Rae, you wouldn't be guilty of discrimination, would you? If I meet all of your eligibility requirements, I would dearly hate to have to take you to court. We both know how that type of thing turns out."

Rae was seething on the inside. If she had a gun in her hand, Rebecca's dead carcass would be soiling her carpet at this very moment. She took several deep breaths, maintaining her composure. She could be patient.

Marsha spoke up, breaking the tension. "Rae, she's right about that. If she can afford the fees, we can't keep her out."

"Thank you, Marsha. I can see *you* have a good head for business." Rebecca's smile was back. Having the upper hand with Rae again made her feel wonderful. It was a pleasant breath of nostalgia.

Rae glared at Marsha. "She can't sue a private club."

"Do you want to take the chance?" Rebecca asked innocently.

Rae stared at her for several seconds. "Fine. Take her money, Marsha. We'll use it to buy plenty of penicillin for the boys."

Marsha rolled her eyes beneath tightly shut eyelids. She was going to slap Rae after Rebecca left. Marsha addressed Rebecca, "Ms. Danforth, did Louise inform you concerning our fees?"

"No. But it doesn't matter." Rebecca opened her clutch purse and took out a checkbook. "Whatever it is, I can afford it."

Marsha's voice became very businesslike and stern. "We require a two hundred fifty thousand dollar annual membership fee, plus ten thousand per visit. Medical treatments are extra."

Rebecca turned and looked at Marsha, slightly shocked. "You're very proud of this place, aren't you?"

"Those are the published rates, Ms. Danforth." Marsha kept her tone even. "*If* you can afford them."

Rebecca glared back at her. "I can afford anything." She started to write out her check.

"I'm sorry, Ms. Danforth," Marsha interrupted Rebecca's writing. "We don't accept checks, only cash, or cashier's checks."

"You won't take my check?" Rebecca asked, this time genuinely offended. She was about to tell both Rae and Marsha where they could stick the whole facility, but she realized she'd be throwing away her opportunity to regularly come out and flaunt her power and influence in the face of her old rival. That in and of itself was worth the money.

"I'm sorry." Marsha smiled. "It's company policy."

Rebecca had one more challenge left. "Whose policy?"

"My policy," Rae curtly declared.

Rebecca smiled at her again, folding up her checkbook and putting it back in her purse. "Fine. I'll contact my bank and make the arrangements later in the week."

Marsha rose, walked over and stood next to Rae. "Very good, Ms. Danforth. Please see Stephanie at the reception desk on your way out. She'll be happy to summon your car."

Rebecca stood up and looked at both women. "Good to see you again, Rae. I'm sure we'll have plenty of time to catch up on everything."

"I'm sure," Rae whispered, with a cold expression.

Rebecca walked to the office door and turned around to face Rae one more time. "You know, Rae? It just struck me. In a strange way, I feel somehow responsible for this center. You may not agree with this, but what happened between us fifteen years ago was obviously the very lesson you needed to learn about real business. I think it shook you out of your biochemical daydream and faced you with the real world. It made you tough, sober, like me. And you're successful now, a realist, like me. In some ways you ought to thank me. If it hadn't been for me, there's a good chance none of this would be here."

Rae couldn't resist. "You know, Rebecca, in a twisted sort of way, I think you may be right about that."

Rebecca opened the door and smiled. "See, Rae. There is something we can agree on. Perhaps we can let bygones be bygones?"

"Perhaps." Rae lied with everything that was in her.

"I know I'm going to like it here." Rebecca stepped through the doorway and was about to close the door behind her. "The tour was incredible. I can hardly wait to try everything out. It was as though you did it all with me in mind."

Rae felt Marsha's viselike fingers clench into her shoulder with painful force. She forced a smile. "Good-bye, Rebecca."

"Good-bye, Rae. Marsha." Rebecca closed the door.

Rae looked down to Marsha's grip on her shoulder. "You can release your talons any time now."

Marsha let go with an enormous sigh of relief. "You really worried me there."

"I thought I did fine," Rae said defensively. "I thought I was almost . . . pleasant. Didn't you?"

"I'd say you almost gave me a heart attack." Marsha walked around her desk and leaned her arm on the winged-backed chair where Rebecca had been seated.

Rae laughed. "I was serious about the penicillin. And make sure whoever gets stuck with her as a therapist has a full supply of condoms."

"Patience, Rae." Marsha held her palm up at Rae. "Remember? All good things come to those that wait."

"I can wait." Rae leaned back in her chair again, massaging her shoulder. "I knew she'd come sooner or later. What do you think she's thinking right now?"

"Who knows?" Marsha looked toward the closed office door. "Probably trying to figure out how to build her own center just like it and put us out of business."

"Let her try," Rae said with a bitter taste in her mouth.

Rebecca Danforth held the receiver of her car phone to her ear as her limousine drove down the long drive of the Women's Center, away from the main complex.

"Hello, David?" She looked out her window as the limo turned left from the main gates and proceeded down the two-lane road, heading back toward civilization. She glanced back at the main complex building, watching it grow smaller in the distance. "I want you to do a computer check on a place called the North Dallas Women's Center. Find out if it's public or private, who has the stock, and what their financial picture looks like. I want to know who their creditors are, who owes them money, the works. This is a big operation. They've got to have a D and B rating. I want everything."

David's voice crackled through the receiver, "What about the Webster Laboratories acquisition? Do you still want that research too?"

"Screw that shit!" she snapped. "This is much better. Secularian Industries needs to broaden its horizons in women's care. And I think I've found what I'm looking for."

"Are you serious?" David asked.

"Dead serious." She faced front, looking at the road ahead. "And you'll never guess the best part. Remember that little flower you picked for me back in Boston? Rae Taylor?"

"How could I forget," David said flatly.

Rebecca couldn't help but break into a deep, guttural, malevolent laugh as her black limo soared down the road toward the city. "I'm about to show you how to make lightning strike in the same place twice."

Part III

THE TINCTURE OF TIME

The thousand injuries of Fortunato I had borne as I best could; but when he ventured upon insult, I vowed revenge. You, who so well know the nature of my soul, will not suppose, however, that I gave utterance to a threat. *At length* I would be avenged; this was a point definitively settled—but the very definitiveness with which it was resolved, precluded the idea of risk. I must not only punish, but punish with impunity. A wrong is unredressed when retribution overtakes its redresser. It is equally unredressed when the avenger fails to make himself felt as such to him who has done the wrong.

—Edgar Allen Poe
The Cask of Amontillado

41

February 1983

Houston, Texas

BRIGHTON, TAYLOR, AND ASSOCIATES WAS OFFICIALLY INCORPO-
rated in January of 1981. For its first two years it carried on
nothing but exhaustive research in three thousand square
feet of office space situated in a glass tower near Greenway
Plaza, on the southwest side of Houston. Rae and Alicia
wasted no time getting started after receiving the thrilling
phone call from Nicole Prescott in Boston. Rae had kept her
promise to telephone Nicole the night of the Christmas
party in 1980, although her first call discovered little more
than an answering machine. But two days later she was
laughing long-distance with her old schoolmate. Rae was
saddened to hear about Nicole's divorce, but glad to hear
she was doing well and sounded so happy. Nicole promised
to check her old files and see if Rae had any grounds to begin
working again in cell mapping and gene therapy.

Nicole's eagerly anticipated return call came a week later,
and what they had hoped for, prayed for, was true. As long
as Rae didn't apply her techniques for any cancer applications, specifically "replicative infirmities," as the wording of
the patent stated, she was free to find other uses for the
process. Nicole went so far as to call the American Medical

Association's attorneys in Washington, and had them verify that cosmetic applications and/or restorative treatment from injury were clearly outside the scope of the patent. The AMA concurred.

This turned out to be both good and bad news. It was good news in that Rae felt as if she had a second chance at life. But it was bad news because she had none of her original documentation on how the process was done. Secularian, via David Stratton, had confiscated it all. All of it had to be reworked, redeveloped, redocumented, retested, and recertified. To add to the problem, since cancer treatment was not the objective, an entirely new system of catalytic regeneration had to be developed for trauma to epidermal cells, nerve tissue, musculature, ligament restoral, etc. But Rae didn't care. She was in her own sandbox again—and loving every minute of it.

Alicia enjoyed coming to work and watching Rae's enthusiasm. It was contagious. From early in the morning to the wee hours of the night she slaved relentlessly at her labors. Alicia often solicited Marsha's help every week or two to drag Rae out of the lab for a day of rest and relaxation. Alicia was afraid Rae would drop from exhaustion after the first year, but was proven wrong by the end of the second. Actually, during most of the second year, Rae slowed her pace a great deal. Much progress had been made with tests on laboratory animals, and also, Rae had hired two capable colleagues. The first, Don Kennedy, was a friendly Rice University graduate with a degree in biochemistry. But it was the other young man Rae took a special interest in, a Cal Tech research specialist named Keith Lambert.

Keith had that lean, well-defined, southern California look—like someone who spent a third of his time on a surfboard, a third of his time in a gymnasium, and the rest doing whatever came naturally. He had light blond hair, deep-blue eyes, and a tan that melted hearts every time he went in public. He also had a 4.0 grade average, with an undergraduate degree from Stanford and a graduate degree from Cal Tech.

Rae had been very matter-of-fact with Keith during his employment interview, but ran into Alicia's office after he left with her face flushed, breathing hard, wanting to know what Alicia thought of him. Alicia had seen him in the reception area before the interview, and pretended to be unimpressed, telling Rae she didn't think he would do. Rae nearly panicked until Alicia reluctantly gave in and let her hire him. Alicia still laughed about the incident every time it came to mind. But they certainly got their money's worth out of the new employee. Not only was Keith brilliant, he quickly became very fond of Dr. Taylor. Alicia didn't have to guess that many late nights in the lab weren't spent staring down the barrel of a microscope or smearing cultures in petri dishes. But Rae steadfastly insisted that the only thing that went on in the lab was chemistry.

"It looks good." Rae leaned away from the binocular lenses of the powerful oil-immersion microscope.

Alicia held a clipboard in her hand and checked off one of her notes. "Is that the last one?"

Rae nodded. "Yes." A wave of excitement went through her. "That's the last one. The rabbit's musculature is completely back to normal. It's as though there was never any damage." Rae laughed. "It even made the scar go away where we made the original incision."

Alicia smiled. "That's wonderful. And Don's report clearly trends the lack of any side effects."

Keith came through the door with three white bags bearing the yellow McDonald's logo. "Lunch, ladies. If you can tear yourselves away from the germs and gore long enough to sit up and take some nourishment."

Rae smiled. "I think we can break for a minute."

Keith cleared off a space on one of the worktables and spread out the Big Macs and bags of french fries. "Voilà!"

Rae and Alicia pulled up a couple of chairs and began stuffing their mouths as they continued their discussion. "Alicia, I think we're ready to try this on some clinical patients."

Alicia's face grew serious. "I don't know, Rae. We don't

have the FDA approval yet. Nicole just started the process a few months ago. And you know it could take years. We could get in serious trouble."

"We have a research license," Rae contended. "All we need are volunteers to sign waivers saying they won't sue us."

"Who are you going to find dumb enough to let us inject them with our experimental serum?" Alicia raised her eyebrows at Rae.

Rae looked at Keith. "Have you got any injuries or scars, Keith?"

Keith backed away from the table with his hands held up in surrender, his mouth crammed with two all-beef patties, special sauce, lettuce, cheese, pickles, onions, and a sesame seed bun. "No way, uh-uh, not a chance on this boy. Forget it, bad idea."

Both women laughed. Rae looked down at her lap for several moments.

"What is it, Rae?" Alicia asked.

Rae didn't answer. She walked back over to the microscope station and picked up a scalpel from her specimen kit.

Alicia saw her pick up the razor-sharp instrument and suddenly felt afraid. "Rae, what are you doing?" She jumped up and raced across the room when she heard Rae gasp, and saw three large drops of blood hit the floor. She screamed, "Dammit, woman, what have you done?"

Rae showed her the back of her hand. Alicia saw a two-inch incision about a quarter of an inch deep. Blood was running down to her wrist.

"It's all right," Rae tried to assure Alicia. "Just bring me a dressing."

Alicia grabbed the side of her head, shouting, "What in God's name do you think you're doing?"

Keith ran over and looked at the wound, grimacing at the sight.

Rae looked calm. "Just get me a dressing. It'll scar over in about a week to ten days. Two weeks from now we'll start the treatments."

Alicia shook her head in disbelief. "Rae, you're insane."

"I'm a scientist," Rae stated flatly.

Alicia went to the stainless steel storage cabinet to collect some gauze and an antiseptic, caustically lecturing, "If I remember correctly, as in all those Gothic horror books I see you always reading, Dr. Jekyll and Dr. Frankenstein said much the same thing. And look where it got them!"

Rae smiled and sat down in her chair. "Tis true. Shelley and Stevenson definitely brought out the inspired passion of a doctor in pursuit of his dream. But since I was a child, my personal favorite has been Poe. I've always felt he reached a greater range of depth between the soul's depravity and virtue."

Alicia looked though the bottom lens of her bifocals as she poured the antiseptic on the open wound with punishing liberality, eliciting a deserved moan of discomfort from Rae. She deserved it for being so foolish. "I hope that hurt. Serves you right."

Rae looked into Alicia's eyes. "Don't be angry with me. I want to know how it works firsthand. This way we'll know."

Alicia wrapped two long strips of adhesive tape around the bandage to hold it secure. "I know you're brave, Rae. But you're a professional, and you know better than to do anything so foolish."

"It isn't foolish," Rae contradicted. "It's history."

"I hope you're right." Alicia stood up and looked at her watch. "I've got to go." She turned to Keith, who still had a pale look on his face. "And you keep her away from anything sharp till I get back. Understood?"

Keith laughed. "That I can do."

As the door closed behind Alicia, Keith came over and sat down next to Rae. "I don't believe you cut your hand." He looked down at the bandage. A few tiny red drops were soaking through. "Does it hurt?"

Rae held up her bandage to his face. "Want to kiss it and make it better?"

Keith pressed his lips lightly on the edge of the gauze. "Better?"

Rae nodded. "Umm-hmm."

"Is that all I can kiss?" Keith asked.

Rae shook her head and leaned over into Keith's arms, pressing her lips into his, tasting the sweet warmth of his mouth.

42

March 1983

Boston, Massachusetts

KATY POLLARD WALKED INTO NICOLE'S OFFICE AND HELD OUT A fresh stack of files. "Here you go, boss. The depositions on Turner Land Developments. Ben and Jerry both say they'll be ready for trial by next week. They just need you to sign the release forms on top."

Nicole rose from her chair, took the stack of folders and laid them in the middle of her wide desk. "Thank you, Katy. Has that idiot Bergen with the FDA returned my call yet?"

"Nope." Katy, hands on hips, shook her head. "I've called him three times this morning."

"Fine." Nicole sat back down and put on her reading glasses. "Get Senator Wellford on the phone for me, if you would, please. He owes me a few favors. He's on the Senate appropriations committee. We'll see how cooperative that pompous ass Bergen is when he finds out he's about to get his budget slashed."

Katy giggled. "I'll get ahold of the senator's office right away."

Nicole called after Katy as she left her office. "Don't call the main number. His private number is in the address book in my purse. Tell him I may have second thoughts about

accepting his invitation to Jamaica if he gives you any shit."
Nicole could still hear Katy laughing after she closed her
door.

Nicole's thoughts went back to Rae. Until her old friend
called from her Christmas party two years ago, they hadn't
written or spoken since Rae left Boston. But when she heard
Rae's voice, it was as though a moment hadn't passed
between them. She was delighted to hear Rae had done so
well in Houston, and was only too happy to help her find out
if she could possibly realize her dream again. The never-
completely-forgotten legacy of Rebecca Danforth still
haunted Nicole from time to time. Rebecca hadn't just beat
her—she made her look foolish and unprepared in her very
first case. Over the past two years, any chance to help Rae
overcome that miscarriage of justice became her top priority.

After that first fruitful week of research, Nicole was as
excited as Rae was to discover that, indeed, her new idea of
research wasn't within Rebecca's clutches. Nicole had put in
over a hundred hours of research in those first five days
alone, called in numerous favors from Washington, done all
the incorporation work, and was now, two years later, in the
process of getting full FDA approval for Brighton, Taylor,
and Associates. That seemingly impossible feat was in its
sixth month. And she did it all for her customary fee—ten
dollars—customary for Rae Taylor, that is.

Nicole could still remember the sound of Rae's joyous
tears when she gave her the news that everything was safe to
proceed in her research. And that made Nicole feel good.
Helping Rae get back into her chosen field somehow made
the weight of her first loss in court, *Taylor* v. *Secularian,* a
little lighter. In her heart she felt a strange obligation for
restitution, even though her mind told her it was irrational.
And even if she had to pull strings at the White House, she
was determined to get Rae everything she needed to be
successful—and now she had the power to do it.

Her intercom buzzed. "Nicole, I've got Senator Wellford
on the line. He says he wants to speak with you personally."

"Thank you, Katy." Nicole hit her speaker phone button. "Hello, Tom. How are you today?"

"Fine, fine," the senator's voice boomed out of the speaker on Nicole's desk. She turned the volume down a bit. "Now what's this nonsense about you backing out of our trip?"

Nicole laughed. "Did Katy tell you that? I was just teasing her," she lied. "She takes everything I say so literally."

"That's good to hear." The senator sounded genuinely relieved.

"So when are you going to call Frank Berger for me?" Nicole propped her elbows on her desk.

Senator Wellford chuckled, "I'll call him this afternoon if you like."

"I like. Threaten him, beat him, take away all his funding. Do whatever you have to, but I want him to process Dr. Taylor's application at the top of his pile." Nicole's voice was jocular, but the senator could tell she wasn't kidding.

"Isn't this a new company? Have they submitted all of the paperwork?" He was obviously fishing for a reason not to cooperate.

"Yes, it's been in for six months now." Nicole was growing impatient.

"Well, I'll see what I can do," he offered diplomatically. "But you must know, sometimes these things take time. Years, in some cases."

"Not good enough, Tom." Nicole leaned down by the desk set, nearer to the microphone, to be heard clearly. She lowered her voice to a sultry tone, "I want results. And if you let me down, I'll call Berger myself and invite *him* to come with me to Jamaica. And then I'll tell him how you two compare in the area of indoor sports."

Tom Wellford burst into laughter. "You'd do it too. Wouldn't you?"

"Are you willing to try me?" She sat up straight.

"Not on your life," came his quick reply. "I'll have one of my staffers get you an itinerary right away. I thought we might rent one of those fifty-foot sailing yachts and do the little islands this time. Get a few gallons of rum, some baby oil, that kind of thing."

Nicole let a pregnant pause pass. "Get me that FDA approval, Tom, and I'll forget to pack a swimsuit."

The senator cleared his throat. "I'll get back with you before close of business today."

"Have a nice day, Senator." Nicole punched the line button, terminating the call. Perhaps Brian had been right. The Senate sounded like it could be a lot of fun.

43

August 1990

Dallas, Texas

SHE KEPT HER EYES CLOSED, DEEPLY DRAWING THE SWEET FRA-grance of the coconut-scented oil in through her nose, expanding her chest beneath the lambent fingers rising up her sides, cupping her breasts, kneading them together, sliding between them, then winding down her stomach again. She felt the hot buttery liquid on his hands burning into her thighs and hips, across her knees, down her shins, and lusciously around her feet. She let out a relaxed sigh as she felt strong fingers probing their way up the insides of her calves, slightly parting her knees. She couldn't stifle a gasp of excitement as the strong hands dissolved the tension in her inner thighs, moving higher and higher toward the one place she wanted touched more than any other.

"Do it," she whispered, almost pleading.

There was a moment of hesitation, a void of desire on the brink of panic, but it was soon placated with gratifying fullness as she felt the tips of his fingers separating the velvety hairs and begin their gentle caresses, cautiously exploring her honeyed recess. As the stimulating caresses continued, a delicious wave of excitement shuddered through her when she felt the heat of his breath poised above her left breast, waiting, teasing. Her back arched up toward the heat, driving the sensitized peak into the moist warmth of his open mouth. The swirling motion of his tongue made her thrash her right leg down against the massage table, biting her lower lip as the long muscles in her legs began to tighten. It was time.

"Now," she whispered. "I want you now."

She kept her eyes closed, a smile of eager anticipation on her lips as she felt him move around the end of the table and climb atop it. The hot breath from his nostrils blasted against her legs, her stomach, her chest, her shoulder—he was almost there. When she felt his swift entrance, her state of arousal was so peaked, her entire body involuntarily went into frantic motion, her hips rocking wildly against his rigid body. Her arms reached around him and pulled his chest down against her own.

She could feel his skilled hands sliding easily over the rich oils on her sides, carefully maneuvering beneath her to the small of her back. With impatient fury his hands and body worked together in harmony with her rocking hips to synchronize the ferocious thrusts with greater and greater force, driving her to a delirious climax in a matter of seconds—a climax that peaked with bone-jarring exertion, every joint straining to the point of pain, an incredible pain, a delightful pain, an intense pressure that spun her equilibrium like a tornado and ground her teeth together with flesh-tearing power. And it didn't stop; he wouldn't let it stop.

She cried out loudly—in ecstasy, in pain, in delirium, in desperation—for more. And it went on. With every euphoric convulsion, she felt him increase his speed, pounding and pounding, deeper and deeper, harder and harder, faster and faster—her eyes came open. The room was spinning, her ears starting to ring, her heart beating its way out through her temples, and the undulating orgasmic waves radiating out from the inferno within her. It kept going and going, her body telling her any instant she would lose consciousness, and she didn't care. She wanted it, she wanted it all, she wanted it to devastate her completely, utterly, discharging every spark of energy in her body.

This was what she had been dreaming about all her life that sex could be, should be, was supposed to be, when it was done right—and the incredible expression of complete gratification her body was now experiencing transformed her dream into a reality. It was too sweet a sensation for her body to contain; the destructive tornado of white-hot passion swept her away again, higher and higher into the air of mindless ecstasy, every ounce of energy, every muscle, every gland, every breath—focused into one massive, writhing, flailing, digging, surging, scratching, pounding, contorting, grimacing, paralyzing—

Unconsciousness.

When she awoke, it was dark outside. Her last memory was in the early evening, just after dinner. It was still light out then. A quiet étude played on the stereo. She was lying in her bed, her hair still damp and matted to her head, her skin still smooth with the lingering trace of oil and the faint scent of coconut. She lay covered with the soft linen sheet and her quilt. She was alone.

He must have put her to bed, she thought. Her entire body ached wonderfully; and in a futile attempt to stretch her legs, she was instantly aware of an extreme soreness in the place that had caused so much pleasure. That made her smile. If she were saddle sore for a week, it would have been worth it. No man had ever been able to please her like that. This place was too good to be true. That thought inspired her to roll over and lift the French-styled telephone receiver off its brass hook and dial the front desk.

She heard Carol's voice, the night clerk. "Yes, how may I help you?"

"Is Marsha Collins still on the premises?" She was still trying to clear the fog from her head.

"Yes, ma'am. She's still here. I think I can still reach her in Dr. Brighton's office. Please hold." She was put on hold and heard more soothing music coming out of the phone. A few moments later she heard Carol's friendly voice again. "Just a second, I'll transfer you."

She heard a ring, then Marsha's voice. "This is Ms. Collins."

"Marsha, I need to talk to you. It's urgent." She had made up her mind. After only four visits to the North Dallas Women's Center, there was no way in hell she was going to let any other person have it—especially Rae Taylor. She had to have it. It was too luscious, too wonderful. "This is Rebecca Danforth. Can you meet me in the Luchesi Salon for a drink?"

Marsha's voice was tentative. "It's nine-thirty right now. I still have some things to discuss with Dr. Brighton. Is ten o'clock too late?"

"No," Rebecca insisted. "That's perfect. I'll see you then." Rebecca knew it would take at least half an hour to make it out of bed and get dressed.

Marsha glanced at her watch when she saw Rebecca enter the elegant salon. It was 10:12 P.M. She didn't like to be kept waiting. But she decided not to say anything about it after she saw Rebecca. She looked ill.

"Are you feeling all right?" Marsha asked with genuine concern as Rebecca flopped down in one of the plush cocktail chairs.

"Yes," she sighed, "I'm fine." Rebecca leaned toward Marsha. "Derek was kind enough to give me one of those hot-oil massages, and I'm afraid I overdid myself a bit."

Marsha smiled. "Derek is in high demand for that. Some say he gives better massages than Brett."

Rebecca leaned back. "Oh really? I haven't met Brett yet."

Marsha shrugged. "He's the expert." Her smile faded. She was not in the mood to chitchat. "So what did you want to talk about?"

"Business," Rebecca said bluntly. "I've had my staff

checking into this place for weeks. And they can't find out shit about it. You've been very discreet. And I like that."

Marsha looked annoyed. "What is it that you're trying to find out?"

"Who owns this place?" Rebecca demanded. "Are you publicly owned or private?"

"Right now we're privately held." Marsha took a sip of her cognac. "The corporate stock is held equally by Dr. Taylor, Dr. Brighton, and myself."

Rebecca looked disappointed. "Any chance you might want to sell out?"

Marsha laughed. "I don't think so. With eight- and nine-figure net profits per annum, it would hardly be a wise business move." She leaned toward Rebecca to rub it in. "Besides, we're having too much fun."

"I can see that." Rebecca returned her smile. This is not what she wanted to hear. "So there's no way to get a piece of this action?"

Marsha looked hopeful. "Well, now that you mention it, we are planning an expansion program you might be able to get in on."

"What kind of expansion program?" Rebecca was eager again.

"Oh, I'm not familiar with all the minute details." Marsha tried to look naive. "Our broker is handling all of that. But I can tell you that we're planning a major upgrade package for the entire complex, including a retirement village and condominiums for clients who wish to locate at the center on a permanent basis."

Rebecca was salivating. "Real estate broker?"

Marsha shook her head. "Stockbroker. Unfortunately, we haven't exactly decided how to proceed. The upgrade is estimated to take almost a billion dollars, cash. And we don't have that kind of money yet. So we're either considering a bond program or perhaps a public stock offering."

Rebecca almost came out of her chair. "You're seriously considering going public?"

Marsha shook her head. "We don't want to. Rae doesn't want to give up any control. But we may have to if we want to proceed with the renovations. Over the long term it may end up making us a lot more money."

Rebecca was quick to agree. "Oh, it would! It would. Definitely. I wouldn't screw around with bonds. You're subject to interest rate fluctuations and all that shit. Plus the government gets twice as involved."

"Really?" Marsha asked as if she didn't know.

"Really," Rebecca stated flatly. "Take my word for it. I've been in the corporate game for a long time. And public stock is definitely the way to go."

Marsha smiled. "Well, your success certainly attests to your wisdom in the business world. Doesn't it? I'll keep that in mind. Like I said, we haven't decided yet. I'm waiting to hear from my broker. He's still doing the financial analysis, and will give us the long-term projections of each option."

Rebecca asked innocently, "So who's your broker?"

"Why do you want to know?" Marsha asked with measured skepticism.

"Because you may want to use mine," Rebecca said quickly. "He's the best. He can get you the best terms with any lenders, has the best attorneys, the works."

"I think Mr. Bodell will do just fine." Marsha nodded. "But thank you for the offer. Was there anything else you wanted to talk about?"

Rebecca shook her head. "Not for now. Thank you, Marsha. You've been most helpful. Who knows? Either way you go, I'll see if I can help you get those condos built." She batted her eyes. "And after this afternoon, I may want to live in one myself."

Marsha chuckled. "That would be wonderful." She cocked her eyebrow. "Although, from what I hear, you're supposed to have enough cash to do it single-handedly."

Rebecca laughed. "Not hardly. But keep the rumor going if you don't mind."

"If you'll excuse me." Marsha got up to leave. "It's quite late."

"Oh, certainly." Rebecca reached for Marsha's hand and politely thanked her again for meeting with her so late in the evening.

Rebecca couldn't wait for morning. By close of business tomorrow, she'd know everything she needed to know about a mysterious stockbroker named Bodell.

44

November 1983

Houston, Texas

"HELLO?" RAE KNOCKED ON THE BEAUTIFUL STAINED OAK DOOR of Alicia Brighton's six-thousand-square-foot home in King's Heights. She didn't hear any answer as she came into the beautiful marble entryway and closed the door behind her. She had seen Alicia's BMW 633 sitting out in the circular driveway, so she knew she was home. It was Saturday; they had agreed to go shopping and then meet Keith and Charles for lunch. Rae had grown concerned when Alicia hadn't answered the doorbell. She found Alicia sitting in the spacious county kitchen, wearing her bathrobe, just staring out the bay window at her flower garden.

"Alicia?" Rae walked over to the table. "Didn't you hear me at the door?" She became alarmed when she saw that Alicia was crying. "What's wrong? What's happened?"

Alicia turned and looked at Rae. Her short black hair, now showing a few streaks of gray, framed a swollen and puffy face. She had obviously been crying for a long time. Her eyes puddled up again when she saw Rae, and a soggy handkerchief in her right hand came up to her runny nose. She wiped it from side to side.

"Oh, honey." Rae came over, put her arms around Alicia's shoulders and rested her chin on her head. Alicia buried her face in Rae's chest and started to sob, her arms trembling, holding on to Rae like a frightened kitten. "It's all right, now." Rae stroked her hair and did her best to be comforting, her insides twisting into knots wondering what had happened.

After many patient minutes Alicia settled down and started to talk. Rae made some hot tea, sat down, and gave her friend her best ear.

"I was talking to Stella Porter, an old colleague from Boston who had relocated to Dallas," Alicia began with difficulty. The more she talked, the more relaxed and lucid she became. "I was calling her about some support documentation for the FDA report Nicole wanted. She mentioned something about Secularian, and I asked if she had heard anything about Donald recently." She started to puddle up again.

"Go on," Rae urged with as much compassion as she could muster.

Alicia took a deep breath." And Stella asks me in surprise, 'Don't you know?' Know what? I ask." Alicia's hands illustrated every word, her right hand still clinging to her saturated handkerchief. "She says, 'Donald passed away of a heart attack three years ago.'" She started to cry again.

Rae's face pinched with concern. "Oh, Alicia, I'm so sorry. I never realized how much you still cared for him."

Alicia did her best to push a half laugh through her tears. "Yeah, well, some things you just grow attached to after a quarter century or so." She wiped her red eyes. "I never should have left. I should have stayed and fought. We had our problems, but maybe I should have just—"

Rae cut her off. "Alicia stop that. You couldn't have done anything more than you did. He was a big boy, he made his own decisions." She suddenly looked puzzled. "Besides, I thought you two didn't keep in touch. You said it was three years ago. I don't understand."

Alicia gave Rae a pained grin. "I didn't tell you the worst

part. And granted, it's only my ex-wife suspicion, but I'd lay money I'm right."

"What?" Rae demanded.

"After I talked to Stella yesterday, I made a few calls." Alicia's words were picking up speed and venom. "At first I didn't believe her. Donald was a marathon runner, an avid skier. He had the heart of a teenager. There was no way I could believe he just had a heart attack at sixty-five. Syphilis, yes. Heart attack, no."

Rae didn't know if she should smile. She decided not to.

Alicia rambled on, "So I made a few calls. And what do I find out? But that our dear Miss Danforth had married him." She shouted, "Can you believe that?" Her voice settled back down. "And he passed away shortly thereafter."

Rae's face darkened; the black feeling of foreboding was back. "You don't think . . ."

"Rae." Alicia looked resolute. "I found out through a few well-meaning friends that Rebecca Danforth, by virtue of her marriage to Donald and his subsequent death, has over fifty percent of Secularian stock and is now the chairman of the board."

"No!" Rae was appalled. "Alicia, that's insane. Rebecca's a monster. But even *I* don't think she'd stoop that low."

"I don't know what else to think." Alicia turned back to her flower garden.

Rae thought for a moment. "I'll give Nikki a call."

Alicia turned back. "What can *she* do?"

Rae walked over to the telephone. "She's got lots of connections. She deals with big white-collar crime all the time. If Rebecca did anything, Nikki may know who can find out for us."

Alicia looked impressed. "You think she'd do that? Nicole's a very busy lady."

Rae dialed the private number of the Cape Cod residence Nikki had given her, expecting to get her answering machine. "If what you suspect is the case, then Rebecca Danforth has got to be stopped. Nikki's the only person I know who might be able to do it."

Alicia shook her head. "Rae, from what I've heard, Rebecca has become a very powerful woman. We could be taking a serious risk. And we've got a lot to lose now. All that research. After what she did to you the last time, I'd think you'd want to stay out of her way."

"Wrong." Rae listened to the successive rings. "If Rebecca took your husband away and then had him killed for his money, then I want to be the *first person* in her way."

Alicia was about to say something when Rae looked down at the floor and held up her finger for silence.

"Nikki? Hi, this is Rae." Rae looked back at Alicia with a pleased note of surprise. She proceeded to take a full ten minutes to explain what they had discovered and solicit her assistance. Nicole told Rae she knew of several good private investigators, and with Rebecca Danforth involved, it would be her privilege to hire one. It took Rae almost twenty minutes to get off the phone.

"Well, what did she say?" Alicia looked eager.

Rae walked back to the breakfast table and sat down. "She's going to hire an investigator for us. The detective she recommended is a woman by the name of Clarice James. Nikki said she's used her on a number of key cases and she's supposed to be very good."

Alicia shuddered. "This is all so sordid."

Rae nodded. "That's our Rebecca."

45

August 1990

Dallas, Texas

THE OFFICES OF MALCOLM BODELL WERE SMALL BUT IMPRESSIVE, nicely appointed, located in a Los Colinas high rise near the DFW Airport. It had taken Rebecca's staff less than half a day to track down the stockbroker, and five minutes to arrange a meeting. Rebecca walked through the modern glass and chrome foyer of his office suite and smiled graciously at his receptionist, an elderly woman wearing too much makeup and cheap perfume.

"Yes?" the ruby-red lips asked. The older woman's eyes blinked behind a thick pair of glasses.

Rebecca only glanced at her. "Rebecca Danforth to see Mr. Bodell."

"Oh yes, Ms. Danforth, you're expected. Right this way." The woman toddled from behind her mahogany reception station and gestured for Rebecca to follow her. She led Rebecca down a corridor of closed offices to a set of double doors at the end of the hallway. The old woman knocked once, then opened the door. "Mr. Bodell, Ms. Danforth is here now."

Rebecca strode past the doddering woman in time to see a middle-aged gentlemen with bright red hair hastily put out a cigarette and rise to greet her. He looked comfortable with his tie loosened and his sleeves rolled halfway up. He hurried to make his way around a desk piled with papers.

Bodell smiled and extended his hand. "Ms. Danforth, I'm pleased to finally meet you."

Rebecca took his hand at arm's length. "Mr. Bodell."

"Please, sit down." He gestured to a burgundy leather occasional chair next to his desk, then looked back toward the door. "That will be all, Harriet. Thank you very much."

"Coffee for you or the lady?" the old woman asked.

Bodell looked at Rebecca questioningly.

"Nothing for me, thank you," she said politely. Rebecca knew it was time to be on her best behavior—unless that didn't work.

"No, we're fine." Bodell waved at the old woman, and she nodded and left, closing the office door behind her.

Bodell sat back down at his desk. "So, Ms. Danforth, I've heard a great deal about you. Who hasn't in Dallas? It certainly is an honor to meet you."

Rebecca decided to let him get the customary ass-kissing out of the way before getting down to business. "Thank you, I appreciate that."

Bodell looked excited. "I can assure you, Ms. Danforth, we handle some of the most impressive portfolios in the country out of this office. You've definitely come to the right place."

Rebecca was about to challenge his contention, but refrained. "Is that so? How lovely. Well, I'm always looking for ways to maximize my investments."

Bodell beamed. "Wonderful! Is there a particular financial goal you've established for yourself, or would you like me to explain our standard product set?"

Rebecca did her best not to laugh. This man looked like a kid at Disneyland. But then he ought to, she reflected. She was one of the richest women in the country. This was probably his dream come true. She decided to continue playing the game. "Oh, I'm keenly interested in a particular investment which I understand you're handling personally."

Bodell looked puzzled. "I'm sorry? What could that possibly be?"

Rebecca gave him her most devastating smile, letting her eyes smolder. "The North Dallas Women's Center?"

Bodell leaned back in his chair. "Oh, yes!" His face clouded. "But how do you know about that? That deal's not public knowledge yet."

"I have my sources, Mr. Bodell." She crossed her legs, making sure her legs slipped out the tall slit in her skirt to give him the full show. "I make it my business to know everything that goes on in this town."

"Well, I'm sorry, Ms. Danforth." Bodell shrugged. "There's not much I can tell you about that deal. It's still very premature."

"Perhaps," she lilted elliptically. "Perhaps not. You can certainly give me some background information regarding its status." She quickly appended, "For future reference sake, of course."

"What could I tell you?" he asked innocently, tossing his red locks to the side.

"Is there going to be a public stock offering?" Her voice was getting impatient.

"I haven't decided." He shook his head. "Probably bonds. I think I can get a fixed note from Cosmopolitan Life Insurance and hold the interest rate down. Besides, the current owners still want to maintain control."

Rebecca shook her head. "Yes, but the commission rate on a stock purchase for you would be much greater than a bond issue."

"Not necessarily," he replied. "That stock could be traded all over the world. I'd have to sell it all myself to make any real money."

Rebecca's eyes narrowed. "What if you could? All to one buyer, one deal, all the shares."

Bodell nodded. "I'd be a much richer man. And probably retire."

"That's right," Rebecca agreed. "So tell me more, Mr. Bodell, and perhaps I may be in a position to find you that single buyer."

His eyes grew wide. "Are you serious?"

She wasn't ready to show her cards yet. "Perhaps. But I need more information. What's the cash status?"

"They've got approximately three hundred million liquid," he said with no emotion. "And it's been in operation for less than two years."

Rebecca became alarmed. She never dreamed the operation could be that successful. The information fueled her obsession all the more. "Three hundred million? That's certified with the SEC?"

"I'll have the documentation in the prospectus." Bodell smiled.

"Net assets?" she asked hesitantly.

He paused for effect. "Computed by our accounting firm, the whole operation is worth about two point five billion."

Rebecca was livid. All of Secularian, all she had built over the last ten years, was worth just under two point five billion. There was no way in the world Rae Taylor, Donald's old ex, and some has-been real estate queen from Houston could have achieved that in so short a time. But she had seen for herself the caliber of the clientele and the outrageous amounts of money the patrons willingly parted with to enjoy its services.

Could it be true?

Bodell shook his hand. "But those are only current figures. The financial analysis I've put together shows that after the one billion is invested in the upgrade, the entire operation will be worth in excess of seven billion."

Rebecca was feeling light-headed. Her heart was pounding, her lungs began to steal gulps of air. She'd rather die than see that little prima donna from Houston have an empire almost three times the size of hers. She *had* to have it. She wouldn't rest until she possessed it. She'd kill again, if necessary, to get it. Rae Taylor couldn't do this to her.

In that instant, Rebecca's thoughts went back to college. She recalled every time she came home and found the apartment cleaned, another reminder of what a pig Rae thought she was; every time Rae offered to help her with her homework, just to rub it in how stupid she was; every time Rae paraded her wretched virginity around the house, never dating, never doing anything, all of it done just to hold up a big scarlet banner labeling her a whore, to mock and degrade her. She remembered *everything* Rae stood for, her fancy degrees, her precious discoveries—all of it, a living symbol of everything Rebecca wasn't.

She would never consciously allow the words of her father to well up within her, lecturing her on what she was supposed to *be* like, and *act* like, and *think* like, to be a lady—what he expected of her, *demanded* of her. He wanted her to be someone perfect, just like Rae.

Yet there was a time when she *wanted* to please him, when she was a little girl, his little girl, from her earliest memories through her first two years of high school. Her thoughts dredged up her first swimming competition. He told her many times that swimming and parading herself half naked in public was degrading for a Danforth. He forbid her to join the swim team. But she did it anyway. She so much wanted to show him that she could be good at something other than being pretty. She won a gold medal at that first regional competition. He took it away from her and threw it away, lecturing her again about her disgrace to the family. But she went back, and kept winning.

She won a diving competition her senior year at the state finals. Her mother came to see her dive and was very proud of her. But he wouldn't come. In tears, she drove home with her mother, determined to show her father the enormous trophy she had been awarded. It was magnificent, almost as tall as she was. It proved she had been right, and he was wrong.

When they arrived at their home, an ambulance and two police cars were parked in front of the estate with their lights flashing. The servants and authorities quickly told them what had happened. When they heard the news, Rebecca's mother had fainted dead away. Rebecca just stood there in angry silence. Ray Danforth had died of a heart attack—before she could show him he was wrong. From that moment, she made the decision to show the whole fucking world they were wrong.

"Ms. Danforth? Ms. Danforth?" Malcolm Bodell reached out and touched her hand.

Rebecca started from a daze, a sudden flush of embarrassment on her cheeks. "I'm sorry." She absently glanced around the office. "I'm not concentrating very well today. You were saying?"

Bodell chuckled. "I didn't say anything. You just sat there staring. I thought you might be ill."

Rebecca blushed even more, rubbing her cheeks with her palms. "No. I apologize. Something you said made me think of another transaction I was involved in." She cleared her throat and composed herself, angry with herself for a moment of weakness. That hadn't happened in years. She wouldn't let it happen again. "Let's get back to business."

Rebecca spoke with Bodell at great length about the financial arrangements surrounding the North Dallas Women's Center. Her mind went into motion sifting the sketchy facts and asking many more questions. After another fifteen minutes, convinced that this man had the power to give her what she wanted, what she needed, she chose to wrap her deadly web of persuasion around him.

Rebecca leaned forward, letting her low-cut dress expose more of her soft, creamy cleavage. She noticed his eyes take the bait. "Mr. Bodell, tell me. Are the owners of the Women's Center *fully* aware of its current value, or its potential value after the upgrades?"

He laughed. "I don't think so. Actually, I'm scheduled to meet with them this afternoon to discuss it. I just received the report from the accounting firm this morning. So just between you and me, what I've told you is kind of talking out of school. I'd appreciate it if you'd keep it strictly confidential."

"Naturally." Rebecca's serene, carnivorous demeanor was back. She leveled her cold eyes, brows knit. "I'll be straight with you, Mr. Bodell. I want to buy the Women's Center. All of it. Every share. If you issue a public stock offering for the current value of two point five billion, I'll put up all of Secularian's stock for you to sell. I can liquefy all my other holdings and take control of all of its outstanding shares. It'll be an even swap. You'll make *double* the commission. I'll break even today, and triple my investment tomorrow."

"I can't just do that, Ms. Danforth." He sounded apologetic. "You ought to know that. That would be a direct conflict of interest. The SEC would nail my ass to the wall."

Rebecca's eyes flashed. *"If* . . . they knew about it. All you have to do is give me a little call before the shares hit the trading floor. I can have people standing by to take them all, quietly and with no fuss."

Bodell swallowed. "That's insider trading, Ms. Danforth. They lock your ass up for that kind of shit. Do not pass go, do not collect two billion dollars. The works."

She shrugged, her voice becoming more hushed and seductive. "Every potential reward has its risks. Wouldn't you agree?"

The air in the room seemed warmer.

"Yeah, but I don't know if that's worth the risk." Bodell leaned back in his chair, growing visibly more uncomfortable with each passing moment.

Rebecca rose from her chair and sauntered over to him, gleefully watching his eyes grow wide with intimidation. She could tell he didn't have a clue what to do next. It was going to be easy, like all the others. She towered over him, letting her long dark hair brush against his chin, knowing even her fragrance would intimidate him all the more.

"I'm only asking for a simple phone call, Malcolm." She reached down and touched his knee with her index finger, slowly sliding her long, ruby-polished nail up his trouser leg. She watched his eyes follow it, swallowing with difficulty. He was starting to sweat.

"Ms. Danforth," he stammered. "Please."

"Please?" She deliberately took advantage of his ambiguous remark. "The magic word. Certainly." She let her fingers meander up to his crotch. "Just one little phone call,

Malcolm?" She began to massage the mound of flesh in her hand, feeling it swell. Men were all the same, her mind told her in disgust. For a cheap feel-good they'd sell their souls. Her senses told her victory was close, she could feel it, she could almost taste it—in a moment another soul would be hers. "You know I'm a very powerful woman, Mr. Bodell, and have the power to make your life *very* comfortable. Very pleasurable. You'd like that, Malcolm. Wouldn't you? A little pleasure—in exchange for a little favor?"

He just pressed himself back into the thick padded chair, breathing with great difficulty. Rebecca took her other hand and lifted his chin, raising it up with her other long fingernail, locking his gaze on hers. Then with both hands she reached down, unclasped his belt and pulled down his zipper. "Haven't decided yet, Malcolm?"

She thought he looked like he was going into shock, his pupils dilating. Keeping their gazes fixed, she pulled the waistband of his briefs down, exposing him. She glanced down. Part of him had already made its decision. The rest of him just sat there, wide-eyed, speechless.

Rebecca's voice dropped to a whisper, "Well, take a few minutes to relax while you make up your mind."

She knelt down on the plush burgundy carpet and teased him with a few darting flourishes of her tongue. His head rocked back against the tall chair. She looked up. "What's your decision, Malcolm? I'm very short on time. Will I get a phone call?"

"Yes," he rasped through clenched teeth.

"Good boy, Malcolm. Wise decision." Rebecca took great joy in giving the red-haired stockbroker his reward. It didn't take long. None of them ever took very long. She deemed it well-deserved, and certainly more than he expected. She laughed to herself after she left. If men thought with their brains half as much as they did with their loins, they might actually be running the world by now.

She felt a shudder of omnipotence as her limousine drove her back to Highland Park. She would call David immediately and start preparations for all the financial transactions. Then it would be time to celebrate. She'd see if David could keep up with the talent at *her* new Women's Center. Soon it would be hers, all of it. And Rae would suffer all over again. She wanted Rae to suffer all over again. It was going to be glorious.

46

December 1983

Dallas, Texas

THERE HE WAS, SITTING ON AN EXERCISE MACHINE, DOING LEG lifts. The first objective was to get his attention. She had made it a point to be noticed from the first moment she emerged from the women's dressing room, wearing skin-tight leotard pants, leg warmers, and a halter-styled cutoff T-shirt that did much more than just show off her devastating bustline, especially after it was moistened with a layer of perspiration. She deliberately went over to an exercise machine directly in his line of sight. It was a horizontal leg press, a machine that worked the inner thigh muscles by opening and closing the legs against weighted resistance. She sat down on the machine, set the weights, then leaned back with her arms bracing her from the rear. It didn't take him more than five seconds to hear the dinner bell ringing.

With each repetition on the machine, she took in a long relaxing breath and let it out slowly. A careful peek beneath her almost-closed lashes confirmed he wasn't missing any of the show. She exaggerated her movements, seductively arching her back and extending her breasts forward. After about twenty pumps a fine layer of perspiration was starting to form. The lure was out.

His eyes followed the hook as she stopped and proceeded to the next machine. It was a bench-press apparatus. It was time for the damsel in distress tactic. She laid down on the bench, pushed the weights up over her head and let them return with a bang. She started to push again, then acted as though it were too much to handle. Out of the corner of her eye she saw her quarry come over to play knight in shining armor.

"Hey!" He grabbed the bar. "You're going to hurt yourself there."

She gave him her most devilish smile. "Thank you. I thought I could do it. I guess it was a little much."

He reached around the machine to lower the weight. "Try a little less."

She shook her head. "No, I think I'll try something else. But thanks again." She walked away, knowing to play the hook a little before it was set. She climbed aboard an exercycle and began pumping. Before long her entire body was glistening wet; her thin white T-shirt was doing its job; and he was looking again. Actually, every man in the health club was looking, but she didn't care. Her goal was very specific. She kept her eyes on him, letting him catch her looking at him, smiling.

He came over, straddled the bike next to hers and began riding. "Hello again."

"Hi," she said, as friendly as possible.

"I haven't seen you in here before." He punched the electronic buttons on the exercycle to start it. "Are you new here?"

"Yes," she said, her breathing hot and labored. "I'm just trying this club out. Is this one of the nicer clubs in Dallas?"

"The best," he panted as his legs began to churn. "I've been a member for about four years. I try to come by after work every afternoon, if I can."

She knew that. She made it her business to know his schedule.

She looked admiringly up and down his well-defined body. "It shows."

He grinned, obviously very pleased with himself. The barbs of the hook were just about set. He looked her over from stem to stern. He was supposed to at that point. "You don't look like you need to work out very much."

She smiled. "You have to, to keep it that way. A firm body requires hard work, discipline, and a lot of determination."

He returned her smile, "Well, you're obviously very determined. So what do you do?" Obviously inquiring about her profession.

She stopped peddling. Time to reel. She ran her hands through her feathered blond hair, then slid her fingers down her body, wiping the sweat into her T-shirt all the more. Her generous breasts stood up firm, each inviting shade now highly visible through the moist, thin cloth. Her voice was hushed, "Anything I want to."

An accepted invitation for drinks and dinner were customary, and it often served to heighten the feeling of anticipation. It did in this case. By the time he bravely asked her back to his lavish Bent Tree estate in North Dallas, he could hardly contain himself. He was an aggressive lover, urgent and strongly physical. But he was good. He took his time when he needed to, and managed to bring her to two memorable orgasms. But when he was near spent, she rolled him on his back and wore him out.

Yet each time she sensed he could no longer contain himself, she would climb off and make him relax. In those times she would talk to him, flatter him on his sexual prowess, ask him questions about his life, his hobbies, how important he was in his job, interspersing each boast with more flattery. She let him brag and boast about anything he wanted, and he loved it. It was typical.

Whenever she sensed he was relaxed enough to continue, she would climb back aboard and draw more and more energy out of his body. She teased him and worked him, never letting him fully catch his breath. For her purpose, he needed to have the time of his life. And he did. That too was typical. After almost three hours, when she was convinced he couldn't hold back any longer, she made him get back on top and work till he nearly collapsed from exhaustion. When the final moment came, both of their bodies were wringing with sweat, lungs gasping, hips locked in furious motions, pressure building, the sheets roughly sticking to their beleaguered bodies as they reached the end together. By the time she felt his warm pulsating climax within her, she had accomplished her goal. He was sound asleep in seconds, still lying between her breasts, still inside her, rapidly wilting away.

With great care she rolled him over; slipped out of his plush bedroom, leaving him snoring soundly; and quietly made her way into the living room with her clothes in her hand. She quickly dressed and stole out of the house to her car. When she arrived back at her hotel room, she picked up the telephone and hastily made a long distance call.

The phone was answered on the third ring. "Nicole, it's Clarice. Did I wake you? Sorry, it couldn't wait. I'm in Dallas, and I've made contact with David Stratton, you might say. Look, you need to get hold of a Dallas County judge. I think we're going to need an exhumation order." She threw her car keys on the nightstand, still listening to Nicole. "Oh, I have my ways. Your friend, Mr. Stratton, was quite talkative under the right circumstances. And you'll be very surprised when I tell you what he's been up to. He's been a very bad boy."

47

January 1985

Houston, Texas

"I UNDERSTAND CONGRATULATIONS ARE IN ORDER." MARSHA raised her freshly poured crystal flute of champagne. "To your success."

All three women took a gleeful sip of the bubbling wine and returned their glasses to the table. As soon as Nicole had called that morning with the news of the expedited FDA approval, they had called Marsha. Marsha suggested a celebration lunch at Shady Oaks to commemorate the momentous occasion.

Rae was absolutely beaming. "Marsha, I didn't believe it. I still can't. I don't know how Nicole did it, but she did it. We're supposed to get all the formal documentation *within a week*, and then we can officially open the doors of Brighton, Taylor, and Associates to the public. It's going to be incredible."

Marsha felt so happy for Rae and Alicia. They were both positively radiant with joy. Only under the extraordinary circumstances of Rae and Alicia's current business venture would she ever have considered letting Rae leave Collins Enterprises. Rae was worth a fortune to her. But this unique opportunity for Rae to get back into her beloved research was the one gift she knew she had to give her friend, despite the cost. She nodded graciously. "Again, I'm very proud of you both." She looked at Alicia with stern reservation, pointing an accusing finger. "Although, I'm holding you personally responsible for stealing my best employee. I haven't forgiven you for that yet."

Alicia smiled, her bifocals rising up as she wrinkled her nose. "I'll not deny it. Rae Taylor is the best."

Even in January, on a sunny day, the weather was warm enough to dine on the flagstone terrace. Rae leaned back in the cool sunshine. "I love it when you two fight over me. My ego enlarges about three sizes."

"Your ego? Or are you just thinking of your boyfriend?" Alicia teased.

Rae's eyes narrowed on Alicia. "You leave Keith out of this." Both Alicia and Rae laughed until Rae noticed Marsha sitting quietly, smiling politely in the atmosphere of their mirth, but obviously quite apart from it. Rae knew something was bothering her. "Marsha, what's wrong?"

Marsha looked away. "I guess I'm just jealous of you two. Since you've been gone, it just hasn't been the same. The economy's gone to hell. Real estate is a joke in Houston, in case you haven't been reading the papers. Foreclosures are like a new fad, even in the high-rent district." She forced a smile. "But listen to me, whining like a baby. This is a wonderful day for you, and I'm spoiling it."

"No," both women were quick to express their concern. Rae chastised her former mentor, "Marsha Collins, this isn't like you. Come on. What's really the matter? We know you don't need the money."

Alicia took another sip of her glass. "Marsha, you've never kept anything back from us. You've told us every juicy detail of your love life, so don't hold out on us with your professional life."

Marsha looked at both of them, internally grateful for the opportunity to dump the landfill of garbage collecting inside her. "It's not that serious an issue, ladies," she lied. "Calm down. I just miss working. I haven't sold a house in almost a year." She took a deep breath, held it for a second, then huffed, "You're right, it isn't the money. It's sitting around that *stupid* office all by myself waiting for the damned phone to ring. Or lying here at the club without pampering a client with hot oil and a hot young man." She threw her hands up. "I'm bored!"

Rae shook her head in amazement. "Those are two words I never thought I'd hear you say."

Alicia looked over at Rae with a mischievous expression. "Go ahead and ask her. It's as good a time as any."

Marsha was suddenly apprehensively curious. "What? Ask me what?"

Rae smiled at Alicia. "Well, it's interesting that you happen to be between ventures at the moment, because after much discussion, Alicia and I have decided to ask you to join us at Brighton, Taylor, and Associates. We really need you. Would you consider it?"

"What?" Marsha was flabbergasted. "I don't know anything about medicine."

Alicia leaned forward. "Yes, dear, but you know about business. And we're short-handed in that area. We desperately need a good business manager, someone who can market our discoveries, develop a client base, handle the legal and financial facets of the operation."

Rae was grinning. "Of course, the job doesn't pay much."

Marsha was starting to cry. "You girls are too much." She wiped her eyes. "You'd let me do that for you? You'd really let me join you?"

"Let you?" Alicia was genuinely taken aback. "We argued the whole way over here on the best way to talk you into doing it. We considered kidnapping and extortion."

"You will help us, won't you?" Rae's eyes were pleading.

Marsha hesitated. She didn't know what to think. Could they be serious?

Rae cocked her head. "It could be like old times."

Marsha burst into more tear-filled laughter. "Better than old times!"

Both Rae and Alicia got up from their seats and hugged their new business partner. The waiter arrived with their meals and patiently stood at a polite distance until they had resumed their seats in a fresh buzz of conversation.

Marsha couldn't believe the euphoric feeling coursing

through her veins. A new challenge, a new opportunity—in an instant, it was like being raised from the dead. She couldn't think of two other people on the face of the earth she loved more than Rae and Alicia. As they went their separate ways professionally, they had stayed very close socially. Rae and Alicia were always invited to her lavish parties, and rarely did a day go by when they weren't at one another's homes or talking at length on the phone. But as the years stretched out, the frequency of their contact had noticeably declined. As Rae and Alicia made greater progress in their research, the more enamored they became with science instead of their old friend. And that hurt. Their invitation to join them in their business was the greatest gift Rae could ever have given Marsha. It was more than she ever could have asked for. She felt as if her family had just been reunited.

"Oh, but there's more news," Rae said with melodramatic forboding.

"What?" Marsha asked eagerly.

Rae leaned forward as if she had the latest gossip. "Nikki said her investigator, after poking around for over a year, is convinced that Donald Bennet's death was not an accident."

"No." Marsha was shocked.

Alicia jumped in. "Yes. She says she can't prove anything yet, and it still may take quite a bit of investigation, but she knows Rebecca Danforth was involved."

"I can't believe it," Marsha protested.

"We can't either," Rae continued. "But Nikki says she either did it herself or hired someone else to do it."

Marsha shook her head in disbelief. "That's hideous. How could she be such a monster?"

Rae shrugged. "I don't know. She's sick. She needs help. But I have to be honest with you. I really hope Nikki comes up with something. It would do my soul good to see her behind bars."

Alicia pulled her fork out of her mouth. "Well, someone

should do something. The woman's clearly a menace to society."

Rae's voice became terse, "You know, if it hadn't been for her, we could have the perfect clinic for women. Imagine a place where women could go and receive any cosmetic treatment to make her *look* beautiful—Alicia's piece of the puzzle." She smiled at Marsha. "Plus has her fill of all the young men she can handle, to make her *feel* beautiful—"

"In your dreams." Marsha laughed, batting at the air.

Rae continued, "Your piece, Marsha. And having the ability to be cured of any life-threatening diseases on the inside, to make her whole life *be* beautiful." She grew solemn again. "It all would be so perfect. But that *woman* took away the best piece—my piece. We can treat the outside, but not the inside. It's the law."

Marsha put her hand on Rae's arm. "Well, the first two parts sure sounded good. Perhaps we could still all die happy with two-thirds of the dream?"

"That's right," Alicia piped in. "Can't you just see it?" She held up her hands like a banner. "Come down to Brighton, Taylor, and Associates for a boob job, a nose job, and a hand job—hot oil optional."

All three women burst into laughter.

Marsha shook her finger at Alicia. "You joke. There just might be some money in that."

Rae shook her head. "Well, right now we just need to figure out how to get some clients and keep our doors open. We can't help anyone until the world knows we exist."

Marsha raised her glass again. "Oh, the world's *going* to know we exist. You just hired the woman that can bring it to you."

All three glasses met with the piercing ring of lead crystal.

48

March 1988

Houston, Texas

"WHAT DO YOU THINK?" ALICIA GLANCED UP AT RAE'S PER-
plexed expression.

"Hard to tell." Rae reached down and tilted the young
woman's face up toward the parabolic examination lamp.
This was the worst case either of them had seen in the last
three years, since Brighton, Taylor, and Associates had
received FDA approval to administer their experimental
treatment to the general public.

Since 1985 they had seen almost three hundred patients,
most of them coming through word of mouth, specifically
Marsha Collins's mouth. Marsha had done a great deal for
the small clinic in Greenway Plaza; and after their first three
years, they actually showed a small profit. But like any new
endeavor, progress was slow and tedious. It seemed to Rae it
moved more slowly than their research. There were so many
details and legalities to observe.

On Nicole Prescott's insistence, each patient was asked to
sign mounds of legal documentation acknowledging the
experimental nature of the treatment, thus releasing the
small women's cosmetic health-care clinic of any liability.
Consequently, fees were kept to a minimum, as were profits.
But with each case came more and more valuable experience, more data, and more documentation. With a constant
methodology of trial and error, they discovered which
methods produced the most desirable results and which

were nominally effective. And over the past year the miracles began to happen.

Most of the cases treated were superficial skin blemishes, age spots, wrinkles, and minor muscle or nerve damage. But the most amazing results came from working with scars and burns. However, the case before them challenged anything they had attempted to treat thus far. The depth of the burns and scarring reached down to the bone. Alicia didn't think it could be done.

"This is another waste of my time. Isn't it?" Sabrina said with disdain.

"I'll tell you if it is," Rae said confidently, looking intently at the black and red discolorations around the woman's eyes. She let go of the woman's cheeks and stood up.

"Well?" Sabrina was prepared for the worst.

Rae walked over to a small metal writing desk in the examination room and took a seat. "Ms. Doucette, I want you to understand, first of all, that I believe we can help you."

"But what?" Sabrina demanded. "I think I've heard this speech before from the plastic surgeons."

Rae smiled. "No you haven't. The problem we face in helping you, is the fact that your injuries involve scar tissue. Scar tissue doesn't regenerate. Our treatment uses regenerating cells to replace unwanted cells to return tissue to its original state."

"So you're saying it can't be done." Sabrina folded her arms indignantly.

"No, dear," Alicia interrupted in a comforting way. "Just listen. That's not what she's saying."

Sabrina looked back at Rae.

Rae nodded at Alicia in thanks. "This may sound a lot worse than it is, but I'll give it to you straight. The first person to ever receive scar treatments was myself, about five years ago. And what we found out was that injections around scar tissue had no effect. And injections of our catalyst serum into the scar tissue itself had no effect."

Sabrina looked puzzled. "Then what did you do?"

Rae took a hesitant breath. "We first had to cut away the scar tissue. Remove it entirely. That's Alicia's job. She's our resident surgeon."

Sabrina grimaced, a look of apprehension spread across her face.

Rae held up her palm. "I know it sounds gruesome. But understand what has to happen. In my case, once the scar tissue was removed, the opened tissues beneath were stimulated to regenerate. At that point we administered the serum, and the tissues that grew back were like the original, not the scar. It works. Look at the back of my hand."

Sabrina glanced over. Rae's hand looked like anyone's hand. "I don't see anything."

Alicia spoke up. "Rae had a cut two inches long and a quarter of an inch deep. She intentionally rubbed the wound for several days to make sure it created a scar instead of closing up properly." She looked over and gave Rae a five-year-old look of chastisement. "The treatments took about two weeks, but in less than thirty days you couldn't tell there had ever been a cut. We've seen the same happen for about a dozen other patients."

"All right." Sabrina's voice sounded challenging. "What's the problem, then?"

Rae crossed her legs and leaned forward with her hands on her knees. "The problem is the extent of damage to your face. If we cut away portions of the scar tissue, the surrounding tissues have to have time to begin the cell-mapped regeneration before new scar tissue forms. For that to happen, the wounds have to stay open. It's not very comfortable."

Alicia looked at Sabrina sternly. "And with the extent of the area of your face affected, if we did it all, you could bleed to death. We'd have to dig away quite a lot."

Sabrina looked disappointed. "So you're not willing to try?"

Rae furrowed her brow, thinking for a moment. "Alicia, what if we went slow, and did it a little at a time? Segregated, say, each ocular region into four segments. Then we work on one segment on each eye for a full week, then move to another segment. That would give each area a full month of treatment before it was traumatized again, and the surface area would be reduced for each operation by seventy-five percent."

Alicia sat back, somewhat stunned. "Rae, you're asking this girl to go through four operations in as many weeks, and have two open wounds on her face for a month. Those wounds won't even close until the fifth or sixth week. Have you any idea what she'd be going through? Think about the risk of infection."

Rae continued to look at Sabrina's face. "You didn't answer my question. Would it work?"

Alicia looked back at Sabrina. "It might. But I'm not going to make that call."

"Then it's up to you," Rae said to Sabrina. "No guarantees. Just a possibility. All, on the other side of a great deal of discomfort. I won't lie to you. What we'll put you through will be very painful."

Sabrina measured the look on both physicians' faces. There was a confidence in their eyes that said they could be trusted. "You don't know the pain I've already been through. If you can give me the chance to have my face back, I can handle it."

Alicia walked over and put her arm around Sabrina's shoulders. "That's very brave, dear. But don't make a snap decision. Think about this. Take some time."

Sabrina flinched away, raising her voice. "I don't *need* to *think* about it! If I wasn't *serious,* I wouldn't have *come* here!" She stood up from the paper-lined examination table and walked over by the wall. "Look, I can't tell you what kind of a hell my life's been like over the last two years. Before my accident, I thought I had everything a woman could want. And it was probably true. Everyone wanted to know me, to love me, to talk to me, to be near me. But after I woke up in that hospital, every person who looked at me got sick. Shit, I got sick when I saw it."

She leaned her back up against the wall; a thin tear had already made its way down to her chin. She brushed it aside with the back of her hand. "The phone calls stopped. The friends who had sent cards, letters, and flowers all stopped coming. And even the one person I thought really loved me found better things to do—just walked away without even a good-bye."

Rae and Alicia exchanged a look of sympathy.

Sabrina held her palms up, her fingers extended. "My life ended at that finish line. I checked out a champion. That's how a racer is supposed to go out." She ran her fingers back through her hair. "But somehow I woke up in this sequel to an incredible life all alone, with nothing but memories. I've spent the last two years watching 'Wheel of Fortune' and making empty Smirnoff bottles. And I don't know what else to do." She leveled her gaze at Alicia. "Doc, if you want to cut this hideous shit off my face, be my guest. It won't hurt me a bit!" She lowered her voice, "And it ain't gonna make me look any worse."

A pained silence held all three women for several moments.

Rae nodded, "Very well, Ms. Doucette. If you don't mind waiting in my office, I need to speak with Dr. Brighton for a moment. We'll let you know how we might proceed in a little while."

Sabrina sniffed once, tried to smile, and quietly left the examination room.

As soon as she was gone, Alicia lit into Rae, saying, "Rae Taylor, what do you think you're doing? You can't get that poor woman's hopes up like that and then send her out of here. We've never had a case as bad as this one. We don't know if the dosage required to affect that much tissue wouldn't kill her, or worse!"

Rae didn't back down. "Can you turn someone like that away without even trying? You heard what she said. You read her letter. You talked with that psychologist out in California. Don't you care?"

"Yes I care!" Alicia's eyes flashed. "How dare you call my motives into question! I'm just trying to be realistic."

Rae shook her head. "Don't be realistic. Be compassionate. So we might fail. It's a possibility! We've always known that! But we might succeed—and give a woman her life back." She shook her head wearily. "Alicia, that's why I went into medical research. I don't want to see people suffer. I've watched it all my life and I know I can do something to stop it. Maybe not a lot, but something. I'm not going to sit by when I have even the smallest chance to make a difference."

Alicia grew quiet. She put her arm around her young colleague's shoulder and pulled her close, apologizing, "I'm sorry, Rae. You keep reminding me of what's really important." She put her forehead next to Rae's. "But you better prepare for a grizzly time. What we're going to do to this girl isn't going to be pretty."

"Opening old wounds never is," Rae said elliptically. "But if a wound doesn't heal right, you know it has to be done to give it another chance."

Alicia smiled with a nod. "You're right." She walked back over to the metal desk and picked up Sabrina's chart. "But I'm afraid even if we're successful, from what she said, there are some deeper scars our serum will never reach."

Rae looked pensive for a moment. "That's true." Then she smiled, "But there *are* different forms of treatment."

Alicia looked puzzled.

Rae gave her a coy grin. "Like when you meet a recent divorcée who has a broken arrow in her heart and you prescribe her a twelve-month dose of Charles?"

Alicia blushed and giggled. "Ah! The best kind of *therapy* I know." She put one hand on her hip. "You know, after all these years, Charles is still on my payroll. He's decided to make a career of it. And considering how many times I've raised his pay to keep him from getting any ideas about leaving, it's no wonder why."

Rae laughed. "You still pay him? I can't believe it."

Alicia shrugged. "It's true. I'm an addict. Without my regular treatments, I go into convulsions." She shuddered. "It's not pretty."

"I thought that happened *during* your treatments," Rae teased.

Alicia gave her an aloof smile. "Maybe." Her brow furrowed with a fresh thought. "You know, we've joked so much with Marsha about adding her special little brand of TLC to our program, but we've never done it. Why don't we give it a try in this instance? I know you and Marsha used it extensively on the front end of your sales campaigns when you were still in real estate, but why not on the back end as part of the recovery process? If ever there was a woman who needed to feel good about herself again, it's Sabrina Doucette." She cocked an eyebrow. "And if it works, we'll get Marsha to start charging for it."

Rae's voice bubbled over with excitement, "It's perfect! Serum for the body, *therapy* for the heart! We'll be rich!"

Alicia folded her arms. "You're wrong on two points. First, we're already rich, and second, *therapy* is also for the body."

Rae slapped her friend's arm playfully. "Alicia, you're wicked."

"So I'm told, dear." Alicia walked toward the door. "But who can we get for her?"

Rae thought about it for a moment. "Jason. Jason Maxwell. Remember? The skier we treated last year? He'll be perfect."

"Yes," Alicia nodded. "He *is* perfect. Good choice." She sighed. "Well, let's go tell our new patient we can schedule her first surgery for day after tomorrow."

Rae looked happy. "I know this is going to work, Alicia. I can feel it. And when it does, we have to get Marsha to find a way to offer this kind of thing to a lot of women."

"That'll take a great deal of work," Alicia pointed out. "Even with Marsha's help. We're still a small-time operation. She knows a lot of people, but not that many require cosmetic treatment. If you're talking about a nationwide operation, that's big business. Big business requires lots of planning, lots of staff, lots of headaches. It's not like you, Marsha, me, Don, Keith, and the bunnies." She suddenly had an idea. "But you know what? Sabrina is a well-known person. If we succeed in fixing her up, I'll bet she could be very instrumental in spreading the word. Let's mention it to Marsha. She'll know what to do."

"That's a good idea." Rae stood up to leave. "Maybe one day we'll see Brighton, Taylor, and Associates written on the side of her race car."

Alicia laughed, then grew serious. "If we can ever get her back inside a race car."

49

September 1990

Dallas, Texas

"I'VE FOUND A POTENTIAL BUYER FOR YOU." MALCOLM BODELL leaned forward from his desk chair, propped his elbows on his calfskin desk blotter and lit a cigarette.

Rebecca Danforth smiled with satisfaction. She knew he'd do exactly as instructed. He was a pawn; they all were. "Wonderful, Malcolm. You work very fast. I like that. Who are they?"

"A Texas consortium that wishes to remain anonymous until they get more information from you about the deal." Bodell blew a puff of smoke into the air, opened a folder on his desk and picked up a note. "Apparently they are one of your current competitors and have no desire for Secularian to know any more about them than necessary, in the event the deal falls through."

Rebecca frowned, trying to discreetly peek at his notes upside down. "Sounds like something I would do. What exactly do they want to know?"

Bodell ran his fingers through his red hair. "Their attorney tells me that they're willing to put up two point five billion in cash for all the outstanding shares of Secularian. But they want to know if you can deliver them all in one transaction. They don't want a proxy fight at a shareholders' meeting."

Rebecca took a deep breath. "I can. I'll have to liquidate virtually all of my other holdings prior to the sale, but you said the Women's Center has three hundred million in cash. I take it that once I get their stock, that money will be mine. Correct?"

Bodell nodded. "Correct. And rather than do an open floor trade, just between us, I've decided to keep this private. Your accountants will see the entire transaction as an even swap, never really seeing the two point five billion. You merely turn over the Secularian stock in exchange for the North Dallas Women's Center stock. The money from my consortium buyer, in essence, goes straight to the owners of the Women's Center. However, on paper it will be seen as passing through your hands."

"Very tidy," Rebecca commended. "I want this neat and simple."

"It will be." Bodell took another puff and set his cigarette in the ashtray next to him. "But there are a few caveats."

Rebecca arched her eyebrows questioningly. "Such as?"

"In order to keep the transaction quiet, I'm going to withhold the stock issue until January, putting the deal into the next fiscal year." He glanced at his notes again. "That way, I won't have to file SEC and IRS reports until April of 1992. And the current owners won't see the actual transaction reports till then either."

Rebecca watched the gray line of smoke ascending up into the air. She nodded. "That's smart."

"Thank you." Bodell smiled. "Also, you need to sit on the stock for at least a year. And don't make any changes in the existing board, personnel, management, or anything. I'm conveniently going to forget to mention to the Women's Center board that the entire issue went to one buyer. As far as they're concerned, every share was sold, *publicly,* and that's all they need to know. They'll have their cash to press ahead with the planned renovations, and you can just relax, sit back, and watch it happen. Remember, the current owners think their sell-out is just temporary. They plan to buy back the outstanding shares after the renovation project from increased operating profits, before it's reevaluated."

Rebecca was still not pleased. "Then I can't let them know I own the center? I *want* them to know."

"Not right away," Bodell advised, raising his hands defensively. "Just be patient, Ms. Danforth. I can't overemphasize that what we're doing here could get us both in a great deal of trouble if the wrong parties found out about it. We can't have any premature attention drawn to your sole ownership. Not yet. If you go making changes right away, they'll know you're in control. And then they'll blow the whistle. Give me time. All I need is twelve months, and then it won't matter. In that time I can bury the transaction so deep in traded hands it will look like you came upon the entire portfolio by gradual acquisition. Then they legitimately won't be able to buy it back. After that, you can make any adjustments you want. Please. You have to trust me."

"I understand," Rebecca huffed in disappointment as she folded her arms. "But I don't like it. Just do what you have to do."

Bodell picked up his cigarette again and smiled nervously. "Well, Ms. Danforth, I do need to get something straight with you. I must insist that my commissions be paid on the date of the transaction, just in case something adverse happens shortly thereafter. If you should inadvertently alert someone, and there is an investigation, I plan to relocate in a hurry, and start my early retirement."

Rebecca chuckled. "We think a lot alike. Very well, Mr. Bodell, you'll get your money—all of it. But I won't slip up. This is too important to me. I'll just be a quiet customer, take my afternoon massages, and bide my time. And when you tell me all is well, I'll make my presence known. *Very* known. And not until. You have my word." Her eyes narrowed. "Besides, I'm sure the anticipation will heighten the pleasure of the moment all the more."

She broke into her dark, malevolent laugh, instantly raising the small hairs on the back of Malcolm Bodell's neck.

50

April 1988

Houston, Texas

THE ACRID SMELL OF ISOPROPYL ALCOHOL SINGED THE INSIDE OF Sabrina's nose as Dr. Brighton used a heavily soaked gauze pad to wipe the excess adhesive tape from around her eyes. She glanced down, beneath Alicia's swabbing motion. On the gray metal table next to her lay the remnant of bandages that had enveloped her head for the last four weeks, ever since the last painful operation. As the last piece of cotton padding fell away, she looked at Alicia's eyes for an indication of what she saw. Alicia's expression didn't change; she kept her eyes set, stoic, professional. Sabrina's heart started to pound; she knew it hadn't worked.

A deep knife of depression mercilessly gouged into her chest, stifling her breathing. After all the operations, all the stinging pain, the constant burning of the injections, antiseptics, antibiotics, gels, and oils applied to her face—it had all been for nothing. It was true, the days of living and walking in public like a normal human being were forever gone, swallowed into the hideous shadows of her mask. She had sincerely hoped this treatment would do *something*. She fought vigorously not to get her hopes up, just as Dr. Burton had warned; but ever since she worked in her father's garage back in Jacksonville, she had always been the eternal optimist, the wild spirit that couldn't be held back, the risk-taker on the bleeding edge of life. And now that once vibrant life lay captive inside her own body, repulsed by everyone, including herself. Her eyes drifted closed upon a welling film of tears.

She heard Dr. Taylor's voice next to her. "Sabrina, open your eyes."

Her expression grew cold and distant as she opened her tear-filled eyes to glare at the two doctors who had built her hopes so high, only to disappoint her like all the rest. However, what she saw hit her like a train wreck. She couldn't breathe. Her heart was about to explode.

"What do you think?" Rae stood in front of the thirty-year-old blonde, holding a wide hand mirror, smiling broadly.

Sabrina's head was beginning to swim. It was a hallucination; it was a fantasy; it was a deception; it couldn't be real—it was a miracle. There in the ten-inch glass reflection was her face. It wasn't the scarred red and black tissues ripped and torn away. It was her face; a face she hadn't seen in two years. Trembling fingers reached up to touch the smooth pink flesh around her eyes. It looked like a new-born's skin; it was soft and supple beneath her quivering fingers. In seconds the rivulets of salt-laden tears washed over the new flesh—*and she could feel it*. She could feel the sensation of her fingers around her eyes. The leathery deadness was gone.

She felt Alicia's arm around her shoulders, firmly hugging her close, laughing softly. She could hear Rae Taylor crying almost as much as she was; but her gaze never left the mirror. Her left hand absently took the beautiful glass out of Rae's hand and pulled it closer to her face. The new skin definitely looked different, but only because it was new. It was fresh and alive.

Both Rae and Alicia jumped when the mirror tumbled out of Sabrina's trembling fingers and crashed onto the floor. Sabrina stood up, her body racking with grateful sobs as she hugged and kissed the two doctors, wetting their faces and necks with her tears, and similarly sharing theirs. After almost a full five minutes of soul-pouring joy, Sabrina began to laugh and laugh and laugh and laugh. It was infectious, and both Rae and Alicia reveled in it along with their euphoric patient. It took the better part of an hour for the three women to compose themselves.

Rae hugged Sabrina once more and looked her in the eye. "Sabrina, there's some things we need to tell you about your treatment."

Sabrina looked at Rae intently. "It's only temporary. Right?"

Rae laughed. "No, it's for keeps." She went to the metal cabinet in the room and brought back a plastic tube of cream. "Here. This is a prescription skin cream that will protect your skin from the sun. I want you to use it religiously for at least three weeks. It's stronger than any sunscreen on the market. Your face is like a baby's. Remember that. The skin will toughen up in no time. But until it does, you have to take special precautions."

Sabrina nodded obediently with an exuberant grin. "Okay. Is that all?"

Rae shook her head. "No, I want you to be very careful not to rub around your eyes. Believe it or not, in a short while you'll see your eyebrows and eyelashes grow back. The hair follicles are still regenerating. Fortunately, because you're a blonde, most people won't even notice." She put her hands on her hips. "But we also want you to know that your treatment isn't complete yet. There's another phase."

Sabrina looked puzzled. "For what?"

Alicia spoke up. "Dear, we understand you must be quite happy with the results of your treatment, but with the kind of injuries you've sustained, sometimes there's damage that goes much deeper."

Sabrina's face clouded. "What are you talking about?"

"How do you feel about going out in public?" Alicia asked candidly.

Sabrina shrugged. "I think I would feel less conspicuous now."

"But not completely at ease," Rae prompted. "Right? Wondering if anyone could tell?"

"I don't know." Sabrina pushed her blond hair back behind her ears. "Maybe I would."

"And how do you feel about going back to racing?" Alicia asked.

Sabrina frowned. "I'm retired."

"That's it?" Rae lifted her hands. "You'll never get behind the wheel of a car ever again?"

Sabrina's voice became solemn, "Not a race car."

Alicia walked over to the storage closet to find a broom for the broken glass. "Sabrina, you're only thirty years old. You're the only woman in history to win back-to-back championships at the greatest race in sporting history. Are you sure that part of your life is over?"

"Yes," she stated flatly.

"Well, perhaps that's true." Rae folded her arms. "What do you do next? Where do you go from here?"

Sabrina shrugged again. "I don't know. I made plenty of money over the last ten years. Who knows? I may try to get on TV as one of those color commentary people."

Rae nodded. "And I'm sure you'd be good at it. But you need to decide what's best for *you*. And it may take some time before you're recovered fully enough to honestly make that decision."

"That's probably true." Sabrina watched Alicia sweeping up the glass into a metal dustpan. "I guess I'll take it easy for a while and see how I feel."

Rae smiled. "We hoped you'd say that. As your doctors, we have a little follow-up program we insist you take advantage of. Phase two of the restoration program. We feel it may help you in the rest and recuperation department."

"What did you have in mind?" Sabrina asked curiously.

Alicia dumped the dustpan into the trash can and turned around. "Well, dear, one of our staff will explain that to you. His name is Jason, and he is going to be your personal therapist for the next few weeks. He'll explain the entire therapy program to you."

"Therapy?" Sabrina looked skeptical. "What kind of therapy?"

Rae tried not to giggle. "It's a unique style of care we're confident you'll find most beneficial. It regards your state of mind and sense of well-being."

"A shrink?" Sabrina sounded disgusted. "I've had my fill of shrinks."

"Oh, no," Alicia corrected. "Not a psychologist. Just a behavioral therapist, licensed by this clinic. Specially trained staff. But don't worry about it for now. As I said, Jason will explain everything."

Sabrina was puzzled, but in light of the miraculous blessing she had received that day, she didn't feel in a position to argue with her benefactors. Alicia escorted her to Rae's office and they made a few phone calls. First they called Marsha, who had to race over immediately and see the results for herself. That just sent everyone into fresh bouts of laughter and tears. About an hour later a handsome young man with dark, wavy hair and deep brown eyes arrived.

"Sabrina, this is Jason Maxwell," Rae said, introducing the young man as he came in.

Sabrina felt a jolt of anxiety grip her heart for a second, wondering if he noticed anything on her face.

"Pleased to meet you, Ms. Doucette." He smiled politely.

"Thank you," she heard herself say, taking his hand politely and shaking it. "But just call me Sabrina." She saw Rae give him an unexplained nod. He caught Rae's eye and nodded back affirmatively.

"Would you please come with me, Sabrina." His smile was warm and charming.

Sabrina looked at the three other women, who all nodded, smiling gleefully to one another as if they had a secret, and gestured for her to go with the man. Forty-five minutes later Sabrina and Jason were pulling into the marina at Houston harbor. She asked after the quiet ride from the clinic, "What are we doing here?"

Jason grinned as he opened the door of Marsha Collins's Mercedes 480SL. "We're going for a boat ride."

"Where?" Sabrina climbed out of the car with hesitation. The sun felt wonderful on her cheeks. It had been so long since she felt that sensation.

"My instructions are to take you for a ride in the Gulf aboard Dr. Brighton's boat." Jason shrugged innocently. "You are supposed to relax, catch some rays, and basically have a great time. If I bring you back without having a good time, they'll fire me. Simple." He leaned over the roof of the car and lowered his voice. "So even if you get seasick, or fall overboard, or if everything basically sucks, you could do me an enormous favor by telling them you liked it."

Sabrina smiled. She decided Jason was all right. "So that's it? You're just supposed to keep me entertained for the afternoon?"

He led her down the wooden dock toward the fleet of boats moored in their respective slips. "That's it. A great job for what they pay me."

Sabrina followed behind him. "They said you were supposed to be some kind of a therapist?"

"They did?" Jason took a set of keys, attached to a small oval piece of red foam, out of his pocket. He cocked his head. "Sure. Why not? If that's what they want to call this, I can work with that."

Sabrina grinned. "I take it you haven't done this before?"

Jason turned down a small strip of dock next to a sixty-foot Sea Ray. "Whatever gave you that idea? I do this for a living, you know." He shook his finger at her. "I'm a professional. Don't try to do this at home."

Sabrina laughed at his serious expression.

He stopped at the rear of the boat, put his foot on the side and looked up into the warm blue sky. "God, isn't this a great country?" Then he smiled at her with youthful excitement in his eyes. "Madame?" He held out his hand to help her climb in.

"You're crazy," she said, giggling as she jumped down into the spacious rear deck.

"Yep." He nodded as he ran forward to cast off the bow lines. "Could you untie those lines in the rear?"

Sabrina cast off the stern lines and tossed them on the gray wood of the weather-worn dock. She turned around and watched Jason quickly climb the chrome ladder up to the flying bridge and stab his key in the ignition. He pushed the throttle forward and turned the key. A dull grinding noise churned beneath the rear deck below her feet. Nothing else happened. He turned the key again, only to get the same result. Finally, with an embarrassed look, he turned around and quickly climbed back down the ladder.

"Remember, you're having a good time," he said, and smiled. "Excuse me." He moved her out of the way and lifted the fiberglass cover shielding the twin V8 engines below the deck. "Oh boy," he muttered. "I'll be right back."

Sabrina watched the swarthy young man go below, heard the sound of rummaging and large objects falling, then saw him reemerge with a metal toolbox.

"This'll only take a second." He set the toolbox down and proceeded to futiley attack the helpless engines for the next forty-five minutes.

Sabrina watched him struggle aimlessly with great amusement. When a full hour had passed, Jason wiped a black streak of grease across his brow and threw a socket wrench down on top of the starboard engine in exasperation. "You stupid piece of shit!"

Sabrina chuckled. He gave her a frustrated glare. She grinned. "I'm having a good time."

"Well, you shouldn't be!" He folded his arms in disgust. "We're stuck, and I'm going to get fired."

Sabrina squatted down next to him. "No we're not. It's just the port starter assembly. Give me that wrench. The nine-sixteenths." She pointed to an open-end box wrench in the toolbox.

"Right," he huffed sarcastically, not really sure what a starter assembly was. "You think you can fix it?"

She nodded. "Umm-hmm."

Jason leaned back and looked at her skeptically, his voice challenging, "Okay, here's the deal. For every minute less than an hour you take to fix it, I have to give you a stellar back rub. Every minute over an hour, you gotta rub mine."

Sabrina's eyes twinkled. "You're on." She leaned over the engine. "Say ready, set, go."

"Ready, set, go," Jason muttered absently, glancing at his watch.

The twin engines roared to life five minutes later, despite Jason's shocked expression and protestations that his previous labor was primarily responsible for the results. That just made Sabrina laugh even more at him. Fifteen minutes later they were cruising out of Houston harbor into the Gulf of Mexico.

It was a gorgeous afternoon; only a few wisps of clouds garnished a rich cerulean sky. The water wasn't too rough, pushed gently by a warm spring breeze. Sabrina sat with Jason on the flying bridge, letting the salty wind blow through her hair as the powerboat knifed through the rolling waves of jade.

Jason looked over at Sabrina with a friendly smile, shouting above the roar of the engines, "What happened to your face?"

A pang of fear tore her gaze to his, her heart pounding erratically. All her fears came crashing down in an instant.

Jason touched his own cheek below his eye. "Did you get too much sun? You look like you've been peeling or something. If you need some sunscreen, there's some down below in the bathroom." He turned his attention back to the waves.

She couldn't believe it. *That was it? That's all he noticed?* He just thought she had a little too much sun. Her heart settled down.

It was true. Freedom had truly come. Another chain around her heart fell away with one long sigh of release. Now it was safe to relax.

Sabrina climbed down the ladder to the rear deck, found a folded lounge chair, opened it and sat back in the afternoon sunshine. She wished she had brought a bathing suit with her, but no one had bothered to tell her about going out on a boat. She was wearing a pair of khaki safari shorts and a short-sleeve white cotton blouse. Remembering the tube of cream Rae had given her, she retrieved it from her purse and applied it to her face. She kicked her tennis shoes off, interlaced her fingers behind her head, and laid back on the lounger. This was wonderful. The doctors had been right. This was exactly what she needed.

After cruising for more than an hour, Jason killed the engines about three miles offshore, climbed down the ladder and threw the anchor overboard. "Can I get you anything?"

Sabrina opened sleepy eyes, her strength drained by the sun. "What do you have?"

"Dr. Brighton stocks just about anything." He started down below. "Cocktail, soft drink, beer, juice." He jovially tossed his head from side to side, affecting a Jamaican accent. "Or might I interest you in one of my world famous piña coladas?"

"Umm." She rocked her shoulders back and forth. "That sounds scrumptious."

"Hold that thought." He disappeared for about ten minutes, then returned with two milky glasses, garnished with a flexible straw. "Wrap your lips around this succulent portion of paradise."

The cool, sweet lactescence was delicious, rich in pineapple, coconut, and the fragrant sweetness of rum. "That's great."

"I know," he said without shame. "I whipped up a whole

pitcher down below. They're like Lay's potato chips. You can't have just one."

Sabrina laughed again. "So are you always this amusing to your patients?"

"Not always," he said with mock seriousness. "But for you, I'm making an exception. Remember that when it's time to tip."

She took another sip, looking curiously into his dark brown eyes. "So how did you get involved with the clinic?"

Jason's smile faded; he didn't answer for a moment. "Well, to tell you the truth, I was one of their first patients. A guinea pig, you might say."

Sabrina was intrigued. "Really? What did they do for you?" She quickly added, "If you don't mind my asking."

"I . . . uh . . ." He gave her a half laugh. ". . . used to be a ski instructor at Breckenridge Resort in Colorado, alternating lessons there in the winter and doing odd jobs for Marsha Collins down here in the summers." He took a difficult breath. "About two winters ago I took a bad fall on a black run one day, and had a most unfortunate meeting with a tree, an outcropping of rock, and a few more trees."

Sabrina grimaced, a faint memory of vertigo and a checkered flag flashing in her thoughts. "So how bad was it?"

"I couldn't walk." He took a long sip of his drink. "They said I'd never walk. I had two disks cracked in my back, plus muscle damage in my legs."

She gave him a sincere look of concern. The jovial atmosphere sank into somber silence.

He sniffed and continued, "They said I was going to spend the rest of my days rolling around in a wheelchair. Said I'd never stand on my feet again, let alone a pair of skis. And consequently, my career took a slight setback." He took a breath and another sip of his drink. "Not too many students want to take lessons from a broken man in a wheelchair. It doesn't *look* good."

Sabrina tried to smile. She knew exactly how he felt.

He laughed. "And then one of my doctors turned me on to a friend of his, named Cal Dominski, a college professor buddy at one of those big Ivy League outfits in Boston. That guy turned me onto Dr. Taylor. Dr. Taylor and Dr. Brighton worked on me for about six months. They tried their experimental treatments on my back and my legs. It went real slow at first, but then things started to happen. Miraculous things." His voice cracked. He took several deeply emotional breaths before he said, "You could never understand how much it meant to me." He looked up at her proudly, his voice still quivering, "You know, Marsha bought me a pair of Fischer Classic skis for Christmas last year. The ones that Franz Klamer uses." His eyes were moist. "And they're fantastic!"

A tear slipped out of Sabrina's eye. "Yeah. I *can* understand that. I really can. More than you might think."

He finished his drink and wiped his eyes. "I'd do anything for those three ladies. Anything."

A shiver of awe ran through her. Who were these women who held such an awesome secret to restore life, straighten crooked bodies, resurrect broken flesh?

Jason reached out to take Sabrina's almost empty glass. "Can I get you another?"

She stared into his warm, brown eyes and nodded. He disappeared again to refill their glasses. Could it be that there really was another person who might be able to understand how *she* felt? Was this that person? Her heart had already answered the question before he returned.

"Did you ever hear about the Indianapolis 500 of 1986?" she asked with difficulty as he ascended the steps carrying fresh glasses.

For the next few hours Sabrina did her best to tell this complete stranger what had befallen her over the last two years. She told him of the pain, the scars, the surgery, the mask, all of it. He listened patiently, nodding with a sincere look of understanding on his face. And the more she told him, the more her soul felt free, the more chains dropped away. With every unveiled emotion, it was as though scales were falling off and she felt more and more alive. She didn't understand why it all came out the way it did, in a liberating catharsis, but it did. And throughout the conversation, Jason Maxwell cried with her, laughed with her, and finally took her hand and held it warmly in his.

Sabrina stared at the young man quietly, feeling his empathy, seeing it in his eyes. She didn't know why it seemed right to do what she did, but it just did. She leaned forward and kissed him softly. He responded with the warmth of his lips, but nothing more. He wasn't there to take; he was there to give; he was there for her. The revelation startled her. Somehow, unspoken, she understood that. It was an uncanny sensation. She hadn't been this close to a man for almost two years. Part of her felt very awkward, almost shy; but the rest of her felt strangely at ease, comfortable. Jason wasn't a sweating teenager, lusting to get her in the backseat of a car; he wasn't a wide-eyed racer, eager to devour her in some athletic event; nor was he a mysterious elder, taking what he could and giving what he might. He was just a young man, with a heart scarred like hers, and healed by the same miraculous power.

She didn't speak; she said it with her eyes; and he understood. As the sun slipped majestically below the horizon, casting brilliant hues of crimson against the deep blue of the Gulf, her eyes never left his as he lifted her into his arms and carried her down below to the forward cabin, laying her softly on the wide, fur-covered spread of the captain's berth.

Her hands eagerly held his cheeks and pulled his mouth into hers, drawing his tongue out of his mouth, cherishing it, savoring it, still sweet with the succulent savor of coconut and rum. She felt his fingers gently stroking her hair, her new cheeks, her neck. She had never wanted to be held, touched, and caressed so much in her entire life. And somehow she knew that he sensed it, knew what would please her, and wanted to please her.

She helped his fingers unbutton her white blouse, and before it was fully open, she hastily guided his face down her neck, across her collarbone, and down to her left breast, arching up to meet him. His face and lips were warm, but the soft inner recess of his mouth was warmer. She bit her bottom lip as the almost forgotten sensation of a man tenderly kissing and tasting the firmness of her nipple instantly revived feelings in her she never thought she would experience again. With an insatiable hunger he alternated between her breasts, igniting more and more dormant passions with every sweet flourish of his tongue.

His mouth planted swirling kisses down her stomach to her waistline, eagerly unbuttoning her shorts with impatient fingers. She was growing impatient herself, as he awakened a bodily urge within her that demanded prompt satisfaction. With the zeal of teenagers they both ripped their clothes off, tossing them at random around the cabin, quickly embracing, trying to touch and taste and sense every inch of the other's body all in the same moment.

In tender embrace she felt his hands firmly massage her shoulders, his teeth softly nibble her earlobe, the tip of his tongue delicately running down the long tendon in her neck, stopping at her breastbone to draw small circles against her flesh. It was intoxicating. She ran her fingers through the silky waves of his dark hair as she rolled over onto her back and let him feast on her body, beginning with each breast, her ribs, her hips, her thighs. She giggled when he ran his tongue down the length of her right leg to her foot and began probing the bottom of her foot. It made her pull her knees up in ticklish reflex, which apparently was what he wanted.

She felt him roll over on top of her, the moist warmth and weight of his chest settling down low, between her legs. The pressure sent a rippling wave of delight through her, and entreated her passions to a heightened state of desire. She felt his tongue press into her navel, drawing circles around it, then tracing a winding trail down, down—his whole body sliding down, farther and farther. A tingling thrill of anticipation shivered up her spine when she sensed his tongue weaving its way through the soft tufts of hair below. But before it zeroed in, gratifying her swelling desire, it mysteriously detoured to the inside of her right thigh. She felt the delicious pressure of his lips drawing on the tight muscle of her inner thigh, now flexed against his left cheek, but it wasn't the right place. His tongue continued making its penetrating swirls, each swirl cautiously advancing up to the top of her leg, but going no farther. It was driving her crazy, so close, yet not there.

She felt the heat of his breath as he *finally,* slowly, turned his head to the exact spot, *yes*—but no, moving past it, stopping at the exact same place as before, but on her opposite thigh, sweetly sucking on the taut flesh pressed against his right cheek. A moment later he turned his head back, this time letting the tip of his tongue swiftly glide over the impatiently awaiting spot—only to disappoint her again, returning to the other thigh. It was erotic torture; his face slowly rotating back and forth, coming within millimeters of ecstasy, then moving past to the firm flesh of her leg, to teasingly demonstrate what she was missing just an inch away. It served to arouse her more than she could stand. Her back arched, attempting to press against him as his face passed. Her entire body was on fire, glistening with a fine layer of perspiration, yearning for satisfaction.

The tempo of her pounding heart and rapid respiration accelerated again when she became aware of an altogether new sensation—gentle caresses with the tip of his nose, just above, and the teasing flicks of the tip of his tongue, just beneath. Sabrina couldn't take the delicious torture anymore. She leaned her shoulders forward in a half sit-up, lacing her fingers behind his head, straining her abdominal muscles, squeezing his face against her with all her strength. She could feel his neck muscles providing firm resistance—and then it happened.

With one darting plunge he firmly thrust his tongue deeply inside her, probing deeper and deeper, with ravenous fury. Her eyes came open for a frenzied instant, but all she saw in the cabin were the blurred images of paneled mahogany amid darting lights and random flares. Her lungs locked into a fierce seizure as every cell in her body unleashed two years' worth of forgotten energy in one ferocious, devastating deluge of absolute abandon.

The penetrating intensity refused to abate; rather, it only increased. Sabrina lost her grip, her upper body rocking back wildly against the fur spread. Waves of undulating sensuality circulated through every taut fiber of her being, to the point of delirious discomfort and exhausting elation. Moments later it delicately diminished in sweetly radiating waves. As her body went completely limp, she felt Jason crawl up between her legs and begin to make gentle love to her.

He held her in his arms and slowly rocked within her for longer than she could ever remember a man loving her, masterfully harmonizing the patient movement of his hips with the ship's undulating motion upon the waves. He gently brought her to several soul-enslaving orgasms, each about ten to fifteen minutes apart, some more deliciously draining than others. Even after she felt him relish his own climax, he never withdrew. He continued to hold her in his arms long after she could tell he had grown lax. He continued to kiss her, and caress her, holding her for many loving minutes until she sensed him reviving within her loins, and making love to her all over again.

When she felt she had enough strength to sit up, she made him roll onto his back and sat up straddling him, gently rocking her hips until the beautiful contortions of another exquisite climax pulled her down into his arms in salty perspiring exhaustion. As soon as her breathing had settled down, she felt his arms gently lift her back into a sitting position, again savoring the titillating rush of pleasure when he took each of her nipples into his mouth, feeding on them, loving them, pleasing them.

He laid her back down and made love to her for hours, never withdrawing; patient, consistent, compassionate. In a near catatonic state of pure ecstasy, she lost count of how many times he had tenderly brought her to the peak of her pleasure. She knew he arrived there himself five times in the course of their enduring intimacy. The last conscious image her eyes beheld before plummeting into weary sleep was the faint light of dawn coming through the porthole. As she drifted into languid slumber, still lying beneath her sleeping lover, still joined to him, her last thought was the desire to wake up sometime in the very distant future and drive a very fast car.

51

May 1988

Houston, Texas

RAE CLIMBED INTO THE HAND-STITCHED WHITE LEATHER REAR facing seat of Marsha's glossy white Rolls-Royce as her chauffeur closed the door. Both Alicia and Marsha sat in the backseat. Marsha smiled at her as if she had a secret. Rae looked at Marsha skeptically. "So what's the big mystery about?"

Rae had received a disturbingly vague phone call from Marsha that morning announcing an urgent meeting between the three principal partners of Brighton, Taylor, and Associates. After Marsha directed John, her chauffeur, to drive them up Westheimer Avenue to the Galleria Mall, she looked back at Rae with great excitement in her eyes. "I've had an inspiration."

Alicia looked at Rae. "She's probably decided on a new perfume at Neiman's."

Marsha gave Alicia a dirty look. "Hardly. I've spent an entire week making telephone calls, talking to bankers and real estate developers, and I have a startling proposition for you two. I didn't want to tell you about it until I had all of the details worked out."

"For what?" Rae was curious.

Marsha paused for effect. "For everything we've ever dreamed about."

Alicia smiled at Rae. "This sounds like it could be better than Gucci number three."

"Be quiet," Rae chastised Alicia. "Let her talk."

Marsha nodded a thank-you to Rae. "Well, as you both know, my first love is developing real estate. And secondly, seeing rich women be happy. Myself naturally among that group, and certainly not necessarily in that order."

Alicia and Rae laughed.

"And I know how much you two really want to help women be healthy and beautiful." She glanced to both of them for some sort of assent.

Rae accommodated her with a nod.

Marsha continued, "Good. Well, I've come up with a plan that I think just may be the *perfect* combination of our various talents. It happens in phases, starting small, but working up to a tremendous potential to reach a great many women."

Alicia frowned and adjusted her glasses. "That sounds delightful, dear. But could you be a little more specific?"

"Be patient." Marsha patted Alicia's knee. "All in due time. First of all, it's going to necessitate our relocating. But don't worry, you'll both quickly see the advantages in doing so. Besides, as dry a market as Houston is now, it'll do us nothing but good to get out of town."

"Where do you want to go?" Rae asked.

"Dallas," Marsha stated flatly.

"Dallas?" Alicia objected. "I have no desire to go back to Dallas."

"Yes you will, when you hear what I have in mind."

Rae and Alicia both continued to stare, waiting to hear something of substance to support their excited colleague's bold assertions.

Marsha pushed her dark red hair back off her shoulders. "Picture a women's center, more than a clinic, an exclusive resort-type affair with the best of everything, adorned to the teeth. We offer an elite clientele a vast array of health and . . ." She added with a coy inflection, ". . . social treatments."

Rae smiled. "It sounds wonderful. But why can't we do it here?"

Marsha frowned. "I'm coming to that. We make our new enterprise the worst-kept secret, so word spreads rapidly. And before long, we have the hottest development in the country where women receive the finest care money can buy."

Rae's expression sank. "It sounds great, Marsha. But it can never be a total-care facility. Only the externals. Remember? An old college acquaintance of mine has possession of the best piece."

Marsha shook her head. "That doesn't matter right now. You'll understand when I show you all the details back at my office. Trust me. Besides, Rae, wouldn't you love to have your old college acquaintance's nose rubbed in the most successful, elaborate, elite, delicious enterprise in the world?"

Both Rae and Alicia nodded. Rae shook her finger. "You have a point there. It might be very nice to park our women's center right under her nose."

Alicia folded her arms. "Well, I think it's silly. I don't see any advantage in doing that."

"You will." Marsha rolled her eyes with a mischievous grin. "You will. And you'll enjoy every minute of it. I guarantee it. But right now I would like to propose a new general partnership, with formal incorporation."

Rae looked puzzled. "Why?"

"It's all part of my plan." Marsha shrugged innocently, raising her palms. "Brighton, Taylor, and Associates is a fine organization. But this new endeavor calls for some intricate behind-the-scenes business dealings, which necessitates a new organizational structure." She assured them, "But don't worry. I'll explain everything as we go. For now, I just want to give you the highlights."

Alicia turned to Marsha. "So what's this new organization going to be called?"

Marsha beamed, proud of herself. "RAM Industries."

"Ram Industries?" Rae glanced at Alicia to note her reaction. "Ram, as in the masculine form of sheep?"

Marsha shook her head. "No, RAM, as in R for Rae, A for Alicia, and M for Marsha. RAM, as in collision, impact."

Alicia chuckled. "Well, at least she didn't take top billing."

"What do you think?" Marsha asked expectantly.

Alicia grinned at Rae. "I think she's just upset because she doesn't like being known merely as 'and Associates.'"

Rae laughed as Marsha turned to Alicia indignantly. "That's not true. This is important for the plan to work the way it's supposed to."

"I'm sure, dear." Alicia nodded apologetically. "Settle down."

Rae caught Marsha's attention. "It sounds wonderful. We want to hear the rest of your plan. Just tell us what we need to do."

Marsha's excitement was back. "Well, in the short term, Rae, you need to get in touch with Nicole and have her draw up a set of incorporation documents and stock issuances in accordance with an instruction package I have back at the office. Then both of you need to get on the phone and start some telemarketing. We need every rich and powerful woman you can find. Call everyone you know, and tell them to call their friends. I've already started, and the reaction I'm getting to initial queries is very positive. The thought of having their own private Shady Oaks, plus having access to your medical care, is a very salable concept." She added, "And if I were you, I would specifically look for those who might take maximum advantage of the medical treatments."

"Why?" Rae asked.

"Because we need a great deal of money. Cash money." Marsha looked deadly serious. She always looked that way when she was putting together an extremely big deal. Rae had learned over the years to trust that look; it always led to prosperity.

"Why do we need a lot of cash?" Alicia was confused. "We all have a great deal of cash in the bank."

Marsha smiled at Alicia. "I'm not talking about land acquisition or construction cash. I have enough to take care of that myself. I'm talking about real money. To do what needs to be done, we'll need about three hundred million dollars of liquid cash and securities."

Rae whistled. "Wow. Why so much? Is it that expensive an operation?"

Marsha shook her head. "Not at all. Our center will be a money maker. It has to be. The cash has to do with how our records look to the government and the general public." She waved her hands. "I don't want to get bogged down in the nitty-gritty right now. We have plenty of time for that. I just want both of you to know that this endeavor will indeed achieve our goals if we're patient, and follow every step of the plan. And when we get back to the office, I'll tell you the best part."

"There's more?" Rae looked surprised.

"Oh, yes." Marsha was loving every minute of her deliberate rationing of information. And it was having its intended effect, driving Alicia and Rae crazy to know what she had up her sleeve. Marsha smiled. "There's much more. And you're going to love it."

52

May 1988

Houston, Texas

AFTER ONE LAST DEEP REV OF THE HIGH PRECISION ENGINE OF THE
cherry-red Ferrari Testerossa, Sabrina pulled up the hand
brake and killed the engine. She leaned over toward the
passenger seat for one more long, tender kiss of Jason's
moist lips before they climbed out of the sleek sports coupe
and walked hand in hand into the offices of Brighton,
Taylor, and Associates.

Sabrina knocked on Rae's half-open door as she came in,
with Jason in tow. Rae was sitting behind her desk perusing
a fan-fold stack of computer paper. "Anybody home?"

Rae looked up. "Sabrina! Come on in. Jason! Hi!"

After hugging Rae and exchanging warm greetings,
Sabrina and Jason took a seat in the two chrome and plastic
chairs in front of Rae's desk, still holding hands. Rae sat
back down in her rolling desk chair. "So how are you two
doing?"

Sabrina looked at Jason with affectionate eyes, "About as
good as can be expected, Doc." She looked back to Rae.
"You *know* he's a lunatic."

Jason huffed with indignation, "Me? *I'm* not the one with
a death wish every time I get behind a wheel. *My car* has a
first and second gear." He leaned toward Rae. "Although,
have you seen the cute little set of high-dollar wheels she
picked up?"

Rae laughed with sincere joy. It made her feel wonderful

to see Sabrina's smile—and Jason's. "No, I haven't. But it's probably something low and fast? Right?"

Sabrina nodded. "Just a toy. I'm saving my money for a real car—with wings."

Rae looked favorably impressed. "Then I take it you've decided to head back to the racetrack."

Sabrina glanced at Jason again. "Well, after a month of your fantastic therapy, I think I'm about ready for anything."

Jason blushed, glancing furtively at Sabrina.

Rae clapped her hands. "That's wonderful! Are you looking for a sponsor?"

Sabrina leaned forward in her chair. "That's kind of why I wanted to talk to you today. I don't need the money. I have enough saved to build a car. I plan to be competing again in a year or so." She glanced at Jason again. "But after what you've done for me and Jason, and so many others. I want to advertise for you. I want your permission to put Brighton, Taylor, and Associates on my car."

Rae leaned back in her chair. "You can't have it."

Sabrina looked shocked. Jason stared at Rae, dumbfounded.

Rae laughed. "You need to have it say, 'RAM Industries.' That's our new corporate moniker."

Sabrina sighed. "Rae, you scared me there for a second." Her eyes narrowed. "Why the change?"

Rae shrugged. "It's a new development in our marketing strategy. In a few months we're relocating our entire operation to Dallas. It's a bigger market, not so adversely impacted by the oil depression here."

Jason asked, "So are you going to continue the same treatments?"

Rae nodded. "Oh, yes. But we're defining our market niche a little more precisely. Marsha has purchased a big piece of property northeast of Dallas on Lake Lavon. We're going for more of a resort theme. There's an old country club there. In fact, just last week Marsha commissioned three contractors to begin new construction. We're going to renovate the existing facilities as much as we can and establish an entirely new era of women's services."

Jason frowned. *"Women's* services?"

Rae gave him a sympathetic look. "For the time being. I can't explain why it has to be that way, but for now it does. But don't worry, Jason, you'll always be welcome, and Alicia and I will always be happy to help you in any way we can."

Jason looked at Sabrina. "You already have."

Sabrina returned his gaze in a warm, silent exchange, then turned back to Rae. "So what's this new place called?"

Rae leaned forward on her desk. "Something innocuous and simple: the North Dallas Women's Center."

"That sounds clinical," Jason noted. "Where does the golf course and the resort part come in?"

"It's supposed to sound austere for discretion's sake." Rae addressed Jason directly. "Only our clients will know different."

"What will be so different?" Sabrina asked.

Rae's eyes sparkled with excitement. "Everything. It's going to be a fantasy come true. Every guest will have a private suite decorated to her exact tastes, private terraces, Jacuzzis, salons, restaurants, a complete sports center, horseback riding, massages, the works. We're not sparing a dime."

Jason huffed, "And only women can go to this?"

Rae winked at Sabrina. "As a free charter member, Ms. Doucette is welcome to bring you as a guest as often as she likes."

Sabrina squeezed Jason's hand. "So you better be good, and maybe I'll let you come."

Jason looked at her, not quite whispering, "I'm always *good.* I just don't always behave."

From the look she saw in Jason's eyes, Rae knew they wouldn't be staying long. She'd seen that look too many times on Keith's face, and it never failed to make her heart race in anticipation of what always followed. She cleared her throat. "Sabrina, I do appreciate your offer to help us get the word out. Please contact anyone you know who could benefit from either our medical treatments, our unique *therapy,* or both. Anyone who could be influential in promoting the center would be welcome."

Sabrina nodded. "You know, I can think of one person right off. I don't know her real well. I've only met her once in person. But if you could help her, a whole lot of people would notice."

"Who's that?" Rae asked, picking up a pencil to take some notes.

"My favorite musician." Sabrina shook her head sadly. "She's a classical pianist. I've seen her in concert a few times. After my accident, her music really helped me. I read in *People* magazine recently that she stopped playing after experiencing some kind of nerve damage, or something like that, in her hand. It made me cry."

Jason gave Sabrina an odd look. "I never pegged you for a classical fan. I thought you'd be into like ZZ Top, and Aerosmith, and guys like that."

Sabrina patted his hand softly. "That was in another life. Tastes change."

"So what's her name?" Rae asked, her pencil still poised.

"Emelia," Sabrina replied. "Emelia Travain."

53

November 1990

Dallas, Texas

GERSHWIN'S "RHAPSODY IN BLUE" PLAYED SOFTLY IN THE BACK-ground around the heated turquoise waters of the spacious indoor oval swimming pool. A few women swam laps from one end of the wide ellipse to the other, while others lay in tranquil repose upon the padded loungers, soaking in the mid-afternoon rays of the sun as it filtered through a domed skylight. The enormous single piece of convex Plexiglas was slightly larger than the circumference of the pool. A uni-formed waiter carefully lifted another chilled glass of cham-pagne off his silver tray and handed it to Rebecca Danforth, reclining on one of the loungers.

"Thank you," she said absently, obliviously accepting the glass, not taking her eyes from the page of the paperback novel she was reading. She brought the glass to her lips and sipped, wrinkling her nose as the chilled effervescence toyed with her nostrils.

"Hello, Rebecca," came a familiar voice.

Rebecca glanced to her left to see Rae Taylor unwrapping a towel from her body. "Why, hello, Rae. Won't you join me?"

"Thank you." Rae spread the towel out on the lounger next to Rebecca's, lay faceup on it, and tossed her fountain of brown permed curls up and over the top of the lounger pad.

Rebecca looked at Rae's body. It wasn't the same one she had back in college. Her arms and legs were tanned and firm. Her full bust line stood at prompt attention beneath a white string bikini. She was stunning. Rebecca smiled in amazement, vainly flattering her rival, "Rae, you're gorgeous. Did you get a late growth spurt or something?"

Rae closed her eyes, letting the sun penetrate into her face. "No, a Christmas present last year from Alicia."

Rebecca rolled her eyes. "Well, tell her she does good work."

"I don't need to," Rae said sleepily. "All the men here do it for me."

Rebecca was starting to seethe on the inside. So Rae wanted to play games? Very well, the last laugh was already in the making. "That's wonderful, Rae. And I'm *sure* it's true. I still can't get over how well you've done here. All of you: you, Alicia, and Marsha. The Women's Center is absolutely fabulous."

Rae looked over at Rebecca. "You really think so?"

Rebecca lifted her eyes, surveying the grandeur of the surroundings. "You don't need my opinion to confirm that. Your guest list is evidence enough. Undeniably, this place is the singularly most exquisite place on the face of the earth for the woman of the nineties."

"I'm glad you think so." A minute of silence passed, then Rae lowered her voice. "You know, Rebecca, not a day goes by I don't think of what you did to me years ago. But I just want you to know that I've learned to go on with my life. I refused to let what you did keep me down."

Rebecca laughed. "Oh, Rae, don't be so melodramatic. What happened between us was just a clash of personalities." Her eyes grew dark. "Besides, I wouldn't be so cocky if I were you. If I *really* wanted something you had, I'd simply take it. And there wouldn't be anything you could do about it."

Rae huffed, "You still talk big. But I think you overestimate your influence these days. Look around you. Could you assemble all these women of power and affluence in one place? Would they do anything for you? They're all my friends, Rebecca. And this is my empire, where you're the guest, merely a transient. You have no say in anything you see. And that makes me very happy."

Rebecca held her temper. "Is that what you came over here to tell me? To flaunt your lovely little resort and gigolo farm?" She set her book on her lap and rolled over to directly face Rae. "Rae dear, if it pleased me, I could come along and buy this place right out from under you, and sell it off piece by piece for scrap. So don't piss me off. Just keep the champagne and pretty boys coming."

Rae smiled. "You're so full of shit, Rebecca. You don't have enough money to buy one of my Jacuzzis. They're not for sale."

Rebecca rolled back and lifted her book, carefully heeding the words of Malcolm Bodell. But she couldn't resist one more stab. "Everything's for sale, Rae. You should know that. It's all just a matter of who you do business with."

54

December 1990

Dallas, Texas

THE JETS OF THE EIGHT-BY-TWELVE-FOOT, KIDNEY-SHAPED MARble hot tub fired into the stillness of the water, instantly churning it to a boiling torrent of bubbles and foam. After closing the cover over the jet controls, Sabrina reached down and turned the thermostat to 110. Rae Taylor sat on one of the bar stools in Sabrina's suite, sipping a glass of sherry.

"Is the car everything you'd hoped it would be?" Rae set her glass down.

Sabrina stood up, wearing a terry-cloth robe. "And more. My engineers went way above and beyond the call of duty. It handles well in excess of two hundred and forty without a shimmy."

"Wow." Rae shook her head in awe. "And you're sure about Indianapolis?"

Sabrina came over to the bar and refilled her wineglass with the room-temperature, aromatic Italian vintage. "The car's done everything I wanted it to do on the test track. It's got the muscle, it's got the moves. I think it's going to be a winner. I've already submitted my application and entrance fees for the time trials in April."

Rae looked at her friend with concern. "Don't you want to try some of the smaller races to kind of get your feet wet again before going back there? Isn't it a little premature to go directly to Indianapolis?"

Sabrina shook her head. "Rae, my daddy always told me you have to get back on the horse where you fell off." She sipped from her glass. "I don't have to *win* to prove to myself I can still do it. I don't really have to finish. But I *have* to compete. And I have to do it on the level I know I can achieve."

Rae reached over and put her arm on Sabrina's shoulder. "I wish I had that kind of courage sometimes."

Sabrina tapped the edge of her glass against Rae's. "Doc, you've got more courage than I'd ever hope to have. I just go 'round and 'round an asphalt oval trying to stay out of everyone's way. You've gone right into the jaws of misery and pain and brought back survivors. That's courage."

Rae felt a warm rush of confidence sweep over her. "That's sweet. You know we'll all be rooting for you."

"I'm counting on it." Sabrina smiled. "I can't drink all that champagne in the winner's circle alone."

The door to the suite opened as Jason came in carrying a tray filled with grapes and cut fruit. "Hi gang," he called out, setting the tray down on the edge of the bar.

Rae saw the excitement in Sabrina's eyes as she looked at Jason. It was inspiring to see two people so shamelessly namored with each other. It made her think of Keith. He was supposed to meet her for dinner in about ten minutes. Rae finished her glass and rose from her seat. "Well, I still have a lot to do before I call it a day. I'll leave you two to enjoy your evening."

Neither Jason nor Sabrina tried to constrain Rae to stay. They hugged her warmly, as usual, and saw her to the door. When the heavy six-paneled door of the suite closed behind Rae, Sabrina's back fell against it, and Jason's lips were upon hers in the next second.

She tasted the sweetness of his mouth. She hadn't delighted in its intoxicating flavor since that morning, and that was too long. She felt his hands sliding the thickly woven cloth of her robe off of her shoulders as the weight of his body pressed firmly against her. It felt good, but she was hungry for more.

She reached down and pulled his short-sleeve sport shirt up to his armpits, the bunched material squeezing between them, up her stomach and roughly over her exposed breasts, as she frantically sought to feel the heat of his body against hers. She wanted the heat, needed it, all of it. He released her just long enough to pull the garment over his head and fling it away. In the next instant she reached out and pulled his face back to hers, delighting in the arousing sensation of his voracious lips sampling her chin, cheeks, neck, shoulder, collarbone, and breasts with quick, nipping kisses—each spot soothed by the sensuous swab of his swirling tongue.

Her bodily desire launched upward with insatiable force and velocity. The thought of waiting to get him into the bubbling waters just a few feet away was utterly out of the question. There couldn't be any more waiting. She had to have him now, right there, without delay. Her breath went short when she felt his fingers begin to explore the warm wetness between her legs.

Sabrina hastened to unbuckle his Docker slacks and slide them down, pushing his low-rise black silk briefs down with them. Her eyes greedily took in the beauty of his aroused body, sensing that his desire for her was only exceeded by her intense craving for him. Her hands grabbed him by the small of the back and pulled him against her once again. She could feel the firm heat pressed flat against her pubic bone, but she wanted it closer, much closer. A fresh wave of excitement rose within her when she felt his hands reaching around her, beneath her buttocks, and lifting her legs off the soft carpet. Her back pressed tightly against the door while his lips consumed the side of her neck. As she lifted her knees, implicitly trusting in his strong arms to support her, she forcefully reached down between them, took him in her hands and quickly guided him in, easily and completely. She threw her head back against the door with a firm thud as the hot penetrating firmness reached its fullness. She wrapped her legs securely around his sides, locking her heels together, her arms clinging tightly to his neck.

The door banged in its jamb with each firm thrust of Jason's hips. Sabrina was oblivious to the loud thumping noise behind her as the muscles and sweet tissues of her body focused on one objective, one supreme goal, building and building, getting closer and closer. The dull trembling in her legs announced its imminent arrival. The quickened pace of her lungs shouted it was within sight. The thunderous pounding of her heart against his chest called out for it with earnest pleadings. The rigid ecstasy suddenly exploded within her, and she embraced it, bathed in it, relished it, tasted it, loved it, and then clung to it as it slipped away.

When her body relaxed and her face fell against his shoulder, she felt Jason lean back and carefully set her back down on the rug, looking deeply into her glazed green eyes. He brushed a blond strand of hair away from her lips, and whispered with deep emotion, "Sabrina, I love you so much."

Her eyes brimmed with tears as a lump welled up in her throat. Her choking words were barely audible, "I love you too." She leaned forward and hugged him tightly.

He affectionately pressed his cheek against hers. "Let's get in the tub and relax. I want to love you all night long—just like our first night." She felt his lips lightly caress her forehead as he softly added, "Like *every* night should be."

55

January 1991

Dallas, Texas

THE BREATHTAKING VISTA OF MULTICOLORED LIGHTS, FORMING the sea of modern civilization known as the Metroplex, shone forth from the inverness cloak of night, slowly panned by the revolving restaurant atop Reunion Tower. The white lights that comprised the ball at the top of the tower surrounding the restaurant went into their panoramic computer-driven display of designs and rotations. Though Rebecca Danforth sat by the window with her dinner companion, David Stratton, she was oblivious to the spectacle.

"It's done, David! It's done!" Rebecca raised a glass of the most expensive champagne the establishment provided.

"Congratulations." David lifted his glass in a toast.

Rebecca shuddered with delight, her blood pumping through her body with renewed vigor, the sensation electric. She hadn't felt this elated since she took possession of the chairmanship of Secularian. "Bodell called me this afternoon. I went over right away and signed all the documents." She lowered her voice, but could barely contain her excitement. "David, I am now the sole owner of the North Dallas Women's Center, and that little bitch Rae Taylor *doesn't even know it.*"

David set his glass down. "So you completely unloaded all of your Secularian stock?"

Rebecca took a long drink from her glass, letting the bubbling wine warmly flow down her throat. She nodded. "That's right. As of today, Mr. Stratton, you officially no longer work for me."

David shook his head. "I can't believe it. We've worked together for so long."

Rebecca smiled. "And I'm sure we will in the future. With the renovations planned at my Women's Center, I'm going to need some sharp executives. Bodell says I have to sit tight for about a year, but when this year is over, Rae, Alicia, and that empty suit Marsha Collins, who thinks she knows something about business, will be in an unemployment line, licking their wounds."

"A year?" David asked with concern.

Rebecca reached over and caressed his hand. "It's not such a long time. Things will just move along as usual. You'll take care of Secularian for its new owners, just like you did for me, and then when I open up the executive positions at the Women's Center, I'll steal you away."

David flashed her a seductive grin. "And what might you do to entice me to come?"

She caught his double entendre. Her eyes darkened. "How does a hot wet steambath after dinner at my house sound?"

He smiled. "That's a start."

She watched his dashing expression change to an embarrassed blush as she kicked off her high heel, slipped her toes up between his legs and began to massage his crotch. She could feel a swelling reaction against the ball of her foot. This might have to be a very short meal.

David straightened his back and pushed her foot away with a smile. "Rebecca, please. This is in public here. Can't you wait until we at least get in the car?"

Rebecca laughed playfully and pulled her leg back from underneath the table. She shuddered again, her fingers spreading out before her. "Oh, David, it's going to be glorious. I can't wait to take possession of my new empire. It'll be so fantastic!"

David looked at Rebecca with a curious frown. "So who bought Secularian anyway?"

Rebecca shrugged matter-of-factly. "Oh, some small-time consortium. I don't really care."

"Who are they?" David asked innocently. "If they picked up all of our stock, they can't be *that* small-time."

Rebecca frowned. "Bodell said they were a competitor of ours, but to be honest, I've never heard of them." She picked her glass up again and took another sip. "But apparently their money's good. They took possession of all of Secularian stock today in exchange for all of the Women's Center stock. And believe me, that was no small feat. They had to have two point five billion to pull that off. Cash."

David shrugged in amazement. "Damn. So who do I work for now?"

Rebecca furrowed her brow. "Some outfit called RAM Industries."

56

January 1991

Boston, Massachusetts

NICOLE PRESCOTT'S INTERCOM BUZZED ONCE. KATY POLLARD'S voice came over the speaker, "Nicole, Clarice James is here."

"Send her in," Nicole replied, directing her voice down toward the telephone set on her desk. She closed a case file on her desk and pushed it aside, then turned around and opened her ostrich-skin portfolio on the credenza behind her. Inside was a plain manila folder containing about a half-inch-thick stack of papers. The tab on the folder had scrawled in her handwriting: *Taylor.*

Nicole watched Clarice James come in and quickly take a seat in one of the two padded leather chairs in front of her desk. Nicole was nervous; she had no reason to be, but she was. Clarice's face didn't betray what she was about to report. Everything was ready for the trip to Dallas, but she wanted to be able to give this one last piece to Rae. She deserved it. She thought of it as the last part of her obligation. Rae didn't need it, but Nicole felt that she herself did. In some strange way, it would make things right again. It would restore a long-ago lost but not forgotten piece of her faith in the system that had been her life for the last fifteen years. It would erase a scar on her own profession —no, deeper, a scar on her own soul, inflicted by a common adversary.

Nicole swallowed with difficulty. "Well?"

Clarice let out a faint smile. "It's your call. I have a veritable library of videotaped testimony of David Stratton in my apartment. It's not prime-time viewing, but edited down, I think the message is pretty clear."

Nicole shook her head and closed her eyes. She never questioned Clarice's methods, but couldn't imagine herself in the same position.

Clarice went on, tossing her feathered blond hair from side to side as she talked. "It may not be admissible in court, but he may sign a waiver on a plea bargain. I didn't get the impression he was the chronically loyal type. The best news is, I finally found the chemist at Secularian. And he can be subpoenaed. I've talked to him. He has no great affection for Stratton or Danforth. He'll testify." Clarice smiled with pride. "And as a bonus, I even found a guy who worked for a limousine service ten years ago who had the wildest story about the bereaved Mrs. Danforth-Bennet concerning the day of her late husband's funeral."

Nicole felt the surge of energy run through her with a confident shudder. "That's perfect. Thank you, Clarice. It's enough. I've already called the Dallas County prosecutor. He's willing to give Bodell immunity for his testimony."

Clarice frowned. "Wasn't that arranged from the beginning?"

Nicole smiled. "No, that would have been entrapment. Besides, prosecutors tend to come and go. We calculated a favorable nod from any D.A., but there were definitely some risks. I picked Bodell just last year, taking into account the possibility of casualties."

"Will the Dallas D.A. indict?" Clarice leaned forward.

"He's just waiting to hear from me." Nicole punched the button on her intercom. "Katy?"

"Yes?" came Katy Pollard's friendly voice.

Nicole leaned toward her desk set. "Call Brian and Joel and tell them to ready the jet. Clarice and I will be arriving at Logan within the hour."

"Will do," Katy replied. "I'll let you know if there's any problem."

"Thank you, Katy." Nicole punched the button again and looked at Clarice. "You've done an excellent job, Clarice. You are definitely the best. I'll be in your debt for quite a while."

Clarice laughed. "Hell, Nicole, this has taken years to crack. Granted, I didn't work on it full-time, but I'm sorry it took so long. Some of the pieces I found early. But I didn't get the chemist's name until about two weeks ago. I didn't think we had a case until I found him."

Nicole shook her head. "It's all right. It was in time. That's all that matters. Come on. It's time to go. You wouldn't want to miss this show for anything."

Clarice rose from her chair. "Don't worry. I'd walk to Texas to see this one."

57

January 1991

Dallas, Texas

REBECCA DANFORTH WRAPPED HER MINK STOLE TIGHTLY AROUND her shoulders, as her freshly waxed black Rolls-Royce pulled through the gates of her recently acquired North Dallas Women's Center, winding down the scenic drive to the stone porte cochere. As she listened to Wagner's Viking anthem "Ride of the Valkyries" on her stereo, she couldn't sit still on the luxurious Corinthian leather seat. It was too good to be true—the Women's Center was hers, all of it, every magnificent, adorned, sexy, beautiful inch of it. It had been three days since she signed the papers. Three days since she reveled in celebration with David Stratton high atop Reunion Tower, and reveled in ecstasy with him later that night in her steambath. Yes, she decided, David would be added to the staff at the Women's Center without delay.

Rebecca had waited three full days, three excruciating days, before approaching the center, because under Texas law, after seventy-two hours, all contracts are fully binding. The words of Malcolm Bodell still rang in her ears about sitting on the transaction for an entire year, but she didn't care anymore. His words were useless now; originally given only to cover his own ass. It was done, final and binding. That was the only relevant fact. She hadn't slept in the past three days; she couldn't. Her ultimate victory was in her grasp, and she'd be damned if she was going to sit around and bide her time for an entire year. Today was the day of final victory.

So what if people found out about the transaction? She'd tell the SEC that Bodell simply made her an attractive offer and she purchased it. If he was dealing improperly, then that was his problem. He'd already collected his tidy commission, and had nothing to complain about. She was just an innocent customer. No, the thought of confronting Rae one last time and laughing in her face was too tempting an event to postpone. Three days had been enough, more than enough, every moment a torture. But it was necessary. For within three days Rae and her comrades could have nullified the deal and walked away. That was the law. Rebecca wouldn't allow that. She had been too shrewd for them, despite her impatience. They didn't know what they were doing in the high stakes game of corporate America. Rae Taylor was about to learn her most punishing lesson of all about big business. And Rebecca was going to savor every dark second of teaching it to her.

Rebecca had envisioned the glorious scene over and over in her mind from the second the pen crossed the *"t"* in Danforth in Bodell's office three days ago. It would be perfect. She would walk into Rae's office with the contracts and portfolio documents under her arm, commanding Rae to vacate *her* new office. Rae would object, and get angry. She wanted to see that anger. She would then calmly show Rae copies of the documents giving her power to do as she pleased with the Women's Center. She would then deliberately burst into black laughter informing Rae of her employee status, watching the look of horror on Rae's poor little face. She would ridicule the piteous bitch, demoting her to a custodian's position and ordering her to go clean toilets. And before Rae had time to start protesting, crying and become violent, she would inform Rae of her intention to fire Marsha and Alicia without delay, but would consider letting them remain if Rae obeyed, like a *good* girl.

And Rae would. Rebecca knew she would. Rae was a *good girl*. She had that martyr syndrome all about her. Rae would take all the shit she could dish out to protect her worthless friends. Stupid woman! Rebecca's heart pounded as the limousine pulled up to the majestic entrance of the Women's Center and stopped. It was going to be so sweet, so perfect. And before her chauffeur could walk around to open her door, the fantasy came to its climax. She knew, in just *moments*, she would have Rae Taylor on her knees begging her for mercy, kissing her shoes and licking her feet. She'd *make* Rae lick her feet. She felt an uncanny wave of pleasure sweep across her lap at the thought of her adversary's lips touching her toes.

And lastly, Rebecca could see herself leaning over and spitting on the groveling, worthless wretch, wishing at that precise moment she had one of her old swimming trophies to shove up Rae's tight little daddy's-good-girl ass. Unfortunately, the trophy that came to mind had been broken into little pieces on an angry night next to an ambulance many, many years ago. The chauffeur opened the door.

It was time.

As she rose from the car, she noticed something odd. The handsome uniformed doorman wasn't at his post. She walked toward the dark sliding glass door of the entrance— and it didn't open. She almost collided with it, but stopped short, her heart starting to pound in confusion. What was going on? She saw a piece of paper awkwardly taped to the inside of the smoked glass. It read:

ATTENTION: ALL GUESTS AND STAFF

The North Dallas Women's Center is no longer open for business. All facilities are closed to all guests. We regret this action, and all clients will be contacted shortly with final disposition instructions regarding your accounts.

Sincerely,
Marsha Collins, Executive Director

Rebecca was livid. Her eyes began to blur as she read the message three more times. Marsha Collins didn't have the uthority to do this! Her mind raced to piece together the acts. They must have found out, and they were running! But it didn't matter—no one had contacted her in the time limit to terminate the deal. The three clever bitches were screwed whether they liked it or not. The deal was one hundred percent binding. Unless . . . Bodell.

Rebecca ran back to her car, threw open the rear door, jumped in and grabbed the car phone, frantically pressing buttons, the telephonic tones resonating through the car. If they got to him in the last seventy-two hours, it was over. That couldn't be! No one was going to steal her victory away, not after coming this far, not this close.

Harriet, Bodell's receptionist, answered the phone with her squeaky voice, "Bodell, Powers, and Blakley. How may I direct your call?"

"Put Malcolm on the phone," she ranted into the receiver. "It's an emergency."

After two rings she heard the red-haired stockbroker pick up his extension. "Malcolm Bodell."

"Malcolm, it's Rebecca." She tried to control her heaving chest. "What the *hell* is going on?"

He was quiet for a moment. "You'd better get over here right away."

"Why?" she demanded, using all her concentration to stave off demons of panic.

"It's not entirely clear," he replied cautiously. "I have something to show you. And it isn't good."

"Dammit, man!" she screamed into the receiver. "Did they back out of the deal or not?" Rebecca held her breath. The next word out of the stockbroker's mouth would determine whether the telephone receiver went gently back into its cradle or was used to shatter the window next to her.

"No, they haven't backed out," he said calmly.

Rebecca suddenly felt as if she'd received a stay of execution from death row. She took several deep breaths of absolute relief, forcing herself to calm down. "Well, then tell me what's going on."

"Like I said," he repeated, "get over here as quickly as you can. You're still in the deal, but it's not good."

"I'll be there in half an hour." She slammed the receiver down without waiting for a reply, shouting at her driver, "Get this piece of shit back to town. Now!"

The tires of the limousine squealed across the asphalt as they careened out of the main gate, racing back toward Dallas.

58

January 1991

Dallas, Texas

REBECCA STORMED INTO MALCOLM BODELL'S OFFICE AND STRODE up before his desk, still fuming with ire, her dark eyes cold, hunting, looking for blood. Bodell stood politely and gestured for her to take a seat. "Hello, Ms. Danforth. Please take a seat."

Rebecca remained standing. "Show me what you've got."

Bodell sat back down, loosened his tie, picked up his cigarette from the ashtray on his desk and took a trembling puff. Rebecca could see he was sweating. He picked up a single piece of typed paper from his desk. "I received this earlier this morning by special courier. It's from Marsha Collins, announcing the resignation of the entire staff at the Women's Center. Everyone, all three hundred personnel."

Rebecca snatched the piece of paper out of his hand and ravenously consumed it with her eyes, the words and characters running together. She had to force herself to slow down and absorb it slowly.

She heard Bodell continue to talk as she read, her heart still racing, "As you can see, Ms. Danforth, they don't give any reason, just a letter of resignation addressed to the new ownership. I don't know what prompted this. I can assure you none of my staff, nor I, have had any contact with them after the final papers were signed." He looked very worried. "You know I wouldn't say anything. It's my ass on the line."

Rebecca threw the paper back at him. "That doesn't make any sense. They obviously know about the deal. Why didn't they just back out?"

Bodell picked the paper up and looked at it again. "I can't tell you why. Maybe they just didn't know they could."

Rebecca looked down at him in disgust. "Marsha Collins may be a stupid bitch, but she didn't make millions selling real estate just by spreading her legs. She had to know *something* about Texas contracts." She walked over and threw herself down in one of his chairs, her mind still wheeling to assimilate the confusing storm of information.

Bodell shrugged. "All I can think of, is that somehow they found out you own it, and they quit out of spite. I guess they figure they can take the cash from the sale and start over someplace else, counting on you not being able to revive the operation without them."

Rebecca's mind focused on Bodell's words. "That's it! But the pathetic little whores are wrong." She raised her voice. "They're welcome to start all over again. But I'll show them. I'll hire an entire *new* staff, a *better* staff, my own hand-picked staff—and make the center twice as prestigious as it ever was." She laughed nervously. "I've still got title to the Women's Center name, the client base, the account files. They'll never catch up." She laughed again, this time with maniacal resonance. "I'll drive them into the ground in less than six months." Rebecca was beginning to feel good again. It was all going to work after all.

So that was it. They were afraid, and running from her awesome power. So they should. They might try and run and hide, but she would wait for them to come out of the shadows to exact her pound of flesh. Rae had succeeded in avoiding the eagerly anticipated confrontation, but Rebecca had the satisfaction of knowing that somewhere, Rae was lying on a floor crying her pretty little eyes out in the knowledge that she had lost again. *Poor Rae.* Whatever Rebecca sought to possess, she possessed. And there was nothing sweet little Rae could do about it, Rebecca thought. Well, Rae and her cowardly comrades could all just die a miserable death and go to hell. She might even put forth the effort to help them get there.

"Ms. Danforth?" Bodell held out the letter again. "There's a number at the bottom where Marsha Collins can be reached. It says to call if you have any questions."

Rebecca leaned forward and grabbed the paper again. "Wonderful! I *do* have a few questions for *dear* Ms. Collins. I'll call her unemployed ass and see who gave her permission to close down *my* facility."

Rebecca got up and stormed back out of Bodell's office without another word.

After he was sure she was gone, Malcolm Bodell picked up the telephone and punched in seven digits. "Hello, Marsha. It's Malcolm. She was just here. I know. Be ready. Are you going to do it tonight? Tell Rae and Alicia I'll be there. I gotta see this for myself."

From the backseat of Rebecca's car she called the number on the letter.

"Marsha Collins," a friendly voice answered.

"Marsha?" Rebecca sounded almost pleasant. "This is Rebecca Danforth." She took a deep breath, letting the anger well up into her throat. "Just *who the hell do you think you are,* closing down *my* Women's Center? I'm going to sue your pretty little ass for lost revenue today, tomorrow, and every day until the center reopens. Are you aware of that?"

"Shut up, Rebecca," Marsha snapped. "I don't take any shit from dried-up whores like you. If you want to talk to me, then you can bring your worn-out, sagging little tits over here and do it face to face." Marsha took a breath, letting the first wave of the attack sink in. "That is, unless you're as nickenshit as Rae says you are, always hiding behind the lemmings you recruit and rut with like a bitch in heat. But I don't think you will! I don't think you have what it takes to show your ugly face in my presence!"

Rebecca felt an eerie calm wash over her. It was time to kill. "Name the place and time, bitch."

Marsha's tone was firm and even. "Seven o'clock. At the Women's Center. Don't be late. And bring that prick David Stratton with you. I have a few things to tell him as well, unless he doesn't have the balls to show up either."

Marsha hung up the phone in her living room, noting she'd have to get the number changed now. She looked up at Rae's and Alicia's shocked expressions.

Rae shook her head in awe. "Marsha, remind me never to piss you off. I've never heard you talk like that before."

"I'm used to selling houses to people in the oil industry. Remember?" Marsha gave Rae a teasing smile.

Alicia laughed. "Is she coming?"

Marsha looked indignant. "She'll be there. Loaded for bear. And everything will be ready. Nicole called before you two got here. Her plane arrives in about an hour."

Rae shivered with delight. "I've waited so long for this night. I can't believe it's finally here."

59

January 1991

Dallas, Texas

BY SEVEN O'CLOCK DARKNESS SHROUDED DALLAS, TEXAS, BEneath a chilling, overcast sky. As another Arctic cold front blew in from the north, the weathermen were predicting one of North Texas's infamous, paralyzing ice storms sometime during the middle of the night. Sand trucks were already preparing for a long night. A razor-sharp wind tore through any garment, numbing the skin within seconds. Rebecca had her driver stop her car as close to the front door of the Women's Center as possible. There were lights on inside. Rebecca glanced at her diamond-encrusted Rolex watch once more. It was precisely seven o'clock. She felt David Stratton's hand on her arm as she grabbed the door handle.

"Rebecca, this is crazy." Lines of worry marred his brow. "Why are you doing this?"

She yanked her arm away, glaring back at him. "Just for the thrill of it, David. I'm going to show these amateur-class trollops the kind of power they're dealing with. They won't make the mistake a second time. Now grab those papers and come on."

Inside the Fortunato Ballroom, Rae Taylor stood between Marsha and Nicole. Rae still trembled with excitement from Nicole's news. Her shakes were intensified by her predawn battle nerves. The enemy was due over the horizon at any moment. She glanced at her watch, then looked at Marsha. "It's seven."

"She'll be here." Marsha smiled and put her arm around

391

ae's shoulders. All three women were dressed in formal attire, long gowns and smartly accented jewelry. This was a very special occasion.

"She's here!" Alicia announced, practically running through the main doors of the ballroom. "Is everyone ready?"

"We're ready." Nicole nodded, quickly looking around the ballroom at the sizable gathering of people. All of the cars had been discreetly parked in the lot behind the main complex, not visible from the front entrance. Many more would be arriving later.

Rae felt her heart beating faster as the rapid click of angry heels paced across the polished wooden floor, growing louder as they approached the ballroom. Her hands were shaking. The fierce clicking stopped before the closed double doors of the ballroom. When the heavy oak doors flew wide, spread to the violent span of Rebecca's arms, Rae's breath stilled for an instant.

This was it.

Nicole watched Rebecca Danforth's eyes as she hesitated in the doorway, obviously startled. Rebecca surveyed the silent faces in the room, panning her cold gaze from left to right, apparently unsure of what to do or say in the first instant. David Stratton stood behind her with a wide-eyed look of alarm on his face. Nicole hadn't seen him in fifteen years. He didn't look much different; perhaps put on a few pounds and added a few wrinkles around his eyes. But he was still a handsome man—for a prick. She saw Rebecca's eyes narrow when they found Marsha Collins. But Marsha was ready for her, stepping forward on cue.

"Welcome, Rebecca, to the North Dallas Women's Center." Marsha took great pains to be as warm and pleasant as possible. She had already decided to play this to the hilt, if not for Rae's sake, then just for the fun of it. This was the beast who had mercilessly injured the two people she loved the most. It was time to make her hurt, and let everyone watch her suffer.

ANTICIPATION

Rebecca walked into the room slowly, cautiously, timidly followed by Stratton, letting the heavy doors silently float back into their jambs. Her voice was measured and tentative, "Marsha, I thought this was to be a private meeting—between ourselves."

Marsha shook her head with a condescending smile. "No. In fact, everyone in this room has a vested interest in being here tonight, Rebecca. It's a special night for us all."

Rebecca glanced around at all of the faces. Half of them she didn't recognize. But she wasn't about to back down, even in light of Marsha's show of force. This was a business confrontation, her forte. She felt a brief surge of confidence. "It doesn't matter, invite the whole damned press corps if you want. I believe you owe me an explanation for closing down my property." Rebecca stood just inside the doorway with her arms folded defiantly.

"*Your* property? Oh, that's right." Marsha took one step closer and nodded with mock deference. "Congratulations on your acquisition. In fact, we *all* congratulate you. It took quite a lot to acquire this place. It was quite valuable."

Rebecca stepped farther into the room, moving slowly toward Marsha, hoping to intimidate her. Her voice was even and professional, crisply rising in volume. "I had the power to do so. I chose to use it." Her dark eyes found Rae. "Despite what *others* may have thought. Remember, Rae? I told you, *anything* I want that belongs to you, I can have. I just have to take it. It's that simple." Rebecca was a little unsettled when she saw Rae smile instead of cringe.

"It's all yours, Rebecca," Rae said softly.

Rebecca's head was feeling light. This didn't make sense. They weren't upset. Her voice became catty, her right shoulder thrusting forward with her chin, her voice loud and venomous, "I *know* what you're planning. You think you can all just leave and start somewhere else. You think I don't have the resources to make this place run? Well, you're *wrong!* You're *all* wrong! And I'm going to enjoy watching you all fail at whatever you attempt to do to compete with me." She tried to laugh but it came out sounding hollow. Rebecca was beginning to sense something was seriously amiss.

Marsha's expression grew grave. "That's an interesting notion, Rebecca. But the truth is, we don't think we would have any trouble competing with this place at all, regardless of what we did. I hate to be the bearer of bad news," her smile reemerged, "but in your case, it's a distinct pleasure." She nodded sympathetically. "I'm afraid you're going to discover very shortly that the value of your new investment has dropped drastically in the last few hours."

Rebecca's eyes flashed in anger. "What are you talking about? What have you done?"

Nicole stepped forward. "Nothing you don't already know about."

"Who are *you?*" spat Rebecca in stark condescension, deeply resenting the interruption. She was about to fire another berating remark when she was struck with a faint feeling of recognition. "Aren't you Nikki Thompson?"

Rae spoke up. "Rebecca, this is Nicole Prescott, my attorney."

Rebecca huffed, "I thought you'd have hired a *real* attorney by now, Rae. I still remember when one of my lame law clerks beat her ass years ago." She absently waved off Nicole's look of irritation, ignoring her completely, and turned back to Marsha. "Explain yourself, woman. What have you done to impact the value of my investment?"

Nicole's eyes flashed with rage, but she quelled her anger with one deep, controlled breath. She tersely asserted, "Rebecca!"

Rebecca looked at the bristling attorney again with disdain.

Nicole's voice was cold and lecturing, "Marsha told you that the value of your investment has decreased due to the resignation of the staff. Apparently you're not aware of the full impact of that fact."

Rebecca shrugged, arrogantly shaking her head. "You think I give a shit about that? You think I need any of these worthless second-rates? I'll hire the best talent in the country and have this place doing twice its current revenue in less than six months."

Nicole laughed, clasping her hands together. "I don't think so. Perhaps I should be a little more specific." She walked over next to Rebecca and paced around her back. "The specific talent you can't replace is Dr. Taylor and Dr. Brighton. Surely, you can hire new domestics, new sports professionals, new cooks, new maids, new secretaries and administrators. But you'll find out very soon that the main attraction to this facility was not the resort, but the unique medical treatments pioneered and administered by Dr. Taylor and Dr. Brighton."

Rebecca quickly became annoyed at Nicole's orbits around her. She boldly spun around to face the brash attorney. "Do you think I need *them?* You've been smoking too much bad dope, sweetheart. Women don't come here to get well. They come here to *feel* good. And the kind of feel-goods they serve here I can reproduce in a *week.*"

Nicole shook her head. "No. The success of this center was heavily weighted upon the combination of specific medical treatments—and an admittedly unique style of follow-up therapy."

A thought came to Rebecca. "Well, if that's the case, *counselor,* then Dr. Taylor and Dr. Brighton must realize that I now *own* their treatments. When I bought this place, I bought everything that comes with it. If the treatments are unique, then I'll make sure my attorneys keep you from ever reproducing them anywhere else." The inspiration boosted Rebecca's confidence. She spun around and glared at Rae, her teeth on edge. "Sort of like déjà vu, right, Rae? You won't compete with me, because I *own* your pretty little ass all over again."

Nicole shook her head once more, and continued her intimidating pacing, "Wrong again, Rebecca. Dr. Taylor and Dr. Brighton only worked for the North Dallas Women's Center as contract labor. Perhaps your staff should have reviewed the personnel contracts more closely before your

...asty decision to purchase the facility. You see, Rae and Alicia are currently employed by their Houston-based parent, a consortium you may have heard of. I incorporated it myself." She stopped. It was time to draw blood. "It's called RAM Industries. All of their discoveries and treatments are patented, licensed, and owned by RAM Industries."

A warm sense of pleasure ran through Rae when she saw all the color drain out of Rebecca's face. It was as though an executioner's blade just passed through her neck and stuck in the wood of the chopping block. Rae's hands were no longer shaking. She was anticipating her turn. It wouldn't be long.

Rebecca's lips parted slightly. *"What?* You're part of RAM Industries?"

Marsha nodded, speaking slowly and deliberately, savoring every word, every syllable, "That's right, Rebecca. RAM, as in R for Rae, A for Alicia, and M for me."

Rebecca's chest began to heave, the weight of the truth suddenly gripping her insides with oppressive violence. David Stratton started to ease away from her toward the door, holding the folder of papers tightly to his chest. Rebecca looked at all of them, glaring from smiling face to smiling face, her voice crescendoing in volume with every livid word. Her wrath erupted, *"You fucking bitches!* Conspiracy! You're all guilty of *conspiracy,* and I'll press charges against you all—*immediately."* Abruptly, she shouted with all her might, her hands lifted in cruel claws, spittle flying from her mouth, *"I'll see you all rot under the fucking jail!"* Her voice echoed through the ballroom.

The stillness was broken by Nicole's soft laughter. "Strike three, Rebecca, and you're almost out. The papers you signed were of your *own free will.* Remember? You signed them in front of Mr. Bodell back over there, as he will testify." Nicole pointed to Malcolm in the rear of the crowd, doing his best to watch but not be seen. "And before all these witnesses tonight you've disavowed any claim to the staff. This place was legally worth what you paid for it only as long as Dr. Taylor and Dr. Brighton were here. The market value of this property, legally and accurately quoted by Mr. Bodell, was based on services provided. But you don't have those services anymore. Dr. Taylor and Dr. Brighton abandoned this place of their own free will—just like Mr. Stratton terminated his relationship with Dr. Taylor of his own free will. Remember? Any jury in the world will be easily convinced that *all* you legally own right now is this facility." She looked around with mock admiration. "It's a nice place."

Rebecca just stood there, stunned, her heart pounding, her blurring mind numbing to the nightmare unfolding around her. *This couldn't be happening.* Her limbs began to feel heavy, resistant to her voluntary commands.

Marsha added, "Rebecca, in your haste to acquire the Women's Center, I assume you never bothered to have the physical assets appraised. So let me give you a rundown on what you bought. You'll find a golf course resort, which I purchased two years ago for six million dollars, plus approximately ten million invested in improvements. With appreciation, it might be worth twenty million—*if* you could find a buyer. The three hundred million cash, you'll find, was borrowed from RAM Industries, and the note became delinquent as of today. But don't worry about that; Mr. Bodell will see that it's paid off promptly."

Marsha gestured around the room. "So what you see around you is *all* you have, Rebecca. That's what you gave Secularian to us for. All of your hospitals."

Rebecca gasped in horror, defensively clutching her fists to her chest.

Marsha looked at Rae and smiled. "And *all* of Rae's original patents." She turned a hard glare back to Rebecca's glazed eyes. "That's what you liquidated all your assets for—to give back to Rae Taylor all you stole, *with interest!* We consider the net profit of just under two point five billion a handsome restitution on your part. Thank you, Rebecca."

Rebecca's eyes clamped shut; her fists squeezed with such

force she could feel her nails piercing the flesh of her palms. She didn't want to hear any more. She didn't understand why David wasn't saying anything, or why they were all *staring* at her, or *why* they did this, or *how* they did this, or *what* they thought they had proven, or *what* they—

Rebecca forced her mind to focus. Her jumbled thoughts spun and whirled, but she forced, she gripped, she fought, until her mind flowed into one vulgar stream of brutal thought. She summoned every drop of her will to settle her breathing. Regrettably, the bitches had drawn the iron gauntlet and struck a fierce blow, but the battle was far from over. They hadn't seen unbridled wrath in the measure it was now about to be dealt. She opened her eyes; all she saw was red.

Control. Maintain control.

"This isn't over, *ladies,*" Rebecca seethed, her fingers still gnarled in white-knuckled fists. "You don't seriously think I'll let you get away with this."

Nicole winked at Marsha. "We already have. And according to the laws of this state, you had three days to back out of the deal."

Rebecca snapped her head toward Rae, her black hair flying off her shoulders, and glared murderously into Rae's unflinching eyes. "This was all *your* doing, wasn't it?"

The moment had finally arrived, just as planned. Marsha, the picadore, had thrust her lance well, and enraged the beast beyond control. Nicole, as the banderillero, had planted her brightly ribboned darts deeply within the creature's hide, drawing its blood and visibly weakening it. Now it was up to Rae's cape and sword to consummate the spectacle.

Rae walked over to Rebecca, stopping two paces in front of her. Since that day in Marsha's limousine, when she first suggested her plan, Rae had lived in anticipation of this exact moment, planning every word, every look, every intonation. And now it was here; the moment had finally arrived. All the anticipation culminated into one final confrontation. Nicole and Marsha gingerly stepped back, both feeling a rush of excitement, sensing the vortex of the battle about to commence, as the matador entered the ring.

Rae gave Rebecca her most pleasant smile, savoring every instant. "I can't take credit for all the planning. The real mastermind was Marsha." She gestured to Marsha, as she had practiced in front of her mirror so many times. "Alicia and Nicole helped put it all together." She lifted her chin defiantly, "But they all did this, all of it, every perfect detail—for *me*. They did this because they *love* me, and because they're my friends." She moved closer to Rebecca, intimidating her with her presence and the confidence in her voice. Rebecca leaned back defensively as beads of perspiration broke out across her brow.

Rae's volume increased as her tone rasped harsh and cutting, "Friends are something you probably don't know about. Do you, Rebecca? They're people who care about your welfare. People who are there for you when you need them. Good people. But you don't know about *good*, do you? You never have been a *good* girl? Right, Rebecca?"

Rebecca violently recoiled her head and spat in Rae's face, thrusting her sharp jawline forward, her face a mask of repulsion, her vehement words dripping with icy venom, "You're not a match for me, little bitch. You're *weak*, Rae! Weak and *inferior*, like you've *always* been. You think you've accomplished something great by stealing Secularian from me, Rae? Do you?" Her chest heaved. She threw her head back defiantly. "Take it. Keep it. I'll build another empire twice as big, and do it twice as fast." Tears of anger began to run down her scarlet-flushed cheeks. "I'll show you." She screamed again with bloodcurdling force, *"I'll fucking show you all!"*

Rae wiped the drops of saliva off her cheek and smiled. Rebecca had that hunted look of a cornered animal. The beast had charged the cape, as expected. It was time to draw the sword. "I don't think you'll get the chance." She looked up at the baroque architecture of the ballroom. "Look around you, Rebecca. Do you see all this finery, all this adornment? It's all just a shell, a facade, a monument to your *failure* and my victory." She looked back at Rebecca's expression of . . . Could it be? Rae thought she detected the nervously dilating pupils, and twitching lips of—

Fear?

Rae moved closer. "Look around. Don't you see now what it *really* is? A sculpted mausoleum, an empty catacomb, an ornate tomb—*your* tomb, Rebecca. It's over. I've waited fifteen years to take back from you what you stole from me. And it's done. Now Alicia, Marsha, Nicole, and I are going to take your precious Secularian, the empire you *worked* so hard to acquire, and we're going to rename it. Very shortly, each Secularian hospital across this nation is going to be transformed into the Hope Clinics I've always envisioned. We're going to sell off every nonessential asset, and turn every Secularian hospital into a smaller version of what you've seen here at the Women's Center, only nationwide. Except now I have my patents back—the third piece of the beautiful mosaic. And whether a woman hurts on the inside or the outside or just in her heart, we now have everything we need to help her." Rae paused with a haunting chuckle. "And the best part of all, which I just found out tonight, is that you won't be around to see it."

Rebecca's breathing was short and spasmodic, bordering on hysteria. Only Rae's last words registered.

"What do you mean, I won't be *around?*" Rebecca snapped with the last trace of poison in her voice. "You think you can get rid of me?" Her eyes burned with fresh fire, and a crazed laugh seeped past her lips. "Is that supposed to be some kind of threat? Is that what you're planning, Rae? To *kill* me?"

Rae smiled, her voice patient and measured, looking for the precise opening for the tip of the blade, "No, not a threat. I don't *want* you dead. I just want you to *suffer,* to *watch* you suffer—the way you made me suffer, and Alicia suffer, and all the others you've stepped on to gratify your own twisted desires."

Rebecca started to interject an enraged rebuttal but Rae shook her head, the cold steel of her voice piercing forward, trampling over her words, "No! Dear, miserable, Rebecca! Not a *threat* at all! A fulfillment of a promise, a fifteen-year-old promise." She raised her hands, gesturing at the vast expanse of the entire center, *"This* is where it ends for you, Rebecca. Don't you see? I've taken away everything you've worked for, just like you did to me. *Everything!"*

"Shut up!" Rebecca screamed in Rae's face, the beast groaning in pain.

Rae moved closer, her voice growing louder, driving the rapier deeper, *"This* is where, in your drunken stupor of power, you failed to even see it happening all around you." She gave a chilling laugh. *"This* is where I make every one of your precious hospitals the fulfillment of *my* dream."

"No! No! No!" Rebecca ranted, pressing her face up to Rae's, nose to trembling nose, screaming hysterically at the top of her lungs, tears of rage running down her cheeks amid spastic sobs.

Rae abruptly stopped, her trembling dagger of a finger raised between them. Her voice was hushed and cold, "I warned you, Rebecca. You didn't watch. I waited, and now it's done." The blade reached the beast's heart with one final pronouncement. *"As I pleased, Rebecca, everything you once possessed—I have made mine."*

The air was so tense, Nicole couldn't breathe. Alicia was trembling. Marsha's mouth was wide open in shock. No one in the room moved. Rebecca remained paralyzed, speechless, her body trembling uncontrollably, her gaze transfixed on Rae's.

Rae had waited so long to say those words. The wait had been worth it. The look in Rebecca's eyes told her it had accomplished all she had intended, and more. The beast lay writhing in its own blood. However, she couldn't resist adding a touch of insult to devastating injury. "You know, Rebecca, for a woman of your imminent stature in the business community, I'd have at least thought you would have read the *fine print* of your own contracts."

Rebecca's mind was a tangled wreck. She had just enough presence of mind to command her body to make a hasty retreat in order to attack another day. She didn't care what it took, how long it took, or who was destroyed in the process. Rae Taylor, Alicia Brighton, and Marsha Collins would die for this outrage. Their only mistake was *not* killing her. That was the only thing that could now keep them safe.

Rebecca wiped her eyes with her fists and composed herself for one last futile barb, her voice weak and desperate, "You're *completely* insane, Rae." She sniffed deeply and huffed, "I'm going to enjoy seeing you locked away in an institution. *All* of you." Her pitiful voice found one more vehement drop of ire, "If you *live* that long." She spun toward David Stratton. "Come on, David, we're going to find a lawyer and the sheriff, and have them all arrested for trespassing on my property."

"That won't be necessary," Nicole interjected. "The sheriff is here. Along with two federal marshals, plus some local and state investigators, agents with the IRS, and U.S. Treasury officials representing the Security Exchange Commission. They'd all like to talk to you. Both of you."

"What?" Rebecca demanded sharply, as some of the faces she hadn't recognized walked up and surrounded her and David Stratton.

Marsha looked at Rae. "Are you finished, Rae?"

Rae shook her head. "No. One more item of business to attend to." She nodded to Nicole, who brought her a plain white, legal-sized envelope. Rae walked over to David and handed it to him. "As the new CEO of Secularian, and your *superior,* I'm officially notifying you of your termination. You'll find a letter to that effect inside." Her expression grew hard. "It's nothing *personal,* David. Just business."

David's face flushed. He looked down at the envelope. Taped to the outside with a two-inch piece of fingerprint-stained Scotch tape was a fifteen-year-old engagement ring. He cocked his jaw arrogantly and glared at Rae. "Cute. So are you *satisfied* with your petty little spectacle of retribution?"

"Not yet." Rae's hand came up so fast and so hard, he never saw it coming. The echo of the slap reverberated through the entire ballroom, startling everyone. David tumbled back, papers flying into the air. He crashed to the polished wood floor with a hard thud, instantly rubbing his reddening cheek, wincing from the bone-jarring force of the blow. Rae looked down at him on the floor. "Now I'm satisfied."

Everyone in the room, with the exception of Rebecca, broke into thunderous applause.

"Rebecca?" Nicole held her hand out to an elderly woman holding a pair of open handcuffs. "This is Ilene Duvall. She's a federal marshal. She has asked to speak with you first."

Rebecca spun around and, looking at the woman, her eyes quickly widened at the site of the chrome-plated handcuffs. "What do you think you're doing?"

"Rebecca Danforth?" The woman lifted the lapel of her jacket to reveal a silver star laminated in plastic next to a picture identification card. "You are hereby under arrest for the murder of Donald J. Bennet. You have the right to remain silent—"

That's as far as the marshal got before Rebecca turned and fled toward the door screaming. Two plainclothes detectives pounced on her and wrestled her down against the hardwood floor. Rebecca didn't stop screaming and cursing while they handcuffed her and dragged her from the premises into an awaiting police car. In the meantime, two other officers had helped David Stratton to his feet and were now holding his arms. They informed him of his arrest as well, and led him away sobbing.

Everyone enthusiastically cheered again as the doors to the ballroom closed, only slightly muffling the vulgar ranting and raving of Rebecca's voice fading down the hallway.

Marshal Duvall came over to Marsha. "That was quite a show. You folks must have really enjoyed it."

Marsha smiled. "More than you could ever know. But we certainly appreciate your help, Ilene, and your patience in letting us have our final say before taking her into custody. You're welcome to stay for the party."

"Party?" the marshal looked puzzled.

Marsha nodded sadly. "Our last one here. The entire staff will be arriving in about half an hour. It'll probably go on all night. Our festivities here at the center tend to be quite elaborate. Plus, with the ice storm coming in, it may go on even longer."

Ilene looked around and nodded, "Well, if I have to be stuck anywhere, this doesn't look like too bad a place."

"It isn't." Marsha gave Ilene a coy grin. "And I know you'll want to meet some of the staff. I'll be sure and introduce you." She thanked the officer once again, turned, and walked over to Rae and Alicia.

Rae threw her arms around Marsha's neck, crying again. "We did it! We did it!"

Marsha looked into Rae's eyes, "How do you feel?"

Rae laughed. "Like I'm ready to conquer the world! Marsha did you see her face when those two officers jumped on her? I'll cherish that memory forever." Her voice grew serious. "Thank you." She looked at Alicia and Nicole. *"All* of you, for all you've done. I'm so happy." Her tears increased to genuine sobs of joy.

Marsha reached over and hugged Rae close to her cheek, feeling the warm moisture against her face. She leaned back and shrugged. "But you know, I'm really going to miss this place."

Alicia nodded. "Me too. It was a shame we couldn't keep it. It would have made a wonderful corporate headquarters for Hope Clinics."

Nicole furrowed her brow. "Well, if you think about it, Rebecca's broke, and she's going to be facing court costs—*big* court costs to keep her pretty little self off death row." She nodded. "So I would expect this place to be for sale in the not too distant future."

Rae grabbed Nikki's hands. "You think we could buy it back?"

Nicole shrugged. "I don't see why not. We've got three hundred million dollars cash coming in from Malcolm, minus his well-earned commission. I'm sure that's more than enough to swing the deal."

All four women broke into peals of laughter as the legion of caterers came through the rear doors of the ballroom and began preparing for the biggest extravaganza ever held at the North Dallas Women's Center. Rae, Alicia, Marsha, and Nicole knew in their hearts it wouldn't be the last.

Epilogue

May 1991

Indianapolis, Indiana

ALL FOUR WOMEN PRESSED AGAINST THE GLASS OF THE SKY BOX screaming their lungs out. The thousands gathered in the grandstand and filling the infield at the Indianapolis Motor Speedway were on their feet watching the comeback of a racing legend, who was, at that very moment, overtaking the leader coming around the fourth turn of the five hundredth lap, heading toward the finish line.

"She's going to do it!" Rae yelled, spilling her champagne down the front of her dress. The bubbling liquid soaked through her bra down to her skin, but she didn't care. Her attention was fixed on the white wing car pulling up even with a red Formula-One racer.

Alicia pounded on the wide sheet of plate glass with the palm of her hand. "Come on, honey! Go! Go!! Go!!!"

Marsha squealed with delight and threw her arms around Nicole's neck when the checkered flag waved over Sabrina Doucette's white racer with the royal blue logo of RAM Industries and Hope Clinics emblazoned on both sides. Sabrina finished half a car length ahead of the crimson entry from the Marks racing team.

All four women lifted their crystal flutes in ringing

triumph to their chief spokesman as she took her victory lap and cruised into the checkerboard winner's circle. Jason Maxwell was the first person to help her out of the car, pull her helmet off, and smother her face with his.

"We do good work," Alicia whispered to Rae.

"You're right," Rae replied. And it was true.

August 1991

Houston, Texas

RAE TURNED HER FACE AWAY FROM THE ROLLING WAVES OF THE Gulf of Mexico and looked at Nicole, lying nude, as she was herself, relaxing on a waist-high massage table parallel to her own a few feet away, on the rear deck of her yacht. Brett was rubbing a steaming handful of coconut-scented oil into Nicole's back. Rae took a deep relaxing breath as she felt Keith's hands work the same hot, penetrating liquid into the backs of her legs. She mumbled, "Are you having a good time?"

Nicole smiled. "As usual, the fun meter's pegged out. Thanks for the ride on your boat."

Rae wrinkled her nose. "This isn't a boat. It's a yacht. Anything a hundred and twenty feet long is more than a boat. Actually, it's probably more like a ship than a yacht."

"What's the difference?" Nicole asked sleepily, as the penetrating summer sun pressed down on her skin, giving her a dark brown tan in exchange for her strength.

Rae shrugged. "I don't know. I just know it's fun."

Nicole lifted her head as Brett's hands kneaded into her shoulder blade. She smiled at him. When the layoff occurred at the Women's Center, per her insistence, she had first dibs on Brett's postcenter employment. It didn't take a great deal of negotiation to convince him to come back to Boston with her for a full-time position as her personal assistant. She hadn't had a decent night's sleep in almost six months. She had decided that's what late mornings were for. She looked over at Rae. "Did you see the paper today?"

"No." Rae glanced over her shoulder at Keith's affectionate eyes. "I was preoccupied all morning. Why?"

"Well, on the front page was the announcement of Rebecca Danforth's conviction." Nicole laid her head back down.

Rae nodded with approval. "Good. Did she get the death penalty?"

Nicole shook her head. "No, just life in prison."

Rae laughed. "That's better. She can spend the rest of her days remembering what it was like to enjoy the outside world and all its blessings. I think I'll write to her now and then just so she doesn't forget."

Nicole laughed. "You're terrible." She reached down, picked up her wineglass on the stand next to the massage table and took a sip. "Then again I may send her a postcard now and again myself." She set her glass back down. "It also said Stratton got ten years for accessory to murder, conspiracy and fraud."

Rae let out a long sigh. *"Poor baby.* He should have stuck with a good thing while he had it."

Nicole laughed again. "His loss."

"My gain," Keith added.

"No, mine." Rae gave him an affectionate smile.

Nicole decided to change the subject to something more pleasant. "So are the clinics doing well?"

"Wonderful," Rae replied with a slight moan as she felt Keith gently part her knees and go to work on her inner thighs. "We have seven hospitals converted, and fifteen more scheduled for this year. Marsha is heading up the renovations and upgrades. Alicia is restaffing. It's wonderful. We offer all ranges of services to the rich and the not-so-rich, but insured. Profits are up by forty-seven percent this quarter alone."

"That's incredible." Nicole was genuinely impressed.

"So what are *you* going to do now?" Rae asked.

Nicole shrugged. "I don't know. I thought I might try to take a run at the Senate seat next year."

"Really?" Rae was amazed. "That's great. If I still lived there, I'd vote for you."

Nicole looked off the tall rear deck of the yacht at the beach two miles away. "Yeah, Massachusetts could use some fresh insight, new ideas, innovative thinking."

"Well, good luck." Rae turned her gaze out to sea as well, relaxing in the delicious summer heat. She felt a familiar pat on her rear. A shudder of excitement went through her.

"Time to turn over, Rae." Keith caressed her side.

Rae sat up. "No, I think it's time to go below." She smiled over at Nicole, then gave Keith an inviting look. He helped her put on her robe and escorted her to her stateroom.

"Are *you* ready to turn over?" Brett patted Nicole's bottom. The hot-oil machine whirred, dispensing a fresh handful of steaming lubrication.

Nicole rolled onto her back, stretching in the warmth of the Texas sun, looking up into Brett's deep blue eyes with a smile of eager anticipation. "You *know* that's the part I like best."